Narcatoe: The Eighty One Worlds

Book One: Snow in Hell

By

Sophie Sparham

GINGERNUT BOOKS Ltd
www.gingernutbooks.co.uk

First Published in 2013
By GINGERNUT BOOKS LTD

Cataloguing in Publication Data is available from the British Library

ISBN 978-1-907939-30-3

Cover art © Emily Sparkes

Printed and bound in Great Britain

GINGERNUT BOOKS LTD
Head Office
27 Sotheby Ave
Sutton-in-Ashfield NG17 5JU

www.gingernutbooks.co.uk

'For Betty, Ken and Yuko.'
'Because at the end of the day, all that we're left with are our stories.'

Thank you:
Sue Sparham
Char Hudson
Emily Sparkes
Takumi Sloan
Chris Penney
Emma Hulland
Michael and Roxanne Preston
Terry Silver
Michelle Gent
Hannah Ziolek
Megan Dodds
Gez Addictive
And all those that were there to lend a hand.

Special thanks to Alina Airline, whose grammar skills saved the day.

Before you even think about reading this book...

Do not take any information contained within these pages seriously, all the scientific and space like facts are very, very made up. In no way is anything mentioned in the book meant to be taken as the truth. As much as I dream of being a super genius, I do not hold the answers to questions about black holes and what lies beyond our Universe. I simply make it up for purely recreational purposes.

Got it?

Are you sure?

Ok then, on with the story.

A Beginner's Guide to the 81 Worlds

Once, and we are talking a very long time ago, there was nothing… and then, there was something. How that something came to be is another story for another time. According to the advance research from many human scientists on the planet Earth, who, may I remind you, have spent years pondering on the creation of man, there was a bang, and then everything appeared. Complicated stuff, I know, but I'm not here to spark off a philosophical discussion about how we came to be, merely tell you stories of people's beings.

From the very beginning, worlds had gradually been created until there were eighty one within the whole of time and space. The Universe, which I'm sure you're all quite familiar with, is one of them. Now the first question I'm always asked is why eighty one? Why not a more well-rounded number like one hundred? Well, as space is constantly expanding, only eighty one have been created. We still have a few human centuries to wait for the next one. As different worlds are being created at different times, they are all different when it comes to development. For example, the world Nillus, number eighty one, is in a dreadful state at the moment, full of unstable grounds and overruled by war.

The Universe, which you may be unaware of, is still viewed as an undeveloped world, lacking adequate travel and knowledge. A lot of things that the people there believe to be myth are in fact living, breathing and extremely real. At the beginning of our story, no human being has found any sign of life, nor ventured out into space for many years.

The funny thing about the Universe is that the human race still believes black holes consume matter, well yes this is partly true, but, if used correctly, they also transport matter. In fact, black holes are the only current known mode of transportation throughout space to take people to different worlds. Every single world is connected via black holes. Each two worlds have their own individual black hole leading on to another. As there are eighty one different worlds, each contains eighty black holes. So you can imagine it's a bit annoying if you end up getting your directions mixed up and fall through the wrong one.

***

The first fifteen worlds to come into existence are the most advanced and knowledgeable of all. They're also host to the most powerful creatures ever known (or unknown, as it may be). These creatures refer to the whole of time and space as 'Narcatoe'.

In this book, the world Haszear - the fifteenth world ever created and where this story is based - also uses this term. Now, come on, let's face it, the Earth would be an extremely dull place to base a story around. Unless of course you are extremely interested in tax revenues, troubled-teenagers who think they are 'street', or how Doris found her knitting club this week. Haszear, if it chose to, could hold the knowledge of the Universe within its palms three or four times, leaving room to spare for those days when it decides to carry many other useless items.

Prologue

Year 3145 - over one thousand years into the future, 12 years before the story begins…

Time was worthless and not half as valuable there as it was on the Earth. She knew it well, for she was one of the few creatures throughout the whole of Nacartoe that would never die. Trust me, being immortal may sound great but it has more cons than it does pros. She had travelled many worlds, witnessed the creation of new planets. Seen more landscapes than one could dream of; touched, seen and heard what many had not. She had seen the creation of life and the devastation of death. She was one of the most educated creatures throughout the whole of time and space. However, it was not enough to satisfy her needs.

"Is this it? Surely we must have some purpose, some task to fulfil?" She sat questioning and questioning; talking to herself on the clouds. It made no sense to her pure mind how corrupt so many worlds had become. She was amazed that people could be so full of greed and selfish motivation whilst the other angels of her world sat and laughed and continued to do nothing. Why? Her mind wasn't innocent or naïve, she was far beyond that. She cared - some would say too much.

The angel had seen so many fall from grace.

But not I, she swore to herself.

She would not fall into such deceitful hands that had carried away so many kind thoughts. For many a human year the angel tried and tried to preach her words across the land, to teach, to come to some form of conclusion… to do something that mattered.

Nothing stood in the way of the task she had set for herself. The only problem was, trying to make eighty one worlds care. It was a huge task, one that she was determined to complete by any means necessary.

That was when the trouble began...

"The court of angels is angered, Silvia. For your bad conduct and craving for mindless power, we banish you to the floating skin of hell. Your fall will commence in a few hours, I suggest you pack a coat.

The crowd jeered and laughed and yelled.

"Please, please, I only wanted to help..."

The crowd snorted and spat and sneered.

"You will be stripped of your beauty and the use of your wings in the Over World if ever you dare to return. We may even turn you into one of them."

The angels pointed and shouted and swore.

"However, the court does take pity on your good intentions. If you wish to return to your place in the clouds you must complete the task we have set for you. Now, I and various other members of the court believe that a few of your ideas were quite, shall we say, valid. So we believe that they should be carried out, tested, so to speak, on a more disposable dimension."

Silence fell over the court.

"The Universe, home to some of the most destructive creatures this court has ever seen."

The silence weighed heavily on the court.

"We have all watched this dimension fall into chaos. Silvia, if you can convert the people of the Universe to good and filter out the poisonous thoughts of those living there, then you may be able to return. Who knows, this may be the beginning of some form of revolution."

The angels gasped.

"But how?"

"That is up to you. Don't worry; the portal to their world shall be shown to you. And you won't be alone in this task; the Devil has agreed that you may use some of the Brontangus to assist you."

"They were frozen for a reason!"

"Oh, don't worry my dear, they'll still be encased in their conveniently mobile prisons, they'll just be put to good use instead of sitting on the Under World's floor for all eternity. Good luck!"

"This wasn't meant to get out of control..."

Chapter 1

Strange Meetings

It was a quiet day, a really quiet day - too quiet. It had been too quiet for a very long time, seven years to be precise. Jade didn't understand it. He didn't seem to understand a lot of things. He took in the smell of the Earth, oh, how he had missed it. His nostrils relished the crisp sea air, the smell of the sand, the clean... wait; no, there was definitely dog mess somewhere near where he was standing. *Never mind*, he thought to himself, *I'm home*. Jade looked over his shoulder, nothing. Surely someone had noticed his imperfect landing. It was strange; his ship was the only one he had seen in miles.

When he had left the Earth, everything had been in turmoil. Chaos and violence filled the streets, now there was nothing. He left the ship where it landed and made his way to the beach. He turned back to take a last look over the ship, it was rusting. Space hadn't been kind to his 'baby'; it needed an overhaul and fast. He ran his hand down the metal of the small pod; it had been his home for the past six years. Surely he should give it some credit for holding up so long. It was about the size of a public swimming pool, small for a ship, but big enough for one person. Jade remembered making it and smiled to himself. Of course it was easy to tell that the ship had been hand crafted, due to the fact that it looked like some form of deformed burger, but that's just getting off the point.

Jade snapped out of his trance, the ship would have to wait. He had to find out what the hell was going on. Unsure what to do with himself; he walked down the island's deserted shores, hoping to spot a sign of life; there was nothing.

The sun beamed down on his dark skin and he smiled, it was good to be back in Bequia but there were issues. The Caribbean island he once knew so well seemed like a maze of emptiness. He rubbed his temples and looked out to sea, maybe something had happened? No he was probably over-reacting. Travel sickness? Yes, that's what it was. But what if it wasn't travel sickness? What if something terrible had happened and the population of the whole planet had been wiped out? Or, maybe he'd been so desperate to return that it was all a hallucination?

"Am I dreaming?" he asked himself. Jade shook his head in confusion. Knowing no other place to go, he headed to his parents' house.

It was a short walk from the beach. Not far, just ten minutes. They'd always loved the beach. They'd tried to stay as close to it as possible and encouraged him to do the same. He wondered what they'd think when they saw him. As Jade turned the last corner, he imagined running into his mum's arms, telling her about his travels. He'd waited for that moment far too long. He remembered his home well; remembered the hanging baskets out front, the beautiful vegetable patch and the smell of his mother's cooking… And it was only metres away.

"Oh my goodness," he gasped as it came into view. His house looked completely abandoned.

He felt the tears slide down his face as he approached the door. The plants in the hanging baskets were dead, the vegetable patches overgrown. He stared at the porch. Instead of parents, there were bunches of flowers with R.I.P. labels attached to them. *When had it happened? Had he really been away for that long?* Jade sat on the porch and tried to compose himself. He wasn't sure if he wanted to go inside. There would be nothing waiting for him. He shook himself. "Come on Jade, you can do it."

Steeling himself, Jade opened the door to reveal a dusty living room. He sighed, and wished someone had come to clean it. He went into the kitchen.

"Well, at least someone's tried to deal with this place," he mumbled to himself, looking at the pile of boxes in front of him. He leaned over the small sink, gazing at the view over the beach. His mum had loved the view.

Something caught Jade's eye, there on the side was a half drunk cup of black coffee. He touched the mug, it was still warm.

His eyes widened as he moved over to the boxes. He opened one up, finding not his parents' possessions, but files, diagrams, books. Someone was using the place for storage space? How dare they? Jade imagined all the awful things he was going to do to the culprit. They wouldn't get away with it, not if Jade Wilde was on the case. He'd make them wish they were never born, he'd-

"Arghh!" Jade screamed as the door creaked open. He was no longer alone.

"Hello?" A feisty female voice called out.

He ran into the sitting room and hid behind the old sofa.

"Well, so much for that idea," he muttered to himself, embarrassed by his cowardice.

"Anyone here?" The voice called again. The female made her way into the kitchen and put her bag at her feet.

"Jesus Christ," he heard her say. "I go outside to catch a few rays and come back thinking someone's broken in, I must be losing it."

Jade raised his eyebrows. He recognised that voice; there was only one person the woman could be.

"Margot," he said, getting up from his hiding place. "You've been an albino all your life; I really doubt that some sun will change that now."

Margot stopped what she was doing and turned around slowly. *It couldn't be.* Before her stood a dark, well-built man, more than six foot tall who made her look like a midget in comparison. It was him, Jade had returned. She looked him up and down again, just to be sure. Jade had always been one to dress elaborately. She glanced at his long blue trench coat, which when unbuttoned revealed his retro 1960s style shirt. His trademark goggles sat upon his dreadlocks, which were accompanied by a captain's hat. If Margot knew who the character 'Captain Jack Sparrow' was she would definitely have teased Jade for trying to become the black version.

She, on the other hand, felt half naked. She wore a red bikini in comparison to his many layers. It wasn't exactly the outfit she pictured herself in when she imagined meeting him again, but he was so very late. It was about the most girlie she ever got when it came to choosing clothes, a dress or skirt were beyond her.

Margot's fiery red eyes glared at the man before her.

"JADE!" she screamed, and leaped into his arms. "Where the fuck have you been? The mission... th - the..." Margot struggled to contain herself. Without thinking, she backed off; forcing her emotions down as she struggled to be released.

"Margot you won't believe - ," he stuttered, putting her down. Her lip ring became entangled with his dreadlocks as her feet touched the ground. It was an awkward moment. It was far more attention than he was able to cope with. He tried to back away.

"Six fucking years man," she said once her face jewellery was free. "I thought you were dead man! No offence."

"None taken," Jade laughed, so happy to see a familiar face. He turned away as his emotions crept up on him again. "Urghh, my parents."

He was gasping, beginning to cry.

"There, there," Margot said awkwardly, patting his shoulders. She wasn't great in that kind of situation.

After he'd regained control of his emotions, he began to question her. "But Margot, why did you come here, I don't understand? What's happening, why are you using my house for storage, where is -"

She sighed. "A few things have changed round here since you left. Walk with me; we'll go for a coffee. No screw that, I want a beer."

"I have no idea what the time is but I am positive that it's way too early to drink."

Margot bent down and grabbed the shoulder bag at her feet. She rifled through it and pulled out a cigarette. Jade sighed, she never changed.

"Don't smoke in my house," he grumbled.

"Fine then," she said, going toward the front door. "Well are we going to move or are you just going to stand there all day?"

She grabbed his arm, pulling him forward. He sighed again, before following her out and along the lonely shore.

They walked along the coast line until they came to a small village. Jade smiled, it brought back so many memories. He had always been fond of the island. Its small population and lack of modern communication meant it had always been a few years behind on technology. He remembered it was one of the last places to begin using spaceships as transport across the Earth. Although as he looked around; he couldn't see any parked and floating in the oxygen harbour above their heads. He turned and stared at her hoping for an answer, but she remained silent and continued to walk until they came to a small wooden beach shack. Margot sat in the first seat she found. Jade sat opposite her.

It didn't matter to him where she went at that point in time; he would have followed her into a pit of lions if he had to. Margot wasn't just his friend; she was his only current link to the Earth.

*

He looked around and watched people as they got on with what they were doing, they all seemed to smile as they talked to one another. The streets were clean; there wasn't a piece of litter in sight. Everything looked perfect, new and efficient. He supposed he shouldn't be too shocked; after all, it wasn't like they were in a capital city.

"Can I see a newspaper?" Jade asked. The man behind the bar laughed to himself in the background.

"They stopped making them five years ago," Margot said.

"But why, what's going on? What happened to the wars? Why is everything so, so perfect? Is this a trick?" Jade's brow was furrowed in confusion.

"Jade, calm down dude," Margot said, leaning back in her chair.

"No you calm down," Jade stood up. "You're acting like a child!"

The customers around them shifted their eyes in the couple's direction. Behaviour like that was extremely unusual.

"Jade, for fuck's sake, sit down and we'll talk about this," Margot said through gritted teeth.

"Sit down? You sit down! Ok you are sitting down, but that's not the point! Margot, the mission! Our space-" his voice became louder, grabbing the full attention of everyone in the shack.

"Ok, time to go," Margot jumped out of her chair and pushed him out into the sunlight. She dragged him onto the open sands and shook him hard. "Jade, we don't talk about it in public! Ok? So calm down before people start asking questions."

She paused. "Look man, people like us..."

"Scientists," he said.

"People like us aren't looked upon so kindly now," she glanced around before finishing her sentence in a hushed voice. "Let's just get back. To be honest I never thought I'd see you again."

Jade fell silent. He had never considered how shocking it would be for her. Good old Margot; always kept her cool, always remained calm; always so relaxed in the most horrifying of situations.

"But what about my ship?" he asked.

"Fuck! Oh god I didn't think," her eyes were wide. "Where the hell is it? Quickly, before everyone comes out of church!"

"Church?"

"Oh for god's sake Jade, questions later."

*

They retraced their steps down the beach. Jade led the way, both of them sprinting. Margot wished he hadn't hidden it so well; it was more exercise than she had done in weeks. They ran past the odd person walking a dog or strolling. Margot tried not to worry, but she knew they didn't have much time. If the ship was found, who knew what would happen. The people of the island stared at them as they passed. Beads of sweat had begun to form on Jade's brow. He sighed; he knew he wasn't exactly dressed for the weather. Jade took off his trench coat and carried it over his arm. It hung heavily by his side, rendering him only a little cooler. He had no idea why Margot was in such a panic and questioned whether he'd parked in the wrong area.

As they reached the woodland, Jade weaved his way through the trees. The Caribbean island was thick with jungle, so thick that it was easy to become lost, but Margot had to be sure they'd find it.

"Ok, Jade where is..." she gasped, looking down at the deep crater in the Earth. At the bottom lay an odd shaped, smoking lump of metal.

"That's your ship?" She couldn't help but laugh as they climbed inside and attempted to start the engine.

"Don't laugh," said Jade. "You helped build it."

Her eyes widened in response then she ran her hand gently down the wall. He was right. Without releasing it, she'd climbed into the very ship that she'd created.

Jade bumped his head against the wheel and accidently pressed a few buttons on the dashboard. A cup-holder slid out and hit him in the face. Margot laughed.

"It won't start," he said with a sigh. "I've tried everything but I could feel the engines failing when I came back down to Earth."

"I don't think this thing's gonna fly again, the engine's fucked, the metal's rusting, the whole thing is falling to pieces, but no one comes to this part of the island, so I think we're safe," she said. "At least until nightfall."

She shook the controls. There was still no response. Jade stared at her.

"Nightfall?" He muttered to himself. *What was she talking about?* Margot had been talking in riddles ever since they'd met.

He left her at the helm and walked down the decrepit hallway to his bedroom to get supplies. He grabbed a hand full of clothes and threw them into the nearest bag he could find. He grabbed a small object from his desk drawer. It fitted easily in his hand. The device was where he stored all the research he had been doing for the past six years. Jade couldn't wait to show Margot what he knew. His research would blow her mind and if handled correctly, could change the very course of history. However, it would have to wait a while. •

"Do you remember making this thing, man?" Margot asked as she leaned on the door frame. He nodded and pointed to a picture which sat on the drawers next to his bed. "Wow," she said, staring at the photo. It was an old shot, taken of them on their university graduation day. Back then, Jade's hair took the form of an afro and his mortar board barely managed to stay on his head.

"I think this was one of the only photos taken of us sober!" Margot shook her head, she was becoming distracted again.

"Of you, maybe," he said.

"Come on, we're gonna have to leave this heap of shit here for now," she said as they walked to the entrance. Margot kicked open the door and it fell off its hinges and crashed to the ground.

"Oops!"

*

Jade perched on the end of Margot's sofa. He felt awkward. It had been a long time since he'd set foot in another human's house. He'd forgotten what to do. Jade supposed he could go home, but he didn't want to return to that place. He didn't want to see the photos or messages of love, remember memories he didn't want to face. His parents were dead, and as far as he knew, he had no other family members still living - there was no place left to run to. He was surprised at his lack of remorse over their deaths, maybe it was the shock, or maybe he'd spent so long in isolation that any other form of life seemed like an impossible concept.

In the corner of the room he spotted a DVD player. For the 31st century, Margot's house was furnished with an odd and eclectic taste, old and new sat alongside each other. She was a scientist of new inventions, she was also a huge fan of technology, and had always relished filling her home with anything from modern gadgets to things she could find from history. No, Margot hadn't changed. She was a traveller that had become lost in time.

He flicked through the TV, it was six o'clock and there was no news, there were hardly any channels at all. That was something he was going to have to get used to. Margot came back to sit down next to him, she handed him a cup of tea whilst she held onto her black coffee.

"Now will you answer my questions?" he said, switching off the television as he turned to her, his expression stern.

"Some of them," she said coyly. Her expression frustrated him. "I'm sorry about your parents. They were old, dude."

Her words were harsh.

"I don't want to talk about them." He sighed. "Margot, what's going on?"

"Well to be honest," she said, putting another cigarette between her lips. "I don't have a fucking clue. It was one year after you left, everything just changed." Jade leaned forward on the sofa, waiting for her to continue.

"I was in New York, working in the lab on research, and that's when it happened. It was kinda quiet at first, then it got louder and eventually everything just stopped. The guns stopped shooting and everyone stopped running and for the first time in years, there was silence." She looked dazed as she glanced out the window to the beach.

"What happened?" Jade asked impatiently, it wasn't bloody poetry evening.

"The Voice," she said. She turned to face him. "This, like, weird Voice thing, I dunno what the hell it is but people seem to think it's like God or something."

"God?"

"So basically, it kept talking and the wars stopped, crime ceased, the media, discrimination; everything that was wrong with the world, it just came to a halt. People began living peacefully, it brought back faith. Now all people believe in the same faith. I mean seriously, church, religion - it's one of the most popular things nowadays. Weird if you ask me."

Jade stared in disbelief. It was wrong, it was all so wrong.

"Things are so different now Jade, there are no rules but everything is so… perfect. It doesn't make any sense and of course, there's no media, so many things have been wiped clean of the world, man. I mean like, police officers lost their jobs and us scientists - well, okay, don't get me started!"

She paused; he could tell there was some hidden reason she'd had to flee the city. "Whatever it is, I don't agree with it though, there're some of us, underground like, that think something's going on, we're trying to work this shit out but I have to say dude, I'm stumped. But I'll tell you one thing: people have been going missing."

Jade stared at the floor, clutching his mug. He just didn't understand it. He wanted to tell her what had happened to him, the worlds he had found. He knew he could either answer so many of her questions, or just create a million more.

"Why did you leave New York?" he asked with trepidation drawn across his features.

"The city that never sleeps is boring without the crime. Besides I didn't really have a choice, I had to shut down our mission, delete the information on the ship. It was too risky." She sighed. "Although I did like the risk, it was the only exciting thing going. But, where the fuck have you been? Our mission was meant to last one year. I honestly thought you were dead."

Jade gripped his mug tighter; he wanted to tell her of places he had been since their separation. He wanted her to know about the advanced knowledge of the many people he had met: their logic, books and lifestyles.

But he couldn't.

Margot's smile faded. She stared at him seriously. He met her glance. His hands trembled in anticipation, but he fought his desire to tell her the truth. It was just too dangerous. He knew what his words would do. Margot was rash; unlike Jade she couldn't just let things lie. The world he knew had gone, things were different and, until he had more of an understanding of what was going on around them, he didn't think it safe for her to take on the information. He couldn't quite believe it himself.

"Margot, I..." his words trailed off and she said nothing further about the matter. She didn't ask him again.

The rest of the evening was spent talking about the past, avoiding anything to do with the touchy subject of science. Evening drew in quickly and soon the night enveloped the sky. Jade stood up and walked towards the door. It was time for him to leave.

With no money and new rules to play by, he was what Margot would call 'screwed'. He put his thick goggles on top of his head once more and fastened the buttons on his trench coat. He went towards the door. As he turned the handle, he felt a hand on his shoulder.

"Stay."

And that was what he did.

Jade awoke early the next morning. He couldn't sleep. His head overflowed with thoughts. The whole of Earth had changed while he'd been away. His advanced knowledge excited him, but what he was going to do with it was another matter. From what Margot had told him, he had come to realise everywhere had advanced in culture and knowledge. He knew he must study his new environment before he could think of opening his mouth. She had told him very little the previous evening. He guessed it was because her knowledge was limited. For a scientist, it was so difficult to accept things without questioning and he understood the frustration it must have caused her through the years. However, there was one thing she'd told him that could be the solution to a lot of his problems. The 'Underground Association of Scientists' or as she called them, the 'UAS', nicknamed by the public as 'Sewer Scientists', were trying to find out what had really been going on with the world. He wondered when he would meet one.

Jade remembered when he had been a well-respected scientist. His first mission had generated great excitement and given the public hope. They had made him feel like he had a purpose. At that moment, he felt like he had been wiped off the face of the Earth.

Margot rubbed her eyes and glanced back towards the door. She stood on the balcony that overlooked the beach and leaned over the side as she put a self-lighting cigarette into her mouth. Margot lived a considerable walk away from any form of village or town on the island. Her home was situated on the edge of the disused floating harbour. She sighed before she breathed in the toxic fumes of the cigarette. It frightened her to think it was one of the only risks available to her now. Margot wasn't scared - she was bored.

The island was a welcome change to New York, but as far as she was concerned, life all around the globe was equally as mundane. She didn't know what had happened to Jade but she was determined to find out. She looked towards the deep jungle of the island and put on her leather coat. Like him, she hadn't been able to sleep well. Margot was worried, The Voice wasn't stupid. It knew that Jade was back. It would be coming for them. "Good morning," Jade said, he sat on a deckchair behind her.

"'Sup dude?" she replied.

"Margot, what's with the language, seriously?"

"It's 21st century slang, I've been taking classes. I had to do something to shizzle my nizzle since you've been gone." She laughed whilst Jade cringed.

"Okay, erm, good point. That sounded a little weird, let's go for a walk."

They strolled across the deserted beach in silence. Margot had said it was too early to talk, to which Jade had replied that it was 10 o'clock.

"Maybe we should go and check on the ship?" Jade asked.

"No," Margot said. "Let's just enjoy the walk, I'll show you around."

Signs of life appeared on the beach, Margot made a point of trying to have as little contact with people as possible. Jade noticed her behaviour but said nothing; he was too engrossed in watching the locals who seemed keen to talk to her. He watched as her face tensed when they invited her to the latest events taking place on the island. Nobody addressed him; the only attention he got was strange glances.

As they walked further along the shoreline, Margot pointed out a small village close to her home.

"I'll take you there after I've shown you more of this side," she said.

Jade nodded. He didn't dare question her further and knew that anything she had to tell him, she would explain when she was ready. Jade couldn't help wondering what she'd been doing all that time.

As Margot proceeded to show him the jungle of the island, trivial conversation took over. Most of it focusing on his umbrella, which he had decided to put up in an attempt to shield himself from the sun.

"Margot, I'm telling you," Jade defended himself. "I had no idea it was covered in purple flowers."

"Okay, despite that being totally the gayest thing I've ever seen, the point I'm trying to make is you should be used to this shit by now; one, you've lived in this temperature all your life and two, this was your effing home!"

"Maybe I don't like the sun; I don't have to, just because I was born here. Things aren't always that simple."

She gave him an exasperated glare; he was in one of his obstinate moods.

"Maybe not, but that doesn't change anything, good is good, evil is evil, and guys shouldn't carry around floral umbrellas."

Jade shook his head: "Gender stereotype, if you want."

For a moment he had thought she was going to make some form of intelligent response.

"Where the hell did you even get that from?" she said.

"The ship, I was unsure of the weather conditions in space."

"You're a douche."

Jade turned to face her. He tried to look as offended as possible, despite not having the slightest idea what a 'douche' was. Goddamn Margot and her language history class! He tried to think of a suitable come back.

"Yeah, well, well…" he floundered, unable to finish. Something had caught his eye further down the beach. Margot looked over her shoulder to see what had caused him to stop. Then she understood. She had forgotten how far they'd walked.

The figure was cold and stone-like. It reached high into the air and looked older than religion itself. Jade forgot himself for a moment and began to advance upon it. It was fashioned in the shape of a person. Upon closer inspection, Jade could make it out to be some form of hooded creature. Although, he wasn't quite sure what kind, as its features were hidden. The only other thing that he was able to see were two haggard wings, sticking out from the creature's back, worn by time and weather. The statue looked out of place. For some strange reason, Jade could imagine it having once been beautiful.

Margot called after him as she followed him down the beach. At last, he decided to stop and let her catch up.

"What is that?" Jade didn't avert his gaze from the hooded statue. Margot glanced from it to him, frowning.

"Let's go, Jade," she said and there was a serious tone in her voice. She tugged at his arm, until he was forced to follow her back towards her house. Margot reached in her pocket and pulled out another self-lighting cigarette, she took a long drag before muttering something Jade couldn't quite catch. She looked uncomfortable as he asked her to repeat what she'd said.

"That's one thing I didn't tell you, man," she said and looked back over her shoulder at the monstrosity Jade had just encountered. "When the Voice took over, things, those things came with it. They're all over the globe."

"But what…"

"Your guess is as good as mine. The Voice calls them 'angels'. Apparently the statues are meant to remind us of all the good in the world. Somehow, I'm not so sure."

They walked back to the house in silence. As they moved, he felt as though it was watching them and feared its hidden gaze, burning into the back of his head. Jade could quite honestly say he had no idea what was going on any more.

He fought his temptation to look back and stare. After all, it was far too late to turn back now.

Chapter 2

Weird Science

Someone once said that no matter where you went in the world, your home would always be your home. Jade thought it was a very inaccurate statement and that person was a great big liar; for his home was not his home any more. The only question that remained was what to do about it? So many things had changed. His family was gone, the Earth had been taken over and the only person who could help him had become a chain-smoking alcoholic in his absence. He didn't understand it; he had been floating about in the Universe for so long surely he must have spotted something? But space was so vast and full of mystery it was difficult to see, let alone find anything.

He searched Margot's kitchen, trying to find something edible for his strict diet. Everything she owned was full of calories and saturated fat, it was disgusting. Her kitchen was like a fast-food restaurant and not a very good one at that.

"Margot!" he called out towards the balcony.

"What?" she yelled back.

"Margot, your kitchen is like a run down version of 'Burger Buddies'!" He shook his head in disgust, leaning on the dark marble work surface. He glanced at the packaging of a sealed bag of hot dogs. God, she was so lazy. Jade screwed his face up as he reached further into her cupboard and pulled out a packet of biscuits. Organisation didn't seem to be at the height of the woman's priorities. Jade went to put the packet down then looked again. It was plain white, containing only the name of the food on the product, nothing else; neither brand, nor label. He picked up the hot dog packet, it was just the same. Jade flung open cupboard doors; he emptied the fridge and rifled though packets. It was all the same. Everything had the same white packaging. He didn't understand; where were the supermarkets' brands? Where was the information which actually said where the food came from? Then a terrifying thought struck him; people had no idea what they were consuming.

"Margot! Margot!" He screamed until she rushed inside. Her expression changed from one of horror to annoyance when he explained the issue.

"I can't believe you're making a fuss over a chocolate biscuit," she said, turning back to the balcony.

"No Margot, that's not the point! Where are you getting your food supplies from? Where are products being made?" he asked. "Your whole house is like it. There are no brands anywhere!"

"Jade, I don't know." Her tone was plain, her face harsh. She seemed to be deliberately concealing something from him. He knew Margot, she wasn't a fool. He needed to know exactly what had happened since he'd been away.

*

Now, readers, up to this point many of you may not understand Jade's overreaction to the peaceful atmosphere on Earth. You may also not understand his and Margot's relationship, or where the hell the scientist had been for the past few years. In fact, you probably have a long list of questions. Well, it is finally time for a few explanations.

The world as we know it had changed a great deal throughout the centuries. So much so that it had become unrecognisable to anyone over the age of sixty. As technology had advanced, many past creations had been made redundant. Things like ships and planes were seen as collectables for the rich eccentrics who had the time and money to invest. Spaceships were the new cars, and had been made so that the average home-owner could fly from island to island with ease.

It was difficult to find a non-multicultural society. Everyone had mixed with everyone, racial boundaries had been severely weakened and many were happy. A lot of languages had also been left behind in the past. English was still spoken all over the world and had an additional twenty four letters.

World leaders were seen as unnecessary and were discarded. Computer systems were quick to take their place. Many weren't happy about the idea, but when the wars stopped, they thought it was for the best. Hard labour was exclusively undertaken by machines. There was no unfair division of labour anymore; everyone was an equal.

Although it had taken centuries, in the late 2900s, humans had agreed upon some form of peace. Jade Wilde had grown up amongst it all. He'd never had any worry or fear that something would go wrong.

Since the age of three, his parents had noticed something odd about their son. The boy was an absolute genius. Before Jade had reached the age of twelve, he had built a perfect and functioning spaceship, worked out the last number of pi and had memorised the whole of the periodic table. His destiny was clear, Jade was to become a scientist.

Scientists had become renowned over the years. They were responsible for finding a cure for every known ailment, creating new modes of transport and preserving the Earth's surface reasonably well. All technological advances were the fruition of productivity between the scientists and engineers. Scientists had become their own breed entirely. Being one meant you had to be the best; some would even say 'superhuman'. Anyone related to a scientist was well respected and the Wildes were very aware of that fact.

Jade was enthusiastic when it was suggested to him, he was thrilled. So much so, that he applied to the University of Advanced Science in New York as soon as he got the chance. Although he didn't like the idea of leaving Bequia, he knew it was the only option available and the one he was best suited for.

However, as he had grown older, he had noticed a distinct change in the way the world had begun to function. The stories of gang wars on the news escalated into full-blown destruction. Yet again, mankind had shown their true colours. It was something Jade Wilde had always feared. With equal power came equal hunger. Corruption and greed soon took over many a human mind. Before humankind knew it, they were back to square one.

Past wars had seemed like myths to Jade. He was scared, scared of going to the cities, to the heart of the problem. There was nothing amidst the buildings but filth and death. Mankind, in his opinion, was outstaying its welcome. The world was plagued by over-population. Food grew scarce and gangs ruled the streets. The world was turning on itself. Jade had seen it coming for a long time. He wished science would slow down. It wouldn't be long before every finger pointed at them. The saviour would soon become the villain.

Then, a few weeks into one of the hottest summers Bequia had seen in years, Jade heard those fateful words.

"Jade!" his mother yelled. "You're in! You're going to New York!"

Whilst Jade Wilde's heart sank, another's, living thousands of miles across the world, soared. That heart belonged to no other than Margot Grant. Finally, the English girl was leaving the life of mechanics behind her and jetting off to New York. Crime was no threat to her, she had lived amongst it. New York seemed like the perfect place to carry out her plans.

Little did Jade and Margot know their paths were soon to cross. It only took two days for someone to steal Jade's bag.

"Hey!" Jade screamed and charged after the culprit. "That has my research in it!"

Suddenly, a blonde haired woman darted out in front of him. She effortlessly overtook the thief, tripped him and retrieved the bag.

"You should be more careful," she had said, opening his bag and looking through his papers.

"I had it covered," Jade said angrily, snatching back his work. "He was just really fast."

"It was a little girl."

"Who are you?"

"The name's Margot Grant. You should know; you sit in front of me in most of our lectures."

From that moment, their friendship was formed. Their education however, was cut short.

The constant fires of New York disrupted the lectures as they tore the city apart. Margot and Jade knew that there was no hope left on the Earth.

"It's no good Jade," Margot said. "If we don't do something now, the whole goddamn planet is gonna be destroyed."

"Margot, Galaxtica 5.0 and its crew were lost as soon as they left Pluto," Jade said. "You know it's our only option, and judging by that, it's just not possible."

"It is, Jade! With your knowledge and my engineering skills we can do it. We can build the ultimate ship and go find help." She slammed her fist down on the lab table to punctuate her determination.

For some time it had been a plan of theirs to travel out of the solar system. If Margot's theory was correct, and Jade was ninety-eight percent sure that it was, they could build an engine which ran just under the speed of light. The machine would bring hope and ultimately, help for all those on the planet.

The albino was well known for believing that life existed outside of the solar system. However, despite centuries of searching, nothing had ever been found. People had begun to give up and the search had ended long ago. But not for Margot, Jade knew that until she found something, she would never stop.

They slaved away in secret in the labs of New York until it was finally complete. Word had somehow got around, and many thought the news was groundbreaking. Margot and Jade were to go down in the history books. The mission for Normad 1 was all set to go. Jade knew that the ship could hold only one and, to the surprise of many, he volunteered himself.

All was set to run smoothly, his course had been charted. His route had been set. Everything should have gone to plan, but alas-

*

"Jade, have you seen my black skinny-jeans?" Margot shouted. "I'm going to be late for work!"

Work. Jade had quite forgotten about work. Margot worked at 'The Shy'; a local bar on the island. How different life was. He wondered how she felt about it. He didn't dare ask. Margot had so much potential; she was such an intelligent person. The last time he'd seen her, she was waving him off from a science lab. Now, she was a nobody; she was stuck on a godforsaken island; out of the field because of mysterious words from the sky. *How had it happened? What had caused the change since he'd been away?*

A sick feeling shot through Jade's body. He needed air.

"Yes, the sofa." he replied slowly. "I'm going for a walk."

The following week sped by faster than Jade could have anticipated. He walked through the washed out, robotic streets of Bequia. Everything was as he remembered it from childhood, yet so much seemed to be missing. The world had lost its liveliness and character. Jade had never been accustomed to the quiet life, but even he knew the days were going too slow.

He strolled through the town, and made use of his purple umbrella. It was his favourite time in the morning, when all the inhabitants were in church praising their beloved Voice. It took place around eight thirty. Margot was one of the few who never turned up. He thought that her absence was breaking some form of law, even though nothing was ever formally announced.

That was what made Jade feel so uneasy about the Earth. Despite the lack of rules, everyone remained in perfect harmony. The world was quiet. The Earth was at peace.

Since his return, he had seen no acts of violence, no drunken citizens or anything of a suspicious nature. People got on with their daily lives, happy enough. What was stranger still was that no one seemed to question anything. The Voice really did have control. Jade sighed; maybe there wasn't anything wrong. Okay, he knew that whatever the thing was, it wasn't a God, but did that mean that stopping the war was wrong? Maybe the 'thing' had helped.

He shook his head. He was over-thinking the situation. Jade stopped in front of the newly-built church and let the choral voices fill his ears. He frowned at the building, with its thick, wooden structures and beautiful stained-glass windows. Every place of worship preached the same words, the words of the Voice. It was voluntary, he kept telling himself. He would not force himself to be part of something he knew, deep down, was wrong.

He had yet to hear the 'Voice'. The power it had over the people of earth was worrying and made the task of explaining to Margot where he'd spent his absent years harder than ever. He had tried so many times to talk to her but he just didn't know how to phrase the things he needed to say. Margot was distant. When she spoke, however much she tried to hide, he could hear the anxiety in her voice creeping through. He knew she knew more than she was telling him. When they had first been reunited, she had spoken to him quite openly about the UAS. It had been the one and only occasion it had been mentioned. He knew she thought she had revealed too much to him while he thought she hadn't revealed enough.

Jade stepped onto the golden sand, and pondered that fact. A lot of the people he had spoken to since arriving home hadn't had the same spark that Margot did. Maybe he was being over-analytical? No. He convinced himself he must be right. They had seemed emptier, less aware or focussed than her. Then again, it could have just been his imagination. Oh how he had missed her. Oh how he wished he could make a clear decision for once.

He was happy to be away from the clueless town. No one had any idea what was happening within the world, let alone their own goddamn village. They didn't know where their food came from, never mind who was in charge of each country. He suspected people didn't travel from island to island anymore. Despite it being a small island, he hadn't seen one ship in the sky since he had arrived.

He sighed, information was scarce. When he thought about it, the only information that he remembered being delivered to the people of the island was a pamphlet entitled 'Your World Week'. He had glanced at Margot's with interest at first but soon found the content provided nothing important. The majority of it had been filled with tips on how to be a good person and ways to 'walk down the path of righteousness'. There were no politics or law to be spoken of, everything within it was good news, happy, random, perplexing stories about the most trivial of things that Jade had rendered pointless to even mention. Such headlines as 'Pensioner Makes World's First Floating Food' – *big deal* he thought, *try going into zero gravity and then watch your food dance above your head.*

He came to his decision before he reached the door. It was time to tell Margot the truth, whatever the consequence. He couldn't bear it any longer. He would not be held responsible for how she would react. Jade nodded to himself for personal reassurance as he stepped into the hallway.

He took his boots off at the door and placed them on the floating tray that took them to the closet. He gulped before making his way up the spiral staircase to the open-plan kitchen. There sat Margot on a sofa in the far corner of the room. Jade paused as he approached her.

"Margot I…" he began, but was swiftly interrupted.

"Jade, I've not been completely honest with you." Her features hardened. Her hands were rigid by her side.

"I'm going out," she said. "If you want to know the truth of the Earth, I strongly suggest you come with me." There was no playfulness, no colloquialisms as there usually would be. Jade said nothing, merely nodded in response and ran to get changed into another flamboyant shirt.

Ten minutes later, Jade was walking across the shores of Bequia in silence. However, Margot walked with him and they were walking in the opposite direction, leading away from the town and the angel statue. She zipped up her black leather jacket as she led Jade into the island's thick jungle.

"Margot, I'm not so sure about this," his voice faltered.

Margot turned back to him; he was standing on the edge of the beach. "Do you want answers or not?" she hissed.

He uttered an inaudible reply, but decided to follow.

The jungle was thick and the ground underfoot was uneven. Every now and again Jade would stumble behind his leader. The trees were so close together that the roots entwined. Jade had no idea how Margot knew her way to wherever the hell they were going. There were no paths marked for them to follow, no markers to guide them. It appeared to him as the most deserted part of Bequia. He jumped as he heard shuffling in the background. What if there were creatures around there? What if she were leading him into a trap? No, he told himself, not Margot.

He continued to follow her deeper into the wilderness, the path became a gentle incline and as Margot reached the foot of the small hill they were approaching, she changed her direction and went where the ground remained flat.

"We're almost there."

He looked up ahead; the trees were beginning to clear. Jade gulped, wondering what Margot possibly had to show him. She emerged through the branches, looking as clean and collected as she had when she had first ventured in. She paused before looking around to see where he had gone.

"Jade?" she called, ensuring her voice wasn't too loud.

No answer.

All was silent around her. She waited a few seconds and then parted her lips, ready to call his name once more when he fell from between the trees into the open space.

"Oh my goodness!" Jade panted. He groaned as he collapsed on to the floor in a heap, pulling out bits of twigs from his dreadlocks. It was obvious he wasn't fond of exercise. Margot loaded her mouth with another cigarette before pulling him to his feet.

"Thank you," he said and placed one foot forward. There was a familiar squelch under his boot. Animal dung! "Give me strength, this is ridiculous."

Margot remained silent.

"These are non-refundable! Margot, are you listening?" but his voice trailed off as he became aware of his surroundings for the first time.

In the middle of the clearing before them, a dilapidated factory loomed. It was made from red brick, which appeared to have faded over time. As Jade approached the building, he questioned the oddity of its sudden appearance. How could he have lived on the island for so many years and not known of its existence?

He stayed behind Margot. The place was eerily quiet, it unnerved him and he switched into hypersensitive mode; stooping his body low to the ground and flinching at the tiniest of sounds. He followed Margot and they circumnavigated the factory, giving Jade a chance to take it all in. The building was huge, at least four floors high, it was taller than some of the surrounding trees. The windows were large and arched with metal bars crossed over the panes of glass on the outside. He thought it may have partially sunk into the ground, by the look of its slanted positioning in the field.

There was no sign of a clear way in. Jade didn't think that would worry Margot. Despite the dirt on the outer body of the building, there was no graffiti or gang signs, which made him wonder how many people were aware of it.

Margot, walked around the building a second time, she paused at a window, lower than the rest, but still above her head. The window was broken; it contained only a few pieces of shattered glass within the white frame. He could see her eyeing it up.

"Margot don't!" But it was too late; she ignored his words and scrambled up the side of the building, using the bricks as her climbing frame. He gasped, there was no way he was doing that - *nooooo way*.

"Jade, are you coming or what?" Margot was standing on the ledge.

Okay, he said to himself, he was going up.

He pulled his goggles over his eyes and rubbed his hands together. Jade took a few steps backwards and ran at the wall at full speed, leaping high into the air. Unfortunately for him, he had never really been the sportiest of people, nor had he had the best aim. The man missed his target to end up at the bottom of the wall in an ungainly heap of limbs and coat.

"Fucking hell," Margot found it hard to contain her laugher. He looked up to see she had disappeared from the ledge.

"Margot? Margot!" He called as he got to his feet, desperately hoping she hadn't left him there. He heard a faint rustling from inside. Out of nowhere, a rope ladder unfurled and the bottom rung landed at his feet.

"Climb up dude, I've got you!" came the albino's voice from inside.

Jade reached the top and squeezed his body through the bars. There was no sign of Margot; he could see nothing at all. She had truly left him in the darkness. The roof was full of holes and was in danger of collapsing due to its age but there still wasn't enough light to see by. He was worried she might have fallen off the ledge. He wanted to edge one of his feet forward, to see how far it went, but he was far too terrified. He reached for his goggles and flicked a switch on the side, turning on the 'night mode'. He flicked another switch on the frame, and one of the two mini torches which sat just above the lenses came on. Purple light burst from it and glared onto the opposite wall. He glanced down momentarily and screamed, flinching away. He was inches from the edge; it hadn't occurred to him how high he was.

"Turn that bloody light off!" shouted a voice from somewhere within the cavernous room. The voice echoed from wall to wall. Jade did as he was told.

"Margot this isn't funny, I'm leaving now!" he turned his goggles off and moved to the window. Below him he could hear more mumbling voices.

"Someone go get him. Margot, he's your friend," a female said. Jade stood still.

"Jade!" Margot's voice echoed in the darkness. "Walk to the right of the ledge and jump, trust me, you'll be fine!"

Fine? Fine! She wanted him to jump to his death and expected that he'd end up in one piece? He didn't think he'd be able to fulfil both of her requirements. His legs shook as he approached the edge again. Not wanting to see the drop below him, he gingerly reached out with one foot until it found the very far right of the ledge. There was definitely no further way to go on the left. He let go of the bars on the window and bent his knees in preparation.

"I hate you sometimes, Margot!" he shouted as he jumped.

Jade's feet found sudden ground. He laughed to himself, realising there was a second ledge directly below the first. His hand reached towards his goggles, he switched them to night mode again. Although their range was limited, he could see it was a much wider platform. He scoped the area around him. Directly in front of him was a set of steps he hoped would lead to the ground. Keeping close to the wall, he moved his way down until he reached the dusty ground. The place appeared empty. The only things that were in motion were the dust particles floating through the thick air. He took a few more steps forward. The room was large and empty. He could make out poles reaching high up to the ceiling, keeping the structure in place. The only noise he heard came from his boots which were treading on the broken glass and wood that was littered around the room. His body began to shake once more. Where was she?

Suddenly something moved in the darkness.

"Hello?" he called out and his voice shook too. Jade looked around him. Something came into focus through his goggles. A figure moved towards him. He wanted to run but he knew it was pointless. She had led him into a trap, his own best friend! *I must stand and fight*, he told himself. The figure began to pick up speed until it was practically running at him. This was it. The person was only metres away when he pulled back his hand in preparation to make a swing. It leapt at him and he hit it directly in the face, watching as it fell to the ground.

"What the fuck was that for?" Margot sat on the floor at his feet, rubbing her face.

"Oh gosh!" He realised what he had done, "I'm so sorry! I thought, I thought -"

"You thought what?" she snapped at him. "It's a good job you punch like a girl or that might have actually hurt."

"I do not punch like a girl!" was his defensive reply.

"Jade we don't have time to talk; we're going to be late." She picked herself from up from the ground.

"For what?" He snapped. He was tired of playing her games.

"You'll see."

Maybe he would, but he was surprised she could see anything. Upon closer inspection she appeared to be wearing sunglasses. That confused him even more.

They walked to the centre of the room, or at least what Jade assumed to be the centre, given his poor vision. He brushed plants and branches away from his face as he went.

"Stand here," Margot directed him to a spot, or rather, a square on the floor within the greenery. He could hear by the echo of his feet as he stepped onto it that it was metal.

"Ok, now hold on," Margot said, gripping a pole attached to the ground.

"Why? Mar..." it was too late.

The floor shot downwards, deep underground.

"AAAARGHHHHH!" Jade screamed and gripped the pole so tight his fingers locked. The set up didn't seem very stable so Jade was very thankful that the descent didn't last long and the floor began to slow down. It stopped in front of two metal doors sunk into the dark earth which surrounded Jade and Margot.

"Get the hell off me," Margot said, glaring down at Jade who was clinging to her waist. He quickly got up and brushed himself down, trying to regain the dignity that he'd lost. He looked up, trying to fathom how far they had dropped. The range on his goggles couldn't make out the top of the shaft. It made him feel queasy. Margot, on the other hand, seemed perfectly fine. She moved towards the doors and typed in a code that he couldn't make out.

"Jade," she said, holding her arm out in a grand gesture as the doors began to open. "May I present to you, the U.A.S."

His eyes widened as he stepped into the room. He stepped out onto a large white platform which levitated in the brightly lit room. He looked around in awe. Over the edge he could see long lines of computers engaged by hundreds of people. To the right were various tables covered in potions, Bunsen-burners and an extensive range of scientific equipment around which people were moving, taking notes and sharing information. The room stretched back and he could make out a few doors in the distance. The doors led to the various laboratories for individual research facilities.

Blackboards were hung upon all the walls, with lecturers standing in front of them, giving talks to small groups of people. People were going up and down the main staircases from the platform carrying files, books and what he thought to be research. He realised the place must be extremely up-to-date as he had never seen or dreamed of some of the equipment. For example, the mysterious orbs which followed some of the scientists around, flashing and scanning various parts of their experiments.

"Saves the more advanced scientists having to record things," Margot said as she noticed the wondrous expression on his face. Margot had removed her sunglasses and slipped on a white lab coat that had been hanging to the left of the door. She handed him one, which he slipped on over his coat.

The queasy feeling returned, he moved away from the edge and turned to face the doors through which they had entered. Above the doors, the wall was crammed with monitors simultaneously broadcasting different images. He pondered for a moment, Margot's house didn't have the channels they had in the lab.

"These are the only channels that actually provide us with real information," she said, pointing at the screens. "They're run by a small media community that's also rebelling against the Voice."

He nodded.

The place was full of noise from conversations about different types of chemicals, to random bangs and crashes in the background from experiments. Jade tried to catch the words of passers-by; he liked what he heard.

Jade and Margot had caught the attention of a large man standing in front of a raised podium in the centre of the room. As the man turned, Jade observed his features; his smooth rounded face, his messy grey hair and his small, beady eyes. He, like the rest, was wearing a white coat, but also had brilliantly white clothes underneath. Jade noticed that he looked tired and worn and, although his smile seemed friendly enough upon first greeting, he sensed smugness, a snide motivation beneath it. When it came down to the matter, he did not trust the man and he had no logical reasoning behind the sudden decision.

"Dr Grant, so glad you could finally join us," he said, with a sharp tone in his voice. He advanced towards them.

"Dude," Margot nodded in return then waved to a girl passing by in the distance who then also approached them. *Wow*, Jade thought to himself, she was beautiful. The girl was carrying a large stack of papers, but was not struggling with the weight. She had dark Asian skin and black hair, which was flowing loose over her shoulders. The long sleeves of her lab coat had been rolled up just above the elbows to reveal two sleeves of heavily detailed tattoos that travelled to the wrist. She had a few more piercings than Margot, Jade noticed. It made him wonder what other things lurked under the little black dress she was wearing but then felt the sick feeling in his stomach returning.

"Hi Margot." she said. She looked Jade over and had to look twice to actually believe what she saw. The first guy on the other hand was a lot less fazed by Jade. Margot had brought him, as she had promised.

"Professor Wilde," the man held out his chubby fingers towards Jade, which he reluctantly shook. "I'm Professor Clarke. So glad you are here at last; we honestly thought you were dead."

Jade smiled politely. He couldn't form a response, for he was too fixated on his stomach.

"Well, I can't believe it, Professor Jade Wilde!" The girl exclaimed, looking from him to Margot. With that comment, the room around them fell silent, all eyes on Jade. It was not good.

"It's good to meet you," she said. She stepped forward to shake his hand. "It's good to have such a well-respected scientist on the team, if you don't mind my saying so, your work on realms and dimensions was fascinating. The fact that you believe life older than us can co-exist alongside our Universe is an amazing theory."

This was all too much for Jade's weak stomach. He opened his mouth in an attempt at replying, but instead, he vomited all over her designer heels.

He had never been very good with crowds.

After the mess had been cleaned up from the floor, Clarke took Jade on a tour around the headquarters. Jade had apologised to the girl and offered to buy her a new pair of shoes. Whatever awe or power he once invoked had surely gone. The balance within the universe had been restored, and once again she, like so many other females, appeared way out of his league.

"He's potty trained I swear, Reenie," Margot muttered to the woman, who just laughed. Jade cringed, trying to forget what had just happened, why did those things always happen to him?

"...now as you know Professor Wilde, we are one of the few science labs still to exist on the Earth. I trust Dr Grant has told you about the U.A.S. collaboration?" Professor Clarke said.

"I, well..."

"Good," Professor Clarke smiled, looking up at him. Professor Clarke was of average height, but most people looked small when they stood next to Jade.

They walked past a group of people occupied with various tasks. Jade felt their eyes look up to glance at him when they passed by. Everyone seemed to be trying to catch a glimpse of him.

"Now, the main aim, Professor Wilde,"

"Oh, you, you can call me Jade," he said, a little embarrassed by the formality of the situation. It was the first time in years that he had been surrounded by such a large crowd. He felt overwhelmed.

"Okay, Professor Wilde," said Clarke, not too concerned by the request. As they reached the back of the room he opened a door which led to a long grey corridor. "Believe it or not, this centre runs under almost all of Bequia."

"That's crazy!" Jade said. "Margot, sorry I mean Dr. Grant spoke to me about the, shall we say, dislike of scientists. Now, surely this so-called "Voice" would do something if it was to find out about this?"

"Exactly," Clarke agreed. "That's why, with new technology, we've managed to create protection for the building. It can't be seen by anyone who doesn't originate from the Earth. Now sir, I don't know if you've noticed but our staff come from all around the globe." They continued walking down to the end of the corridor which led to a lift. Jade shuddered, hoping it wouldn't travel as fast as the last one. "...So, we use these." Clarke finished as he opened the door. Jade smiled when he saw what the man was talking about. He stood in the middle of another corridor; one wall was made entirely of glass and looked out to an underwater space. It was a parking area for small underwater cars, much like the land versions that had been banned under the Voice's ruling. Jade stared at the rows and rows, held down by anchors. He couldn't see the ends of the ropes holding the ships; they descended too far to see.

"Professor Clarke, what have you been researching here? Dr Grant told me she suspected something about this 'Voice' but she never elaborated on the subject."

"Well, we don't believe it is any form of God, as you may have already guessed. Our main aim is to work out what is going on with the world in these confusing times," he said, then quickly added: "Your ability is well known in the scientific community, we've been waiting for your return, Wilde. I was hoping you'd be able to assist our research, what with your ship..."

It was obvious that he had no idea how far Jade had gone, no one did.

Jade didn't reply, just gazed out beyond the glass.

The ships made him feel so small, so powerless. The science seemed so important, much more important than it had when he had left. Maybe the new world was not all bad, it had allowed the people who worked there to truly appreciate what they had. They had all come together, to fight whatever the Voice was, to unify their scientific knowledge, for science was their true passion. He smiled as they retraced their steps. It was a place that, although may be completely against the law, was bringing people together to work as one. It is what the Earth needed, what humans had been missing. Technology had made people lazy; they didn't have to work to get anything. The people had been thrown into a situation with nothing left to depend upon but themselves. Jade shook himself back into reality when he realised Clarke had been trying to communicate with him.

"...Wilde, are you listening?"

"Oh, yes sorry."

They were in one of the individual research facilities. He looked around for a moment, spotting Margot and Reenie in deep conversation.

"Don't mind Professor Wilde," Margot smirked. "He often goes off on some form of philosophical thought tangent."

"I see," Clarke replied coldly, turning the conversation back to Margot and leaving Jade in his broken daze. "And how did he manage to find you?"

"My ship landed on the Earth just last week," Jade explained. He watched as Reenie and Clarke's eyes grew wide in amazement.

"It is not possible," Clarke said.

"I don't understand, doctor," Jade said and glanced at Margot in annoyance.

"Professor Jade, you must understand, no one has been able to fly a ship, let alone leave the Earth!" Clarke said.

Jade's eyes narrowed, Margot had not told him. Why she had concealed so much from him was a complete mystery.

She reached for a cigarette.

"No smoking, Grant!" Clarke snapped. "You mean to say you've been out in space all this time?"

"Well, erm, yes."

"But how? How did you go unspotted? How, wha-" Clarke's character had completely changed. He was not so smooth, so cool-headed, he was in shock. Reenie on the other hand, was not intimidated at all. She was cool, composed, unimpressed. She leaned back and spoke to Margot. Margot stifled a laugh.

"It is settled!" Clarke said, finally able to gain control of his senses. "He is what we've been looking for."

Jade made to speak but something told him to remain silent.

"Don't worry, Professor, you don't need to thank me, your presence here is thanks enough." Professor Clarke gave a menacing smile in Jade's direction, before turning to Margot: "A word please, Grant."

Margot nodded and followed him outside the office, leaving Jade alone with Reenie.

Reenie ignored him and continued working. She was so calm, a lot more 'together' than she had been earlier. But her neutral expression also brought out a serious air about her. Like Margot, she was a strong-headed woman. Jade liked that.

He also liked the fact that she continued to remain silent and he was then able to try to listen in on the conversation outside.

"… Are you sure about this?" Clarke's voice was muffled.

"Perfectly sure," Margot replied.

"I mean this is not natural, should you test it on someone else first?"

"He's the perfect specimen."

"Excuse me, you're in my way," Reenie broke the silence and ended Jade's snooping.

"Sorry," he mumbled, moving back so she was able to open a cupboard. "Look, I do apologise about the ermm, shoe incident."

She frowned. He looked down to her feet, which were in a bright pair of yellow wellies. He gave an awkward laugh: "They ermm… sort of suit you."

She made no reply, and left Jade to try to listen to the conversation outside once more.

"…but we don't know what this can do. This is very powerful stuff, Grant."

"I don't see why everyone's so fascinated by you," Reenie said and Jade sighed at her words. "I mean yeah, I admit your research is amazing, but since you left, Margot and I have been working together, you know? I'm her new partner here."

She made it sound like she was working for the police force. Deep down, the comment hurt him, it stung his heart. *Margot had a new partner?* He and

Margot had been working together since they'd met. He supposed he'd have to accept that times had moved on, she had moved on and he'd be selfish to expect that she'd waited for him all those years. He remained silent, not wanting to know more about the many years that he had missed out on.

Suddenly, the door swung open, revealing Margot and Professor Clarke, who looked more flustered than when they'd left minutes earlier.

"Right then, everything seems to be in order," Clarke's face was stern as he spoke. "I'll be in contact, Professor Wilde, expect a call in the next few days." Reenie looked to the ceiling in response. He turned to Margot and nodded as if his words had some underlying meaning.

"Well, I didn't expect that," Jade was still in shock as they retraced their steps back through the thick jungle.

"What, the U.A.S. or the fact that you puked all over Reenie's designer heels?"

He put his hand to his face at the comment and held it there a while.

"Come on, you have to admit it was some funny shit, man!" She taunted him as they reached the shore. The beach was dotted with people, strolling up and down the coastline. Jade hesitated, wondering if anyone else was aware of where they had just been. Something flashed past the corner of his eye, causing him to jump. It was like a white light flashing past his line of vision. His goggles had picked it up instantly.

"It's fine," Margot said and smiled at him, she hadn't noticed anything. She reached into her pocket and put another cigarette to her mouth. It lit at the touch of her lips and Jade coughed at the smoke. That was one part of the Earth he could really do without. He glanced back to see if he could find where the light went. There was nothing there.

"Margot, did you just see that thing?" He said, looking around him.

"See what?" Margot said. "Jade, I think you need more sleep."

She stared at him for a moment as they stepped out of the jungle and onto the sand.

"Yeah, maybe you're right." It seemed stupid of the Earth to believe in something like the Voice. *People never change*, he thought, they needed to believe in something, to keep magic and hope alive. However, Jade, on the other hand, did not.

"Margot," he hesitated as he spoke. "Margot, erm, what was it that you and Clarke were talking about?"

She turned to face him, her red eyes burning, "That, that was nothing Jade. Don't worry about it."

But he did worry, he worried all too much.

That night there was an urgent knock at the door, too panicked for Jade's liking. He didn't question it; he had known Margot too long and understood that those people weren't going to be your everyday type.

"Shit, one moment!" Margot shouted, "Jade, get the door will you?"

He sighed; he was in the middle of tying his dreadlocks back. He went downstairs with a deal of reluctance. At the front door he pressed the large blue button by the side of it. Margot had told him it was the latest in security technology and something that was fitted within all modern households. Inside the door was a camera which took a 3D holographic snap shot of anyone standing on the other side. He thought it was useful; it was good to be sure of any visitors, especially if they were bailiffs or Jehovah's Witnesses. But Jade wasn't sure of the visit at all. He was surprised at the photo that dropped through the letter box. It revealed an image of Professor Clarke and Reenie. He put it down and opened the door. The man and woman hurried inside. When he saw them for the second time, he noticed the contrast between the characters. Clarke's huge stomach hung over his belt and his hair, long and white, seemed even messier than when they had first met. However, Reenie looked more radiant than earlier, he noticed her dress complimented her curvy physique. Jade smiled at her and she gave him a nod before following Clarke up the spiral staircase in search of Margot. He saw that both of them were still wearing their white lab coats from before.

Margot came out of the kitchen. "You're earlier than expected." She gave them a suspicious glance.

"We have to try this tonight," Clarke said. He sounded serious but his face wore a constant frown, so Jade could never quite be sure what mood he was in.

However, Margot seemed to read him easily. She looked taken aback as he spoke, "What's happened?"

"We've come straight from the U.A.S. base. It's nothing to worry about but we think someone's on to us. Looks like someone found the building after you left today, something that wasn't quite human," Reenie looked down as she spoke.

"Really?" Margot exclaimed. "This is amazing!"

"No it is not amazing. If it's true, it means the Voice is on to us," Clarke sighed. "The point is we need to try the experiment. If it works, it may help."

"Here?" Margot asked. They both nodded.

Jade was about to speak but Margot put her arm out to silence him. "Okay guys, did you bring the shit?" Margot glanced at their coats. Jade was confused. Reenie dipped her hand into the inside of her coat, revealing a small medicine bottle.

"Here's 'the shit' as you so call it. I still think that using him is a bad idea," Clarke said, looking at Jade who seemed to have missed the last part of the conversation. He was more interested in what Reenie held in her hand.

"Margot, what's that?" he asked. Reenie threw the bottle over to him.

"Open it," she commanded. He twisted the lid and found that he couldn't get past the child lock. Margot sighed, took it from him and poured the contents out into her pale hand, smiling as she did so.

"Dude, this is it!" her fiery eyes filled with wonder as she stared down at the pills.

They were nothing like Jade had seen before. He had a feeling that they weren't drugs for medical use either. From what he could make out, they were in the shape of eyes, with ocean blue pupils and a deep black iris. The colour on them seemed to float about, mixing together. He thought that to be impossible, probably just a trick of the light.

"Margot, what's going on? They don't look like pills you can buy from shops!" Jade gave her a stern look.

"It's something me and Reenie have been working on. They're my own invention. I call the drug 'Face'."

"'Face'?" Jade raised his eyebrows.

"Yes, it works a bit like shrooms I guess, only instead of giving you pointless and random hallucinations, the aim is to give clear visions of the future to those that take it." She paused. "I've been researching the Native Indians of America and looking at their hallucinogenic drugs. Peyote was one of them, or as the English called it, The Devil's Root." She sounded far too enthusiastic for Jade's liking.

"May I ask why?" He asked in a grave tone.

"So I can mix it with modern ingredients," she said as if it was the most obvious thing in the world. "These little babies give you a glimpse into the future or the unknown or something else, I'm not certain, because I haven't exactly tested them out yet." She mumbled the last part of the sentence, hoping he wouldn't hear. He did.

"Margot!" He glanced around in shock, looking at Reenie and Professor Clarke, whose expressions remained rigid.

She continued in her historical slang. "How cool is that, man? I mean these could change everything. I've been working on them for so long now and tonight we can finally find out if they work!" She jumped in the air as though performing a kind of victory dance. The others seemed a lot less enthusiastic.

"Margot," Jade repeated. "No wonder people hate scientists around here, you, you… wait a minute who's testing these things?"

Then he remembered her conversation with Clarke at the U.A.S. base earlier and, upon this realisation, his eyes widened with horror.

"Shut the hell up, Jade!" The other two in the room were taken aback by Margot's passionate tone.

"Now are you gonna test them out or not?" She continued to yell at him.

Reenie and Clark were quiet and extremely awkward amidst the quarrel, despite trying to appear relaxed. They exchanged a look, trying to convince themselves that it was the right thing to do.

"But everything you told me earlier, the angels! If, if the Voice finds out," he stuttered as he tried to shout back.

"Screw the fucking Voice!" she cut in, trying to calm herself down for the next statement. "Jade, this is really important, we need you. This may help us find out a lot of information and since you've spent time away from the Earth, it'll probably reveal more to you."

She gave him a moment to reflect.

"So are you gonna try a pill or not?" she asked. They were inches away from each other's faces.

"NO!" He shouted. But it was too late. As he opened his mouth to reply, she had already pushed it inside.

Jade moved to the leather sofa and sat down. He felt strange and not the good strange that he was widely renowned for. He glanced around in search of the others. The room began to spin. Before long, he was surrounded by vibrant colours which polluted his view and danced around to form new and different shapes before him. He wondered how long the effects of 'Face' would take to wear off or whether or not it would even work.

"Margot, I'm going to kill you!" He shouted, but she was nowhere in sight. He thought about it and he wasn't sure if he had even opened his mouth in the first place. He looked around. He was no longer in Margot's house but on the beach close to where his ship had landed a week ago.

"Hello?" He called out. There was no reply. The orange ball of a sun was setting in the burning sky. Something seemed wrong, it was darker, the atmosphere felt cold and lifeless. Unsure of what to do, he ran down the beach.

Jade stopped; he felt the ground beneath him shake violently. It grew to a critical stage. Something was approaching him, something big, and by the sound of it, something uncontrollable.

Jade screamed… his hat flew off his head. It blew down the beach and he forgot the noise as he ran after it. Finally, it stopped on the cold shore. Without thinking, Jade bent down to pick it up. He frowned, the noise had stopped. Suddenly, a horrible thought occurred to him as something caught his eye. He gulped, as he turned towards it. It was dark and grey and stood right before him. *The angels, they were... moving?*

It couldn't be possible, he thought, as he tried to look underneath the hood of its cloak. It raised its arm and he realised that it would be a fine time to run. Jade sprinted across the beach and dived into conveniently placed bushes. Before his very eyes, two of the huge stone structures were moving across the quiet beach. They were a lot quicker than he thought but their pace was unsteady, inhuman.

From what he could see of them, they still seemed as beautiful as before, but behind the piercing eyes, he saw something cold and empty he turned away. That was when he heard the screaming. When he looked again, he saw they were carrying people in their slender hands, but they weren't just any people - Reenie and Clarke.

Jade tried to run and hide but his feet didn't want him to move. The angels' haggard wings opened out and they flew away into the night, leaving the sandy shores of the Caribbean behind them. Before he knew it, he could feel himself leaving the ground.

Jade floated in the air like a helium balloon. He wasn't sure it if was the wind or just the drug that caused him to follow the two creatures and their victims.

He raced above the motionless sea. He couldn't understand how nature could seem so calm. Jade wondered where they were going, what they were doing or more to the point where Margot would be when he woke up.

It was pitch-black, the night was upon them. The only thing that told him he was still travelling over sea was the reflection from the only light visible, the silver moon. He let out a gasp, realising the direction they had taken. The angels had led him right into the heart of the Bermuda triangle. He wasn't one for superstition, but it was beginning to get strange.

That was when he first spotted the light in the distance. It looked white, almost godly. The angels were flying straight towards it. Then bright colours began to swirl around, dancing into the centre of his eyes once again.

"No! Not now," he shouted, again unsure whether the words left his mouth or not. The scenery began to change.

He found himself face-down on a cold, stone floor. He sat up. If it was a vision then why was it so painful? Unsure of what had happened; Jade tried to look at his surroundings, which were blurred. Then something caught his eye. He couldn't quite make out what it was at first. All he knew was that it had the same godly light he saw earlier.

Finally the room began to take focus, it had high stony walls and heavy chains across the arch windows situated high up just below the dark ceiling. He could hear the faint humming of a female voice. The voice was filled with sorrow, if only he could make out the words it was trying to say. A dark figure appeared from the corner of the room, walking towards the light. Jade couldn't distinguish if it was male or female.

"She is coming, and her army."

"Who is coming?" A female voice asked. It seemed to come from all sides of the room.

"Margot Grant."

Jade blacked out.

Chapter 3

The man who fell to Earth

"Jade? Ja-a-ade." A faint voice echoed in the background. Jade Wilde was regaining consciousness.

"JADE!" Margot yelled. He jumped.

Jade opened his eyes to find a familiar face surrounded by a mass of white hair looming over him. Whatever he was lying on was hard and uncomfortable.

"Urghh," he moaned, rolling over and opening his eyes. He was face down on the kitchen floor.

"Well, he's not dead." Margot said in a sarcastic tone.

As his eyes came to focus, he saw her move to the other side of the room and grab her leather jacket.

"Whaaa?" He was dazed. What had just happened? Was he still dreaming? Jade turned his head, towards the balcony. Sunlight was streaming through from the French doors. *How long have I been out cold for?*

"What time is it?" he groaned, trying to get to his feet. It didn't work. His balance was off, he was unsteady and he fell back onto the floor. His stomach felt heavy and his head throbbed. It was like waking up from a heavy night of drinking. He could feel his body shake as he tried to stand.

"For god's sake," Margot sighed, pulling him upright then going to the kitchen counter. "You're such a bloody drama queen."

Jade's memory began to return to him. He glared at her, "You, you..." He stuttered as he tried to form a sentence. But Jade's words were much like his balance; unstable. Margot walked over to him, handing him a glass of orange.

Jade smiled, but his face soon displayed an expression of disgust. He rushed to the toilet and vomited.

"Does he always do this?"

Jade cringed as he heard the voice complaining in the next room. Reenie hadn't gone home. Margot laughed in response as she peered around the bathroom door. "Dude, you alright?" he asked.

"You drugged me!" He shouted.

"You're putting me off my cigarette," Margot complained, going back into the kitchen.

"Look, I'm sorry dude, but I really, really needed to test it out." Her voice took on an air of sympathy. He grumbled to himself. He *always* let Margot talk him into things. His memory drifted back to when she persuaded him to take ecstasy 'in the name of science'. Jade sighed.

The two female voices drifted through from the kitchen. Whatever they'd been discussing previously seemed to be about him.

"Well, what a waste of a night." Reenie sounded annoyed.

"How was I to know it wouldn't work?" Margot moaned.

"It was your research. You led the project, you said it would!"

"I didn't know he'd collapse." Margot said.

"Hey, I could have died!" Jade said through his retching.

Both women ignored this comment.

"Look," Reenie said, beginning to sound desperate. "It doesn't matter anymore. The drug was a fluke. We'll just have to try something else."

"Does no one care about me?" Jade called.

"Shut up!" Both women yelled.

"Well I'm not happy!" He said and he wobbled back into the kitchen. Margot snuck a look of annoyance at Reenie, who smiled in return.

"Jade, you didn't happen to have a vision last night did you?" Margot asked.

"How dare you!" Jade said, but the albino didn't have time, she was already annoyed and Jade's reaction wasn't helping her already fiery temper. After all, from where she was standing, the experiment had been a failure. He didn't seem to remember anything and if he did, he wasn't telling her.

From the way he was reacting to the situation, it was probably out of spite. Margot glanced at her watch.

"Going to work, see you later, meet you on the beach at five," she spoke rapidly as she closed the door behind her and Reenie.

"Now just wait a moment Margot Grant!" Jade called after her. He bolted down the spiral staircase, but missed his footing and ended up in a heap on the floor.

He sighed, why was nothing simple?

The remainder of that day passed by in a sluggish haze Jade sat on the sofa with a small device in his hand, the device that he always carried around with him. He smiled as he watched it project 3D holograms of the places he'd been in that small ship. The world of Zirus seemed so far away. He let his memories drift back there, to a time that was safe; a time where he didn't have to think or care. Jade felt silent tears falling down his dark face, he shut his eyes and raised his hand to his forehead. It was the first time he'd been left alone long enough to contemplate what had happened to him. Despite being enthusiastic about returning, he knew he didn't belong on Earth. Nor did he belong on Zirus. There seemed no place left in the eighty one worlds for him to feel at home.

Jade was lonely, lonelier than he'd ever felt in his entire life. Every friend and family member he'd ever known had disappeared except Margot. She was the only one left, and he felt she was turning on him. Could he trust anyone? Must he be left alone with the heavy burden of knowledge? He could have stayed. He could have lived his life on Zirus with those intelligent creatures. But he didn't. He returned to Earth, with its terrible technology and a power-hungry angel trying to gain control.

Why did he ever come back?

Deep down, he knew the answer.

Jade wiped his eyes. *Stop it, stop it now.* He sniffed, closing the Jonovicator and slipping it back in his pocket. It was too much. "Enough," he said gently. "Enough."

Suddenly a sharp pain shot through his brain. *What has happened to me?* he thought, rubbing his head. Jade recalled Margot's comment about visions, but try as he might, he could remember nothing. He knew he argued with her, knew he felt ill, knew he was given the pill, but then what? Had he just collapsed?

The pain returned, only stronger. He clutched his head in agony, the small metal device fell to the floor and then he remembered; he had left the kettle on. *Goddamn it.* Margot was going to kill him. He walked to the kitchen and tried to put the events of the day before out of his mind but they kept flashing up throughout his brain. The U.A.S. under threat, the strange blending of colours of the pill, why he could never seem to get the parting in his hair quite right, they were all major issues. Had the angels on the beach found the lab's location?

No, he told himself, it was protected, Clarke had told him. But did he really trust Clarke? Maybe it was his fault. Maybe he had broken the security as he'd come from outer space. Jade's head was swimming with thoughts. He paced back and forth, playing with the numerous, pointless gadgets which seemed to take up the majority of space on every shelf in the building. Something was troubling him, not his knowledge or Margot's rash behaviour, but something else. If only he knew what. He knew he had seen something the night before, something dangerous.

Before he knew it, it was time to go and meet Margot on the beach as arranged. He felt like his body was changing, mutating. It was probably nothing. Jade knew all too well that he was prone to overreacting. He had once evacuated a whole building because he thought he'd seen some form of beast, which Margot had discovered, turned out to be a spider. But this feeling was different, he felt like parts of his mind were being blocked out for some reason. He would get up and walk into the kitchen then fail to remember the journey or his need for being there. He hoped the side effects would wear off soon.

He stepped outside and Margot appeared minutes later, deep in thought. She said nothing to him and they walked across the sandy shores in silence. The sun was beginning to set in the burning orange sky; it complimented Margot's pale skin and matched her fiery eyes.

"I'm sorry," Margot said and turned to him as they walked further away from the quiet village. "What I did was completely wrong. I know I used you."

She sounded like she meant it.

"It's okay," he said.

"It's just… this could change history, I volunteered you. The others were, well, too scared." She then added: "I just want to know what's going on Jade…"

But Jade's thoughts had trailed off, his brain was hurting again and he remembered.

It all came back to him in an instant, the light, the room, the beach. Oh god, the beach. What happened? It faded as quickly as it came. Something terrible - It had gone again.

"Jade?" She sounded concerned. "Are you okay? You're shaking. I told you not to eat that left over pizza."

"It's not the pizza," he said. He realised that his hands were gripping onto his dreadlocks. He let go and he began to stutter. "It's, it's-" He knew he had to tell her.

"Yes?" She leaned closer to him, grabbing his broad shoulders to steady him.

But what came out of his mouth was not what he had first intended. "I wasn't lost in space Margot, I, I went to a different world!"

She burst out laughing, muttering something like 'me too Jade, me too'.

"No Margot it's true, I swear to God or the Voice or whatever. It doesn't matter anyway because this proves that whatever this 'Voice' is, it's definitely not a God, nor should it be your religion!" Jade could feel his voice rising with excitement. He knew his words sounded overly dramatic, but everything he was saying was the truth.

The smile on her face turned to intrigue. Her red eyes widened as she let go of his shoulders and looked out into the ocean, as though she wasn't able to face the reality.

"Stop it," she muttered.

It took him a moment to realise she was addressing him.

"Margot!" He pulled her around to face him. She felt his tight grip on her shoulders, their faces just inches apart. "Please, please listen to me. You were right about the Voice, about other races existing, this proves it."

Her eyes glared into his, their stare never breaking as he told her what she had been waiting to hear since he'd arrived. The story of what had happened whilst he was away.

"I'd been travelling on the mission for a while, four months I believe, but still hadn't found anything. Even with the new speed upgrades on our ship, space seemed as empty as we thought. I had left the Milky Way and was making my way across the vastness of the Universe and that's when it happened.

"At first I thought it just to be a malfunction with the ship, a glitch but then I realised, the engines had completely shut down. Well, there was nothing I could do, I tried to restart them, fix them, restructure the system, everything. But I didn't have the right tools. So I just sat there, motionless and kept thinking to myself of the slow death that awaited me. I was going to die alone, in the middle of the universe and all I could think of was you, Margot. You were the only person that kept me alive, made me wonder and hope for a way, any way I could just to get to you.

"I'm not sure how long I sat there for, it seemed like days and yet I was still floating, hoping for some force to move me, pull me towards something and then, I saw this huge black hole in the distance and that's when I knew I was going die. Oh well, I remember thinking to myself, at least it will be quick, at least it will be painless... well, hopefully it'll be painless.

"The closer my ship was pulled towards it, the longer I sat there frozen to the spot. Well, it would have been a lot more dramatic and Oscar-winning if the force of the hole hadn't caused my ship to shake. It flung me around the walls of the vessel. It shook the whole ship. I didn't do anything, I just waited. And then, it stopped."

"It stopped." Margot sounded unconvinced. "You probably just hit your head, Jade. I expected you, of all scientists to know that black holes..." she said, but he wasn't listening.

"The next thing I recall was gazing out of the window and seeing the most beautiful sight. I thought I was dead for a minute or so. It was a sky,

Margot, but not like any I've ever seen before in my life. It was like an ocean, a beautiful, turquoise ocean, filled with all shades of purple and blue rock clusters and stars. And then I looked down and saw planets, many planets all shades of reds and yellows. That's when I realised, that it *wasn't* my universe. It was like a whole new universe, a different part of space and I'd found it.

"Well, new world or not, it still didn't resolve the problem of the engines. It was pure luck that some locals from a nearby planet had decided to go travelling and found me. To be perfectly honest, I was quite unsure how they saw me at all. Their ships travel so fast you see, much faster than any ship any human has invented. Even faster than ours! And what was even more astonishing to me is that theirs was just a local vessel, it was common for any person of that world to have one and their personal ships weren't limited to their own planets either. Oh Margot, the technology of the people there is so advanced, you'd absolutely love it! They know so much and yet they remain so peaceful, it vexed me at first. Well anyway, the couple took me to the main planet and they treated me like some form of important guest. The only drawback was that they can't actually breathe their own air, but don't worry it was ok, they fitted me with..."

"Jade!" Margot shouted, interrupting his train of thought. She pulled away from his grip and looked out to the ocean, her voice softened as she spoke. "Look, I've given you some pretty strong drugs. You must be experiencing some form of side effect."

"Margot," Jade tried to interrupt.

"Come on, man, let's go back to the house. At least there I can examine you properly."

"Margot."

"For god's sake Jade, come on!" She grabbed his wrist in an attempt to move him back down the shore. The sky was darkening.

He remained where he was. "You've got to believe me, I'm telling the truth!" At his protest, the albino turned around, loosened her grip and leaned in towards him. Her face didn't have the expression of wonder it had a few moments ago, it was stern and desperate. The words she spoke were harsher than before.

"Jade. Please, stop telling lies."

He backed away, disgusted at the comment, at her tone of voice, but most of all, the fact that she didn't believe him. Then a thought occurred to him.

"I can prove it! My Jonovicator," he said.

She acknowledged his statement with a puzzled look.

"The small silver object I'm always carrying around," he explained, as he delved his hands deep into his pockets. "It's not here! I must have dropped it."

"Oh, how convenient," she said, her tone heavy with sarcasm.

Margot forgot her past accusations, forgot all about her drug, she even forgot about any form of reputation she may be losing by acting the way she was about to. She looked wild, like a snow tiger. Her hands shook, with what Jade first assumed was shock, but then realised was anger and impatience. Her hair seemed to stand on end as she screamed at him: "Ok Jade, Ok," she paused for breath; he knew that was Margot when she was trying to contain her anger and he was thankful she was trying to hold back. "Take me to it."

She grabbed him and he jolted forward and almost lost balance. He knew he must obey her. Margot pulled at the sleeve of his trench coat all the way home. Once the couple had reached her home, she flung him and the house key at the door. The key hit him hard at the back of his head, rattling his skull, unsettling his already disturbed mind.

Jade staggered inside, shocked by her violent behaviour, he dashed upstairs to try and locate the device, the Jonovicator.

It wasn't where he thought he had left it.

He searched around the living room, throwing gadgets about. He delved deep in the underbelly of the sofa, sifted through the pile of books - nothing. Margot's black boots stomped up the stairs. Jade cringed, he wasn't sure what was worse, the vital secrets of other worlds being revealed to the Earth or the wrath of Margot when she knew that it had gone missing.

"Well?" she asked, her white face turning red. "Where is it?"

Jade's eyes widened, he stuttered as he spoke, "Well, ermm… erm. It's, it's…" he was beginning to panic. "There may be a slight issue; it seems to be g-"

"This it?" she said, holding a small round object in her hand.

He stepped closer to get a better look. "That would appear to be it, but where…"

"Kitchen counter, really you should stop misplacing things." She sighed, throwing it to him. He caught it most cautiously, completely contrasting her approach to the item, for fear it would fall to the floor.

"But I didn't-" he muttered to himself, certain he had not left it there. Ah well, he thought, he must have forgotten it earlier. His memory after all, had been diabolical that day. Although, adamant that something wasn't right, Jade decided to let that thought go for the moment. It was his time to prove to Margot what he had been saying was one hundred percent true.

"So…" she broke the silence. "What exactly does this thing do?

That was his cue. Jade held the flat circular screen in front of him, pressing a button on the right side; he twisted both ends of it in half, separating it down the middle. To the left of the object there was one red button and one yellow;

he explained to Margot that one was activated to record sound, the other created a 3D hologram of the surrounding area. He separated the two sides; they opened like a large tape measure, revealing a wide, flat screen, complete with a complicated menu of links and buttons. Margot's eyes were fixed on the object, as he touched the screen, finding the correct pattern of links; he finally came to what he was looking for. The machine contained everything. It was a vital part of him. On it, Jade kept his journal, his memories and his deepest thoughts. That was why it was so important he kept it close; it was the outer shell of his inner self.

He suddenly felt shy, almost embarrassed. He felt like he had built it up far too much. Jade felt his face turning red as his finger prodded the folder labelled 'Zirus'. A long list filled the screen; he followed it to the picture section.

That was it.

Still awkward, he flicked through the many holographic images he had stored from Zirus, letting them light up the room for a few seconds each. Some were of the turquoise sky; some were of the communities that inhabited the red planet. Some of the people, their form appeared human, but their sky glowed every vibrant colour in the rainbow and more. Some were fluorescent green, others fiery red. The holograms may have only lit up a small portion of the room but they set alight Margot's thoughts and they blazed through her mind.

She was filled with anger and joy, which she found she was compelled to convey. Margot was not one for showing her emotions in public or in the company of friends, so to hide her overwhelming feelings; she took a few steps backwards and paced up and down before sitting down on her leather sofa. Jade, unsure of how to react, closed the Jonovicator and sat next to her.

Both stared into the room. There was nothing to look at, nothing to distract them. The sun had fallen into the depths of the rich orange sky long ago and neither of them had bothered to turn a light on. Not a word had passed between them but each knew what the other was thinking. Jade, determined to break the silence, began to speak.

"So erm… yeah…" he stammered and he shrugged his shoulders awkwardly. He had no idea of where to begin and knew if he continued to talk he would just stumble even less gracefully over his words. She turned her head towards him, glaring at him with eyes of stone. If her eyes could speak they would be yelling many blasphemous terms. She stood up and went to her bedroom. He remained in the dark and listened as she clattered and threw things about. Finally she appeared, a silhouette, standing in front of the light from her bedroom. She walked into the living area, put on her leather coat and a pair of Doc Martens.

"Where are you going?" Jade asked, scared of what she might do.

"I need time to think." She didn't look directly at him, instead her eyes remained fixed on her shoes as she tied them up.

"Margot?"

"Just back off, Jade," she said sharply. She opened the door, "I'll be back by morning."

This is it, he thought to himself. *She's going to Clarke, or Reenie or worse, to try and contact the Voice! Or maybe she wasn't going to do that at all, maybe she might... no she wouldn't. She's too strong to end everything over something as trivial as this.* But it wasn't trivial, not to Margot at least. It was important, life changing. Margot had wanted to make a discovery like that her whole life and there it was, right before her eyes. Maybe he had said too much? He lay on the sofa in the dark hoping, praying for her safe return in the morning. A storm picked up, shaking the trees that circled the house. Jade sat and listened to the waves hurling themselves at the beach, the rustling of the bushes as they were thrown about on the shore and then... it was morning.

Jade opened his eyes. He turned over and fell hard on the living room floor. He had forgotten that he fell asleep on Margot's sofa. *Shit, Margot!* He looked around the room; she wasn't back. He dreaded to think where she would have gone. The faithful sun glared through the French doors of the kitchen; the weather seemed to be the only thing that Jade could be certain of and even that had let him down. Pathetic fallacy or what? He picked himself up, stretched and stepped outside onto the balcony. What he saw came as some surprise; the beach was filled with people. It was the busiest he'd seen it since he'd arrived.

Then he realised why.

It must have been the storm; the shore was littered with pieces of debris. Trees and cars had blown over, beach huts had collapsed and windows had been smashed. Although shocked at the mess, he was amazed at the spirit of the community for attempting to tidy and salvage what they could. Some things never changed. He glanced at the objects that covered the beach; it was mostly brick, glass and wood but there were a few interesting items such as cans, bicycle tyres and someone's underwear. He laughed, looking at the range of coloured boxers that everyone commented on as they passed and imagined the embarrassment of the person who owned them. Jade paused. He hadn't taken his washing in the night before.

Jade rushed outside and began to collect what he could. He was beginning to wonder if he was some form of embarrassment magnet. He sighed as another person strolled past trying to hide the fact that they were in a fit of giggles. He grumbled to himself and observed his immediate surroundings to see if he could spot any more. *Nope*. He'd gathered all the items and lost most of his dignity in the process. He looked into the distance; a familiar figure caught his eye. Margot was strolling back.

He saw that her eyes didn't once move to the ground as she navigated through the rubble. She evaded the masses of people as she weaved, almost in slow motion. Margot's white hair blew gently in the wind as she moved towards him. She was in deep contrast to the ant-like humans that surrounded her; she never stopped to help, never stopped to ask questions. In their minds, they were the only two people on that beach. The sounds of everyday life were drowned out by the acknowledgement of one another's presence; the shores were hauntingly quiet. The people were just ghosts, dancing around them as if it were all a lucid dream. It occurred to Jade that the storm probably hadn't crossed her mind, but looking at her, he could see an entirely different kind of storm, another darker, more violent storm that unleashed havoc deep in the core of her mind. As she drew closer, her face wore a grave expression, her features more aged, like she had somehow grown older overnight.

She stood in front of him. "Dude, we need to talk," her words slurred slightly, she'd been drinking.

Jade clenched the underwear in his hands tighter. "Let's go back into the house."

Once inside, Margot began to pace, deep in thought. She paused at the double doors. "Jade," Margot said, keeping her eyes fixed on the sky, "I've been thinking all night-"

"You've been drinking all night," he muttered under his breath.

"Don't interrupt!" Her voice was stern. "Look, man, we have to consider our options here. I mean, we could go down in the history books for this!"

Her face lit up as she imagined the glory they would receive. "We deserve this Jade, we've worked so long to try and prove this!"

"Margot," he went to her side. "You've not... you've not told anyone about this?"

"Of course not, but what if we did? We could be unstoppable; we could finally take this thing down!"

"I'm not following..." Jade sounded unconvinced.

"Well, man, you said it yourself yesterday. You went to another world! This not only means that the spaceship was epically built, but also that this whole religious Voice bullshit is, well, bullshit! What I'm trying to say is that this thing must just be from another world and if we tell the scientists…"

"Look," Jade said wearily: "The images on the Jonovicator won't prove anything. I want to keep this quiet. Anyway, who's to say that there's more than this other world I visited?" He was beginning to wish he hadn't opened his mouth in the first place.

"You did, in your journal," she said with a smug look, throwing the Jonovicator back at him. "I've been studying that thing all night."

"You had no right to take that!" he snapped, catching the device clumsily. It was too late now. Every secret had been unleashed.

"Ok Margot," he sighed. "What do you want to..."

She held up her hand to silence him. A faint ringing had begun downstairs.

"Oh bloody hell! Not now," Margot said, putting her hands on her hips. "Well come on then!"

Jade, had no idea what she was talking about and thought she was still addressing him. A small blue pod with four pointed sticks for legs; shot up the spiral staircase, like a lovable pet and halted at Margot's feet. Jade realised it was what was causing the noise. As he looked closer, he could see the obscure object vibrating.

"It's good isn't it," Margot said. "I modernised the old telephone, they said it would never catch on but I kinda like him."

She bent down and tapped it once. It stood still and its rear opened up. A long pole rose up out of the pod, the top of it unfolded to reveal a small screen. Margot inspected the screen. "One moment, I really need to take his."

Jade didn't reply. He couldn't believe the timing of the call. However, he had to admit that although the invention may be pointless, it was impressive.

"Reenie, timing's not your thing is it?" Margot said, pressing a button on the device. However, Jade watched the features of her face drop as a distressed Reenie appeared on screen.

"Emergency meeting at the lab. Now."

"Dude, what's happened?"

"They've... they've taken everything!"

scientists are the only ones we can trust, what if they turn on us now?"

He paused. "And the angels! If the Voice did this, they'll know! The Voice will hunt us down!"

"Jade!" Margot shouted: "Pull yourself together! The scientists are on our side! And as for the Voice and the angels, they're not going to get us!"

"How Margot?"

"Because I've come to a decision, we're leaving." She paused to let the statement sink in.

"The island?"

"The Earth," she said. She stared at him. "We'll fix the ship up and go. They won't know until weeks after we've already left."

"But – but," Jade began, but then realised he had nothing to say.

"It's not safe here anymore." Margot raised her eyebrows.

"But – Reenie – Clarke..."

"Oh, don't worry; we'll make sure we see them one last time. But under no circumstances are we to tell them we're leaving. Got it?"

Jade tried to calm his thoughts. "I hate to sound pessimistic, but Margot, you said it yourself, no one has managed to leave Earth, we don't even have the tools to finish the ship."

"Oh, Jade," she said and laughed. "What the hell do you think I was doing all night?"

Jade's eyes widened. "You? You did all this? How? With who?"

"No, you dumbass! For goodness sake, Jade you're meant to be one of the brightest minds of our generation." She covered her face with her hands, as if to emphasise her annoyance. The next words she spoke were slow and patronising. "Listen. Last night, after a few drinks, I decided to come down here,"

"I'm not a five year old, you know," he grumbled.

"Look the point is, I took what we needed for the ship. Okay, it may not run to its maximum capability but at least we can get her started."

"Margot, have you lost your mind?"

"Have you lost yours?" She argued back.

"This isn't a good idea!"

"What isn't?" A familiar voice replied. They turned to see Clarke standing in the doorway. The features that weren't hidden by his hair looked worn and tired. It was obvious that he hadn't been sleeping.

"Well Professor Wilde?" he asked in a patronising tone.

Jade felt like a child.

"That depends, Professor," Jade said. "Many things aren't good ideas, like wearing paper clothes or putting my white shirt in the wash with Margot's red bra, which, let me tell you, didn't turn out well." Jade laughed nervously and looked around the room. Clarke folded his arms, he was growing impatient.

Margot elbowed Jade hard. "What Jade is trying to say is that me trying to quit smoking is a bad idea seeing as we're so stressed at the moment." She pulled a cigarette out of her pocket and placed it in her mouth. That infuriated Clarke. He pulled it out, threw it on the floor and stamped on it.

"Dr Grant! You know my no smoking policy and yet you continue to break it, and at a time such as this?"

Jade had to admit, it was a pretty good excuse and it distracted Professor Clarke from asking further awkward questions. Even though Jade towered over him, he still felt a sense of fear when he talked to him and was grateful that he wasn't in Margot's position. She, on the other hand didn't seem to care, which riled Clarke even more.

"I strongly suggest you both go home." He finished, out of breath.

"With pleasure," Margot said. She smiled as she walked past him. Jade began to follow but was stopped by Clarke.

"Professor Wilde, I apologise for my attitude, but as you know, times are incredibly stressful at the moment."

Jade nodded in agreement. Clarke paused for a moment, looking him up and down. Jade tried to remain perfectly still.

"Professor, we never did have that conversation on how you made it back to Earth." His lips curved into a smile as warm as physically possible for Clarke. "I am extremely interested in your story; perhaps it would be possible if you were able to join me for a drink to discuss the matter?"

"Professor, in these dark times," Jade began.

"It would seem like a good idea to try and get some answers. Don't you agree?"

Jade nodded slowly in reply and watched as Clarke's white teeth began to show. "Good."

Margot poked her head back round the door. "Ermmm, excuse me, Clarke, since we're doing the whole drinks thing, I'd best join you, you know to make the situation look slightly less gay."

"GET OUT!"

It didn't take much persuading for the two of them to leave the building. They both had much to talk about and many decisions to make.

"You're right, Jade," Margot said as they stepped through the undergrowth. "He's on to you; he thinks you had something to do with it."

"Should we go meet him?"

"Yeah maybe we can find out some information, at the end of the day he's just trying to protect..."

But Jade had stopped listening, his mind had moved on to bigger worries. The albino had a point; leaving did seem the most sensible thing in the world, what other option did they have? There was nothing left for them on the planet, especially for him. Margot was probably the only person he had left in the world and if she was leaving, he would be leaving with her. He had spent too long in isolation to revisit its lonely gates and once again imprison himself inside. The past few days had made him realise so much about himself. He knew that he was lucky enough to be one of the few people on the planet who could choose whether to be lonely or not. He wasn't going to make the wrong decision again.

Jade had worked hard for his career, his position and he was beginning to think that it had all gone to waste. He would be forgotten, like every other poor human that had disappeared for one reason or other. He glanced at the mirror on his Jonovicator and adjusted his goggles over his dreadlocks.

Have I really wasted the best part of my life?

He glanced at his feet. Yes, it was true, she wasn't the most conventional of people, or the most polite, or even the most social for that matter, but she had probably done more living on Earth than he had whilst he was on the ship.

Jade sighed, deep down he knew what he must do.

It was time to start a new life.

"I'm ready," he said.

"What for?" Margot looked at him in confusion.

He realised what he was about to say could sound quite bizarre, out of context.

"Let's leave, together."

"Professor Wilde, I could not agree with you more."

For the next few days, Jade felt like a top-secret spy. It was due to the double life he and Margot had taken on. By day, he worked at the U.A.S; helping to rebuild the labs and contribute to the research. By night, he and Margot worked hard to repair what was left of the ship. With more and more supplies coming in to the U.A.S, it was easy to steal an odd valve or so to further improve their ship which now had the potential to operate. He may be tired but at least he knew they were making progress and Clarke seemed too busy to notice anything. However, Margot often recounted to Jade how pleased she was that someone had broken in that night and taken every camera and tape. As much as she could handle Clarke, she'd hate to imagine his reaction if he knew what she'd done.

Meanwhile, Jade pondered over what her reaction would be if she knew he'd taken her supply of 'Face' that day.

He wasn't sure why he'd done it. To be honest, it had seemed a pretty pointless action considering everyone was complaining about what a waste of time the whole experiment had been, but Jade knew different. He wasn't sure why, but he had a feeling his mind knew more than it was letting on. He sighed to himself, realising that it sounded crazy. It was crazy.

Although busy, Jade had devoted some time to thinking about what happened that evening. The conclusion was that there was no conclusion, not at that point in time anyway. However, he would not stop trying, not yet. The only reason he believed the drugs had actually taken effect was due to the weird feelings and reactions that had taken place in his body. He felt alienated, distanced from the human world. Since taking 'Face', he didn't seem to walk, but glide from place to place. It couldn't be too obvious; Margot hadn't seemed to notice the difference. Then again, it wouldn't help when you've already got a reputation for being an eccentric character.

The days began to blend into one, the less sleep the pair got. A week had passed before Margot said the magic words: "Right dude, I think we're done."

She strolled down the corridor that ran through the middle of the ship. It was beginning to look more and more like a holiday home. She smiled, glancing at Jade's collection of pictures that hung on both walls. *What a sentimental bugger*, she thought.

Jade was sitting in the front compartment, trying out the new camouflage feature.

"It works, it actually works! My precious works!" He yelled.

She shook her head, *that guy is having major sleep deprivation issues,* she thought.

The camouflage gadget was the latest installation to the ship and one of their only methods of escaping without being seen. They had combined minds to make it work. With Jade's ideas and Margot's advanced knowledge of technology, all seemed to be going well. Their amenability had always been something that surprised most people due to their argumentative nature. However, when being told of it, Margot had laughed off the remark and said that there was no one else she could picture herself working with. She frowned at the thought. She frowned, because she knew it was true. Margot shook her head. Sometimes, like sleeping dogs, it was best to let certain emotions lie. It was definitely one of those times. She stepped back into the room she had been most interested in when she first entered the vessel. Jade's bedroom had changed somewhat. For once, it looked reasonably tidy. She ran her fingers over the dark walls. The picture of the two of them was still on the cabinet at the bottom of his bed. Looking around, she opened the top drawer which revealed a large photo album. Margot sat on the bed and flicked through it. She could feel her face breaking into a smile as she glanced at the moving images. Most of them were of his family, in the early days. She kept turning pages until she came to a section with her name on it. Shocked, Margot kept turning. He had kept and dated every photo.

"Margot? Where are you?" Jade's voice called through the vessel.

"Coming," she replied, pulling out a picture and placing it in the pocket of her leather jacket.

"It a shame my drug didn't work," Margot pondered as she cleaned the bar. "Maybe we could have got a good look at the bastards that broke in."

Jade sat at the opposite side, gripping a glass tightly in his hand.

"Keep your voice down," he muttered. He was feeling particularly strange that evening. His head pounded as he took another swig of his pint.

"Relax, dude," Margot said, pouring another.

But he couldn't relax, or at least he found it very hard to relax knowing the task at hand. Jade had been trying to keep a low profile all evening, but his attempt to blend in made him only look more conspicuous. You must understand; it was difficult to blend in when you were about six foot six and dressed like some sort of cyber pirate.

"Jade, stop doing that thing with your hand, man."

"Excuse me?" Jade was startled.

"No, not that! I mean stop, like, putting your hand over your mouth when you talk and for god's sake, you can take your goggles off as well. Oh, and take that sunhat off!" Okay, he admitted it; he may have veered in the wrong direction a little when it came to blending in.

"Jade," Margot leaned back in her seat. "Look, everyone's leaving. I'm closing early tonight for your meeting with Clarke."

Jade took her advice, looking around him as he took off the large floppy hat. She was right; he was a strange sight to behold. He couldn't help it; he'd been paranoid all week. It wasn't long before they'd have to leave this bar and then… he didn't want to think about it.

It was only nine o' clock and most people were departing. Jade found it odd to think that when he left, the government were struggling to control the amount of drink and drugs being taken. Now, it didn't even seem like an issue. The two of them were sitting outside under the wooden shelter of the beach shack. Most of the pub was set outside, but there was a small indoor area in the centre, where the bar was situated and used during the cold season. Around them, torches had been lit as the sun had started to set.

"He should be here soon," Margot said. She tapped her fingers on the table in impatience. "So should Reenie."

Jade felt sorry for her, knowing that after leading such an eventful life, it must be hard to accustom yourself to a quieter, more peaceful one. She had always been one for choosing the more dangerous route. Many had thought her sick to do so. Once upon a time, Jade had been amongst that crowd. Now he supported her, no matter what the cost. Jade knew that although Margot would never admit to it, the risk of danger made their escape even more appealing to her.

A man from the behind the bar approached them. "I'm gonna go now. Here, I'm letting you lock up." He threw the keys on the table. "Don't get up to too much trouble, you two."

Margot stood up and ruffled his ginger hair. She laughed sweetly, too sweetly for Margot, which indicated to Jade that the gesture was fake.

"Me?" Margot smiled. "I'm as innocent as your pet kitten."

The man winked at her before walking away. She smiled back, muttering 'wanker' under her breath when he was out of ear shot. Jade tried to contain his laughter. The last few people were clearing out, meaning their meeting point would be private.

The two of them had been torn over whether to tell their boss about their escape plan. It was a controversial topic. Although it may have assisted in their getaway, the risk seemed too great. If Jade had learnt anything from her, it was to trust no one.

"What happens if he brings the topic up?" Jade asked nervously. "What happens if he already knows?"

"He doesn't." Margot sighed. She got up and walked around the room, collecting glasses and putting them by the bar side.

"They'll be here any time now," she said, glancing at the selection of bottles hanging up in rows. "Fancy a drink?"

Four hours, two minutes and three seconds later (exactly)...

"Well, I give up." Margot's words were slurred. She leaned over the bar. "I have no-o-o idea where they are."

"Yeah," was the only word that Jade felt able to produce in response. He pulled his Jonovicator out of his trench coat pocket and checked the time. Something didn't seem quite right. Jade had felt woozy all day, he'd felt that way all week. He stared at Margot, his body swaying. Jade gripped the table. His vision was blurring, his head beginning to pound.

"I don't get it!" Margot raised her arms in exasperation. "He seemed well up for seeing you days ago! I mean it is rather silly..."

Jade tried hard to concentrate on her drunken rant but Margot's words were fading.

"Margot!" Jade said, trying to grab her attention before falling forward onto the table.

That was when he saw it all again. The beach, the angels. Reenie and Clarke. *Oh no – REENIE AND CLARKE!*

He gasped, jumping back off the table.

"Jade?" Margot was concerned. "Are you ok?

He nodded, but he wasn't okay. He wasn't okay at all. He was in shock. Jade tried to steady his trembling hands.

It worked! 'Face' had worked all along! And now the scientists were to be taken like the rest!

"You're shaking," Margot stared at him suspiciously. He didn't reply. He was consumed by his own shock. She sighed and tried to pull herself up from the table.

"Too much tequila," he said, breathing heavily.

Margot nodded knowingly, to indicate she'd been in that situation many times. And at that moment, her expression changed.

"Jade, I... I *have* missed you, you know," she said, turning away, trying to steady herself. "Look, you know when, when I said that, when well you know; when I moved here, it was for a reason?"

He knew he had to tell her. Before it was too late...

"Margot, there's something I have to tell you," he interrupted.

"Don't fucking cut in! What I want to say was,"

"But Margot this is important."

"Okay, well, obviously you're thinking the same thing."

"Margot."

"Jade."

They both paused.

"I lo..."

"'Face' works! Reenie and Clarke are in danger! Now, what, what did you want to say?"

She fell off her stool.

Jade was scared he had sent them on a wild goose chase as they set off across the sands. Everything was quiet and in perfect order. The scientists moved as quickly as they were able to, taking into account the amount of alcohol they had consumed.

"REENIE! CLARKE!" Margot yelled. There was no reply. Nothing stirred in the darkness. The atmosphere was eerie on the beach at night. Jade pulled his goggles over his eyes and switched to night mode.

"Jesus, Jade. I need to get fitter." She was panting but still put another cigarette in her mouth.

"Maybe it's best if we keep quiet, shhhhh," he whispered. Then asked loudly: "What are you doing?"

She was putting on the sunglasses she had been wearing the day he'd first seen the U.A.S.

"These things are night vision," she said. "Another brilliant invention by me."

"Look, I'll check out this way and you stay around this area," he said, picking up pace along the shore line.

"Fine with me!" she called after him, before slumping in a heap on the floor.

His eyes shifted from left to right, still nothing. The silence worried him more than anything else. It was strange how the shoreline contrasted between day and night. The days were made for families and filled with innocence. At night, it looked like the ideal location for a murder scene. Sunlight was a powerful thing.

Jade knew he wasn't far away from where the angel was situated. He tried to make himself alert.

Why couldn't what he had seen, be false?

He gulped as his eyes searched the open area that lay ahead of him. All was quiet. The angel should have been just around the next corner. Jade dashed around the bend, he was gasping for breath. Just as he bounded across the sand, something stopped him dead in his tracks. It was... *gone.*

Jade's pulse was racing. He spun around on the spot, checking for any movement. The beach was just as still as before. It didn't make any sense. The ground began to shake again; only this time it wasn't a hallucination. Jade stood still. He had found what he was looking for.

From a small clearing in the thick jungle, two stone figures were approaching the sands. In their hands the figures carried the two people he and Margot had been searching for. He knew what he must do. It was time to be honourable, to face his fears, to defend the Earth. However, after brief consideration, he decided to do the complete opposite and darted back down the beach, waving his arms and screaming hysterically. After all, he had a whole lifetime to be heroic, why do it all now?

Margot lay on the cold sand. She wasn't sure why, it had seemed like an amazing idea at the time. If Jade asked what she was doing, she'd say she was covering more ground by searching the sky. *Yeah*, she smiled, *that was a good enough excuse.* Margot felt the Earth beneath her vibrate.

What the hell was that?

She sprang to her feet. Breathing deeply, she examined her surroundings.

In the distance, a figure was running towards her, making horrific screaming noises.

It was one of them.

"No you fucking don't," she muttered, grabbing its arm and flinging it on the sand.

"Margot, it's me!" Jade yelled, writhing in pain on the floor.

"Oh. Sorry Jade," she said, pulling him up off the sand. "Dude what were you..." She stopped mid-sentence, realising what he'd been running from. The two stone figures were advancing.

"Okay, maybe we should run," she whispered, standing stock still.

"Good idea," he agreed, taking her hand and pulling her away. They ran across the shore trying to be as silent as possible. The stone angels followed.

The house wasn't far away. If they could only reach it, they might stand a chance, but Jade was growing tired and even with his goggles, it was hard to find his way in the dark.

"Help!" A female voice echoed in the distance.

Margot came to a halt.

"We have to keep going," he tried to urge her forwards, but her eyes were fixed on something. He followed her gaze. The angels had stopped following them, they looked as though they were about to take flight. He sighed, almost relieved.

"They have Reenie and Clarke!" Margot shouted.

"No Mar-" but it was too late, Margot was sprinting back down the beach. He followed her, desperately screaming for her to turn around. He knew it seemed cowardly, but Margot wasn't like him, she acted on impulse. He knew they'd have a better chance if they waited until they got in the ship. If they just waited, at least until morning...

The stone figures turned their heads slowly. They had found another victim. Margot didn't care; she kept running, getting closer and closer, hoping to come up with a plan on the way. She shouted for them as their screams pierced the perfect sky. Jade continued to follow, crying out reasons for her to turn back.

It was too late.

Out of nowhere, a huge cold hand clasped its fingers around Margot's abdomen and lifted her from the ground. The angel examined her; its dark eyes peered out from underneath the hood. It then muttered something in a language that wasn't familiar to any of them. Whatever it had said, Jade knew that its decision had been made. He had to act quickly. But what could he do? He felt helpless. Without any thought, Jade ran up to the figure and kicked at its huge legs. That was a big mistake. The creature bent down and grabbed him, bringing him face to giant face. He could feel its icy cold breath against him.

"Okay," he muttered, petrified. "This is bad."

It turned to its companion for support. Jade caught Margot's eye, the game was definitely up. *We are going to die.*

The angel had made up its mind and threw him into the undergrowth of Bequia. It seemed effortless, the way a human would toss paper into a bin. The angels had got what they came for. They unfurled their mechanical wings. Jade lay in the bushes, shocked, disoriented and unable to move. The ground was still once more. He turned his head and watched powerless as Margot was lifted away from the island.

His only hope was now just a small dot, disappearing into the night sky.

Chapter 5

Into the Darkness

Margot felt queasy as she hurtled through the sky in the hands of the angel. Normally she was fine with travelling, but it was a different experience. The angel holding her maintained a tight grip. She thought about trying to break free. It was tempting, but looking down at the dark ripples of the ocean, she decided it was better to play along, just for the moment. Disoriented, she tried to see where they were going. Margot looked back at Bequia; she knew she'd probably never see that small island again. She looked forward and realised the direction they were travelling.

"You hooded twat, we're heading straight to the centre of the Bermuda Triangle! Have you never heard the myths? We're as good as dead!" She yelled at the stone structure. The angel made a low rumbling sound, which, in that particular situation, was the equivalent of a laugh.

She looked around for Reenie and Clarke, for signs of life in the darkness. There was nothing. Nothing stirred in the quiet abyss of that unpredictable evening.

That was when she saw it: the light; and the angels were headed right towards it. The closer they flew, the brighter it became, until not even her sunglasses could shield her eyes from its God-like glare.

*

Jade woke up to find his dreadlocks tangled in the bushes.

"Margot?" he groaned, trying to stand up. He turned slowly to see a group of people gathered around him in a small semicircle. Jade rubbed his face and felt a cut on his lip. He must be a rare spectacle in terms of what the people had become accustomed to.

"He's okay!" A man shouted.

"What's the time?" Jade asked, as he glanced into the perfect blue sky.

Once on two legs again, he hesitated for a moment, feeling pure pain throb through his body. He had to screw up his eyes and clench his fists to save from crying out in agony. That feeling served as a cold reminder of the previous night's events.

He was lucky he wasn't dead.

The group of people didn't move on like he hoped they would. Jade looked around them, feeling like an animal at the zoo. Suddenly something caught his eye. There it stood: the hooded monstrosity.

Unmoving, in the exact same position as before and no one knew the god damn difference! Sorry, Jade thought to himself. *I shouldn't have cursed, not even in my head.*

No one but Jade knew the creature's true nature, of the dark evil it hid from the world. And what disturbed him more, was that every person on the earth carried on with their mundane lives, unaware of the danger that surrounded them. Then Jade did what he wouldn't normally do, and acted with complete irrationality.

"What have you done with them?" He yelled, pushing through the group of people and running straight for the angel. "Don't play games with me!" Jade picked up a rock and threw it at the creature. Anyone would think at that point that Jade had lost enough dignity, so a little more wouldn't really make any difference. He proceeded to kick and punch it as hard as he could, as though he was hoping that it would somehow cause the angel to give him all the answers he needed. The surroundings had fallen silent, with the exception of one woman crying out: "He's destroying our Ruler's statue, the monster!"

Jade stopped what he was doing and turned around. Everyone on the beach was staring in his direction.

"I'm not crazy!" He yelled at his newly acquired audience, and then added uncomfortably: "I... I thought it was somebody else... I have an extremely tall family," and with the last remark he walked away with his hands to his head.

Still subject to strange looks, Jade decided it was best to return to Margot's house to think of a plan of action. Whatever they had done with her, they wouldn't do to him. Jade wouldn't be brainwashed by the simple planet with twisted secrets any longer. He was going to find her, and he knew exactly where to go.

*

Margot lay face down in the cold grass. Her head pounded as she came to. She rolled over slowly and opened her eyes. It didn't make a lot of difference. She was still unable to see anything. Wherever she was, it was dark – more than dark, there was an absence of light that she had never experienced. She opened her eyes, closed them and opened them with no difference. She put her hand to her face and waved it about, she could feel it was there, almost touching her nose but there was no light to see it by. She ran her hands across the ground, collecting the items that had fallen out of her pockets. She was shivering, and realised that the drop in temperature was something else she hadn't had much experience of.

All of a sudden, there was the faintest change in the lack of light, a sort of twilight that had come on instantaneously rather than gradually, she could see things – not much, but more than before.

Margot sat up; she saw a large, rectangular shape sticking out of the ground in front of her. It looked like some sort of gravestone. At last regaining her vision, she could make out a whole row of them, darker shapes in the blackness.

Margot jumped. How the hell did she get into a graveyard? A feeling of panic rushed through her body. *Where was the angel? But more to the point, where was she?* Suddenly something caught her eye, something that made the whole situation ten times stranger. In the distance, the dark clouds broke to reveal the blue sky. She had to shield her face for a moment to let her eyes adjust to the light as it flooded over the mountains as though someone had held back sunrise only to let it arrive in one go. It mesmerized her. Margot looked closer and saw directly under the bizarre parting of the clouds stood a range of mountains. They were so tall that from that angle it looked like the peaks touched the sky preventing the dreary clouds, where she was, from spilling over into that beautiful land beyond. That place looked a lot more inviting. It was almost like there was a barrier directly between the bright world and dark land that surrounded her. The mountains were the bars of her midnight prison, the force that not even light could pass through. She wasn't sure what or why, but something about the light entranced her and urged her to get out of the darkness.

She didn't understand how the night could change so rapidly into day.

Then she heard shuffling behind her.

Margot looked around the graveyard. At the other end, a tall figure appeared to be digging. It knelt down, making its elongated figure smaller. The silhouette of its body looked so strange and twisted; it was like watching a magic trick. Margot began to shake; it was trying to pull a large object out onto the grass. She gasped and at the sound, the figure stopped to scan the empty graveyard.

Margot decided it would probably be a good time to run. Although she was no coward, she wasn't stupid. It was a dangerous situation. She tried to get to her feet but it proved more difficult than she thought. Her arms were stiff and rigid and she was sure one of her ankles was sprained; how, she had no idea. What she did know was that she wouldn't be able to make the quick getaway she had hoped for. Maybe if she moved quietly, maybe it wouldn't - it was too late. The creature had spotted her and had started to advance upon her.

The only sound she could hear was a metal shovel being dragged across the grass. It was getting louder. She was frozen with fear. Unsure of what to do, Margot glanced back towards what the thing had been digging up. It looked like a large box or no, she refused to believe it was a coffin. It all seemed too far-fetched. She felt like she was in a low budget horror film. The figure was getting closer and closer until it was mere metres away. Margot tried to search for weak points on its body. If she couldn't move, she'd have to fight it. From where she was standing, she could already see it walked with a prominent limp. That was a good start. Margot remembered her sunglasses and rummaged through her pockets to try and find them. The figure was still approaching. She knew they were somewhere on her person. It was beginning to pick up the pace. If she could only hurry up, the figure was getting larger and larger. Margot gave up, shaking her head she looked up and there it stood, towering over her.

The next few moments seemed like the longest of her life. There they stood in silence, staring in awe of one another. The creature dropped its shovel. Margot could see that it wore high PVC stilettos and ripped and laddered tights. She moved her eyes up the disfigured body, trying to take in every detail possible. The figure was lanky and thin and appeared to be leaning to one side which indicated to Margot that it was deformed or crippled in some way. The skirt it was wearing was splattered with what Margot hoped was dirt and water.

She looked up to the top half of the body; Margot could make out long, black hair and some sort of gothic corset. It was between her and the meagre sunlight so it was almost impossible to make out the figure's face. That was something to be thankful for. Suddenly, a large hand grabbed her leather coat and pulled her off the ground with such force that she didn't have time to consider moving. Before Margot knew it, she was at face height with the thing.

"What are you doing here?" it said.

Margot was taken aback by the low, croaky voice. It definitely wasn't a woman, although on the plus side he did have an American accent.

"I don't know! I think the question is what the hell are *you* doing?" She asked but at the same time she didn't believe that she wanted answers.

He was puzzled; it was his turn to be taken aback. That was her chance.

Margot spun herself around, making the man lose his grip on her coat.

Ha! She thought as she hit the ground. Putting her hand in her pockets once more, she finally pulled out her sunglasses. She turned and felt the pain shoot through her body, but she knew she'd have to keep going; it may be her only chance to escape.

Margot turned to run, completely forgetting about the gravestone that was planted directly behind her. She collided with it head-first, before even putting on her sunglasses. She slipped, hit her head and was once again out cold. It was an off-day for her.

The figure scratched his head in confusion.

*

When Margot awoke for the second time, she felt like screaming. If the first situation had been bad, the second was worse. Her arms were tied, and she was hanging from some sort of hook. She was in agonising pain as the weight of her body pulled down on her arms and shoulders. Margot looked around; she wasn't the only thing hanging up. She gulped. Many others, she would call them 'things' for now, surrounded her, hung in the same position. The only difference was that they didn't appear to be moving. She had to get out. She tried to see if she could locate an exit in the large room. Her heart lifted when she spotted a huge open door, leading to the dark of the outside world.

A flickering candle caught her eye; she turned to her left to see a much smaller doorway. That one seemed to lead further into the building. It also appeared to be the only thing she could see that was emitting light. Suddenly, she heard clanking and the clicking of heels. The strange man appeared in the doorway, his silhouetted figure looked like he was carrying something long and pointed and it wasn't a walking stick.

He bent with difficulty as he stepped through into the room. It was apparent that whoever had made the place hadn't had him in mind. Then again, who purposely designed houses for people who look like they should be an extra from 'The Addams Family'?

"I have something for you," his deep, monotone voice echoed throughout the room. Margot hated to imagine what it would be, the guy's birthday gifts must be horrific. The man walked towards her in the same menacing fashion he had in the graveyard. He placed the long object he was carrying on a small wooden table that stood beside where she was hanging.

"Shit," he muttered to himself.

It was obvious he had forgotten something important. "I'll be back shortly," he said, sounding unenthusiastic.

Margot waited until he had gone back through the door before she started wriggling around. She tried to break free, rocking the rope from which she hung back and forth. It was exhausting, but she needed to escape before his return. Who knew what he'd do to her?

"Come on," she mumbled, keeping her eyes on the door. He had tied the rope tight, making it difficult for her to move at all. Finally, Margot was able to untangle one arm. She swung herself around and reached for the sharp pole on the table which was a sword of some kind and used it to untangle and cut the rope that held her other wrist in place.

Margot dropped to the floor with a thud; it was covered in straw. It was as if she was in a barn. She then remembered the other figures hanging around her, reluctantly she stepped forward.

She had to get out. Margot ran to the open door, but before she got the chance to escape, the strange man was returning. The entrance was a lot further away than she had realised. If she ran, she was sure to be seen and even though she could probably out run him in daylight, she couldn't see a thing in the dark. Margot hid behind the nearest hanging object. Pulling it towards her, she gritted her teeth as she felt its cold rotting limbs press against her body. It was no animal.

"Where are you?" The man's voice echoed throughout the room. She poked her head around the corpse. He was standing where she had just been hanging. He placed the forgotten object on the table. She hated to think what it might be.

"Human?" His voice echoed. "You won't get very far."

The man's voice was still monotone. He ran his fingers through his long black hair as he searched the room. Margot heard unsteady footsteps heading straight towards her. *Don't panic, don't panic,* she thought. She tried to convince herself to stop being so stupid and man up. However, it seemed to be one of those situations where panic was unavoidable. Whatever Margot was doing, she knew she'd have to act fast.

The man checked behind each body in turn. Margot gulped as she heard the click of his heels growing nearer. *What was he going to do with her?* He was almost upon her when she swung the body in front of her so hard it hit him full-on in the upper torso. He staggered. The distraction was just what she needed. Without hesitating, she pelted towards the door with the flickering light, bouncing off dripping bodies on the way. Margot reached the door and slammed it shut. Panting heavily, she slumped against the frame trying to make sense of the situation. Her eyes darted over the room. She had found the source of the light from earlier. Around the window ledges were rows of tall candles. Margot thought it would be a good idea to grab one, as the rest of the house appeared to be in darkness. Before she crossed the room, she noticed an object on the floor, Margot screamed. It was a half open coffin. Before she could compose herself, the door burst open and in walked the huge man.

Margot bolted. She had no idea where she was running to; she didn't care, just as long as the direction led her as far away from him as possible.

She saw a doorway at the other side of the room and took it. Once again she was in pitch blackness. Margot ran through a series of rooms, bumping into or climbing over anything in her path between her and the next door. It was hard to see what anything looked like in the dark and she didn't bother looking at interior décor. All she knew was that everything she touched was covered in dust.

She turned left. She turned right. She ran up and down stairs, constantly looking behind her. The place was like a maze.

Margot kept running until she could run no further, she reached a dead end.

Margot smiled to herself as she closed the door. *No one fucks with me.*

Feeling her way around the room, she thought it was a good idea to build a barricade. She was in the top right hand corner of the house, not that she knew it at the time. She was more concerned with what she could pick up. She believed herself to be in a bedroom, she felt what she thought to be a wardrobe and chest of drawers. *OUCH!* She bashed into something, she'd found the bed. At least that confirmed her suspicions. She ran her hands up one of the poles on a corner; *a four poster, very traditional.*

Margot moved her hands up the sheets. *Maybe she could use this to block the door?* She stopped, feeling a lump rising from underneath the sheets. It felt oddly like a-

"Hello again."

Margot screamed, pulling her hand away in horror. He had been lying on the bed all the time. He got up as she backed away towards the door, but it was proving hard to open. She was trapped. However, Margot Grant wasn't going down without a fight.

He got up off the bed and she lashed out violently. Margot moved to the opposite side of the room, shaking the bed frame. The posts didn't feel secure, they were old. *One good yank and the wood should crack.* There was a huge crash as the four poster bed collapsed. Even if the lights had been on she wouldn't have been able to see the man for all the dust that enveloped the room like a swarm of angry bees. She dropped to the floor coughing, unable to breathe. Whilst down there she searched the floor. Margot felt a long pole that had broken off the bed. It would do. A light flickered on in the room.

She clambered to her feet and began knocking down everything she could.

She could see the room was filled with many strange objects; slimy substances in jars, stuffed animals and pieces of bone. The walls were white and crumbling. She imagined the room would have looked grand once upon a time.

The man reached out his arms. Margot feared he was trying to grab hold of her.

"What are you doing to my house?" He put his hands on his head as he inspected the mess. "Could you please stop doing that? Some of these items are collectables and can't be replaced."

Margot stopped dead in her tracks. He was standing there with his arms folded waiting patiently. Dropping the pole on the floor, she answered: "Yes, sure, sorry."

"Thank you," the emotionless voice replied. "Just to let you know, you've made a terrible mess."

He walked off, as though bored. Margot stood in silence, the only sound was the buzzing of the light. All of a sudden she was confused. The guy seemed a lot less threatening than before.

"Wait, wait, wait," she said, running in front of him and blocking his way out. "Dude, what the hell is going on?"

She grabbed hold of his arm. In the light, she could finally get a proper look at his face. His long thin features were all covered in pale make up. Apart from the dark eyes that sat nicely aside his pointed nose. They were terribly smudged with black and grey eye shadow, which gave him a vampiric edge, with deep red lipstick that covered much more than his mouth.

A terrible thought crossed Margot's mind: "Look you, don't try any shit! You rape me and you'll wish you were never born!"

"You mean I'll wish I was still alive." The response surprised her. He looked out into the distance. "I hate it when they're still warm."

She shivered, but wasn't frightened. Margot wondered if he always said everything in that monotone fashion, it wasn't the most comforting manner. He picked her up, moving her out of the way of the door. That time, she didn't scream. Instead, she said, "I'm not a doll you know!"

"You know, you humans are much easier to deal with when you're dead." He mumbled to himself as he began to walk back down the stairs.

She quickly followed. "Hello? I'm talking to you."

"Your tea is terribly cold now by the way," he added, ignoring her words.

"Wait… tea?"

"What did you think I forgot; a knife?" came the emotionless reply.

"I thought," she paused. "Never mind what I thought. I suppose I'm not usually accustomed to being hung up!"

"You are an extremely rude guest, running off like that. I don't understand it, that's how I've treated every other human; you're the first to complain."

"Yeah but they're normally dead," Margot muttered to herself as they approached the candlelit room. She glanced at the floor; the coffin still lay half open.

Able to get a proper look at the room, she realised it was a kitchen, or at least, had been at some point. Everything from the tiled floor to the broken windows was covered in a thick layer of dust and grime. A small, gnarled wooden table, surrounded by mismatching, Gothic chairs, acted as the centre piece of the room.

Margot surveyed the room, looking at the array of rotting food, half-eaten on the work surface or lying behind open cupboard doors. She shuddered; food wasn't the only thing lying around. The room, like the others she had seen, was also cluttered with strange items. The décor's finishing touches were various arrangements of dead or wilting flowers, which had been placed in oddly shaped vases next to the cracked windows; presumably so they could reach the sunlight. *Pfft, what sunlight?* Margot thought to herself. However, the one thing that really stood out to her was a picture that sat in pristine condition in the centre of the window ledge. She screwed her eyes up trying to get a better look.

It was a woman with long black hair, wearing a white dress. It was impossible to determine the actual colours as it was a black and white photo.

A banging sound caused Margot to divert her attention elsewhere. The man was bent over the coffin, trying to prise open the lid.

"Hey I'm still here you know!" Margot felt almost neglected. "You never answered my questions, now I want answers!"

The transvestite reached for a crowbar.

"What were you doing in the graveyard?"

"Finding someone to fuck," he replied as though it was the most natural thing in the world. Margot sighed, why had she bothered? The man was clearly insane.

"Well, where am I?"

"You're not in the Universe any longer," was the croaky reply. "Sorry about that."

"What do you mean, not in the Universe?" Margot couldn't believe what she was hearing. Before she had time to delve further into the subject, he said: "Now help me with this lid."

He still hadn't looked up from what he was doing.

"Dude, you are joking, right? No, no I am not gonna help you screw a dead body!" She didn't understand how he was so blasé about everything.

Margot leaned on the edge of the table with her head in her hands. "Stupid bastard angels," she muttered to herself. Life had never felt more confusing than it did at that moment. Where had the angels taken her? Was it the land of the Voice and if so where were Reenie and Clarke? There were so many questions that needed answering.

He stopped what he was doing and walked over to her, patting her gently on the head. Margot looked up.

"I'm sorry but you're not very helpful. So if it's all the same to you I'm going to head to that light place I saw and try and find my way from there," she said.

"No, human, you're not meant to be here," he said. He stared into space for a while. It was hard to tell what he was thinking; his expression remained blank. "Come with me, I think I know someone who can help you."

Margot smiled as she noticed the white and blue china tea set placed on one of his grimy trays. He had been telling the truth. Margot sighed; she hated accepting help from anyone. Plus it was obvious that the guy was completely, mentally disturbed, but what other choice did she have?

It may be the only chance she'd get.

"Margot," she held out her hand as a friendly gesture. He looked at it, unsure of what to do.

"Barbie," he said.

*

Jade stormed the house, searching for clues, answers, anything he could find. To be quite honest, he had no idea what he was meant to be looking for. Nor did he have any idea of what to do. Jade wasn't a man of action. He was a man of science, logic. But he was going to ignore all that and let pure instinct take over. Getting in the house had not been easy. Margot had taken the keys with her, leaving him the only option of climbing through the window. Jade didn't execute the break-in in the most heroic way. He had to explain to many passers-by that he wasn't breaking and entering. Although, since he already looked suspicious, his words didn't seem very convincing.

He felt an excruciating pain, deep down inside himself. The pain was not physical, yet hurt more than breaking any bone. He had lost Margot again. She had been his partner, his companion, his best friend and now she had gone - again. They had been separated, just like before. Jade felt anger run through his body, he clenched his fists and narrowed his eyes. He was going to get her back. He didn't care what it took. Jade wasn't going to be alone again. It all had something to do with the Voice, he was sure of it. There was no point going to the U.A.S. He couldn't risk any more lives and they probably would call him crazy anyway. *No, it's up to me and me alone.* He had a plan. He was going to head straight towards the heart of the beast.

Jade Wilde was going to follow the angels.

*

Barbie reached down to pick Margot up as he led her through the dark building.

"It's okay, really, I can walk," she said, as his huge hands reached towards her. The transvestite went towards a Land Rover parked by the side of a winding road. She had no idea where they were travelling, but something told her that he didn't live far from where she had first found him.

The car was surprisingly new.

"I didn't know they still made these." She said, looking around the vehicle. It was the first time she'd ever sat in a car. It fascinated her.

"If you know the right eccentrics, they do," the transvestite replied.

Barbie told Margot about his love of shopping in the Universe and how she should feel extremely lucky to be sitting in the car. She sighed, at the moment she felt like the unluckiest person alive. Margot looked out of the window.

"By the way," Barbie turned to her, throwing two items into her lap. "I believe these are yours." She glanced down at her sunglasses and packet of cigarettes.

Thanks," she said, putting one in her mouth. "How did you know I was hiding in your bedroom?"

"I didn't, I just reckoned you needed time to cool off, so I thought I should go read or something."

Suddenly there was a loud bang that shook the car. Barbie brought the vehicle to a halt.

"Shit, I think we hit someone!" Margot shouted.

"Please let them be dead," Barbie muttered as he opened the door. He turned back to her: "You stay here."

Margot sat in silence. Outside, she could hear shouting. She wished she was able to see what was going on. Barbie had told her to stay put, but she was never really one for abiding by the rules and the voice outside didn't sound very happy. He could probably use the help, she told herself, knowing full well that she just wanted to be in on the action. Leaning forward, she opened the door and crept outside.

"I'm gonna get dis bleedin' dog put down! He's pissed off now, the bastard. Oi get 'ere!" A strong Irish accent called out from the darkness. Margot tiptoed around to the front of the car. She was unable to contain her shock at the sight in front of her. Barbie was kneeling over a man lying in the middle of the road. His features were hard to see from her point of view, but what she did see reminded her of the bark from an old tree. His skin was deeply wrinkled, making him look ancient. However, his old features weren't the cause of her shock. The fact was that the man was disfigured. The crash had rendered him badly injured. He was bent out of shape like a folded piece of paper. Margot glanced in horror at the blood pouring from his chest and arm.

"Barbie! We need to call an ambulance!" She was scared it was already too late.

Barbie looked up. "No, he'll have healed in a few minutes."

As enthusiastic as ever, Margot thought, then she paused for a moment, "Healed?"

She stared as the old man clicked his bones back into shape and slowly stood up.

"Who the hell is tha'? I thought the women you bring home don't breathe, let alone talk." The man reached out his hands, feeling for something to hold onto; he was blind.

Barbie supported him but the man shrugged him off.

"This defies every rule of science," Margot muttered.

"Wha'do ya think you're doing? Now where the hell is my dog? It's the fifth time dat dog has tried to kill me dis week!" Barbie sighed as the man stumbled around like something that had just been trodden on.

"This is Margot," Barbie said. "She's a human. I'm taking her to The Halo and Harp."

The man held up his hands to protest but was stopped by the sound of a bell on a collar. A dog ran out from the wilderness of the night, Margot stared at the animal. The RSPCA would have had a field day. It was a golden retriever; standard for a guide dog. However, she'd never seen any guide dog look like that one.

Flesh fell from its bony structure of a body. She was scared by the idea of the creature wagging its tail for fear of getting covered in whatever hung from it. Its ribs stuck out at all angles and the bones in its legs were starting to show. Despite all that, it acted like any dog should, bounding around, excited by the new company.

"Fuckin' wanker's back," the man grumbled as the dog stood by his side. Margot didn't understand the problem. The dog seemed innocent enough. The man looked completely unharmed. Even the bloodstains on his shirt had vanished. Remembering Barbie's last comment, he turned to where he thought Barbie was standing, "Now wha' did you say 'bout a human?"

"This way, Frank," Barbie said.

Frank jumped, realising the croaky voice was directly behind him. Margot found it difficult to hold back her laughter. Barbie glanced at her, failing to see the humour in the situation.

"Yeh skirt wearin' idiot! Don't make the same mistake as last time!" Frank yelled, his accent was more pronounced when he became excited Margot noticed.

The transvestite, seemingly unaffected by being called a 'skirt wearing idiot', shrugged his shoulders.

"Come on, Frank," Barbie opened the door to the Land Rover for the angry man to climb in the back. He declined help from both passengers and proceeded to fall flat on his face, missing the car.

Finally on the road again, Barbie explained Frank's situation. She had gone past the point of being shocked by anything. Whatever happened next, she was just going to go along with it. What else could she do? Margot lit another cigarette and tried to give Barbie her full attention which, due to his personality, wasn't easy. Believing what he told her wasn't easy, either. "It's not easy being blind and having a guide dog which is part demon," he continued.

Margot raised her eyebrows.

"I've known Frank for years; he's had that dog for ages. I don't think anyone wanted it." Barbie turned to the dog which was lying on the back seat. He lowered his voice. "That dog's been trying to kill him ever since he got him, bit of a shame really. Demons are always hard to trust. Frank's okay though, although he has got a bit of a temper."

Sure, Margot thought. *He seemed absolutely lovely, the height of eloquence.*

"How did he do that... that thing?" She asked.

"He's a healer, doesn't matter how much he gets hurt. I've hit him three times this week and he's been fine." He turned to the old man in the back. Frank sat with his arms folded; his eyes were blank and empty.

"Stop tellin' dis human about my personal life! I'm blind, not deaf! And stop measuring things in human times!" he moaned.

Not a bad response, thought Barbie, *better than his usual replies.* As Frank experienced near death situations on a daily basis, he was never in the best of moods. Margot turned to him angrily, but refrained from saying anything. Instead she focused her attention outside the window. It was a total waste of time as she couldn't make anything out. The bright light in the distance contrasted with the darkness and made it hard for her eyes to adjust. Wherever she was going, she hoped there would be answers there for her.

*

Putting as much 'Face' in his pocket as he could carry and quickly grabbing a few supplies, Jade marched out of the house. It was dead on midnight and although it was risky, he knew he'd never be able to escape in the day time; people would try and stop him. The U.A.S. would try and stop him. He had made excuses earlier as to why he couldn't go to the lab. He feared their suspicions, but after the disappearance of their leader and two of their best researchers, he was sure they had greater things on their mind. Jade tilted his tricorne as he left the house; he had bigger things to worry about, too. Though the hat wouldn't disguise him, it made him feel cool and very secret agent-like.

He remembered Clarke distinctly say space travel was prohibited. Jade pondered on that restriction. He supposed if the angels did catch him then at least he'd have a chance at finding Margot. A strange feeling suddenly washed over him and it had nothing to do with 'Face'.

Margot.

He was so worried about her. Jade had though that coming back to the Earth would make him feel complete again, but now she was gone... He sighed. If only he had told her. No, it was too late now, he had to focus. Jade pushed the thoughts to the back of his mind as he made his way quietly towards the forest on the island. Well, almost quietly, he managed to catch his trench-coat on a tree and ended up falling over. In the words of Jade, *it was one time.*

The night was silent. Only the faint sound of the ocean accompanied him as he crept across the beach. He was close, all he needed to do was cut through a familiar path of trees and he'd be near the ship. Jade looked around the beach; further down the shore he could see the angel. It was frozen to the spot. He smiled to himself; all was going well, so far. Then, like before, the ground began to shake. Jade froze. A familiar rumbling in the distance was getting closer and closer. He turned to see the large hooded figure moving towards him yet again.

*

The Land Rover came to a halt. The three of them sat in silence as Barbie switched off the headlights, rendering them in total darkness. Margot reached for her sunglasses and put them on. She could hear the faint sound of voices and music coming from somewhere nearby.

"Okay, Frank, let's go find Damien, he'll know what to do," Barbie turned to the man. Frank's arms were still folded.

"You're makin' a big mistake if ye ask me," Frank's face looked like a storm. Humans only brought trouble in his opinion.

Margot stuck her fingers up at him. Barbie quickly gestured for her to get out. As Margot closed the door she saw they were in a small car park next to a run-down building. She had seen it before when she lived in Britain; it looked very much like an old fashioned version of a pub. The building itself was tiny, she would be surprised if Barbie was able to stand up inside. The tiled roof was slanted and caving in at one side, the windows were small and steamed over and the stone walls that held the building together were crumbling. The music was louder. She was sure the tune sounded like *The Macarena*. Margot had a feeling that it was their intended destination. She followed Barbie around the side of the building to a rotting wooden door. Above it a sign swung, squeaking on its worn hinges. She could just make out the name: 'The Halo and Harp'. Margot rubbed her head. Well, at least the place would have living people inside. Barbie held the door open as Frank went past grumbling, followed by his murderous dog. Margot followed closely after, curious of what awaited them.

The smell of smoke and alcohol hit her as she walked through the door. Margot waited in a small porch, furnished with a distastefully garish red carpet. The sort of carpet her Grandma might own. Margot put a cigarette in her mouth as she waited, not daring to step inside the main room of the building without Barbie. She stared at him. For the first time, she realised he was a lot less ugly than she had first thought. He had the potential to be quite beautiful. She pictured him with perfect make up; smoky black eyes, daringly red lips and a clean gothic outfit.

Frank had already stepped inside and Barbie was keen to follow. It was funny, Margot thought, that he couldn't find his way inside a car but could get into a pub with ease.

"Let's go," Barbie said and motioned to the albino to follow.

Margot's mouth dropped open as she stepped through the next door. It was like walking into a TARDIS. 'The Halo and Harp' was much bigger on the inside. Margot glanced up and realised she couldn't see the ceiling. She removed her sunglasses, the bright lights and candles floating in the centre of the room hit her hard. It was such a contrast to outside. It was like nothing she had seen before. The bar, in the shape of a perfect circle, sat in the centre of the room. It seemed normal enough, however, looking up she saw another bar directly above that one. And then another. That continued until the bars, like the ceiling, disappeared high up into the pub. The bars themselves were made of a yellow wood. Margot was guessing that was the 'halo' reference, and they contained every sort of drink she could think of and many more. They were all listed on a huge blackboard which took up the majority of the wall on the left. The drinks were an array of different colours, some smoked and others were frozen or on fire. She changed her mind about being thirsty.

Huge, adjustable stools with built-in ladders surrounded the towering, cylindrical structure. They were occupied by all sorts of people sitting, spinning or climbing towards their chosen destination. Margot's eyes followed Frank as he found one of the ladders and began to climb it until he reached what she believed to be the third level. It was definitely better than anything they had on earth. She watched as he spun around expertly, like someone on a public library ladder organising books, towards a smoking green drink in a long, thin glass.

"We were gonna have a long horizontal bar but it's easier for staff to see the over-aged drinkers this way," Barbie replied to Margot's confused expression.

Yeah, she thought, *because that makes perfect sense.*

She saw not everyone was using the ladder-seats, many people with huge wings hovered in the air above them. Some sat at tables and chairs floating around the room. The people that filled the building were probably the only thing that shocked her more than Frank's extensive drink order. She knew why she kept being referred to so explicitly as 'human', she was probably the only human there. The place was filled with strange looking creatures and people, from small goblins to a bright blue and orange couple that had had one too many and were making-out as they danced in the air to the cheesy music. It was fair to say, like Barbie, many of the people were Gothic and dark in appearance. She felt like she was on the set of a cheap Halloween B-movie. All she had to do was wait for a stupid, blonde female to walk into the scene and die horrifically. *Wait a moment…*

Next to them was a set of stairs for customers who wished to venture deeper into the room and get away from the hustle and bustle. However, Barbie led Margot to a set of stairs on the right. They led to the balconies that were level with each bar. The balconies were dimly lit and circumnavigated the bar area. Margot sensed that the darker characters hung around those parts. She saw figures standing in dark corners whispering to one another and passing packages from under their cloaks. Barbie moved her on, leading her up yet more flights of stairs. Had Margot been the stereotypical impatient child, demanding to know 'are we there yet?' Every ten minutes, it would have felt like they had been walking for hours. As a matter of fact, they had been walking for exactly twenty nine minutes. For a place that had such an incredible flow of people, Margot would have thought they'd own a lift. Barbie paused for a moment at the top of one of the staircases.

"Just need to check something," he muttered, opening a red door. She followed him out onto another dim balcony. It felt good to be out of the narrow staircase. Margot watched as Barbie bent his enormous body over the wooden railings and looked towards the ceiling. However, the balcony wasn't like the others, it revealed the top of the pub for the first time. Margot imitated Barbie, leaning over the creaking railings. The ceiling looked strange, more like a sky. It was made of what appeared to be dark storm clouds, swirling in a whirlpool. There was an occasional bright flash, accompanied by intermittent thunderous grumbles. The thin mist that lingered near the top of the building was clearing, giving Barbie a better view of what he was looking for.

A far grander, more exquisitely decorated balcony came into view; it overlooked the entire pub; only of course on the conditions that you had the eyesight of a hawk and could actually gaze down that far amidst the bustle. A man leaned on the railings and looked down over the edge at the people below, he caught Margot's eyes and they stared at each other for a few seconds. She almost felt in awe of him, although would never admit it. His bleached blonde hair blew in front of his pale face. He ran his fingers slowly through it, creating long messy spikes.

Barbie tapped Margot on the arm. "We're in luck. He's here."

Margot felt she already knew who he was talking about.

Her heart pounded as they finished climbing the last few sets of stairs. Margot might finally get some answers. As Barbie opened the last door, they walked into a huge room that opened out onto the balcony she had just been staring at. It was also dimly lit, but what Margot could see, was more elaborate in its decoration than the main part of the pub. She walked past small groups of people, following Barbie towards where the man was standing. Damien looked quite ordinary from the back, which automatically made him stand out from the crowds. His black trench coat fell to just above his knees. As they approached him, Damien turned to them, focusing his attention on Margot. He was dressed entirely in black. Each piece of his outfit seemed to adhere to a formal Victorian dress code.

"Barbie, why is there a human here?" he asked the question sharply. Damien's gaze never left Margot's as he narrowed his eyes so they matched his sharp features.

She stepped forward angrily. "I want answers."

Damien remained perfectly calm, he picked up his drink from the side and swirled the white liquid around the glass.

"Angels dropped her off at the wrong place, she needs our help," Barbie said.

Margot glared at him, she didn't *need* their help. Barbie's blank expression contrasted with the smirk Damien was wearing. Margot's red eyes stared at the overly large canine teeth in his mouth.

"Look, it's fine. I don't need anything, now if you don't mind I'll be on my way." As she turned to walk away, Damien rested his cold hand on her shoulder.

"Give me a few minutes." He smiled coolly, his clear voice sounded like it belonged on radio. Everything about him was so suave, each of his actions became one, single, flowing movement. It appeared effortless.

"Well, that went well," Barbie said. Margot wasn't sure whether Barbie was using sarcasm or being serious, it was so hard to figure out his moods at the best of times.

"I thought you'd be coming back home with me in a body bag," he continued as their eyes followed Damien. "He must like you. We never get humans here, so your blood is a rarity to a vampire."

She didn't reply. She wasn't really listening. Margot smiled as she watched Damien walk away. He was the complete opposite to Jade. Confident. There didn't seem to be one faltering nerve within him. However, unlike Jade, he was unfriendly and downright rude. *Good, this would be a challenge.* Margot stopped in her tracks.

Jade!

*

Jade's heart beat hard in his chest. He wasn't sure which direction he should turn. The angel was gaining on him. There wasn't much time. It was stupid to turn back; he risked getting caught no matter which direction he ran. Jade clenched his fists and sprinted between the trees. He was going to find Margot, no matter what it took. He pulled his goggles over his eyes as he ran through the forest. The sound of crunching vegetation filled the air. The angel had entered the forest. At least it would be harder for it to see him under the leafy coverage. He pushed himself forward, through the trees.

Jade ran towards the spot he had left the ship. It was nowhere in sight. *Oh, where did I park it, where did I park it?* He hit his face on something solid and he fell to the ground. Rubbing his head and picking up his hat, Jade got up to inspect what he had run into. There was nothing in front of him. He had run into thin air? It was bizarre. A thought occurred to him. The ship was in camouflage mode. He fumbled in his pockets, trying to find the key. *Got it,* he thought, feeling the cold metal between his fingers. Jade did a small victory jump, before clambering inside the ship.

The roar of the engine made him smile. He and Margot had put in a lot of work and she ran like a dream. The ship flew out into the open sky, catching some of the branches of the trees on its way up. Jade flew in the same direction he had seen the scientists being carried the previous night, straight towards the centre of the Bermuda triangle. The angel, still on the ground, looked up, confused by what was happening. It hesitated for a moment then the creature spread its wings and followed Jade into the dark night. Jade turned up the engine to full after seeing how much it was gaining on him. He had to hand it to the creature, it was fast. Its huge wings allowed it to pick up speed faster than his small ship. He gulped as a warning sign flashed up on his screen. That wasn't good. Yep, that stretch of sea was definitely living up to expectations. The ship wasn't used to so much power and the engine gave out. Jade's heart dropped as the ship fell into the darkness.

The angel swooped down, still on the chase. They'd been flying so high that Jade hadn't seen the blinding light directly below them. Nor had he seen the amount of angels in the air, like jellyfish of the sky. Jade smiled, he may be falling to his death but on the plus side he had reached his destination. Suddenly the angel grabbed his ship, the sudden force throwing him against the smooth floor of the vehicle. He felt the large hand crushing the outer chassis. Redecorating had been a waste of time.

"You'd better pay for that!" Jade shouted, knowing that it would change nothing. He realised that the angel hadn't stopped falling. It had picked up so much speed that it was unable to stop itself. It had lost control. They were headed straight for the light below. Jade had seen many lights and that was nothing like any of them.

Having had no idea what he was looking for, he guessed it was the place where Margot had gone. Jade closed his eyes as they fell. He didn't want to imagine his fate, so instead he conjured images of happy, innocent children running though fields in the summer, playing fetch with their pet dog. He sighed, not even the thought of little Fido could prepare him for what he was about to endure. The ground must only be a few metres away. He waited for the explosion. He waited for his own death. He kept waiting... why was nothing happening?

They were still falling, but he failed to understand why they hadn't hit the ground or the sea. Jade opened his eyes, realising the tension that had built up in his face was quite painful and pretty unnecessary. Surely he should be dead? Yet, he was still falling, clutched in the grasp of the stone creature. He dragged himself to the small circular window of his ship, scared to look outside.

He was falling through a picturesque pink sky. Although there was no way that the sky belonged to the Earth. The sky slowly changed from purple to a deeper blue the further they fell. Below him he could still see the blinding light, surrounded by pitch black. It was getting larger and larger until he could make out that it was some form of land.

This land was covered in blue bottomless seas, sandy beaches and emerald green countryside. Even the built-up areas looked silver and clean. Jade remembered his situation. He was plummeting to his death at God knows what speed.

Without warning, the angel hit the ground and exploded, tainting the perfect countryside.

And all was quiet once again.

Chapter 6

The Wake Up Call

"Okay." Damien smiled and closed the door. The room fell silent. The four of them stood in a small room at the very top of the Halo and Harp. It was used for storing the most expensive drinks in the building. Margot thought it was the only reason Frank, who was sulking in the corner, had agreed to come along. It was almost certain that the place was closed off to the public, but Damien seemed to be both known and respected by a lot of people. Margot sat on a large crate and put a cigarette in her mouth. She looked round at the dysfunctional group; a necrophiliac transvestite, a drunken, regenerating, blind Irish man with a murderous dog and a satirical vampire. The scene was growing ever more bizarre. Margot sighed; she managed to get herself into the most peculiar of situations.

"You shouldn't do that," a cold voice whispered in her ear. "It's extremely bad for you," Damien took the cigarette and crushed it in his hand before taking out a packet of his own and putting one in his mouth.

"Hey!" Margot turned to him, furious at the lack of control she had. Barbie placed an enormous hand on her shoulder in an attempt to calm her. She understood the gesture, it was one of those *don't fuck with that man; he will rip your head from your body and quite possibly your upper torso with it* gestures. She took the hint.

The door swung open.

Margot turned, interested to know who would walk in next. She continued to stare at the door in suspense. Still, nothing happened. Margot looked around the room in confusion.

"Hurst! Just the demon I wanted to see," Damien said and smiled, leaning back on one of the crates. She heard a cough and Margot followed Damien's eyes downwards to see a small, strange man.

Despite being extremely short, Hurst had very distinctive features. His nose was long and pointed and his large ears stuck out either side of his head. His dark eyes however, were pin-sized and hidden behind circular sunglasses. Hurst's skin was red, which contrasted to the simple, black garments he wore. They complemented his long black hair which ran down almost the length of his back and was neatly tied in a low ponytail. The only thing that did take Margot by surprise was the large, silver Christian cross that hung around his neck. You, dear reader, may compare him to a small demon version of Ozzy Osborne.

"What do you want, Damien?" Hurst asked. His tone was cold; his voice was high and grave. Damien said nothing but pointed and smiled in Margot's direction.

"God moves in mysterious ways," muttered the demon as he examined her with his beady eyes.

"Excuse me?" Margot was taken back. "Did you just say God?"

"So," Damien interrupted, leaning further back on the crate behind him. "Do you reckon Arabina will be up for a visit?"

Before the demon had chance to answer, Margot repeated: "Did he just say God?"

Hurst spun around. "Yes, why?" the demon's squeaky voice rang in her ears.

"But you're a demon!" Margot tried to hold back her laughter. The others, with the exception of Barbie, shot confused looks in her direction.

"I know," he pondered for a while, lost in his own thoughts. "I have a strong feeling that I may be going to a place darker than hell."

The word hell shot through Margot's brain, taking precedence over the rest of her thoughts.

A horrible realisation suddenly struck her: "Oh god, I'm dead! I knew something was wrong! The Voice has finally taken me to hell!" She was beginning to think that all her past beliefs were wrong, that Jade had lied. There were no other worlds. Everything she had worked for had been a waste. The Voice...

"Close," Damien whispered. "Welcome to Haszear, Margot."

"Brilliant, so I'm dead," Margot's body slumped. Frank, who was amused by her dampening spirits, began to laugh.

"Thanks for that input, Frank," Damien sighed, his face breaking into a shadowy smile once again. "But really, it's not Margot's fault she's uneducated."

"Uneducated?" Margot tried to keep her temper but she had a feeling he enjoyed messing with her.

"What do you know of Heaven and Hell, Margot?"

"Do I look like a frigging bible?" She snapped. Margot took a deep breath before answering again. "Only the basics."

Damien ignored her first answer but Hurst gasped, clearly shocked by her tone.

"Well, what would you say if I told you that every human story about Heaven and Hell was based upon this world? I say *based*, there are large differences. The angels currently reside in the Over World whilst the Demons and much darker creators."

"Reside in the Under World, here, yeah I get it."

"Almost," he said and grinned. "Except we're not in the Under World."

"Then where are we?"

"We're on the floating island in between. What humans might call 'No Man's Land', what many of us call Manchester."

Margot burst into laughter. She could see the resemblance.

"I see nothing funny about that," Damien snapped.

Barbie glanced at Margot, she knew he understood.

"Its proper name is Manhaden," he said, before letting Damien continue.

"Our world is much older and a lot more powerful than yours, as you have already witnessed. People like us don't have to rely on apparatus such as your so-called 'technology'. Now, don't ask me why. Probably because of some of our residents' constant visits to Earth," he said and glared at Barbie. "The people of your world seemed to get our world mixed in with their religions. Anyway, they get us mixed up the most with Christianity I think, and none of us, with the exception of Hurst, believe in such things. Our world is like any other. We have bosses like you have world leaders, Satan and Gabriel for example, but these people aren't what you think they are, they're different to what your tales make them out to be. Barbie told me he found you in a graveyard, Margot. So no, you're not dead, we live and die just the same as you, only I'm guessing we have a lot longer life span."

Margot tried to contain the relief percolating within her. For the first time in a very long time she felt happy, not necessarily to feel alive, but to simply just be living.

"I'm alive." Her words were the softest they'd been all evening. If Margot was able to convey her feelings without embarrassment, she would have probably run to Damien and kissed him before streaking through the pub.

"Yes," came his simple reply and his face broke into a cold smile. It was strange to think of that place as real. Margot had heard many stories.

"It's funny; I would have thought I was in hell," she muttered.

Damien heard her and said: "Try telling Silvia that." Although he said it under his breath, she heard it. So did Hurst who shook his head, a worried expression on his face.

"Now yer got what yer came for, yer can go," Frank grunted in the corner. His demonic dog was lying by his side. He gestured to where he thought it was sitting, which happened to be completely the wrong direction. "And take this thing with you."

She didn't need persuading. Margot wasn't like Jade, she was impatient. If the circumstances had been different, Margot would have been all for exploring and researching. However, just then she wasn't thinking with her scientific mind; she was in survival mode. Yes it was true that the world was fascinating. At that moment she didn't care about the history of it, nor was she interested in the origin of its people. She just wanted to find Reenie and Clarke and get out.

A lot of things still didn't make sense to her. Damien had explained where she was, but he had failed to mention what was going on. Why had the angels from their world taken her friends? Where in the world were the scientists? It was very apparent that humans were scarce there, but surely they would be used to their appearance by then.

"Well, thanks for your help and all that, but I'd really appreciate it if you'd ask your stone angels to give my friends back," she tapped her foot as she spoke.

"Ahh now, that's a different matter," Hurst squeaked fearfully. "That has nothing to do with us!"

"What? I don't understand! This is *your* land!" She glanced round at the group. There was definitely something crucial she was missing.

"You don't realise how lucky you are, do you?" Damien's smug faced turned to her. "The humans will be in the light now. It's where they take them all, hence why I am deeply surprised to see you here."

"Well, let's go get them back then! I've seen it in the distance; it can't be too far…" Margot shouted. She assumed he meant the place she had seen earlier over the mountains. It was beginning to make sense. Damien and Frank laughed at her comment.

"What's so funny?" She folded her arms in annoyance.

Barbie stared at her with his emotionless eyes. "No one returns from the light, they're as good as dead."

*

Jade clambered out of the ruins of his space ship. The burning daylight hit him so hard he thought for a moment he had been blinded. Jade groaned. He turned his head away, felt his goggles protruding from his head and pulled them down over his eyes.

His groan became a yelp as he remembered he'd left them on night mode. After turning it off, he reached for his tricorne which lay crumpled on the golden sand. He sighed and dusted it off before placing it back over his filthy dreadlocks. It took him a while to take in the events that had just happened.

After regaining the full extent of his memory, he examined his hands and body. How come nothing was broken? He'd hit the ground hard. The unfolding events were getting more surreal by the minute. Jade turned to look for the angel he had been following. There it lay, dead beneath the blazing sunlight. He thought maybe it would be a good idea to inspect it. Swallowing hard, Jade edged closer. He stopped, and frowned.

The angel was dissolving into the earth. He watched as it began to fall apart and crumble into dust. That was *not* normal. Then again, after what he'd experienced, nothing shocked him anymore. Jade sighed and turned to his ship which was also beginning to dissolve. That had been his only escape from there. *Now what am I going to do? How the hell do I get out of here?* He thought of all his clothes and supplies that were inside. Suddenly, something emerged from the pile of the angel's ashes. At first it looked like white mist or a small cloud. Whatever it was, it whirled around in the air, leaving a vapour trail behind it. Jade's eyes followed it as it danced through the sky, climbing ever higher. Then it stopped. Just like that. He continued to stare at it, still trying to make out its shape. Jade noticed a strange feeling in his stomach, the *thing* spotted him and zoomed back, heading straight at him. His nauseated feeling increased as it spun around him, picking up speed.

He screamed and flailed his arms, helplessly trying to bat it away. An icy sensation came over his body. However, it wasn't the only thing that was icy. A sinister laugh emanated all around him and echoed in every corner of his mind. He gripped his head with both hands. The laugh was like no laugh he had heard before. It wasn't a laugh of joy or happiness, but a smug, merciless and bitter laugh. A laugh, that if he had to liken it to a human made him think of a dark villain on a superhero film; although no film had ever made him feel quite like that. Under the laugh, he could make out weaker voices, whispers, but was unsure of the words being spoken. Abruptly a piercing scream filled his skull and he gasped, collapsing backwards onto the warm sand. The thing tired of him and floated away. *Well, that was strange.* The mist paused once again; Jade cringed, hoping desperately it wasn't going to come back. Then, without warning, it dived into the calm sea.

Once again, he gasped. So much had been going on he hadn't even absorbed his surroundings. It was the first time he had thought of where he'd landed. Jade climbed to his feet and turned on the spot. *This place; it's… it's… beautiful.* He was standing on a beach, not too different from the one back home on Bequia, although the sand seemed more pure. It was so unreal, almost animated. Behind him, perfect green hills rolled on for miles, rich with vegetation.

There was no one for miles around, or at least it felt that way. For a moment, Jade felt at peace, as though he had finally become one with the world. The sea sparkled and shone a deep crystal blue as the sun beat down on its calm surface. Jade gazed beyond it and his mouth fell open as he took in the vista of a long range of mountains which ran for miles into the distance. The mountains he could deal with, but the blackness behind them was something else. It scared him; made him feel trapped. He didn't know what the blackness could be and he feared he didn't want to know. If Christopher Columbus had seen it, he would have jumped for joy. A terrible thought stuck him, maybe he was dead.

What if the fall had killed him? After all, he had felt no pain; he didn't seem to be hurt. Jade thought hard. The place seemed like a paradise to him. *It could just be… No.* He told himself firmly: *You're just getting carried away.* Surely it couldn't be heaven? That would disprove all his research and more to the point; someone like him wouldn't be allowed in heaven. He'd get stopped before he approached the gates. Jade decided to try to think logically for a moment. He must be in another world. That was much more plausible and the only option he had left to believe. He had been to other worlds before, but never seen anything quite like it. Jade pulled out his Jonovicator and scanned the area. He had to keep his wits about him. He had to be ready for anything.

"Ouch!" Jade yelled as something hit him hard on his side.

"Oh, sorry!" A girl, obviously unaware he was standing there, looked awkwardly at the floor. For a moment, he thought she was Margot, due to her bleach-blonde hair, but as she looked up, he saw that the girl's face lacked the feistiness that was always present in Margot's eyes.

"No, don't worry, it's okay!" Jade said quickly, scared that he might offend her. Then he thought for a moment. "Wait, you're a human… You *are* a human…aren't you?"

"You're really strange," she replied with a confused look in her blue eyes. "Look, I don't know what planet you're on, but we're missing the party."

"Obviously not yours," he muttered. Jade paused. *Party? What party? And why is she human?* He had never been in another world that contained human residents.

"Well, are you coming or not?" The girl called, making her way further down the beach. He sighed; it wasn't as if he had a choice. Jade took a deep breath and followed her. Something told him he definitely wasn't dead and hopefully neither was Margot. She must be around somewhere. All he had to do was find her.

*

Margot couldn't believe what she was hearing. No one but her was shocked by the last piece of information. No one seemed to care. From what Damien had told her, Reenie and Clarke might as well be dead.

"Well, thanks a bunch," she muttered, turning to leave. Margot chose to ignore what he had told her. She was stubborn. She didn't need their help. Margot would do it alone.

"Bye then." Damien smirked as she walked past him. Frank sniggered, and not discreetly. Margot gritted her teeth. The room seemed overcrowded with useless people.

"Wait," Barbie's words rendered everyone frozen. "We should help her."

"Well, aren't you the motivational speaker," Damien replied icily. "And what do you suggest we do?"

It was clear Barbie hadn't thought that far ahead. "Look, we're in as much trouble as she is and I know everyone here knows it. If we don't do something soon there'll be nothing left."

"Barbie, I think you're missing the point," Damien said with a sigh.

"Take her to the Cathedral, I bet Arabina could explain everything she needs to know." Hurst suggested; he was more nervous than ever. Margot watched as he tapped his long fingers together and twirled his hands in his palms.

"For god's sakes, do we really have ta go dat far? I mean, it's just a human." Frank said. Hurst had obviously feared his response for when Margot next looked down, he was twisting the long sleeve of his top harder than ever. Everyone, bar Frank, who was more interested in his drink, seemed to be looking to Damien for support. However, his expression gave nothing away and despite his annoyance, he remained cool and calm.

"I'm still here, Frank!" Margot shouted. "What is it with you guys travelling to places to explain stuff, anyway? Can't you just tell me *here*? And who's Arabina?"

Hurst drew in breath audibly. It was obviously someone he considered to be important.

"She can always stay with me." Barbie offered.

"Barbie. You live in a slaughter house, somehow I don't think that will give the right impression," Damien said and Barbie shrugged in response.

"The Cathedral it is." Damien's face broke into another sly smile. Margot pondered the motives behind his unusual facial expressions, but at that point, decided it was best not to question them. She looked skywards as small groups began to leave the room. Damien remained where he was. As Margot stepped past him, he held out his pale arm beckoning her to wait behind.

"Be grateful, Margot," his icy voice rang in her ears. "I wouldn't be helping you if I didn't owe Barbie a favour."

Damien's eyes were cold and menacing. "Humans are seen as very disposable creatures around here."

Margot paused before she answered. Not once since she arrived there had she considered the severe danger she was in. It reminded her of what Damien was really capable of. Good looking or not, he was a killer. Margot glanced at his prominent canines that were once again bared as if ready for the kill. She'd have to be more alert.

"Oh, don't you worry, I'm sure I'll be fine," she said, putting another cigarette in her mouth. Damien was taken aback by her confidence, it was very unusual. She was either very brave or extremely stupid.

"You'll need that attitude for where we're going," he said as he turned and walked towards the door.

Margot felt awkward as she sat in the back of the Land Rover, squashed between the contrast of creatures; Frank with his dog, and Hurst. Damien sat in the front with Barbie. He was muttering directions to him every now and again and Barbie would nod his head before turning down another bumpy road. Margot tried to make out the words he was saying but he uttered them so soft it was hopeless. Instead, she turned her attention to the window. Darkness continued to engulf the car, preventing her from seeing any of the surroundings. The only thing visible was the light cast from the long mountain range on the left. Margot smiled as Barbie turned the car in that direction. Soon, it was no longer a mere view from her side window. Before she knew it, it towered in front of them. She had a feeling that near to that formation would be their end destination.

Hurst gulped: "I hate going so close to the border."

A sudden thought occurred to her. Margot reached into her leather jacket and pulled out her sunglasses.

Once again Margot fixed her eyes outside the car window; shapes appeared in the darkness. For the first time since she'd been there, she was able to see her surroundings properly. Purgatory had a very Gothic feel to it. The landscape was bleak and barren. Margot saw run down ghost towns, overgrown countryside and barren wastelands as they continued to drive. The tall trees were gnarled and menacing, almost like something from a Tim Burton film. Every building they passed looked lonely and abandoned. She couldn't deduce much from the architecture, it didn't really seem very important at the time. It was all unkempt and empty, there didn't seem to be much life anywhere. Margot was beginning to grow worrisome. *Where* was *everyone?* The pub earlier had been full to the brim. Maybe people ventured somewhere else during the day? No, she had heard Hurst say they were scared, the whole lot of them.

"Arghhh, it's horrible!" The demon suddenly cried out next to her. He covered his eyes. Margot turned to look. She saw what it was that shocked him. A building began to appear from behind the landscape. It was the first time Margot laid eyes on the Cathedral.

It stood behind a thick layer of fog. It was the strangest thing she'd ever seen. Apart from the blue sky behind the mountain, the Cathedral was the only thing that emitted light. Margot looked on in awe as the crystal material from which it was constructed glittered in the darkness. It changed from pink to purple and to blue. In context, it was rather unfitting amidst the darkness. It was ornate but toy-like, perhaps resembling something you'd find in the girls' toys section of an outdated home catalogue. Overly large was an understatement, it looked more like a castle rather than a religious building.

Margot stared at it, watching it change colour, mesmerised. As the crystal was transparent, she was able to make out some of the interior as they got closer. Like the exterior, inside was also made of crystal; however it featured a vast array of colours. Margot tried to focus her eyes better. She could distinctly make out the crazy-paving glass floor which was changing from a light pink to a subtle blue. It was like the crystal had been made out of a mood ring, one which had fluctuating moods of its own.

Margot had seen some strange things that evening but the Cathedral had to be the strangest. It wasn't particularly the appearance of the Cathedral, but its matter of placement. Even she had to admit, it looked out of character in that land and the others seemed to agree. Barbie mumbled a range of hyperbolic phrases to describe the building.

"If you'll both be quiet for a moment, you'll realise that this is the security disguise to put off intruders," Damien spoke with calm but his words harnessed a sharp edge. Margot noticed he was quite unaffected by the whole situation.

Hurst covered his eyes, "Why has she put that on?"

"Due to the current situation, it seemed appropriate." Damien said; he was obviously annoyed by their amateur-like behaviour.

The mist approached at speed until it engulfed the Land Rover. Once inside the mist, Margot saw the Cathedral was transforming. The crystal lost its sparkle and filled with a muddy brown. Although it maintained form, it looked less like a fairy tale fantasy and more a medieval reality as the seconds passed. Rows of long turrets pointed towards the black sky. They stood most un-parallel and were falling apart. Margot watched as a few pieces of slate fell to the ground. Three huge archways stood at the front of the building. The centre one was taller than the rest and had two large, ugly gargoyles, placed on either side. Above them hung a huge clock; or what she thought was their version of a clock. The numbers she was used to seeing were replaced by hundreds of strange symbols in three different rows around the outside of the face. In the centre many different hands spun at various speeds. Margot sighed. She knew there'd be a catch. Nothing in that land could look beautiful for long.

"That's better," Hurst gave a sigh of relief. For once, Margot half agreed with him. The building massive; it was easily the same size of the inside of the Halo and Harp, however, it looked far more grandiose. Margot wondered who inhabited the strange building.

The Land Rover rolled to a halt and the mist cleared. Outside in the darkness nothing stirred as Margot cautiously stepped out of the car. However, that place had a different atmosphere than before; everything seemed peaceful, relaxed - almost holy.

"Everyone, hold back for a moment," Damien commanded. "She's around here somewhere."

Margot looked around her. The position of the Cathedral had been carefully chosen. They were surrounded by tall, green hills. The grass was dull and patchy in places and the mountains and light sky behind them loomed in front of them. The narrow dirt trail they had driven down seemed unfitting as an entrance to that mysterious place.

"She? Who's this *she*?" Margot asked as she stepped forward. Barbie put his hand across her chest and shook his head. Meanwhile, Frank let his dog off the lead.

"Hope that kills yer!" He muttered.

"It's fine," Barbie tried to reassure her. "She just has a reputation for being temperamental."

Damien walked across to the other side of the building where a tranquil river meandered between the hills down to a lake, Hurst followed. They paused between the first trees Margot had seen with leaves growing on them. Damien leaned against one, staring hard at the lake. His eyes were fixed on something that was slithering across the dark surface. Hurst jumped and nudged him; he had seen the thing too.

"Arabina!" Damien shouted across the still waters. A large snake lifted its scaly head from the surface of the water. The eyes were focused directly on the pale vampire. Without warning, it dashed across the surface of the lake towards him and Hurst was petrified as the serpent homed in on them. No sooner had its green scales touched the ground as it began to metamorphose. Margot swore under her breath as the serpent changed shape, growing four legs and a tail. As its fur turned a shade of silver, white teeth grew from its muzzle and hung long and prominent. The wolf stood for a moment then howled at the non-existent moon.

Margot's sudden list of expletives was returned by a blank gaze from Barbie. *What was this, some sort of messed-up magic show?*

"Wha' just happened?" Frank hobbled around in circles.

The wolf skulked past Damien and Hurst, more interested in what other visitors were there. Frank's dog bounded up to it, clearly glad to see another canine.

"Can we not just see you in human form?" Damien sighed, unimpressed. He and Hurst followed the wolf towards the Land Rover.

"Fine," came the cold reply.

Margot swore it had come from the animal. Suddenly the wolf shed its coat and transformed yet again. It stood up onto its hind legs. Its front paws, which swung in the air, were beginning to look more like arms. Margot's mouth fell open as the wolf changed into a woman. Her long, dark chocolate hair flowed down her back and complimented her golden brown skin. Margot noticed that she was a piece taller than Damien but that could have something to do with the tall black stilettos that she wore. The woman did seem larger than average size, but still had a perfect figure. Her tight, devilish red dress clung to the top of her body and around her torso, flaring out below. Margot noticed how daringly low cut the dress was. It was the sort of thing that she stayed well clear of. The woman's dark eyes pierced right through Damien's and her red lips broke into a smile. He however, remained calm and returned her look with an icy stare.

"Really, there's no need to show off to new company," Damien said.

Arabina chose to ignore the comment. She looked furious as she turned away from the group of people.

"Now, can one of you please tell me why I had to drag my ass out of that pool?" She spoke with a strong Latino accent.

Hurst's small eyes widened to twice their size until they almost looked normal. He bowed as low as was physically possible for him. Barbie and Frank also bowed whilst Damien folded his arms and nodded his head. Showing respect seemed to make him feel awkward.

"Barbie found something in your graveyard." He gestured to Margot.

Arabina's eyes narrowed. She stood in silence for a few moments. There was aloud 'pop' and she disappeared, leaving a thick cloud of red smoke where she had been standing.

"Well," Damien sighed, "so much for-"

"For what?" snapped a voice. The Latino accent behind Margot was so close, it made her jump.

"Jesus!" Margot exclaimed as she turned to find herself faced with Arabina's large chest.

"What's happenin'?" Frank shouted, pointlessly looking around him. Arabina glanced upward in exasperation. "Calm down, Frank."

"Where've you been, Arabina?" Frank asked. Margot noticed he wasn't being rude to her. On the contrary, he seemed quite happy to be in her presence.

"Questions later," she replied, uninterested. Instead Arabina turned her full attention to Margot. Barbie took a step back as she began pacing around her.

"Interesting," she rested her hands on Margot's shoulders. "A human on my land and a female too."

"Arabina," Damien said with a tone of warning in his voice.

"What?" she said, she sounded like a misbehaved child. "I only wanted to play with her for a while. You can have her back afterwards."

Her hands moved down Margot's front, around her chest.

"Get off me!" Margot shouted fiercely.

Hurst gasped, shocked at her rudeness. "How dare you?" he began but was interrupted.

"Oh, I'm sorry man! She can play with you if you want!" Margot yelled back at him. Hurst winced, embarrassed.

"Enough," Damien's voice was quiet but stern. He turned to Arabina. "You can't go around sleeping with every female species you find. Now will you kindly show us inside?"

Arabina sighed, stepping away from Margot. "Fine. Follow me."

Margot thought the interior of the Cathedral was just as cold as the outside as she entered the large room. Everything was elaborately decorated; all the stone had been carved with strange and beautiful symbols and markings that seemed to run throughout the building. The thick oak door was as heavy as it had seemed from the outside. Barbie was the only one able to hold it open long enough for everyone to get inside.

Like The Halo and Harp, the building was lit by candlelight. Long twisted stands stood in every corner of the room and large holders hung in long rows down each side of the arched roof. Margot glanced up as she walked through the rows of pews. The ceiling was adorned with a huge stained glass window in the centre. It was so high up that Margot found it difficult to work out what the picture was meant to be. At the bottom, a large, elaborate altar stood in the centre of a raised platform. Arabina went to stand behind it, smoothing her hands down the golden design on the front. Behind her were three long arched stained glass windows. It was easy to make out what the image was meant to be. She had never been a believer of any sort of religion but what she saw unnerved her. It was not God or the Virgin Mary, but instead, a large picture of Satan breaking out from under a huge rock. Margot looked again, the picture was moving. The long flames danced in the background as the figure of Satan lifted his mighty arms in the air in rage. Underneath him, lots of small dark creatures were crawling from out of the ravaged ground, trying to get away while they had the chance.

"So," Arabian leaned over the altar as she spoke. "How can I help you?"

Margot held back her laughter, Arabina reminded her of a shopkeeper which amused her in the ever-unfitting settings of the peculiar world.

Hurst beamed. He hung on her every word. Frank however, was less impressed and slumped on a pew in the corner while his dog sniffed around. Barbie stayed close to Margot's side.

"I see the Brontangus have been very careless indeed." Arabina continued, glancing at Margot.

"The Bront- what?" Margot said.

"Yes," Damien replied. "Silvia's been extremely busy recently."

"Who's Silvia?" Margot tried to cut in again.

"I don't know, Damien, how is it that out of everyone in Manhaden, you always know where to find me?"

Damien smiled.

"Don't tell me we're in the Chapel!" Frank exclaimed, a shocked expression on his face. "Dis place has been lost for so long."

"Well, what can I say?" Arabina sighed. "I took some time out."

"I'm sorry," Margot began calmly. "But can you please explain WHAT THE FUCK IS GOING ON?" Her voice echoed throughout the Cathedral to become the only sound as her blonde hair fell in front of her pale face, adding to her frustration. She couldn't take much more of it.

Hurst screamed, putting his hands over his overly large ears. Her cursing was unnerving him. "Do you know where you are or who this is?"

"No actually," Margot took deep breaths. "I don't have a clue what the hell is happening as NO ONE WILL TELL ME!"

Barbie and Frank remained silent, and Hurst turned in the opposite direction, a look of horror on his face.

"Tell her, Damien," Barbie spoke out. "She needs to know."

"It's not like you to get sentimental." Damien spoke in a patronising tone. "Well, where do we begin? Ahh yes, introductions: Margot, this is Arabina, she's related to someone even you might've heard of."

"Really?" Margot replied, by her expression, she was unconvinced.

"Say hi to Satan's daughter."

Margot took a few steps back. Surely that couldn't be correct?

"Do you have a problem?" Arabina asked, obviously irritated at Margot's silent response.

"No," Margot began, trying to hold back her laughter. "It's just Satan never had a daughter in the bible."

"Margot, what did I tell you?" Damien asked, aggravated by her attitude. "The Bible is your version of events. What you humans believe to be real. This is the reality."

The rest of the group were growing uncomfortable. Margot realised why Hurst seemed so anxious.

"My father was a whore back in his day." Arabina looked into the distance, almost in admiration. "Anyway, he already rules over the Under World so, needing someone to look after Manhaden, he gave the island to me. All this land is mine. Some of my brothers weren't the most trustworthy."

She smiled smugly over the power she had been given.

"Margot, Manhaden is the floating island in Haziera that is situated between the Over and Under World," Damien gestured up and down as he mentioned the two. Margot sighed; she knew where they were usually situated.

"This world is like one huge sky," Barbie muttered. "Oh, and Haziera is the name of this world."

"I gathered that, Barbie," Margot muttered and then turned back to

Arabina.

"Look, I think I get it okay? I'm not bothered who rules what; I just want to find my friends. OKAY? Some angels took them."

"The Brontangus," Arabina said; she wasn't looking at Margot any longer; instead she was staring towards the back of the room in what Margot's grandmother would have described as 'in a dream'. The room fell silent for a few seconds.

"Yeah, whatever you want to call them." Margot said, irritated. "Anyway, since you're not the best of friends, if you could just give me a few tips, I'll go over there and get them myself and then we'll be off. I don't suppose you have a ship I could borrow as well, do you?"

"How dare you!" Arabina's daydreaming was over. "If only it were as easy as that."

Margot sighed. Although Hurst kept letting out gasps, she didn't feel threatened at all. She knew the danger she was in and yet she chose to ignore it. Damien continued to smile his coy little smile. Little did Margot know it was a grin of admiration. He was enjoying watching her strong character; none of the others would ever dare talk to Satan's daughter in that manner.

"Wait," something clicked in Margot's head. Why hadn't she spotted it before? It seemed so obvious. Everything that was happening on the Earth and she just happened to find herself there. It was no coincidence. "This doesn't have anything to do with the Voice, does it?"

Hurst screwed up his demonic face. Even Barbie took a few steps backwards. Margot listened to his long heels click on the dark stone floor. She soon realised why. Arabina shook with anger, Margot was worried she may erupt with fire from some part of her body.

"THAT BITCH!" She screamed.

Frank, who had no idea what had been going on, jumped out of his skin.

"One day, one day she's gonna have it coming to her! I tell you I'm gonna kick her white ass right off this fuckin' island!" Without warning, Arabina grabbed the altar and threw it. Margot made a dive to the left to avoid it falling on top of her. She was shocked, unaware that Arabina was so strong. It was not how she'd imagined the rulers of different worlds; she'd thought they have more decorum. Hurst ran towards the altar, and tried to restore it to its original position. It was impossible, it dwarfed the demon. Margot suppressed her amusement. Arabina was pacing back and forth, talking to herself in Spanish. She stopped, closed her eyes tight and tried to compose herself. Damien went over to the organ in the corner. The silver piping was covered in thick cobwebs. It hadn't been played in a long time.

"Maybe it's time to consult a more powerful force?" He asked, patting the organ.

"Good point," Arabina said, taking deep breaths. It took a lot of effort for her to be reasonably polite towards him in conversation. She walked over to the organ and reached down to a small cupboard under the keys. Margot frowned, that wasn't a usual feature of the instrument, but then again, what was normal? She stared in awe, wondering what would happen next. What could be more powerful than Arabina? Would she conjure some strange spirit, or worse, her Dad?

Just when Margot thought her questions would be answered, Arabina reached into the organ and pulled out a large, green bottle and two glasses.

"Drink, anyone?" She said.

All heads apart from Margot's nodded.

"Just a small one for me," Barbie's monotone voice seemed even more boring when amplified as it bounced off the walls of the Cathedral. "I'm driving, remember."

Margot couldn't believe what was going on. She was trying to talk about serious matters and they thought it was time to have a drinking session? How irresponsible were those people? She thought about it, the scene seemed oddly familiar; it reminded her of the meetings that she and Jade used to have whilst working on projects in the lab. She remembered the countless times when she would pull out beers from under the table and get mind-numbingly drunk. However, because she was the one on the receiving end, she felt sympathy towards Jade, wishing she'd paid more attention to him at the time.

The group seemed to have forgotten she was there. Margot couldn't figure out the people. Unless - *was Arabina trying to change the subject?* From what Margot had heard earlier, something was definitely wrong in Manhaden. She remembered Frank's question to Arabina and how angry she had become at the mention of the Voice and Brontangus. She also remembered something about Silvia? The puzzle pieces were slowly clicking into place in her head.

"You're avoiding the subject on purpose," she looked to Arabina directly. "You're scared aren't you? That would explain why you went into hiding."

For the first time that evening, Margot felt like she had the upper hand.

Arabina was in mid conversation and tried to shrug the comment off. "I don't know what you mean." She snapped.

Margot knew instantly she'd hit a weak spot when her eyes dropped to stare at the floor and she shuffled on the spot uncomfortably.

"So this Silvia," Margot began, putting another cigarette between her lips. "What did she do? Upset Daddy's little girl?"

"Margot-" Barbie looked up from his drink. Once again the tension in the room was building.

It was too late. Barbie's attempt to cut in had failed miserably. Margot had stepped way over the line, miles over. Had it been possible to quantify how far, there would have been a considerable circumnavigation of the earth involved.

Arabina turned to face Margot. There was a prolonged crunching as she crushed the glass she had been holding between her dainty looking fingers. The Cathedral fell silent once more. The clicking of Arabina's heels seemed as tumultuous as earthquakes as she made her way over to where Margot stood.

"I suggest, you take your nose elsewhere, human, you've forgotten who you're talking to," she said coldly. Both pairs of red eyes blazed.

"And you forget that you said you'd help me." Margot bit back.

"Not my problem," Arabina shrugged in a dismissive manner. "In case you haven't noticed, no one here cares what happens to you or your friends. I'm surprised you made it this far!"

"You know what," Margot looked around her. "To say you're all so apparently powerful, you are some of the most useless people I've ever met. Screw you all, I'm doing this on my own." She turned and stormed out of the Cathedral. Arabina gave an exasperated last look and went to pour herself another large drink. Damien held out his glass.

The others looked at each other, unsure of how to react to the situation. All except Frank, of course, he was more focused on the beverage in front of him. After another long silence, he spoke.

"Now listen here,"

"She's gone, Frank," Damien said.

"Oh bollocks."

*

Jade followed the girl. He wasn't sure where she was going but she seemed to be picking up the pace. Was it some trick? He couldn't be sure. However, he did know that following her was probably his only option. Where else was he to go? Margot had always told him he was too trusting, if only she was with him, she'd know what to do.

The young woman led him away from the beach and into the foliage. Jade heard voices all around him for the second time. The path through the undergrowth was getting darker. The pale blue sky and land disappeared, replaced by overgrown bushes and thorny trees. It had definitely been a bad decision. He felt his hands tighten into fists as he continued to follow the girl deeper into the undergrowth.

"Not far now," she mumbled. Her accent reminded him of Margot. He smirked, they couldn't be more different. Jade looked ahead of him and saw rays of sunlight just metres down the dark path. Wherever they were heading, they had almost reached their destination.

Jade braced himself. Their exit was approaching fast and he had no idea what to expect. Okay, he told himself, remember your Jujitsu. *Wait.* He thought, he hadn't learned it beyond twelve years of age and had only gotten to white belt. *No.* He changed his mind. *Just sound threatening and then run for it, in no way do anything embarrassing. And don't show your weaknesses!* The voices were getting louder, although he couldn't make out what they were saying. The girl had climbed out of the darkness and he would have to follow. He bit his lip.

"Okay, who, erm, who wants a slice - I mean a piece, yes, a piece of this?" He called out, expecting a crowd of people ready to rip him in half. Instead, he was met by a crowd of people who never faltered, let alone turn their heads to the clumsy commotion. Jade looked around. He was standing at the poolside of an up-market hotel. Some people lay on sun beds, some swam lengths in the pool. Others were feasting on from the bar and buffet.

"Sorry!" The girl said; it was obvious she hadn't been listening. "I thought I'd take a shortcut, I hope that was okay?"

"Right," Jade said slowly. "Yes, of course."

All of a sudden, he felt unprepared. The cloudless blue sky once again smiled down at him. The bright rays warmed his black skin. He ran his hand through his dreadlocks on the back of his head, unsure what scene he had walked into. Every person there, like him, was human. That confused him.

"Hey everyone!" The girl shouted out. "This is - erm. What's your name?"

"Jade," he replied, then thought about what he'd said. "NO! Wait a moment!"

"Everyone, this is Jade!" The girl said spreading out her arms, as though encouraging people to come over and speak to him.

"Okay, what's going on?" Jade said as a large cocktail was thrust into his hand. "If you're going to capture me now you can just do it and remove your human suits."

The crowd around him laughed.

"I… I was being serious!" Jade was frustrated.

"Capture you?" The blonde girl said. "You're on holiday!" The crowds were still roaring with laughter, trying to settle down so they could hear his reply.

"Well, okay, what are we celebrating?" He was confused, how did he get from running for his life to being taken to a garden party at a hotel? *Oh well,* he thought, *I've had a hard day, surely one drink wouldn't hurt?*

Too many hours later…

"Limbo, limbo, limbo!" The crowd chanted.

"I'll show you how low I can go!" Jade jeered. The crowd was silent as he attempted to beat the record set by the last turn. He bent his legs so far back that he was surprised he wasn't lying flat out on the ground. Jade was shocked he was even still in the competition due to his height. He cleared the bar by millimetres and the crowd cheered.

"AND JADE WILDE WINS THE CHAMPIONSHIP!" A voice called out.

"Yeah! I WON!" Jade shouted. He'd never won anything in his life and was elated. He attempted a victory dance as a huge golden trophy was passed to him. He looked up; the sky was still the perfect blue it had been when he had fallen out of his ship. That puzzled Jade. They had been playing for a while; surely dusk must be upon them? Although for the moment those thoughts could wait.

"Did you see that?" He asked the blonde haired girl.

"Yeah, it was awesome," she said and with a hazy look in her eyes, smiled at him.

"You may wanna take that coat off now, though," she said, nodding at Jade's royal blue trench coat.

He smiled genuinely for what felt like the first time in a long time.

"Nah," he laughed. Despite the temperature, Jade never seemed to get hot. It was the same on Bequia, he had no idea why. He took one of its corners and used it to polish the trophy's golden surface.

That should do it, Jade thought, looking at the shiny metal and expecting to see his smiling face reflecting back at him. However, what he saw was nothing like himself. In the trophy a pale woman with fierce red eyes glared back at him. Margot's face broke into a smile on seeing his. Jade dropped the trophy. It hit the floor with a clank.

"Sorry," he muttered, bending down to pick it up.

"Are you okay?"

"Yes, I… just need a walk," he said, turning tail and leaving the party behind.

A dark woman looked up from the bar. She watched Jade leave, picked up her bag and followed.

It didn't take Jade long to find the open countryside again. The hotel was on top of a cliff overlooking the coastline. Jade remembered climbing a small hill but he didn't realise it had been so steep. He turned to his left to see a small town in the valley. He didn't want be near people at that moment, so he turned right and took a footpath further into the countryside. Jade took deep breaths as he walked. It had been Margot, he was sure of it. Maybe she was trying to contact him? Maybe it was a call for help? Or maybe she was - he didn't want to think about it. *No, of course she wasn't, she couldn't be dead.* He refused to let that thought stay in his head. Anyway, how could he be sure what he saw was real? How did he know any of it was real?

He was in the middle of a field with long, uncut summer grass, sprinkled with meadow flowers. He sighed; if he was stuck there, at least the world seemed peaceful; there were no strange angels or stupid restrictions. In some ways, he was happy he had ended up there. At least the people actually seemed to like him. Where Jade had come from, he'd been an outcast all his life, but the people he'd met lately seemed to enjoy his company. He shook his head, he was being selfish. Margot would care if she was with him, it wasn't her fault. It wasn't the time for self-pity. A breeze was beginning to pick up from the north, making Jade shiver. He was getting closer to the end of the trail; the end was the cliff edge. It seemed pointless to walk any further, he might as well go back and apologise. However, just as Jade turned, something caught his eye which encouraged him to turn back again. He paused in utter bewilderment. *It couldn't be.* There, standing on the very edge of the cliff, smiling and waving, was *Margot.*

"Margot?" Jade's voice was soft. The breeze on the cliff picked up, blowing the meadow flowers towards her. They were like inviting fingers, pointing towards the cliff's steep edge.

"Margot!" Jade shouted. Abandoning what was left of his senses, he ran at her with open arms. She looked so pale, a lot paler than usual, which was really something, considering she was an albino. Her skin seemed to glow unnaturally in the light, but he knew it was definitely her. He could recognise her anywhere with her signature black clothes, leather jacket and bleach-blonde hair. His eyes widened as he noticed the heels of her boots were hanging over the cliff edge. As he grew closer, he could hear small sections of it breaking away to fall into the depths of the crystal clear sea below.

"GET AWAY FROM THERE!" He screamed. The edge was further than he thought. Margot ignored his words; she laughed and swung her body back and forth as though it was some sort of game. He was only metres away, if he could just get there and make her stop. He knew she was reckless, but it was too much. It was too late; Margot waved her hand one final time before spreading her arms out and leaning back.

"NO!" He screamed, watching her fall. He'd been so close - just inches away. Jade had to take a few steps back to prevent himself following her, although, the thought seemed very tempting.

He watched her fall through the air. Jade braced himself, prepared to see her body torn to shreds on the sharp rocks below. He wasn't sure if it was his eyesight or if Margot was getting more transparent the further she fell. He gasped, she was; Margot was fading like light dying from a bulb. She became more transparent until she disappeared altogether.

"JADE! WHAT ARE YOU DOING?" A voice screamed behind him. It was so loud that it made him jump and he almost fell to his death. His feet were centimetres from the cliff edge. He hadn't realised how close he'd actually got.

Behind him, woman was making her way over to where he stood. Her skin was a shade lighter than his and her arms were covered in sleeves of tattoos. Although he had never seen her without a white lab coat on, he instantly recognised Reenie.

Had he imagined the past few minutes? Jade hoped it had been a hallucination for Margot's sake. His own sanity could wait. After the count of three, he glanced down at the rocks. There was no body. He had a feeling that even science couldn't work that one out. He didn't know whether to cry like a child or sigh with relief. Glancing over his shoulder, he decided to do neither. Reenie was fast approaching.

"Jade, what's happened?" She asked.

Jade was shocked at her tone of voice and he had to look up to double check it was her. It was probably the first time Reenie had spoken civilly to him or chosen to speak to him at all.

"Body – someone fell – down cliff," he couldn't produce a sentence. Reenie understood what he meant as she followed his gaze over the edge.

"It's okay, there's nothing there," she said in the same motherly tone. Reenie attempted to put her arms round his shoulders, but due to his height, decided to settle for his waist. His lips curled into a smile. It would be rude to admit he didn't mind the female attention. With some difficulty, Reenie persuaded him to move from the cliff edge and she seated him in the long grass near the centre of the field. Jade sat down without argument. A sense of complete hopelessness fell over him. He was lost, confused and despite Reenie's help, still felt completely alone. Jade was ready to throw in the towel, but knew that despite how much he wanted to, he was going to keep going until he found her.

Chapter 7

Earthquakes

"What the- Where the- What's going on?" Jade's words spilled out of his mouth, rather than forming sentences. "Where's Clarke?"

"Jade, just calm down for a moment," she said, sitting down next to him.

"Reenie, what's going on? Where are Clarke and Margot? How did you manage to find me? Where are we?" He tried to get to his feet but she pulled him back down. Jade realised he was shaking.

"Jade!" Reenie's voice was strict. "Will you just sit down for a moment? I don't know where they are, okay? I don't know."

She stopped, and saw the disappointment on his face. Jade hoped she might have had at least some answers. "Look Jade, yesterday I was in the same situation as you. Do you think I know what's going on?"

"Sorry," he muttered, he looked down at the grass. "I just thought, oh, I don't know what I thought."

Her voice lost its sharp tone. Reenie looked at Jade and her face became a sympathetic frown. "I just saw you whilst I was sat at the bar and when you left I thought it would be a good idea to follow you, it's a fricking good thing I did. You could have been killed. What the hell were you doing?"

Jade felt the muscles in his throat tighten. He wanted to tell her, but how would she ever believe him? She'd think he was mad. He shook his head, and closed his eyes. Jade didn't want to think about it. Maybe it was time to change the subject to something more important.

"Reenie, you don't think we're…" he paused; he didn't want to believe the words he was going to say, "…dead?"

She was shocked by his serious tone. "No Jade, of course not."

He wasn't convinced that she believed what she was saying. They both looked around in awkward silence. The wind was dropping, everything became still, peaceful.

"Where are we?"

"Beats me." She turned to him. "It's pretty good though."

Jade glared at her. Those weren't the words he would have used. *Is she really that naïve?* But before he could to respond to her unusual comment the ground began to shake dislodging more rubble from the cliff. After a brief delay, the debris could be heard sloshing into the sea. On land, the trees dropped leaves and some of the flowers lost their petals. The vibrations of the earth were not the work of a natural disaster, but rather a voice that Jade had been waiting to hear since he returned home.

"As always, The Voice is welcoming to its new residents and would like to inform them of a few simple rules. Residents must remain in their sleeping quarters from 1am until 6am; residents must not attempt to swim out into open water nor in any lake that isn't man made. This is due to safety reasons only. Feel free to carry on with your holiday!"

So that was it? That was 'The Voice' that he'd heard so much about, the thing everyone believed was their god. He could see why it was so easy to think it. It was probably the purest voice he'd ever heard. It was so soft, so beautiful. He shook his head. Jade knew he mustn't let it get to him. But he was feeling a strong sense of trust; it was the most heavenly thing he'd ever heard.

"NO!" Jade said in a loud voice.

"Jade?" Reenie had a look of fear on her face. He knew she was thinking the same thing.

"I'm fine," he lied. "Reenie, just don't, don't - just be careful okay?"

Reenie seemed to be on the same level, gleaning total understanding from his confused utterance. She nodded before asking: "Have you got a room, yet?" Jade knew she was trying to change the subject; she was scared.

He shook his head.

"Well, come on then, let's go get you booked in! You can stay at the same place where we were earlier, that's where I am," she glanced at a black watch strapped around her wrist. "Jesus, is that the time? It's 12, come on we haven't got long."

"But it's not dark!"

"Jade it's never frigging dark," she looked skywards as though that piece of information was universal knowledge - he supposed it was if you lived there.

So many questions raced through his mind, but he had a feeling they were going to remain unanswered for a very long time.

*

I don't need anyone. I can do this on my own. I will find them on my own. I'm not weak. I don't need anyone. I DON'T NEED ANYONE. Margot's thoughts ran through her head until it was the only phrase left. She hoped it would soon sink in. Like Jade, Margot had been isolated throughout her life; the difference was, she actually liked being by herself, or so she told everyone.

In the distance, she heard the screams and cries of creatures she had once believed didn't exist. They didn't scare her. There was a war waging in Margot's mind, too violent to allow her to be concerned with such trivial fears.

Margot sat in the darkness of Manhaden, she hadn't got very far. She had stationed herself on one of the hills that surrounded the Cathedral. The hill was by the lakeside where she'd first met Arabina. There was no method in her madness, it was closest; she let fatigue make the decision. Her lack of sleep meant she wasn't prepared to venture out much further. Once alone, Margot's mind began to wander dangerously into her sub-conscious.

If only he were here.

I don't need anyone.

He'd known her better than anyone…

I don't need anyone.

… there was still so much she hadn't told him.

I – DON'T – NEED – ANYONE.

She fought back feelings she'd spent so long stifling, she hadn't realised how strong they were. However, Margot had come to believe her own lies. She liked being alone, she enjoyed having minimal emotional range. From a young age, Margot had been used to being self-sufficient. It was the way she worked best.

She snapped out of her train of thought, in the ether, something was moving. Margot may have been wearing her night vision sunglasses, but their distance was limited and much of her vision was shrouded in darkness. She was quiet. Out of the nothing, she heard an ear piercing scream that didn't sound far from the hills. Her thoughts raced as she decided what to do. Should she run? But where could she go? There wasn't anywhere to run to.

"Human!" A familiar voice called from the shadows. She let out a sigh of relief, glad for once, to hear Barbie's deep grave-voice. She didn't reply. "Human, I heard you." Barbie searched the darkness for movement. His crippled figure made its way into her range of vision. Barbie's blank face looked at her and his twisted fingers flexed as they waved at her in an awkward fashion. She raised her eyebrows but continued to stare back at the barren surface of the ground. Barbie wasn't used to entertaining company, so became interested with the long ladders that ran down his tights.

There must be something he could do to start a conversation, he thought; something that she would like. He thought of things that humans liked. Margot sounded American and he'd been to America lots of times. It was his favourite place to visit on the Earth. There must be something he could remember that those people liked. He thought hard on it for a while.

"Now traditionally I'm supposed to make a speech, tell some funny stories, as this is my friend's special day. When I say friend, he's more like a brother-"

"Barbie?" Margot looked up to see Barbie parading around in front of her. "What the hell are you doing, man?"

Barbie stared at her in confusion. It hadn't had the effect he was hoping for. "I was being the *best* man," he said, justifying his actions as though it was the most obvious thing in the world.

"Why?" Margot was even more confused.

"Well, I thought you humans must like them or you wouldn't call them *the best*. I thought it would cheer you up." His flat voice made her laugh and he thought he had done something right for once; Barbie sat down next to her. It was the best form of comfort he could manage. They sat together for what Margot thought was an eternity. She was deep in thought, her mind failed to register what was going on around her. She didn't hear the screaming and shouting, banging and crashing, the fires burning, the explosions, the sinister laughing and cries for help.

"Oh Barbie, what am I doing here?" She looked out into the distance and sighed. She was exhausted and fed-up by the constant confusion, which was no more resolved that when she had first arrived. She covered her face with her hands. Barbie turned to her, unsure of how to deal with the situation. He reached out his icy cold fingers and touched hers, pulling them away from her face. Margot winced as he patted her hard on the head.

She could hear the disturbances from all around them. Somewhere in the distance, glass shattered followed by a faint wailing. Margot looked behind them, she could see flames.

She failed to see how Barbie could be so at peace once she realised what was happening around them. Havoc was unleashing itself from all angles.

"And this is meant to be the safe side?" Margot mumbled to herself.

"Don't worry human, none of the things you hear will be able to get inside the mist. They wouldn't dare approach the Cathedral if they thought it looked that ugly." Margot suspected he was trying to reassure her.

"Oh, thanks Barbie, that's very comforting." Barbie didn't notice the sarcasm in her voice.

"As long as you stay with me, I'll keep you safe," he said.

"Oh yeah, I'm perfectly safe with the guy who thinks dressing up like a woman and sleeping with dead people is a normal way to live."

He stared at her.

"Sorry, I didn't mean that," Margot apologised. Then she thought about what she'd done. Had she just said *sorry* out of choice? The air must be getting to her. Margot was such a proud person; it was something she'd never do. Barbie wasn't listening, however. He was preoccupied with things that caused physical pain rather than emotional.

Margot felt the ground below her feet tremble, loud rumbling could be heard. She looked up at Barbie, following his line of sight. He was staring at the mountains beyond the Cathedral. Although it was hard to see, Margot was sure they were also shaking.

"Is it an earthquake?" she shouted to Barbie over the noise. She wasn't sure if he replied, nor if he heard her. The sound was so loud it drowned every word that came from her mouth. If it was an earthquake, it was not like any she had felt before, it was deafening. Barbie looked at her and without any hesitation, picked her up over his shoulder and sprinted down the hill.

*

"Well, at least humans are good for something!" Arabina laughed. She was leaning her body over the golden altar. Small lines of white powder had been scraped into rows in front of her and her eyes were dilated. "What did Barbie say this stuff was called?" She turned to Damien who was sat in a corner drinking a green liquid from an exquisitely engraved china cup.

"I have no idea; it was from somewhere called America. I believe it's called 'Coating' or 'Co-canion'." He said.

Arabina pointed towards the altar and offered him a line. He smiled at her but the smile was sinister. Her eyes captured his glare and he lost himself for a moment. She turned away. "Frank! Drink from the other bottle, that's window cleaner!"

Frank was leaning against the organ; he hiccupped and mumbled something indistinguishable before getting to his feet to find the other bottle. Arabina shot a concerned look at Damien. "Sometimes I wonder if he's saving that dog a job."

With assistance from his demon canine, Frank stumbled towards them, sporting a huge smile across the surface of his tree bark-like face. He was carrying two bottles - one for them, one for him.

Hurst, the only one who wasn't enjoying the festivities, shot the three of them dirty looks from the other side of the room. He had a lot of respect for his leader but couldn't deal with her increasingly rebellious lifestyle.

"I dunno what your problem is, my little muchacho," Arabina said when she spotted his look of disapproval. "Your nose is bigger than all of ours put together, you could put it to good use."

Hurst turned away as they laughed. He didn't see what was so funny. However, their laughter didn't last long. The tremble of the earth made them silent.

"What was-" but before Arabina had time to finish her question Barbie burst through the double oak doors. "Barbie; have you gone completely loco?" she yelled as he made his way down the rows of pews.

"We need to move now." The urgency of the situation was lost in his non-tonality. However, Barbie's words bore force as three faces of horror returned his blank expression.

Margot, still flung over Barbie's shoulder, was shouting a wide range of expletives. "Get the hell off of me! Barbie, I mean it! Put me the fuck down! NOW!"

Barbie dropped her head first onto the stone floor.

"Oh good, she's back," Damien said sarcastically, his hand over his eyes, expressing his displeasure to the group. He focused his attention on Barbie before asking: "What is this all about?"

"The mountains, they appear to be on the move again."

Damien was at once concerned. He went to the nearest window; each spike of his hair seemed to be more upright. Margot realised he had caught sight of the ground outside because his eyes widened.

"We need to leave immediately," Damien's smooth voice was still calm; yet bore a sense of urgency.

The ground trembled so hard, Hurst fell back. Several glasses, once perched on the side of the altar, smashed on the floor.

"It's okay, guys. Chill…" Arabina laughed, she seemed unconcerned. "This place is safe, no need to-"

A large crack shot down the stained glass window. Everyone fell silent and recoiled, backing away from the window, staring at it. Even Frank, with guidance from Barbie managed to move back a few seats; he clutched a half-empty bottle.

She laughed again. "See… see I told-"

The window shattered.

Shards of glass sprayed across the rear of the Cathedral, covering Arabina's sleek body.

"What te hell is going on?" Frank shouted, scrambling to his feet.

Damien's face stared in horror as a huge rock loomed closer to the window. As strange as it seemed to Margot at the time, the mountains were most definitely moving and were pulling up everything in their path.

There was another loud smash as the wall collapsed. Huge waves from the river crashed through, flooding the floor, gushing to where the group stood. The building was collapsing.

"Maybe it would be a good time to move!" Damien shouted pointing to the doors at the far end. The back of the Cathedral collapsed in on itself; destruction making its way up the large room. Hurst didn't need telling twice. He ran round in circles, unable to see the doors at the end. Frank also seemed confused of which way to run. Margot watched as he ran into the wall, cursed, regenerated, clambered to his feet and did the same thing over again. She laughed; it reminded her of the instructions found on a shampoo bottle. *Break bones, curse, repeat* with more violence.

Damien pushed everyone towards Barbie.

"Take them to the exits! Go with him! Head for the hills!" He yelled at Margot. She didn't argue, she grabbed hold of Hurst and made her way to the double doors with Barbie and Frank.

Damien headed the opposite way, searching for Arabina. She didn't take much finding. She had positioned herself in the middle of the room, with her arms wide open, her eyes blazing red. She looked like a Captain, ready to go down with the wreckage of her ship. He ran towards her, dodging pieces of debris from the high ceiling.

"Arabina," Damien sighed: "Stop being self-righteous and get out!" It was a command, not a request. Water flurried around his feet, pulling debris into the turbulent flow. If they weren't crushed by the building, they'd be swept away by the sheer volume of water. Towering rock formations, which had to be the foot of the mountain range, had reached the huge stained glass window at the very top of the building. It hurtled down in sonorous shards and just missed the tip of his nose.

Arabina continued to laugh, ignoring his warnings. "Damien, you know I can't die!" Damien rolled his eyes; he knew that, despite her mocking. He just didn't want to put it to the test.

Margot and Barbie were inches from the doors when a huge beam dropped from the roof and blocked their exit. She punched the air in anger; she knew full well that she had less chance of survival than all of them. However, she wouldn't let it faze her. Margot turned to Barbie who was standing behind her. "Help me – move this!" she yelled. Barbie nodded, but Margot's eyes flitted to what was going on behind him.

She stared in awe as she watched Frank's dog bounding about in the chaos. Margot finally understood what he'd been talking about. She watched as the demonic guide dog dodged rubble and wagged its tail in the carnage. More of its decaying skin fell to the ground as the building collapsed. Barbie held its drunken owner in one arm, whilst trying to move a beam in the other. The Irish man cursed, demanding to know why he was in some sort of war zone.

"Oh, shut up Frank!" Margot yelled, desperately pushing the beam. She had to bend down to allow Hurst to climb on her shoulders; the surging water reached up to his neck. Finally after much effort, they shifted the beam enough to allow themselves access to the door.

Margot wrenched it open and almost threw Hurst outside. Barbie followed behind, but before he had chance to step beyond the door, Frank's dog unleashed its true nature. Its eyes, once dark and calm, became a nasty blood-red and its skeleton outgrew its skin. Margot watched, dumbstruck. Even though the dog didn't grow beyond the size of the building, it grew enough to cause considerable damage. However, it wasn't the change of the dog's appearance that caused disruption, but rather what it did next. It all happened in a few seconds; it was so quick she doubted anyone could have done anything to prevent it. Without warning, the dog dived on top of Barbie, knocked him to the floor and grabbed the blind man from his grasp. Margot watched in horror as Frank was dragged back towards the mayhem at the far end of the Cathedral. Barbie pulled himself out of the rubble and attempted to follow him, which took him back into the demolished end of the room.

"Not again!" Frank grumbled. Margot thought he didn't seem at all surprised by the situation, he sounded very much like he expected it. She ran back inside the building and tried to follow them. Barbie waved his hand in warning, to try and get her to go back. She ignored him and ran to his side.

"Where is he?" she yelled.

Barbie shrugged, they searched the apocalyptic surroundings. A fire had broken out and thick grey smoke filled the room. Choking, Margot decided to drop low to the floor to try to enable herself to get a better view. Low down, just above water level, she spotted Frank half covered in debris, lying still on the Cathedral floor.

"Over there!" Margot pointed to a group of half destroyed pews. "On the left."

Barbie followed her instruction without hesitation. His long heels kept getting trapped beneath the water. When he reached Frank, only half his body was visible, his legs were covered by the fallen ceiling and his head was submerging under the water. No matter how much they scrambled at the debris, they couldn't dig him out. More of the Cathedral crashed to the ground and the mountain was fast approaching.

Margot heard Barbie's croaky voice through the thick smoke. "We need to turn back or it will crush us both."

Although she hated to admit it, he was right. Their task seemed hopeless. They muttered their apologies before turning to make their way to the open door, leaving Frank's crumpled body unconscious on the Cathedral floor.

It seemed to be a much shorter journey to the end of the room since the mountains had cleared half of the building. *Almost out, almost out, almost out…* Was the only phrase running through Margot's mind.

"I think this is going to collapse," Barbie said as they made their way across the room. Margot looked up, he wasn't joking. The whole thing was coming down. Every step they took, they risked death by falling debris. The door was only metres away. *Almost out… almost …almost-* with one leap Barbie and Margot dived out of the archway and collapsed onto the grass outside.

Margot gasped, breathing in as much of the fresh air as she could. She was on her hands and knees in front of the building. Margot saw that next to her, Barbie had got to his feet.

"We need to get as far away as we can; the place is going to collapse."

She didn't argue, she followed him to the hill next to the path they had driven down earlier that day. She was coughing so much she was scared her insides would become external. Barbie was quite unaffected by the event; Margot kept forgetting that he wasn't human. He grabbed her arm and pulled her to her feet. Normally reluctant to accept help, she didn't argue. She noticed Barbie's limp had become more prominent, maybe he had been hurt after all. Before they were halfway, Margot heard a loud crash. The colossal mountain range annihilated the Cathedral as if it was made of cardboard.

She couldn't get her head around what had happened; it wasn't physically possible. Mountains didn't move. Margot shook her head; she had to remember she was in a different world. They reverted to silence again. Margot felt something in the dark, both figuratively and physically; and something told her Barbie felt it too. Although not a word passed between them, his lack of expression was painful to watch, she had an inkling that he was waiting to see who had survived the cataclysmic destruction.

It was hard to see what was going on from where they emerged. Thick black smoke billowed from the scene, it was impossible to make out anything. She turned to Barbie, who was standing very lopsidedly next to her. His arm was outstretched and pointing to the wreckage. A dark figure walked towards them and it looked like it had something in its arms.

Margot's eyes were transfixed.

She heard a squeaky voice behind her. "There they are! I see them, it's a miracle!"

Margot slipped her sunglasses out of her pocket and put them on to see a filthy looking Hurst making his way towards them. She had a strange feeling that his words weren't directed towards her and Barbie. Hurst was also looking in the direction of the figure that loomed ever closer. Then Margot realised who Hurst was talking about. Out of the smoke came Damien carrying a very annoyed Arabina.

If anyone was watching from afar, they, like Margot would believe the scene was romantic. It was for about a minute or so, until he dropped her in a heap on the ground.

"Come on, then!" Hurst screeched, running down the hill.

Barbie shrugged. "Don't worry human, we're safe, they're not gonna move again for a while."

Margot let out a huge sigh; somehow Barbie had managed to answer the question before she had asked him.

"Shall we?" he croaked.

Margot nodded. They made their way towards Damien and Arabina.

It was a decision she instantly regretted; she and Barbie walked into a full-blown argument.

"You are probably the most awkward person I've ever come across." Damien snapped at Arabina, who was still lying on the floor.

"Besa mi culo, puto! Vaya tener relaciones sexuales con un burro!"

Margot had no idea what that phrase meant, but coming from Arabina's mouth; it was bound to be rude.

Damien rolled his eyes. It was clear he wasn't focussed on the conversation. Margot could see that his eyes were fixed on the mountain range. He wore a grave expression. Arabina on the other hand was in full-flow.

"Why did you do that? After I *specifically* said no, leave me?"

Margot had a feeling she hadn't seen the scale of the damage yet. Damien held his hand up to silence her.

"Don't worry your highness. Don't worry, I'll help you up." Hurst offered, he rushed to her side and held out his pointed fingers.

"Oh, fuck off Hurst; I am capable of standing by myself." Arabina snapped. Hurst backed off looking hurt. Pulling herself up, Arabina continued to rage, "DON'T YOU DARE SILENCE ME! Who the hell do you think you are Damien? I am Arabina, Satan's daughter, ruler of Manhaden, dweller of the great Satanic Cathedral and you have humiliated me!"

Margot found it hard not to smile, the angrier Arabina got, the less bothered Damien became. He kept his eyes in the distance, she wasn't even sure he was paying attention to his so-called leader.

"I am sorry, but I'm afraid there are rather more pressing matters at the moment," Damien replied, not turning to face her. "I don't think you'll be living anywhere for a while."

"Really? Really? Well would you kindly tell me what the-" Arabina turned round, and fell to her knees. "My home..." She let out a high pitched noise somewhere between a squeal and a scream. It was a monstrous sound and Margot had to cover her ears for fear of it causing serious damage. The sound was torturous, like a soprano opera solo on a scratched record.

"I'm gonna kill her!" Arabina screamed. There was a loud noise and she disappeared again, leaving behind thick red smoke.

"Well, at least we're all here," said Hurst, laughing nervously. "Wait... where's Frank?"

A pang of guilt hit Margot hard. She may not have liked the guy but she didn't want what had happened.

"We tried," Barbie began. "But he was crushed. We couldn't get him out in time." Hurst covered his mouth and looked away.

Damien appeared unaffected.

"Well Barbie," he said. "You certainly know how to be discrete don't you?"

"He'll be okay," Margot said, trying to reassure herself. "He's got that power, he'll just re-generate himself or whatever that shit is that he does. Right?"

Damien turned on her. "He is currently suffering a fate worse than death. Think about it Margot, you're a scientist."

"How did you-"

"His body will keep repairing itself only to die instantly." He paused. Margot could tell he was growing more and more frustrated. She glared at him. How did he know she was a scientist? She'd never mentioned it before - or had she? It was hard to remember the conversation in the car. Margot sighed. What did it matter anyway? It wasn't going to change matters. She looked around at the group; everyone was filthy and full of varying emotions.

Barbie's makeup was more smudged than it had been; the only eye shadow he wore was the filth from inside the building. Hurst's long sleeves more resembled rags. His entire outfit had been saturated by the dirty water. Margot dreaded to imagine what she looked like; she ran her hand through her hair, pulling out shards of glass. It was official, she thought, dusting herself down; they all looked a complete mess. All except Damien, who seemed to be able to pull off any sort of look, making it sophisticated. He was one of those people that could revisit the nineteen nineties; then wear his outfits in the year three thousand and still make them look acceptable. Yes, even his hair was immaculate and stylish.

"Right," Damien took a deep breath, wiping the dust from his face. "Is everyone okay? No terrible injuries, I hope." It sounded a lot more sarcastic than he'd intended. Something was faltering in his cool façade.

"I broke my stiletto." Barbie shrugged, examining the bottom of his left shoe. That would be the reason for his exaggerated limp, Margot thought.

"Oh brilliant, Barbie," Damien replied sarcastically. "The last satanic chapel in Manhaden has been destroyed, Frank is as good as dead, we could be on the brink of apocalyptic war and you've broken a heel."

Margot wondered if she was the only one that noticed Damien's cool, carefree attitude was no longer coming across in his speech. She saw him clasping the top of his arm. Damien met her gaze and dropped his hand; he gave her a stern look that only she noticed.

"Well, what do you suppose we do?" Barbie asked.

Damien opened his mouth to speak, but before he uttered a syllable, he was interrupted.

"I tell you what we're gonna do. We're gonna attack that bitch," Arabina's Spanish accent rang out in the darkness. She wasn't in range of Margot's sunglasses but Margot could see her.

Arabina's bright red eyes were burning vividly. She reminded Margot of a nocturnal creature, their eyes reflecting light in the dark. Arabina approached until she finally came into Margot's view. She wasn't filthy at all; in fact Arabina looked like she had just come from an A-list world premiere.

"Will you just calm *down*," Damien raised his voice then added a quiet: "For a moment."

"Coño!" Arabina yelled and pointed at the mountains.

Margot didn't know what she'd said but it sounded impressive. She looked different to before. Margot knew that she had been just annoyed back in the cathedral; Arabina was different because she was distressed. It seemed that the problem was more than just her home being destroyed. Whatever she was saying in Spanish, she obviously didn't want Margot to understand. However, the fact remained that in mere minutes, thousands of years' work had been destroyed. It was no accident.

"Okay, do you want to tell me what's going on or should I take another wild guess?"

Margot approached Arabina; she ignored the reaction of those around her. There was a reason behind it and she wanted to know what it was. "Well?" Margot said.

Arabina sighed. She sounded as if she was bored of the albino. Raising her hand to her head and closing her eyes, as if she was suffering from a mild headache, she said: "Oh, someone else do it! It's too much for me to bother with." She slumped down on the grass, holding back her frustration.

"Basically," said Hurst, keen to follow his mistress's orders. "Up there in the sky live some of the most powerful creatures in all of Nacartoe, the angels." He paused for dramatic effect, but when Margot raised her eyebrows and folded her arms, he decided to continue swiftly. "Anyway," he squeaked. "Angels can't die and a lot of them can travel between worlds and remember; our world has been around for a very long time so they've witnessed a lot."

Margot was unimpressed. "Hurst, where is this going?"

Hurst ignored the comment. "There was an angel..." He looked over at Arabina, and screwed up his eyes before he said the name: "Silvia."

Arabina's fists clenched, but Hurst carried on: "She believed that the state of things within worlds were getting worse as time went on and tried to change things. But you see, Silvia was a bit of an extremist and she did bad things." Hurst kept glancing at Arabina as though she was a lethal bomb about to explode.

"Then," he continued gingerly: "The angels found out about this and they were going to give her one of the worst punishments known in Nacartoe - throwing her out of the Over World. But they realised that her intentions were good. After thinking about it, they decided if she wanted to regain her place in the clouds she would take part in an experiment."

"This experiment being...?" Margot prompted.

"Well." Hurst twisted his ragged sleeves. "They said if she could make one whole world peaceful and live in harmony, she could go back up to heaven. Of course she was excited to do good and they chose a world they believed nobody would care about, a world that lacked knowledge so she'd be able to play about with it. They chose world number 56."

"Bad times for them! So which unlucky world got that sprung upon them?" Margot asked.

"Well actually... it was well you know, The Universe." He laughed nervously and took hold of his cross.

Margot's eyes widened, she bit her lip ring hard. "So that voice..."

Hurst nodded: "...was Silvia."

"Well. Well... what has she been doing?" Margot was panic stricken.

Damien stepped forward. "We're not quite sure how she's been doing it but we believe she's been brainwashing humans."

The past few years of Margot's life were beginning to make sense. All that time, while everyone on Earth had believed it was their 'God', she had known better and she had been right. A small rush of pride ran through Margot's body. She was right. When everyone thought their saviour had come, Margot knew it had been something else all along, toying with and manipulating them. She could see why they had chosen their universe. *Humans were underdeveloped. They were mostly stupid. They were also the most destructive species known to man,* she thought. *They were the most destructive species known to the angels. Humans not only destroyed Earth, they destroyed each other, and they ultimately destroyed themselves.* It was becoming clear to her just how futile humanity was.

There had been many years of war on Earth during her childhood. It was the reason for the ship, the reason for hers and Jade's partnership. She couldn't remember a time when war wasn't waging on Earth. Margot frowned, she hated to admit it but they sort of deserved it. What sort of race turned on themselves? They should be battling people like Silvia, protecting their planet, not fighting each other. It was their fault; being so violent gave Silvia the need to be there in the first place. They were the corrupt ones, not her.

Margot thought for a moment, "Hang on a minute, it still doesn't explain what just happened or where my friends are OR why that place over there is lit up like Vegas!" She pointed at the light beyond the mountains.

"Didn't you hear Hurst?" Damien gave Margot one of his patronising *'are you stupid'* looks. "Silvia was thrown out of the Over World; she had to carry out this operation somewhere."

"So you mean over there, is like, her headquarters?"

"Indeed," Damien sighed. "When Silvia fell into Manhaden, she created a large crater and shifted the land, creating a circular mountain range known as The Torgeerian. There is a portal on the Earth that connects to this place. It was an easy access point, where no human ever goes and hence it made it more appealing to 'carry out the operation,' if you like, here. Barbie uses it a little too much."

Damien glared at the transvestite for a few moments before focusing his attention on Margot again. "I believe it is called the Bermuda Bi-sex-u-angle sorry the Bermuda Triangle."

"Okay..." Margot put her hand in front of her mouth to hide her smile. "So basically she's been taking them and..."

"Putting them back in their world, yes." Damien said with a smile. "The leaders were taken first to avoid any problems, then anyone else who fell out of line."

"But what exactly are they *doing* to them?" Margot asked.

"Who knows," Damien shrugged, looking away.

"And these stone angels, sorry the Bron-"

"The Brontangus are helping her, yes." Damien's voice was cool. Everyone shuddered at the mention of the name. Even he looked unnerved for once.

"Those thingies. That's right; I knew I almost got it right." She looked in turn at their sombre faces. "What?" Margot folded her arms, "What's wrong now?"

"I wouldn't talk about them so lightly if I were you, they're scum. They're the worst creatures to roam this world!" Hurst raised his voice as he spoke.

"Enough," Damien snapped. They fell silent. Damien turned, Arabina had disappeared again. He shook his head; that sort of conversation always got her riled up. It was a dangerous decision to explain to Margot. He glared at Hurst and the demon bowed his head.

Margot looked around before she spoke. She was reluctant to ask another question due to the heavy atmosphere, but then again, it had never stopped her before.

"So, why don't we do something? Go over there?" She said as though it was the most obvious decision to make.

"My point exactly!" Arabina shouted from behind her. It was clear that she was way past boiling point. "We'll go in there, destroy her and take back my land…" she trailed off, on what she believed to be a full action plan. Margot found it hard to hold back her laughter. Arabina didn't know much about Earth.

"Your highness… I, I don't think we can find twenty hundred fire-breathing octopuses on Earth." Hurst screwed up his eyes in fear of her reaction. Arabina was disheartened.

"Look, to be honest," Margot began. "I didn't *really* anticipate doing the whole 'save the world' cliché. I just want my researchers and scientists back so we can sort out the mess on Earth. You guys are on your own!"

"Can we call at the shop on the way, see if I can get another pair of shoes?" Barbie asked.

"EVERYONE STOP!" Damien yelled. Margot gasped, it was the first time she had heard him shout. "Margot you have no idea what you're up against, the light is *dangerous* to humans. It changes them. You're too underdeveloped and powerless to take that sort of glare from an Angel and Arabina, we're hardly an army. Look at us. You of all people should know that our floating island is well renowned for its darkness. How will our people cope? Then there's the other matter, of why you haven't tried this before."

"Yeah that's a good point dude, why haven't you?" Margot turned on Arabina.

Arabina looked embarrassed. It was a bit like watching a teenage girl admitting they had a crush on a boy to her friends. Only Arabina was trying, without much success, to conceal her reaction.

"Well," she began, hesitant. "I can't overpower her, because good forces always overcome evil ones, by our ancient laws and traditions."

"That's a real rule?" Margot sniggered.

"Of course!" Arabina snapped, offended. "It was written by the Angels years ago, so that should we try to overpower them we would fall! The rules were made at the beginning of the world."

"You guys need updating... seriously. I mean, look at you, none of you are evil," she waited for a response. No one spoke. The group looked around at each other, then at Margot.

"Oh, you'd be surprised," Damien said and smiled, bearing his large canines.

Margot raised her eyebrows; she wasn't going to show her weaknesses. Instead, she would look unaffected.

"One more thing," she decided it would be an excellent idea to change the subject. "You still haven't explained why the mountains moved. Even here I'm sure that's not normal..."

"Allow me," Arabina stepped forward. "I don't know how, but for some goddamn reason, that woman is pushing those mountains out and taking more of my land. The more humans those... *things*..." she paused, gritting her teeth: "Bring in... Well, not this time muchachos, I will no longer be sent into hiding! I'm going over there whether you're with me or not!"

Margot's heart leapt. *Finally*, an action plan! That was what she had been waiting for since she arrived. She had to go along with Arabina, Margot was unsure how but she knew it was her only way out of that place.

"Yes!" She said, almost too quickly. "I agree."

Damien laughed in response. "Arabina, you can't honestly listen to her..."

However, it was clear Arabina had made up her mind, as she was striding away. She gave a sly smile as she listened to Damien's words slip further and further into the background.

"Arabina... Arabina! You can't be serious about this venture..." Damien glared at the group.

"Well come on then, you don't think we're going to leave her do you?"

They followed their fiery leader towards the mountains.

Chapter 8

The Imperfectionist

Somewhere amidst the clouds, a figure soared above golden sands. The figure wasn't anything usually seen in the Earth's sky. The figure flexed its heavy stone wings, they were awkward and stiff and it struggled as it advanced to its destination. The sky was darkening. The air was growing icy. The creature grew closer.

What made the creature eerie, despite its hidden features, stone-gargoyle texture and mysterious air, was the fact that it was carrying something in its giant hands. A person, caught between the creature's fingers. What the person had done was unclear, but they appeared intoxicated or comatose as they hung limp in the creature's grasp. The creature smiled.

Its hungry eyes cast over the bright landscape. It was empty. She'd kept her word; it was safe to go down. Slowly, the Brontangus circled lower until it came to an empty street in busy city centre. Its large hands screwed up into tight fists as the man fell to the concrete. Brontangus weren't well renowned for their empathy, they were taught not to feel. However, the Brontangus had been trained to spot imperfection in the loneliest corners of the world. The man would find his way from there and if he didn't, it was his loss. Knowing the job in hand was done, there was only one other place where the creature could go.

It opened its wings and took off, over the hot ground. The light became unbearable after a while, even to something that held such great power. It had to return to its master, she'd be wondering where it'd got to. The Brontangus rose into the air, it wasn't cold, the clammy, thick atmosphere clung to the creature's stone form. The Brontangus flew north; high above the cities and towns towards the outskirts of Izsafar and the Torgeerian mountain range. He soared over scenery humans could only wish to experience. Very few travelled to that part of the island and even fewer to its destination. It was somewhere that the faint of heart feared to tread. The creature turned its stone head. All was quiet. Below, several shades of green filled the forest's wild pallet of colours. Vines hung between thriving trees while large tropical flowers, with their vast array of colours saturated the invisible floor. The forest, like other beautiful things, concealed cruel truths; however, the flight was not over yet. The Brontangus continued through the sky, flying close the jungle's steep cliff edge and then… it found it.

A cascading waterfall hung from a large rock. That was it. That was the entrance. Its cold eyes glanced at the sun-kissed water and in a few seconds it had gone. The Brontangus dived over the edge of the pool, swimming with the strong current. However, the creature didn't stop there. It continued to swim deeper until the pale blue water was almost black with lack of light. It continued, deeper still. Before long, a small, glowing red spot appeared; the light was coming from the bottom of the pool.

The Brontangus had swum as far it could go. However, the usual sandy sea bed was nowhere in sight. Without hesitation, the Brontangus outstretched its stone arms and pulled itself through the hole in the rock to the other side; below Arabina's floating island. It had almost reached its destination.

The angry red sky of the Under World stretched on for miles below. It was difficult for the creature to see the tainted floor; even more difficult was the task for those on its floor to reach the top. The sky had been given the nickname the 'Sky of Hell' and any living creature that was unlucky enough to venture below Manhaden could see why. It was an endless torrent of air, not just filling the space of Haszear, but putting as much distance between its dark inhabitants and the rest of the world.

The crimson and grey clouds crashed and thundered, as though crying out in agony. They twisted and turned around the creature, trying to make its movements difficult to execute. Anyone else would have struggled, but the Brontangus was no average dweller of that realm, it knew what it was doing. Around it, it could see more of its kind. Occasionally, they'd meet in a break in the cloud and then disappear back into the maze. The clouds began to untwist, revealing its master's home; the castle.

The building had a dark, sinister undertone as it floated amongst the clouds. The grey stone looked as old as time and the windows were dark and jagged. The one enclosed in its high walls, was no villain, on the contrary, she was an angel. The Brontangus continued to move through the sky, aiming for the marble floor in front of the imposing building. There, it joined in line with the other stone figures. All stood silent; waiting for their commander.

The grand interior was unexpected. She stared out of the window, her fingers playing over the keys of a grand piano. *They had arrived.* The sound of heels echoed through the building: from the lonely turrets, along corridors and empty halls, until at last they arrived at the doors.

The Brontangus watched as one door creaked opened and a great light beamed through the gap. The light source emanated from the angel herself. Everything about Silvia was overpoweringly pure white. The light she emitted was so bright, it was impossible to see her features. It was possible however, to make out that she was wearing a long dress.

Not one of the monsters dared to move, even speak in her presence.

"Well, well," she said as she moved along the marble floor. Her voice shook the underground sky. It echoed around them and penetrated the minds of the creatures. The voice was powerful, like none any human had heard. Some of the creatures grew restless.

"Patience," she said. "The games have only just begun."

*

"Do we have to walk much further?" Margot panted, clutching her aching sides. The group had been walking for hours, it had dawned on her that the idea didn't seem so good after all. Margot looked down; her night vision didn't even reach the bottom of the mountain. She had no idea how far up they were. Maybe it was good that she couldn't see. Barbie limped at her side, whilst Damien strode in front; constantly stopping them as Brontangus flew overhead. She knew he thought the trip was a bad idea, but for some reason, he refused to argue against Arabina's rule. He was the only person who dared challenge her. However, there were more pressing issues on her mind than the vampire's leadership skills, such as the sheer drop behind her. Arabina had transformed herself into some form of winged creature and she swooped down to land on a nearby rock pile. The mountain was a barren landscape. It was not surprising that there was no trace of footsteps no rough trails, just desolate, un-navigated terrain.

"What's going on?" she said, transforming back into her human form, the only form which exemplified her annoyed expression. "We're almost there now!"

"We can't be." Margot stopped dead in her tracks. She saw the rays of light bounce off the rocks and into the darkness. She frowned and without a second thought, began to climb towards them.

"Margot," Damien said, pulling her back. "Everyone will wear a pair of these from now on," he said, handing out sunglasses.

"I've got my own," Margot said, but Barbie thrust a pair into her hands.

"Trust me," said Damien, sliding his onto his pointed face. "You'll be wanting these." He turned to everyone. "Keep a low profile, the Brontangus could be anywhere."

Barbie looked at Margot. His blank face was just the warning she needed. She had to keep a low profile. Arabina decided it was a good idea for them to set up camp while she scanned the outskirts. Margot had a strong suspicion that the Demon was merely buying time so she could think of a plan. Margot watched as Barbie made a small fire, while Hurst marked out the way they had come from a crumpled map in his pocket.

"Right, gather round!" The silence was broken by Arabina's abrupt tone as she swooped back onto the rock and changed into human form once again. They gathered around the small fire. "Now the plan is this: I'll go back and alert the rest of Manhaden and we'll have an army to invade the land tomorrow."

Damien was beginning to get frustrated with her spontaneity and interrupted. "You know we don't stand a chance going in head first like that. I think a few of us should survey the area first, set up some form of base, and then start to infiltrate."

"Ohh, but that could take weeks," Arabina moaned. She sounded like an impatient child.

"My… my lady," Hurst squeaked. "I believe Damien is right, that is far too impetuous and if she's as powerful as you say…" He gulped, unable to finish his sentence.

"We'd be dead in seconds," Barbie's mundane reply silenced them all.

"Putting aside Barbie's usual sunny disposition, he does have a valid point." Damien said as he looked at Arabina. "We need to plan this carefully."

Sensing another full-blown argument was about to break out, Margot decided it was time to go on a solitary walk. She got up and slipped away unnoticed as voices began to rise in anger. *Those people are idiots.* She thought. *How stupid are they?* Keep a low profile Damien had said, not start an argument. The journey was pointless, judging by the fact that they couldn't agree on anything. Even if they were on a one way street, she bet they'd still argue on which direction to turn. The rays of light grew more frequent. Margot followed them further up the mountain. She felt increasingly vulnerable as her body became more exposed. That was when she saw it.

Her first glimpse of Izsafar.

Her eyes widened as she edged closer to the precipice of the mountain. It was beautiful. Margot stared out at the human paradise below. She clutched her sunglasses, forgetting their importance. Margot was unable to believe that what she was looking at was meant to be enemy ground they had come to eliminate. She turned back towards the dark wilderness. She put a cigarette in her mouth and thought… what if she was on the wrong side? After all, she didn't know the people she had travelled with, they could be leading her on, tricking her. Maybe it was time to run? They were confusing times amidst even more confusing places. It was hard to know which side to be on, while to work out what to do next. But what if Damien and Arabina were telling the truth? A horrible thought hit her. *Did fighting for them make her evil?* It was something she'd not thought about. They weren't exactly on the righteous path, they were, after all, defending Satan's daughter. Margot gazed back towards the peaceful land of Izsafar, she wanted to run away, leave those people behind…

"But what about the human?" Barbie's question broke Margot's train of thought. Suddenly the conversation was becoming interesting again.

"What about her?" came Damien's cold reply. She crept into audible range of the group and positioned herself against a nearby rock.

"We'll keep her with us until we can decide what to do with her," Arabina said. Margot's mouth fell open, were those people going to do something to her?

"I just wondered… it's very dangerous for her over there," Barbie spoke once again.

Margot smiled, he seemed to have her back.

"She knows the risks," Damien said.

"Where is she, anyway?" Arabina snapped. Margot's blood ran cold, she felt guilty for listening to them talking about her, as if she was eavesdropping. Without thinking she ran back to her original position over-looking the mountains and tried to look casual. There was still time to escape. Maybe she should…

"Something wrong?" A calm voice whispered in her ear. Damien stood directly behind her. "Because I could have sworn I told you not to wander off."

She turned towards him, his face was stern and he said: "You weren't thinking of leaving were you? You do know you wouldn't stand a chance on your own."

How did he know? Were her thoughts that obvious?

"Damien," she began.

The vampire noticed the view across to Izsafar.

"You shouldn't stare too long, it may," Damien paused. "Enchant you." He looked out over Izsafar. Margot noticed he was holding his arm close to his side. She turned to face him with her back towards the cliff edge.

"We're fighting for the Under World; doesn't that make us the bad guys?" She had to ask. "It's not a question of who the *bad guys* are," he sounded disgusted, using the colloquialism. "This situation is far beyond morals now, it's about choice and how the humans in that land are severely lacking, and so are we."

She hated to admit it, but his words reassured her. She didn't reply; she didn't have to. Unseen by Margot, Damien shot a guilty look to the floor; one of his brief seconds of weakness.

"You're hurt," She said, nodding at the arm he was still holding.

He shrugged, "I'm fine, Margot."

Margot ignored his comment.

She took another step towards him and put her hand on his injured arm. He didn't flinch, but the black trench coat was cold and wet. He'd been bleeding. She paused, did vampires bleed? He obviously did. She was so close to him that Margot could feel his cold breath brushing across her neck.

"If you'll just let me…" She stopped and looked up. His eyes glared down at her, but the glare was more inviting than anything else.

"Damien," Margot's voice was only just higher than a whisper. His mouth curved into a smile as she turned to face him fully. She moved closer, not quite sure what she was doing. Damien moved one of his hands to her hips and moved it up and down her back. Their faces were centimetres apart; their lips grew closer and closer until they finally met. He kissed her lightly at first, but it became more passionate. She knew she should resist but it had been such a long time since anyone had touched her like that. Damien's hand explored Margot's body, it moved up her body while his mouth moved down. He unzipped the front of her leather jacket and moved his mouth to her neck, teasing the tender skin.

Without warning he withdrew and looked her straight in the eye. "I do apologise for this Margot, but you were right. I am in a weak position at the moment and you can help me." His menacing smile was not intended to reassure her. Margot returned the look with a confused one. *What did he mean?* Then he leaned in and bit her neck hard. Margot gasped, she felt the blood drain from her body.

"Fuck," she whispered.

Then she screamed so loud that Damien could hardly make out the words. "Get the hell off me!" Margot lashed out at him, trying to fend him off by punching him as hard as she could. She cried out in pain, it only made his grip harder. Margot could feel the full extent of his long canines lodged deep inside her.

A figure appeared, Arabina approached them.

123

"Can't you guys keep it down? Low profile, remember?" she said. Then saw what the commotion was about. She froze, but like Damien, her mouth curved into a smug and menacing smile. "I knew she'd come in useful!"

Margot knew there was no point in screaming for help. No one was coming. She fought, not noticing how close her heels were to the edge of the mountain side. If she were any paler, she would be translucent. Finally, Damien retracted his teeth. His lips flickered and curved up as he moved in on her once again. His pale hand gripped hard on her shirt to steady her balance and prevent her from falling.

"You know Margot, you're a lot weaker than I first anticipated, but don't worry, you're too useful to..."

Margot lashed out once again making him lose his grip on her top. She broke free, but from the severe lack of blood, dizziness overcame her and she lost her footing. Margot fell back and before he could grab her, she plummeted off the mountain edge.

"How unfortunate," Damien said, unperturbed by the situation. "At least she'll be able to find her friends."

Arabina smirked but suddenly her smile faded.

"Ermm, Damien," she said in a worried voice. "Won't that give away our position?"

Damien glared at her. "Ahh, yes."

*

Jade sprang up. He could have sworn he heard a scream. Whatever it was had since faded. He was panting and covered in a cold sweat. *It was just a nightmare* he told himself, but something about that dream had seemed so real. Jade ran his hands through his dreadlocks. Since he'd taken that stupid pill he felt like he'd been losing his mind. Someone had been falling, he was sure of it. *Forget it,* he told himself, *or you will go crazy.* He looked around the dark hotel room; everything seemed to be where he had left it. Hauling himself out of bed, he went over to the double doors that lead to the balcony and edged the curtain back. The light shot across the room. He gasped and covered his eyes.

"Arghh," he moaned, rubbing them hard. "Does it ever get dark here?"

A thought suddenly struck him; he should be tracking his progress. Jade walked back over to the bed and opened the small wooden drawer at the side. There at the bottom, lay his Jonovicator next to the packet of 'Face'. He picked it up and pressed a small button on the side.

"Day two in Izsafar," he said in a low voice. "I know I missed out day one but I was busy, so I guess this sort of is day one, no, no scratch that."

He shook his head and pressed the button again. "Okay, day one, take two or day two, take one... I don't know. Anyway Jade's journal or log. Log sounds better. I'm in a strange new place called Izsafar. Still no sign of Margot or any other sort of creature, in fact, strangely, everything is quite normal. Reenie has put me in a hotel room on the coast. All the humans here seem happy, but from what I've seen they don't talk about Earth, to be honest they don't really seem to think about a lot of pressing matters. None of them seem to work here. It's a conundrum. Yes. Extremely obscure. Something is definitely wrong. I'll have to investigate further."

"Jade?" a confused voice came from the doorway. Reenie was standing in the shadows of the room dressed in a small back night dress. "Who are you talking to?" Jade dived back under the bed sheets. He slept naked.

"Jade, are you okay?" she asked again.

"I'm fine, I was just talking to..." He paused before uttering: "Myself." He punched himself hard. If there was a prize for appearing like the biggest freak, he'd win it hands down.

"Right," she said, unconvinced. Without warning, she bounced into the room and jumped on the bed next to him. Jade hid the Jonvicator under the sheets; it wasn't the time to tell her what he was doing. Not until he knew more about the situation he was in.

He turned a bright shade of red; he had never encountered a situation like it and felt awkward. Unless he counted the time where a girl had stumbled half-drunk into his room at university - and even that had been a mistake.

Jade Wilde was no stranger to women, in fact he was widely known by them and therefore they did their best to stay away. It would be the first time a female, bar Margot had stepped into his bedroom. It was rather odd.

Reenie looked around the room, as if expecting to see someone hidden in the corner.

"You really were telling the truth," she muttered under her breath, almost disappointed.

Jade screwed up his eyes in embarrassment.

"Look get dressed, okay? There's going to be loads of entertainment in the city today, I think it's like a carnival or something! The voice has organised it so it's going to be good!" she said.

He was so glad she changed the subject. Reenie left as quickly as she came in, she jumped off the bed and rushed back towards the door.

"Reenie," he called, just before she left. "How do you think we get home?"

She burst into laughter. "Jade what are you talking about? We are home!" She shook her head as if he'd said something crazy. "You really are strange."

"Yeah," Jade laughed in response. "I don't have a clue what's going on."

Chapter 9

The Carnival

The South West of Izsafar was renowned for its beautiful coast line and soaring temperatures. It was the kind of place holiday makers flocked to. It combined coast and heat with luscious greenery. Long, white sandy beaches stretched along it, covering the outskirts of the land which led out to the tranquil sea, isolating the dark mountain range in the distance. Above the shore, long white cliffs, covered in wild flowers, stood waiting for the next person to tread their walkways and trails. Wild meadows stretched for miles, hiding all sorts of wonders.

That side of Izsafar contrasted to the big cities in the centre of the land. It had very few occupants and even fewer places to house them, but the residents who lived there managed to party continuously, as Jade found out. He knew he was lucky to find a hotel room, but he was unsure whether he could keep up with its inhabitants' demanding lifestyle.

The South West was one of the most peaceful places of Izsafar. It was a place where one went to think, reflect, relax and party, all while taking in the rays of the hot sun.

Margot burst through the calm surface of the sea, gasping for air. The sunlight that hit her as she surfaced shocked her so much she became engulfed again until she steadied herself. She had been in darkness for what felt like an eternity. It was such a dramatic contrast to the other side of Manhaden that she had to shield her eyes, opening them just millimetres at a time to try to accustom herself to the new blazing surroundings. In her weak condition, she struggled to swim and was desperate to reach the shore. She looked like a drowning cat as she flapped her arms and legs in a desperate attempt to get back to land. Margot was panic stricken, not only was she temporarily blinded, she didn't have the strength to swim. She could feel her body relenting to the power of the currents. Margot looked up at the surface as she sank. Her vision grew darker... the light was fading.

A loud cry came from nearby. "Someone's in the water!"

"Get her out, now!"

Before Margot knew what was happening, she was hoisted out of the sea and onto a wooden floor. There she lay; face down, coughing and spluttering. Around her she could hear muffled voices muttering phrases she couldn't quite catch. She felt hands sit her upright. Margot's body swayed as a man with kind eyes and a brown beard looked at her.

"It's okay now missy, you're safe." He sounded like an old fashioned pirate. Margot looked around. From what she could make out, she'd been pulled onto a boat. The wooden floor she sat on was clean and polished whilst the bridge in the middle of the deck was a brilliant white. It was obviously new, she felt terrible for what she was about to do.

"I think I'm gonna hurl," she moaned, putting her hand on her throbbing head.

"Move her to the side of the boat!" The same strong hands picked her up and thrust her to the side. She felt her knees buckle and her body swayed as she attempted to remain upright. The hands remained firmly around her sides, holding her up. Margot could feel something warm and wet running down the back of her head.

"She's lost a lot of blood," the man holding her called, before muttering: "How did you get there?"

Margot turned around and stared up at him. He was a lot older than she was. She guessed early to mid-fifties, patches of his dark brown hair were turning silver. The wrinkles on his face were deep which said to her that he'd had a rich life, full of vastly interesting experiences. Either that or he'd just partied too hard in his youth. Margot didn't know, nor did she care at that point, she was comforted that he was there to help her.

"Sir, what do we do with her?" another voice said. It sounded younger, more nervous.

"Eric, let her sleep for a few hours below deck before we moor up and go and make her some food!" Before Margot even reached her quarters, she collapsed into a deep convalescent sleep.

*

Hurst paced back and forth, wincing occasionally and throwing his arms in the air.

"What do we do… what do we do?"

"*You* can shut up for now," Arabina snapped at him.

He hung his head in shame. The group hadn't advanced from the cold mountainside. After their mishap, they knew it wouldn't be long before they had to do something. With no solid plan formed and no army to speak of, they were, as Barbie liked to put it, 'fucked'. He looked even more glum than usual as he stamped out the small camp fire, scared it would attract unwanted attention.

"Well, this is *your* fault, what do you propose we do?" Arabina shouted.

Damien remained silent, he was wearing aviator shades and his hand was perched on the side of his face, in some sort of thinking position.

"Maybe," Barbie spoke. "No… no I don't think a bunch of flowers would change Silvia's mind would it?"

Damien rolled his eyes behind his sunglasses.

"I don't know why you look so smug," Arabina turned to him. "You've not had any better ideas."

"Actually," Damien said. "I have."

*

Margot looked out over to the mountains; how she wasn't dead, she had no idea. One thing that Margot did know was that she was never returning to those stupid people or that ridiculous place ever again. Her white hair blew in the wind as the small boat sailed back to shore. She was feeling a lot better. The older man, who had introduced himself as Wolf, made sure she had eaten and had loaned her a clean white shirt. The boat was small and cosy. The inside, like the outside, was spotless, but very old fashioned and was minimally decorated. Wolf lived aboard with his son, Adam. Together, they spent their time sailing the waters of Izsafar. He was a cool and collected man, who, by the sounds of it, never set foot on the land if he could avoid it. Like Margot, he wasn't the most social type.

"Feeling better?" he said, joining her on the side of the boat.

"Much," she said and smiled at him. Margot was grateful for his kindness, without him, she'd certainly be dead. However, she didn't say that, Margot wasn't one for showing gratitude through words. Instead, she opened her packet of cigarettes and offered him one.

"They'll kill you, you know," he said, pushing the packet back towards her.

"Yeah well," she shrugged. "So will falling off a mountain."

Wolf chose to ignore the comment, believing she was still concussed.

He ran his fingers through his thick hair. "There's a river just up here that leads up into a town a few miles away from the main city. We'll part ways there."

"Why would I want to go to the city?" She asked, trying to sound innocent. Margot intended to make that her destination.

"Don't play games Margot, you know perfectly well why," his eyes met hers. He lowered his voice to prevent his son from hearing. "It's a very good place to start looking for your friends, lass."

"Wait... how did you..."

"Intuition," he said with a coy smile.

The boat turned and made its way up the river that flowed between wild countryside and the island. Margot looked around; there was still no one in sight. An odd sensation ran through her brain. She felt light headed and woozy, but also happy. The happiest she'd felt in a long time. Her smile widened the further they travelled. She almost forgot how she had arrived there in the first place. Margot could hear voices in the background, not just Wolf's, many voices; women's, men's and a few children. They were approaching the town.

"Margot," Wolf tapped her on the back. "It's bright out. Don't forget to put these on." He produced the pair of sunglasses Damien had given her.

"Okay, okay," she sighed as she put them on. Suddenly she felt her mood drop. Everything around her fell back into the horrible perspective she had been so used to. She felt like jumping off the boat and letting the water have at her carcass. But, being Margot, she said nothing and tried to act normal. She realised what Damien had meant by his comment.

The light had made her forgetful, feel at ease. She understood the vampire's warning, but had ignored it, even if it did make her feel like a naughty child for disobeying him. The man watched her in curiosity.

"Are you okay?" Wolf asked.

"Of course," Margot smiled back, wishing she had told him the truth. She disembarked the small wooden boat and headed into town.

"Just follow the path," Wolf called to her, as he and his son moved back down the river. "I'm sure we'll meet again someday."

She waved in return, knowing full well they probably wouldn't. Margot sighed; it was time to find Reenie and Clarke.

The quaint riverside and wild moors were a distant memory in a short time. The countryside became more urbanised the further she walked. Margot looked around her, watching as she passed small villages which became small towns. There was an odd atmosphere; something she couldn't quite put her finger on. It was quiet, far too quiet for her liking. The Voice had done a good job, it resembled Earth well. Margot continued walking, until she saw a group of people following the same path ahead.

"Come on," she heard one of the men say. "If we don't get to the city soon, we'll end up having to turn back."

Keeping herself hidden, Margot followed close behind them until she found what she was looking for.

At last, the city. She sighed in relief, letting her leaders get a good way ahead. Margot went down an alleyway between two skyscrapers they had led her to. She had found the main stretch. It was just like being back in New York, before the existence of the Voice. It wasn't anything special. The city was, like every other city, full of dirty streets, pollution and sky scrapers, topped off by litter drifting around the streets. If anything, to the normal human, the city seemed more run-down than any on Earth, but to Margot, it was home.

She liked the risk, the adventure, the grimy streets and even grimier people. If it was where Silvia had put all the so called 'corrupt' humans, then that was where she was most happy. Unlike most humans, what she had been missing the most was *the danger*. She loved the idea of having to watch every move she made, keep her guard up at all time; and she'd need to do that more than ever. It was like being in a real life action film. Margot had always thought she belonged in the C.I.A. If she wasn't so much of a rule breaker, it might have happened. She had to hand it to the Voice; Silvia made pretty good replicas of things.

The only thing that Margot did find strange was the lack of transport. Normally, in an average Earth city, pedestrians filled the old roads while the sky was rammed with ship traffic struggling to get to their destinations. However, it was different, the skies were unoccupied. Margot looked up at the few ships that sailed the lonely air. Those models must have been nearing fifty years of age, perhaps more. They were not the latest technology had to offer. Maybe that flaw in Silvia's knowledge wasn't as incidental as it appeared.

A man walked past her with a glum look on his face.

"Morning," she beamed.

He shot her a filthy look and spat on the floor.

"I frickin' love this place!" She smiled and jumped off the ground, just a little skip but anyone who knew Margot knew she didn't get enthusiastic about a lot of things. That was a rarity; it took a lot to make her happy and the process normally included an advanced chemistry set or a large collection of illegal drugs.

Her encounter made Margot wonder if the people there saw what she saw.

Who knew, maybe she'd see some sort of utopia when she took her glasses off. Margot put her hand up to the frame around the lens, ready to remove them. One quick peak wouldn't change anything and she'd put them straight back on afterward. A gaggle of people rushed by, bustling to their destination. With that, Margot forgot about her original intentions. "Hey!" she yelled after them. "Watch it!" Many people on the street turned to look at her. She glanced down at the concrete; she had forgotten how busy it was. She bit her lip ring hard, repeating the phrase *low profile, you idiot* over and over in her head.

Something she couldn't comprehend was the difference in the people. Many seemed as if they were intoxicated, unsure of their actions. Some, like the man she had passed earlier, was shifty-looking; he kept a low profile and looked as though they were trying to hide illegal substances. But none of them seemed to be fully aware of their purpose or what they were supposed to be doing. She watched as they dashed back and forth. Then she realised that most were running in the same direction. Margot paused for a moment, making sure it wasn't her mind playing tricks on her. *Nope,* large quantities of the city's residents were making their way to the end of the street.

"Come on!" Margot heard a voice shout from nearby. "Or we'll miss it!"

Miss what? She stood back and watched as another group of enthusiastic people dashed past her.

She pondered. Something weird was going on, the question was whether to follow them to the apparent place of interest, or search the area whilst they were occupied. She had to be careful, Margot knew how powerful Izsafar was, it could be Silvia playing mind games with her. She looked up and down the street, it was almost too easy. There was no sign of the Bronatangus or any other reinforcements. There didn't seem to be any authority at all. *Was breaking in really that straight forward?* She had at least expected some form of fight, challenge, but no, nothing. Margot wiped her brow, it was excruciatingly hot. She slipped off her leather jacket and clean shirt, to reveal a small, white top. When it came to clothes, it was fair to say she was a very monochrome individual. The only other colour ever found in Margot's wardrobe was probably a food stain from a night out.

"Reenie, where are we going?" A familiar voice called.

Margot's red eyes widened. She was sure they could probably open wider, but that sort of strain would usually be reserved for sights such as horror films and naked old men.

Jade.

Jade Wilde was here? And by the sounds of it he had found Reenie. Margot couldn't believe what she had just heard. She spun around so fast she almost lost balance. More people were making their way down the street, a lot more than when she'd first arrived. If she didn't move fast it would be impossible to find him, if the crowds continued to grow exponentially as they seemed to be doing. Without considering the consequences, she made a dash for it, dodging the groups of people along the way. *Where was he?* She ran, looking in every direction. Margot slowed her pace as she saw the end of the street.

Out of breath, she paused at the T-junction she rested her hands on her thighs to steady herself. She really needed to quit smoking. After the brief rest, Margot concluded that she must have been hallucinating. She shook her head. It had sounded so real. Across the other side, black bars, tipped with gold reached high into the air. Behind the bars was one of the most beautiful parks she had seen in a long time. The grass was emerald green, cut to exactly the right length that grass, in her opinion, should be. The park was filled with oaks, ferns, silver birches and trees that were so exotic she had no idea what they were. Flower beds acted as centre pieces on paths. They were filled with every flower you could think of, and many you couldn't. In the centre, she could see a large narrow lake that stretched down the park. Parts of the lake were hidden by leafy trees. Margot watched as the water glistened in the blinding light of Izsafar.

She looked down the street to her left where the crowds were headed. She sighed, there was nothing to do but follow. After resuming her usual stance and stern facial expression, she turned left and became one with the crowd. She passed more of the tall, run-down buildings, takeaways of all nationalities and robot-operated shops. The park on her right was bigger than she had first thought; it continued on by the side of the road.

The sun beat down on Margot's neck and back. She was surprised it wasn't burning her white skin, she felt like she was on fire. Something caught her eye. A few yards in front, a tall man stood above the rest of the crowd. His long black dreadlocks hung down his back with a tricorne sat on top of them. His dark skin was hidden by a midnight blue trench-coat. Margot could only just see the collar through the hordes of people.

So it *was* him. She smiled to herself, unable to distinguish whether she was feeling smug in her deductions or if she was simply happy to see him again. She wasn't going to run up to Jade and make a scene - partly to maintain the low profile, but more important, to protect him. She knew Jade all too well and didn't want to drag him into another one of her messes. Jade was a good person. She was the one that had led him into trouble. She was the one that had led him astray. Because of her, he had spent the prime of his youth alone in space. Another pang of guilt hit Margot hard, similar to the one when they lost Frank. She shook it off and kept her eyes fixed on Jade.

The crowd were bearing right and Margot soon lost sight of him. Before she knew where she was, she found herself walking through two large black gates, tipped with the same gold as the fence of the park. She was inside. It was deserted at the top half, but crammed full of all sorts of people at the lower end where she stood. Looking around, she saw bright, flashing colours and lights coming from a huge variety of carnival rides and stalls that filled the field. A horrible noise, like terrible microphone feedback, ran through the airwaves.

"Welcome one and all to the very first and long awaited Izsafar Carnival!" A man boomed. Margot saw a stage, and that was where the voice came from. "Now, as you all know," the man continued. "The Voice has outdone herself by organising this event! There are so many things to do today, have a go on the flying dodgems, morph into an animal or take a step into our virtual video game! There's a wide range of products you can buy, from amazing technology to an array of interesting substances."

Margot raised her eyebrows.

"But first, on the main stage, an act that has made a last minute booking, and we're so glad to have them, all the way from the north jungles of Izsafar, put your hands together," he paused for effect. "It's Margot's Magical Circus!"

Margot's eyes widened, it was too much of a coincidence. No, she told herself, there were lots of Margots in the world; it was stupid to think that the act was named after her. She stared at the empty stage. Ethnic music burst from the high stacks of speakers which towered over the sides of the stage. A puff of thick white smoke appeared on stage. It cleared to reveal a woman, who could only be described as a belly-dancing gypsy. The woman was wearing long, loose trousers and a small boob-tube that showed off her perfect figure. Her back, face and black hair were all wrapped in a shawl made from different pieces of cloth. Margot snorted, the woman danced in a provocative manner and she introduced other members of the performance. Something told Margot that it definitely had nothing to do with her. With that in mind, she felt free to explore without being noticed.

She turned to leave and ended up walking straight into a man standing behind her.

"Watch it!" A bald man with a strong American accent shouted as his hotdog fell to the floor. She got ready to make some angry and uncouth comment, but after looking at his face, found herself unable to speak. Margot's mouth dropped open. She knew the man; her Dad had known the man. Her Dad had worked with him. He was the reason that her dad had gone to jail.

"Sorry," she muttered, walking backwards. The bald man stared at her; it was obvious that he could still remember her face. Before he had chance to say anything, they were intercepted by an out of control flying dodgem that was flying so low they had to duck to prevent themselves being hit. The dodgem was piloted by a middle-aged couple that had just begun to break out into an argument.

"Honey, maybe we should stop and ask someone for directions back to the arena?"

"Goddamn it, woman, will you shut up and let me drive?"

"Sorry!" the woman shouted at Margot, as the dodgem lifted back into the air. "He's not normally this cranky, I think it's because he's not had his painkillers today!"

Margot wasn't listening; it was the diversion she needed to make a break for it. She had to admit it was funny seeing one of the most notorious gangsters in America in possession of a hotdog. The carnival was becoming dangerous. Her eyes scanned the outskirts of the park, confirming some of her worst fears. She knew many of the people - and not for the right reasons. She could write a long list of the criminals that were spread around the park. Some gangsters, others murderers, others who had done things too terrible to even contemplate, let alone mention. Margot moved past them, hoping they wouldn't remember her.

It was no secret that Margot had always been fond of breaking the rules, but the question was: how far would she have gone? That was one question she was in no hurry to answer.

They said it was hereditary, in the Grant family genes. Margot liked to believe it was her own love of recklessness that had led her down that path. In her eyes, there was no deep meaning to her erratic behaviour, she thought it was complete and utter bullshit. In her youth, Margot had done many things she regretted, many things that she'd tried so hard to push to the back of her mind. Her father had been a terrible man. At first she had put it down to stress and frustration with his difficult job. Then she blamed her mother before turning to herself. Margot wished he hadn't hit her mother, wished he hadn't smashed up the house or played poker and snorted cocaine in the front room, but most of all, she wished she hadn't got involved. Moving to America and getting out of his car company had been the best decision she'd made. His voice still rattled through her head: "You can do great things Margot, great things." They were the only kind words that she'd ever heard come from his mouth. Most other phrases started and ended in cursing or blinding insults and usually followed with an act of violence or some item being smashed. Margot closed her eyes; it was time to leave the park.

She stared at the front gates, which were occupied with many shifty looking characters. Behind her, 'oohs' and 'aahs' filled the air. Margot shifted her gaze between the two locations. Surely it'd be safer to attract less attention if she put herself in the crowd and made a break for it when the act had finished. Checking behind her, she made her way towards the stage where the gypsy woman was engaged in all sorts of acrobatics above the crowd. They cheered as she swung high in the air, her feet attached to two long ribbons, tied to the ceiling. As everyone gazed upwards, Margot kept her head down, walking further and further into the crowd.

The woman on stage disappeared again leaving behind the same trail of white smoke as before. The audience gasped, then cheered when she reappeared on stage. The woman lifted her hands in the air before taking a low bow.

"Now for my next act, I need a volunteer," she said, as her tall masked assistant wheeled a large blue box onto the stage. The gypsy's eyes scanned the audience, looking for her victim. Margot wasn't paying attention and she pulled a cigarette out of her leather jacket.

"You. Come onto the stage."

Margot looked around her to see which poor person would have to make a fool out of themselves. No one moved forward. What she did see was many different pairs of eyes staring right at her.

"Oh, great," she muttered sarcastically.

"Are you deaf, pale woman?"

People took strides away from Margot, leaving a circle, where she stood, in the middle.

"I'm okay thank you," but it was too late. From being the centre of attention in her empty circle, she was hurtling through the air, carried by what seemed like a cloud of smoke. She was dropped to the stage floor.

"Ouch," Margot moaned getting to her feet. She turned to look at the audience and gasped. They stretched for miles and miles. The park hadn't seemed that big before. Her eyes narrowed as she studied the faces, all eagerly awaiting her participation.

Before the act could continue, there was a scream. The crowd and the performers fell silent.

"MARGOT! MARGOT IT'S ME!" In the centre of the crowd, Jade Wilde was screaming at the stage. Margot watched as he tried to push past people to get closer to the front. It was like watching a fourteen year old at a My Chemical Romance concert.

"Do…you…*mind?*" The gypsy woman sounded offended. "We are trying to carry on a performance. Can this wait?"

Jade laughed nervously, he looked at the angry faces glaring at him.

"Erm sorry," he said. "Sorry everyone; my fault!" He looked straight at

Margot and attempted to mouth communications. He failed, due in part to the fact that they had about five hundred people between them. "Margot - you - and - me – will – talk – later! Later." He repeated the last word slowly as though she hadn't already got the embarrassing message. To make things worse, Jade then added a 'thumbs up'. Margot covered her eyes with her hands; the situation reminded her of an overly proud parent at a school play.

The gypsy woman seemed just as embarrassed and she studied the ceiling before she continued.

"Okay for my next trick, I shall make – what is your name?" She asked.

"Sarah," Margot lied. She realised at once that would make Jade look even more stupid.

"I shall make Sarah disappear!"

Margot felt two large cold hands grip her shoulders. It was not good. The tall assistant wore a long black hooded coat, reminding her of something the grim reaper would choose as an outfit. She glared up at the white mask. It was blank apart from the elongated black smile that stretched up to its cheeks.

"Sarah, please step into the box." The women gestured to the blue box in the centre of the stage. A smaller assistant was sliding the door open. Margot didn't have much of a choice. The tall man behind her turned her body around and shoved her inside. Jade, who was watching from the audience, took in a short, sharp breath as the door slammed behind her.

Once again, Margot found herself in the darkness. The box was cramped; she didn't even have room to turn around. All that was left to do was wait and listen to the woman's voice outside.

"Okay everyone; on the count of three, one..."

Margot wondered how they were going to do the trick. She couldn't feel any door behind the stage.

"...two..."

Surely an assistant would come to her?

"...three."

Margot was confused... nothing had happened. It hadn't worked, she laughed to herself, people really were stupid! However, just as Margot put her hand on the door to let herself out, the wooden floor beneath her disappeared.

She screamed as she fell underneath the stage. It was moments before Margot hit the ground. "Oh," she muttered as she got to her feet, it wasn't nearly as far as she had expected. Outside she could hear the crowd in wild applause. She rubbed her head as she looked around. She was in a dimly lit basement. The walls were old and peeling of their many layers of paint. It was outlined with bronze pipes and cobwebs and the white ceiling above her was cracked and looked like that too could fall away. The room itself was empty.

Margot couldn't see much else apart from a set of stairs in the top right hand corner and a few piles of boxes which, on closer inspection, contained old stage costumes. The door at the top of the stairs swung open.

The silhouette of a tall figure walked down the stairs. Margot dived behind the boxes, in a pitiful attempt to hide. The figure had seen her. It was the same assistant that had put her in the box.

"What do you want from me?" She screamed at him. He didn't reply, instead, he continued to walk towards her, limping. Then something clicked in Margot's mind.

"Barbie?" She asked. The man lifted his mask in response, revealing a long pointed face, smudged with heavy makeup.

"Human-" Barbie began.

Margot felt a hard blow in the middle of her back, and fell to her knees. She lashed out, flailing her arms, which were grabbed by what felt like several other hands and bound behind her back.

"Hello *Sarah*," a strong Latino accent came from behind her. Margot stopped struggling, she knew who it was. She heard the click of heels and Arabina stood in front of her, taking off her long shawl.

"It was *you*," Margot said through gritted teeth. Arabina grinned.

"I've made up my mind," Margot said. "I don't want to work with you guys anymore, get it?" she flipped onto her back with her legs in the air then jumped to her feet. Margot kicked Arabina hard, and the Demon fell backwards.

"Sorry, Barbie," Margot said before also kicking him. It wasn't a powerful kick, but it bought her enough time to get to the stairs. She was so close just a little further and she'd be free. Free to finally be with Jade, to find an escape route, a way home.

The door crashed open again. At the top of the stairs stood the person she loathed the most. Damien.

"Well, what a strange turn of events," he said sarcastically, as he walked down the steps. Margot knew she was cornered. She sighed as she felt Barbie's cold hand grab her tied wrists.

"Human, please stop attacking us, or we'll get caught."

"Listen to Barbie," Damien said. He pulled a wooden chair out and motioned to Barbie for Margot to be placed on it. She didn't put up a fight. She might have been angry, but Margot knew when it was time to quit. She didn't stand a chance.

"Now Margot, if I'm being perfectly honest, we're not too happy about working with you either, but as we have established here, we're all on the same team. It would seem silly to make more obstacles for ourselves, don't you think?" Damien circled the chair.

Margot narrowed her eyes.

"I think soon you'll be thanking us."

"Why the hell would I *ever* thank you?"

"Margot, did you really think you could march into Izsafar right under Silvia's nose? It won't be long before she comes looking for us. I expect she already senses we're here and when she does come, at least you'll be protected."

"I can look after myself, thank you."

"Oh really?" Damien leant close to her. "And what exactly is *your* plan?"

Margot didn't reply. Instead she maintained the disgusted expression she had worn earlier.

"Exactly," Damien said in a smug voice.

The tension in the room was mounting. Margot felt the glare of the hostile eyes upon her. She was surrounded. Barbie stood behind the chair; his hands resting on her shoulders. She wished she knew what he was thinking.

"So," Damien continued, taking off his stage costume. "What did you think of our little disguise then?"

"I think the name was a great idea," Margot said. She had changed her tactics and tried to mimic his calm and collected attitude. It didn't quite work.

"Well the idea was to attract your attention. The name was easy. I just thought of the most egotistical and attention seeking person I knew, and I chose you, Margot," Damien's patronising tone was really starting to get under her skin.

"Really? Well if I ever need to create the biggest idiot show, I'll make sure to put your name in the title!"

"Witty as usual, Margot," Damien took a step backwards.

Hurst burst through the door. His hands were flapping about in front of his face, which was covered in a nervous sweat. It was clear he was anxious to tell them something.

"Damien!" He said, gasping for breath as he fell at the vampire's feet.

"Yes, Hurst," Damien glared down at the Demon.

"She... I think she knows we're here, we- we- need to leave." His small body was shaking.

"And how exactly would she know?"

Hurst pointed a long finger towards Margot.

"He wants to see – her. The man; the man with the long black hair."

Margot's body tensed. She knew what he was talking about. Jade was trying to get inside; he was looking for a way in. He was looking for her. Margot's heart leapt. Damien, who was obviously on the same wave length, muttered: "Professor Wilde."

"Where is he?" he turned to Hurst, who quivered at his feet.

"Erm, erm…" Hurst stuttered, cracking under the pressure. Margot watched as he played with his hands. "Outside."

"Oh, you're so descriptive, extremely useful at a time like this." Damien was growing more sarcastic by the minute. "Okay everyone, it appears we have to leave - and quickly."

They gathered items from around the room: bags, equipment, anything they could carry. Except Arabina, she stood in silence with a pensive expression upon her face. Margot twisted her mouth into a smug grin, she may be the one strapped to the chair but seeing Arabina looking vulnerable was something of a rarity.

"Erm Damien-" Arabina said.

"Not now," he replied, not even bothering to glance in her direction. "Oh, Barbie, deal with her." He pointed at Margot. Barbie lifted her from the chair and put her over his shoulder.

"Are you going to put me down?" She said.

"Margot," Damien rubbed his forehead. "Do we really have to do deal with this now?" After a few moments he said, "Fine. Let her down, but Margot, I'm warning you," his voice was smooth and cold. "Any trouble and I will have to kill you."

Margot didn't reply. She wanted to, she wanted to bite his fucking head off, punch him, kick him, knock him to the floor and do unspeakable things. She was sure that one day she probably would, but at that moment the group had other things on their minds. Margot had to focus. Hurst ran up to the door, cracking it open and looking round in all directions. He nodded at Damien, the coast was clear.

"Damien," Arabina began, but once again she was interrupted.

"Okay everyone, new disguises, choose something from the boxes and try and show as little of your faces as possible without looking like the rest of the circus. Remember, blending in is the key."

The group took various clothes and hats from the boxes. Many looked like they belonged at the carnival. Margot thought the idea was getting worse; it would attract more attention. Barbie, on the other hand, seemed to be in love with his flowery dress and straw hat which he wore with pride. It was clear the group didn't know a lot about humans, especially when it came to fashion. The transvestite had chosen the best outfit of the lot and that wasn't saying much.

"It's like trying to train the Under World's monkeys," Damien shook his head. "This is just not working is it? We're moving from circus to pantomime. Hurst is the only one here with red skin, give him the hood. Everyone else grab a cloak or some garment to hide your face."

He shot them a look, suggestive of the fact that they were all idiots. Deep down, Margot thought he was probably right. Barbie grabbed a green velvet cloak and threw it over Margot's shoulders. Hurst grabbed a baseball cap and pulled it down low, hiding his face, however, his nose still stuck out.

"Arabina you're going to need to transform your body to something more human looking, if she's about, she's going to recognise you a mile off," Damien said. There was no reply. "Arabina?" Arabina had moved further back and was deep in the shadows of the room, where the dim light faded to black. Even though Margot's vision wasn't brilliant in that light, she swore that she had seen Arabina stumble. Something wasn't right. However, Satan's daughter gave Damien a reply that sounded no different than usual.

"Give me a chance!" she said, before her body began to morph into another. Margot watched as her silhouette changed shape. Her red dress became small, less elaborate. Her body thinner, her legs longer. Margot had a feeling she was using it to her advantage. Arabina and her new body walked forward. Her skin was a lot whiter but looked like it'd had quite a few bottles of fake tan applied to it, giving her some colour. Her hair was still long and straight, but blonde and only a few shades darker than Margot's. Damien looked at her choice of clothes. Her denim skirt was well above her knees and her boat-necked top was exceedingly low. There was no change in her fiery eyes or beautiful face which was the only thing that identified her as the same person.

"Brilliant, we no longer look like intruders, just your pimps." Damien said. Margot stifled a laugh but she wasn't amused for long.

Arabina swayed. She took a few steps back to try and steady herself. The room was silent, their eyes fixed on Satan's daughter, watching her every move. Even Damien was concerned. That worried Margot, if *he* was unnerved, then something must be wrong.

"Arabina," he said, stepping forward. But Arabina didn't answer him. Although her eyes were fixed on his, she was looking right through him, almost as if he didn't exist. She was gazing longingly at nothing.

Everything happened in slow motion. Arabina collapsed; Damien hurried towards her and grabbed her shoulders as she fell to the floor. He knelt down, holding her in his arms.

"Arabina," his tone was frantic.

Margot could hear the panic in his voice. He turned to the rest of the group, who were motionless, apart from Hurst who was bounding in panic-stricken circles, imploring the rest of them to do something.

"She's losing energy," Damien said, regaining his collected tone. "This world is more powerful than I thought."

"Damien," Barbie said. "I think I saw human ships behind the stage. Maybe it would help if we took one?"

Damien's smile returned. "Brilliant."

*

Jade banged his fists against the stage door. Its metal surface rattled with each blow.

"Just – let – me – in!" He shouted, hitting it as hard as he could. On the other side of the stage, the carnival was nearing its end. Jade knew that in a few hours everyone would be gone and he would lose his chance. There were so many questions that crossed his mind, so many things he wanted to ask her. His fists were red and sore. Next to him, Reenie stood with her arms folded.

"She said her name was *Sarah*, it *wasn't* Margot," she said, irritated.

"You weren't *there* Reenie, I know what I saw," he said. Jade knew what he had seen, it was definitely her. Reenie's negative attitude planted the terrible seeds of doubt in his mind. What if it was a similar incident to what had happened on the cliff? Maybe he was losing his mind. Jade stopped and leaned his head against the door. He stood in silence.

"Jade," Reenie said. "You're gonna make yourself ill!"

She approached him, trying to pull him away.

"I know," his breathing was heavy, "I was just so sure."

"Come on."

The metal door opened. Jade, who hadn't moved from its side, was hit in the face once again, he fell backwards.

"I do apologise about that," a pale, blonde man stared down at him. Something in his voice, told Jade he wasn't sorry at all; he seemed quite the opposite. He walked past him without a second glance. Jade got to his feet, ready to protest but he saw the woman with her arms around the man's shoulders, using him as support. Reenie shot a confused glance at him as the couple moved to the gate leading to the staff's oxygen harbour. A thought struck Jade:

"Hey! Wait!" He ran after the man. Reenie cringed, but followed.

"Yes?" Damien snapped. He turned around, he glared at Jade.

"Ermm," Jade felt nervous, the man obviously wasn't happy to talk to him.

"I haven't got all day," Damien said.

"You, you got inside, you're staff. I need to get in." He tried to sound as tough as he could. Maybe if the man thought he was dangerous he may be more inclined to listen to him.

"In case you haven't noticed, I've got bigger issues to deal with." Damien gestured to Arabina. The woman didn't even look conscious. Her eyes looked tired and empty. The man had to keep a tight grip on her to stop her from collapsing. There was no way she could support herself.

"Alcohol abuse." Damien answered Jade's question before he'd asked it.

"What, where, where are we? It's so bright, am I dead?" She stood upright slowly, rubbing her eyes. "Where is she? Where's Margot?" She asked; a tone of anger in her voice.

Damien pinched Arabina hard.

Jade's eyes widened. "What about Margot?"

Reenie, who had stood back, put her hand on Jade's shoulder. He ignored her.

"Who's the guy with the goggles?" Arabina asked, still dazed.

"Jade," Reenie said. "Leave them be."

She took his hand and tried to move him back. He continued to ignore her.

"She said *Margot,*" he said.

"As in the circus," Damien said. The angrier Jade got, the more obstinate Damien grew, however, he also had a conscious Arabina to contend with and the situation was only getting worse. He nudged Arabina again, trying to give her the hint to be quiet.

"Ouch, Damien, will you stop hitting me?" She said.

Jade raised his eyebrows, but Reenie was begging him to leave. His dark eyes met Damien's cold glare. They stared at each other. It was no good, Jade thought, it was going nowhere, he was wasting his time.

"Right well if you don't mind, I'm going to try again," Jade said through gritted teeth.

"Be my guest," Damien eyed the open door.

"Goodbye," Damien said, he turned around, still clutching Arabina.

"Damien get off me, if you think for one moment..." Arabina said but Damien put his hand over her mouth and turned his back to Reenie and Jade, who were staring at him, bewildered.

"Well they were... strange." Jade muttered, staring at the couple.

*

Damien approached the oxygen harbour with caution. His hand was still over Arabina's mouth. She was struggling under his grip. He dreaded to think about the noise she was going to make when he took it away. Around him, small earth ships were parked up and hovering in the air. It had been a long time since he'd used one of those things. He looked up; it wasn't going to be easy. Damien looked around him; the street next to the park was empty. Everyone was still occupied with the carnival.

"Okay, clear," Damien called out. Around him, Barbie, Hurst and Margot appeared from the nearby trees. Damien smiled, his distraction had worked well. He had managed to keep Jade talking long enough so that everyone could sneak past him without being noticed.

"Get off me!" Arabina yelled, managing to escape Damien's grip. He put his hands down, annoyed and disgusted to have kept hold of her.

"What the hell is going on?" Arabina yelled. Yep, Margot sighed, the old Arabina was definitely back.

"Oh, your majesty!" Hurst dropped to his knees. "Are you hurt? Do you need some water?"

"I need a fucking explanation," she said, furious, then added: "Get off me, Hurst!"

She shook the Demon off. He was clinging to her leg as though scared she might collapse again. Barbie and Margot inspected the ships to decide which one would be the easiest to climb into from the surrounding trees. Possession of the key caused the vessel to float to the ground, allowing the passenger to step inside. It would be a lot trickier without the key. Then there was the alarm system to consider. Margot was an expert in those matters. She knew what systems were placed where and why. Her Dad's business had not been wasted on her.

"That one," she said. She could barely hear herself think over Arabina's shouting.

Barbie nodded, "The XRay R4, good choice, old, easy system." He croaked in response.

"Too old," Margot narrowed her eyes.

"She doesn't sound very happy," Barbie turned to look at Arabina.

Margot laughed at his monotone voice. 'Not very happy' seemed to be a bit of an understatement. She was screaming and stomping around like an unruly toddler.

"How's it looking, Barbie?" Damien turned his attention to the transvestite, deciding to ignore the tantrum.

"Not bad," Barbie replied. "Give us half an hour."

Damien frowned; he wasn't used to human measurement. "A while." Barbie corrected himself and Damien nodded.

"I'm going for a walk," Arabina said. Hurst put his hands up to protest but before he said anything she shouted: "Don't try and stop me, and no I'm not running away!"

"Whatever, go," Damien said, frustrated. His eyes were fixed on the ship.

Arabina, not happy with the lack of attention she was getting, stomped to the front of the building, out into the main part of the carnival. She smiled as she moved around the stalls. It felt strange to be one of them. She was used to being treated differently, worshipped, spotted or guarded wherever she went. It was nice to have freedom from that for a while. She walked further, past the carnival to the lake, away from the noise and commotion. It was peaceful; she wished she could stay for longer. Arabina stared down at the surface of the lake, the water rippled in the gentle wind that was picking up. She sat down beside it, under the shade of a tree. She took in a deep breath; she was finally starting to calm down. The anger inside her was starting to dissolve.

"Hey, are you okay?"

Arabina jumped as a pale woman stepped out from the shade of the trees a little further down from where she was sitting.

"Yeah," Arabina said in her abrupt manner. She continued to stare at the lake. She cringed; she still had her Latino accent. That wasn't going to add up.

"You shouldn't do that you know," the woman said and moved closer. "We're not supposed to go near the water."

Arabina stared at her. She was a pale girl, extremely pale. Her black hair and clothes accentuated her skin to a ghostly white. The woman wore heavy make-up, consisting of dark purple eye-shadow and dark lipstick to match. *Oh god*, Arabina thought: *it's like a shorter version of Barbie.*

"So," the woman said, sitting down and lighting a cigarette. "What's up?"

She offered the packet to Arabina, who accepted with a nod.

"Just thinking," Arabina said, enjoying being awkward. "Why are you here? Perving on me?"

"Maybe," the woman replied, smiling. Arabina's heart skipped a beat. She did *not* expect that; she had to keep her cool.

"Are you falling for all this bullshit?" The woman asked, looking around the park.

"I don't know what you're talking about." Arabina yawned and lay back on the grass. The woman leaned over her, her black hair falling to brush Arabina's face as she did so. Arabina smiled as their lips grew agonisingly close.

Just before they touched, the woman drew back. "The name's Lucy." She smiled then backed off and stood up. Arabina clenched her fists as the woman walked away. She tried to think up a name.

"Evie," she shouted, sitting up.

Lucy turned around. "Nice," she said. "Well, see you around, Evie."

"Maybe." Arabina smiled too. She lay back on the grass. Yep, she thought, she definitely still had it. A strange feeling bubbled in the pit of her stomach; that was no ordinary girl.

"And just what was that all about," a cold voice came from behind her. Arabina jumped. She sat up, to see Damien.

"God, how did you get here?" She jumped to her feet. "You scared the crap out of me."

"Yes well…" Damien said, but he wasn't looking at Arabina, his eyes were fixed on the girl, who was disappearing into the trees. "You ought to be more careful next time *Evie*."

They walked back in silence, Arabina, smiled to herself for the duration. For her, the journey was finally becoming a success.

*

Jade sat on the edge of the empty stage; his legs swinging, his spirit breaking. What was going on? He pulled out his Jonovicator once more. "Professor Jade Wilde, day three. Margot has been spotted, well at least I think so." He was perplexed.

There was a loud creak behind him as Reenie approached. Jade put the Jonovicator away and added: "Note to self, stop leaning on doors."

"No sign Jade," Reenie put her hands on her hips.

"I just don't understand it, Reenie," he said, staring out into the distance. "She was here, I *saw* her."

"Yeah, well, she ain't no more. God knows where she could be now." Reenie sighed: "Jade, even if Margot *is* here, I hate to say it but she hasn't come looking for you."

He looked up at her. Margot's sighting seemed to have brought her back to reality, away from her dream like state. Jade wondered how long it would last. He hated to admit it, but Reenie was right. His heart sank.

"Besides, even if she is here, she's probably just as lost as we are."

His expression changed. "Exactly. And I'm going to find her."

Chapter 10

Room 115

There was a storm blowing in the skies of hell. If that storm came to Earth, the media would have a field day, if not for the destruction. The storm had been picking up for days; it was almost time and she knew it. The envious clouds burnt the red sky, consuming every sign of light, twisting the air as they awaited more victims. They were no longer calm and beautiful as they had once been. They had turned black with hatred. Like the creatures that lived amongst them, they were immortal and were growing tired of Haszear's strange ways.

It was cold, colder than it had ever been before in the Under World. Ice and snow filled the castle grounds, giving it a palpably haunted atmosphere. It was a strange sight as the snowflakes fluttered down, diluting the deep red sky. The new snow seemed so out of place; unlike the lands it drifted upon, it was pure; for only the young are truly innocent, and as the snow fell to the ground, it changed, becoming tainted by its knowledge of the new earth, growing filthy from the soil, marred by memories of the sordid history.

However, nothing truly dies and nothing truly disappears. As the snow outside the castle window melted, Silvia knew it would soon return, ready to freeze her again. How could something so beautiful be so cold and fleeting? She watched it for a few seconds longer as it danced across the castle's highest tower before being consumed by the dark clouds. The tower was her favourite; she liked it because it was so isolated. It was away from *them*.

Not many had seen their true nature. She had. Only she and the true devil knew what it was like. Silvia shut the window. *Their stone eyes; their long mechanical wings* - she tried to distract herself from the thoughts, from the grotesque souls beneath the hoods. They would sit there forever, tortured for all eternity. But she wasn't like them, she wasn't the same. Silvia hadn't sinned, *she* wasn't sinning. They had threatened her, the angels. They were going to make her one of them, tear her soul from her body. That was the original plan, but Silvia was different, or at least she kept telling herself so. She wasn't a robot; she wasn't a copy, the same by-product as they were. She wasn't *evil*. The angels must have made a mistake even thinking about doing that to her. What did they know? They didn't know her at all. It wasn't a simple matter of good and evil, things were much greyer than that! In the game of right and wrong, it wasn't a case of one or the other. If anyone were to climb into her head and listen to her thoughts they would think her hypocritical in the extreme.

She knew the truth would surface soon. She was waiting to be exposed. And when that day came, she would be ready. Sometimes extremist ways were the only ways that worked. Someone had to act and she was the only angel who dared to carry out the task.

Silvia looked around the bare walls of the castle, trying to distract herself with something, but like her, the interior was desolate and empty. She sighed, running her fingers through her long white hair, as she continued to think. Maybe, just maybe, she could change.

There was a knock at the door.

"Your majesty," a dispassionate voice said. Somewhere outside, a servant stood, not daring to enter the room. "He's here."

Silvia sped down the spiral staircase of the gloomy castle. It felt darker than it had before. Change was afoot. She could feel it. She rushed through the rooms of the castle, down the stone corridors where the red carpet was the only element of colour. She tried to keep to the outermost of the building as much as possible, where the rooms that let in the most light through the tall, arched windows were, but not today.

The rooms in the castle were sparsely furnished; it was no home, it was operational, and Silvia was running to its core, the Great Hall. One of the biggest rooms in the castle, it was situated towards the front entrance of the building. There was a reason for its location.

Silvia stood at the very end of the hall leaning on a white chair that had scriptures and strange pictures carved into its ancient sides. All she had to do was wait; wait for him to show up so she could shout at him for letting her down. He was one of her most faithful servants - a deviant and clever servant in whom she could bestow almost all of her trust.

She paced the floor, her body glowing hot with rage when she thought of the day's events. She was no longer scared, but angry. Angry with the lack of attention they had paid. Angry with the fact, that that woman thought she could just slip right through her fingers. There was another knock.

"Enter." Her voice made the very walls of the castle shake. At the far end of the room, the two large wooden doors swung open. A Brontangus slid inside; its cold presence was enough to make any human shiver, even from the opposite side of the room. Silvia was not interested in the creature, but more in what lay behind it.

Metres away from the stone monster, a hooded figure followed. If one had just seen the figure passing in the street, many things about it would not be clear. People assume to know so many things about people upon first glance. Gender, looks, whether the being is human, it all remained a mystery to the innocent bystander... but Silvia knew exactly who it was. She had been waiting for him.

"You took your time," she said, turning away from him to face the window. The Brontangus approached the bench and attempted a half bow before gliding out of the room to leave the two of them alone.

"Good things are worth waiting for," he said. He didn't remove his hood, he didn't need to.

"Oh really?" Silvia tensed her hands. "Then can you please tell me why you haven't caught her yet?"

Her hair was floating higher above her head than normal. He put it down to anger, her face burned bright white and he was unable to see her features.

"Like I said, time," he replied.

"We haven't got *time*. For some reason she's not affected like the others." She took a deep breath to calm herself. "Just hours ago I got a report from one of your workers telling me that the water had been tainted by a human species and then I'm told *she* has disappeared again!"

She paused for a moment: "Margot Grant was meant to have arrived in Izsafar three human moons ago and not only has she turned up late but she's turned up on her own accord!" Silvia faced the hooded figure, she was taller than he was but it didn't make her any more intimidating. He stood stock still, waiting for her to speak again.

"Now tell me," Silvia continued. "Why would a human choose to come here?"

"You're not honestly insinuating..."

"Of course not!" It is far too early for that but, it is most curious. Something is going on and I have a feeling that *she* may be involved."

The man behind the hood knew she was no longer talking about Margot Grant. Silvia was talking about a much more powerful force: Satan's daughter.

"She wouldn't dare," he said.

"She'd be a fool to do so, but I know Arabina, she *is* a fool." Silvia turned away. "It was just a thought at first, but I can sense it. Something's different."

"What do you want my team to do?"

"*You* have proven your incompetence! I have already taken matters into my own hands, but nevertheless, even if this is a false alarm, Iszafar will still have to be searched."

"What have you done?" There was a hint of fear in his voice.

Silvia smiled before continuing her speech: "When was the last time Grant was spotted?"

"The Brontangus tell me, a man named Jade Wilde swears to have seen her at the Carnival yesterday. However, he is an eccentric and may be wrong. There were no other eyewitnesses who can confirm it was her. According to our information he was her ex-work colleague, but he hasn't been living on the Earth for years."

"Interesting… Bring him to me; I have a small job for Jade Wilde."

"My lady, a question."

Silvia nodded to give him the go ahead.

"If Arabina, does decide to step foot in Izsafar, surely she will die?"

"It is a strong possibility; it will most definitely weaken her. Anyway, that is not our main concern at the moment. Just make sure your people search Izsafar, the Brontangus too. See what you can find."

"And Margot Grant?"

"Oh, the wheels are already in motion, you can be sure of that."

*

Margot turned over, rubbing her eyes. She hadn't slept so long in a while, it was extremely satisfying. Opening her eyes gradually, she attempted to get up.

Margot screamed and fell off the sofa. Barbie's bare rear was inches away from her face. She knew it was a bad idea to go tops and tails, especially with somebody who had huge legs and was twice her height. Margot looked around the small room of the cramped ship. It was just like being at university all over again. The place was full of junk. Whoever owned it was pretty disgusting she thought. She stepped over the clutter that Hurst was sleeping in. Margot looked down the small corridor, leading to the bedroom. She knew Arabina was the daughter of the Underworld, but seriously, why did she get all the perks? At least two of them could have shared that bed, but no, she was stuck sleeping on the most distasteful orange sofa, in a room full of crap. She shivered to think of the amount of bacteria in the place. Putting on her sunglasses, she opened a metal door.

It wasn't as bright as it was on the South West coastline. There was so much greenery it blocked most of the sunlight out. Margot rather liked the North jungles of Izsafar. The trees stretched high into clear sky. There were no paths or roads and no sign of anyone for miles. The group were isolated. The lack of life forms unnerved Margot, everything was silent. Unlike Earth, there were no birds singing, no creatures rustling around on the jungle floor. Margot was disappointed to find no larger predators looking for animals to eat.

It wasn't nature, it was artificial.

She stepped onto the quiet ground, the dead leaves rustled beneath her feet. Silvia had tried so hard to create a perfect landscape and she had almost succeeded, it just wasn't *real*. It didn't have the same feeling that the nature of Earth had, what made the Earth so wonderful was the imperfection and entropy. The things that had gone wrong gave it character. Margot stood under the trees and she realised that it was Izsafar's greatest flaw. Perfection was a flaw.

There was a rustle nearby. She turned to her left to see Damien leaning on one of the trees, surrounded by shade. Margot glared at him.

"Morning," he said.

"Hey dude," Margot replied through gritted teeth as she placed a cigarette in her mouth. His eyebrows raised behind his aviator shades.

"Now, now Margot, you need to control that temper of yours."

"Temper! Oh, I'm sorry I must have completely over-reacted when you sucked my blood then kidnapped me." She stopped. "This isn't right. My friend Jade was back there. Why couldn't we bring him? I think you're doing this just because you don't like me!"

"Me? You're a child. Something like this was bound to happen, we are at war. Things have to be sacrificed. He is just a man."

Those words hit her hard. Jade just a man? *Just* a man? Damien didn't understand, he would never understand, he wasn't human. Margot realised it was the first time she had properly thought about Jade since leaving Bequia. She felt selfish. How could she forget about him? If only they had taken him with them.

Stop it. She told herself, trying to push the thoughts to the back of her mind. She was showing weakness again, maybe not to Damien, but to herself. *I'm not weak*, she thought. She had trained herself not to think about those things. Emotions got in the way, slowed people down, prevented true potential. The greatest of men had fallen into their clutches and been defeated. Margot Grant would not. *Damien's right*, the cold, inside voice said. He's just a man. There are many men in the world and many are completely worthless. But deep down inside, there was a dark, stabbing, empty pain that Jade had always been able to heal; that he would be able to heal if he'd been there. She couldn't help herself muttering under her breath.

"Well if you ask me, it's fucking unfair. Biggest fucking sacrifice ever."

Damien must have heard the comment because he turned round to her.

"You know *nothing* about real sacrifice or hard choices, *nothing*. This is the first unfair thing that's ever happened to you, so maybe you should just hold your tongue in your overly large-mouth for once."

Margot was stunned. She had a strong desire to punch him in the face, but thought better of it. How dare he judge her like that, he didn't know her. She looked directly into his cold, blue eyes, searching for some sense of humanity. Anything at all... There was nothing.

"Human, Damien," A croaky, monotone voice interrupted. Margot hadn't noticed Barbie heading towards them; she'd been much more occupied with the heated debate. "I think there's something you should see."

"Good or bad?" Margot asked.

"Knowing our luck, probably bad," he said and shrugged his shoulders.

"I guess it was worth a try," Margot sighed.

"Human, please be quiet now," Barbie said and lead them to a gap in the trees where the light beamed down, leaving an odd shaped circle. He didn't tread in it, instead he stayed back, hidden deep in the undergrowth.

"What is it?" Damien whispered, he sounded annoyed. Barbie didn't answer, just pointed a long pale finger high into the air. "Ahh, I see."

Large groups of Brontangus were swarming in the sky. It looked like the air was saturated with large, ugly birds. As the jungles of Izsafar were all on high ground, the group had a great view of the open sky and land for miles. From that distance, the skyscrapers and endless buildings looked like the only thing they could contain was ants.

"What are they doing? What are they holding? Are they?" Margot said.

The creatures' devil-like claws were clutching limp objects. The objects, had arms and legs, hearts and souls.

"This doesn't make any sense," Damien ignored her, a frown on his face as he stared.

"Morning muchachos!" Arabina shouted, jumping out of the spaceship. "It feels so good to be back in this body."

"SHHHHHHH!" The three of them turned on her.

"What?" To their annoyance, she yelled: "How dare you! How dare you talk to me like- oh, right." She glanced up at the sky.

Suddenly, the trees shook. The tremor was so violent that they struggled to stay upright.

"Drop to the floor!" Damien shouted. Nobody argued. Everyone, even Arabina, fell to the ground, lying as flat as they could. The sound of iron wings was alarming as the sky above them turned black. Margot turned her head, eager to see what was above them. She wished she hadn't.

Margot stared in awe as the Brontangus flew above her. She strained to hold her breath, fearing that if she allowed herself air, she'd use it only to scream. She looked at Damien, who was lying face up, also staring at the creatures. There was no fear in his eyes, just pure hatred. She didn't like that look, that look meant they had to be heroic. Because Jade was involved, it was a different ball game. She cared about the events of Izsafar just that little bit more. It also warmed her to the idea of teaming up with the rest of the group, or as she had started calling them, 'The Manhaden Rejects'. The last of the Brontangus passed overhead and she heard a collective sigh of relief.

"What do you think they're doing?" Arabina said, getting to her feet.

"I don't know, but they're definitely not starting a fraternity club!" Margot replied.

"They're doing their job," Barbie said, still staring at the sky. "They're bringing more humans to Izsafar. Yesterday, I heard a human say they had to get back before the curfew. That must be when they come out."

They turned to Barbie, dumbstruck at his statement.

"Back to the ship," Damien said.

There are times in a person's life when they must stand back and accept defeat, accepting the fact that there are forces out there more powerful than them. However, Arabina still chose to ignore it and continued with her plans of mass destruction.

"...then I'm gonna bring my armies over the border, find her base and destroy it. Oh we're gonna kick her white ass so bad."

"I can just imagine Arabina opening a can of 'whoop ass' on Silvia and how badly it would fail." Margot muttered to Barbie, whilst the devil's daughter continued her threats in the next room.

"A can of what?" Barbie asked, as he steered the ship through the trees. They had left the jungle and were returning to green fields and quaint meadows in the Northern Quarter of the West coast. Occasionally, Damien would leave the babbling Arabina and go to the cockpit, muttering directions to Barbie. Margot smiled, she liked knowing more about something than Damien, and what was even better; she knew it bothered him. Every time he slid into the room, she made sure to give him a smug look. Technology was her thing; and Margot knew what she was talking about.

Barbie made sure to keep the ship low, trying to attract the least attention possible. Damien instructed him to fly on the outskirts of the island, next to the sea. There were hardly any Brontangus there, and to Margot's surprise, when one did pass overhead, it ignored them. Either Barbie's 'quick and skilled flying' had fooled them or they were choosing to ignore the ship.

The temperature began to rise and the white sandy beaches were again on the horizon. Margot had a horrible feeling they were back where they had started in Izsafar. She was right. Meanwhile, Arabina decided to conjure up another ludicrous plan to undermine Silvia.

"... and after Damien has got her cornered, I'll finish her off and I don't mean sexually either." She gave an evil smile. "Barbie!" Arabina shouted to the front of the ship. "Where are we going now?"

"We're running away." Barbie replied.

"Yes we're – wait, we're what?" She burst into the cockpit. "Why are we back on the West Border of the Torgeerian mountain range? Turn us back now!"

Margot wasn't sure if she found Arabina amusing or scary at that point.

"Sorry Arabina," Barbie replied. "Me and Damien both agree-"

"Damien!" Arabina yelled so loud, it caused Barbie to lose his grip on the wheel. The ship jolted and Margot was thrown sideways. They were flying over South West Sea and Margot worried that had Barbie not grabbed the wheel in time, they would have been under it. They approached the mountain range, the pitch black sky revealed more of itself.

"Sorry," Barbie said, before putting them on the right course again. Damien made his way inside the cramped cockpit.

"Well, well, well," Arabina began.

"Kindly shut up a moment," Damien said, retaining his calm persona as he leaned over the transvestite's shoulder.

"Barbie," he said, he didn't look at him but instead stared out of the window. His eyes narrowed. "Please turn the ship around."

Barbie turned to face him. "First you tell me one thing then you tell me another, it is very confusing for me you know."

"Just do it, please."

"Dude, what the hell?" At first, Margot thought Damien was succumbing to his Queen's orders. But she knew him far too well; he never listened to any orders given by Arabina. She followed his eyes to see what he was staring at. Then she saw.

Coming towards them at full speed were two Brontangus.

"Oh dear," Barbie said, picking up on what was going on. The creatures were advancing upon the ship at an uncomfortable speed.

"Barbie, the ship, if you please." Damien nudged the transvestite, who was dumbstruck by the situation. Margot didn't know how the vampire could remain so calm. The ship swung round at Barbie's control. There was a loud bang that came from behind them. Margot and Damien went to check it out.

"Ouch," Hurst said, as he slid down the wall opposite the sofa. It was obvious he hadn't been prepared for the sharp turn. "Change of plan then?" he squeaked, clambering to his feet.

"This ship should think about investing in seatbelts." Margot said, suppressing her laughter.

She looked out one of the windows, hoping to catch a glimpse of where the Brontangus had got to. It was no good, the angle was too steep, she couldn't see a thing.

"Where are they?" Damien called to Barbie; he attempted to do the same as Margot. Both he and Margot returned into the cockpit.

"Gaining," Barbie's reply was short. They were speeding back towards the lands of Izsafar. Margot looked out of the rear window and gasped. She wished Barbie wouldn't understate everything. The Brontangus had gained on them so much that she was sure if they strained hard enough, they'd be able to touch the ship.

"Can't this thing go any faster?" Arabina asked.

"Not unless you wanna blow the engines all together," Margot replied. "We're pretty fucked to be fair."

"We're not fucked yet." Barbie said, turning to Margot. "And you're all very distracting, so if you don't mind-"

"BARBIE!" Arabina and Margot screamed together. They were metres away from colliding with another ship. Margot grabbed the wheel, jerking it so that the ship entered into a nose dive and missed the other vessel by inches.

"Pull it back, back, we're falling!" Arabina yelled. The ship was heading for the sea. The transvestite's hands were trembling. He had to react quickly, but the wheel didn't want to move.

"Barbie!" Arabina screamed. They were advancing fast upon the blue. Margot really hoped it floated.

"Got it." Barbie pulled the wheel back just in time.

"Where are the Brontangus?" Damien asked. Margot looked in the rear mirror. One was still following, but the other...

She saw large chunks of wreckage falling through the sky and crashing into the sea.

"Now he's falling behind, yes!" Arabina rejoiced. She paused. "Wait, what's happened?"

Outside, loud bangs could be heard.

"Oh dear," Barbie said, glancing at the mirror.

'Oh dear' didn't cover it. Margot gasped again as she looked out the window. High above them, the remnants of a huge explosion filled the air. They may have dodged the creatures, but the other ship hadn't been so lucky. They had collided, destroying each other in the process. The things falling through the air in all directions were parts of them. Although she wanted to, Margot couldn't look away; she stared in disbelief at the destruction. Then, she wasn't sure if she imaged it but for a split second she thought she saw something small and white rising from the Brontangus's stone body. Whatever it was, it wasn't solid. It shot high into the air before disappearing into the sky.

"Something's wrong." Damien said and he frowned as he stared out of the ship's front window. "That was another ship, another *human* ship."

"Yeah, and...?" Margot shrugged.

"Meaning that the Brontangus are out after curfew. They're looking for something."

There was another loud bang. However it came from their ship. Margot caught a glimpse of something red in the corner of her eye. She turned, not wanting to imagine what had just hit the ship. Blood streamed across the front window; and unfortunately it wasn't the only substance.

"Fuck," was the only word Margot was capable of producing. Right in front of her eyes, a human arm was stuck on the front window. She stifled the scream that she so desperately wanted to let out. Margot looked at the others, looking for their scared or horrified reactions. Nothing - no one batted an eyelid.

"Calm down Margot, violence is mandatory where we come from. Most of its residents take part in things like this every day." Damien sounded like a teacher talking to a child reluctant to dissect a frog. Margot could hear the smugness behind his voice. She wished he'd stop it.

"Well, look at that," Barbie said, in his usual mundane voice. "Now I'll have to put the windscreen wipers on."

A sense of normality descended, they had escaped yet again. Hurst slumped against the metallic sides.

"So, still want to run away?" Arabina taunted. "Looks like we're not going anywhere." Everyone, even Hurst, glared at her. Her smile faded. "Well then," she looked awkward.

The entire ship shuddered.

"What *now*?" Arabina yelled. Warning lights flashed red on the instrument panel. The ship began to lose altitude it plummeted through the air.

"There's a wing on the roof!" Hurst squeaked. Margot's eyes widened. She glanced up at the ceiling. It was beginning to cave in. Hurst screamed. The ship spun out of control.

There was a large splash as the Brontangus's wing fell into the sea. But it was too late, their ship was uncontrollable. They were going to crash.

Margot screamed as the ship entered an obscure loop-de-loop.

"I'm losing her," Barbie said, he sounded as mundane as ever. "The ship can't take that sort of weight. It's blown out the engines."

They were getting nearer to the white sandy beaches.

"Is there an eject button or something?" Damien sounded more impatient than scared.

"We may have accidently ermm… disconnected the safety features," Margot said, she screwed her eyes up and shrank in her seat. She could feel her voice rising as she spoke. Margot wasn't sure if she was more scared of Damien's wrath or crashing to her death.

"Well done, Margot, you have shown us that yet again you are another brilliant asset to the team," Damien said sarcastically.

The ship hurtled through the air. They had passed the beaches and were flying over the countryside.

"Damien, this is really no time for sarcasm!" Arabina yelled at him. Her body, like Hurst's was pressed against the ship's sides.

"We're gonna have to land this shit heap!" Margot shouted, diving directly behind Barbie. "Arabina," she screamed. "Do some magic shit. I dunno, make the ship try and keep balance. I'll land the fucker!" They stared at her. The ship jerked violently once again.

"Please," Margot said. For the first time in her life, she actually sounded serious. "Please Arabina, just trust me."

Suddenly, she felt the sides of the ship turn red hot. Margot shot a glance at Arabina. She had her eyes closed and both her hands placed flat on the ship's side. They were metres away from the ground, but they appeared to be a little steadier. Barbie removed his hands from the steering to allow Margot to take charge of the wheel.

"Brace yourselves!" She shouted, pulling it back. Damien looked to the ceiling. A loud crash filled the quiet meadows. It was all over.

Margot opened her eyes. Her hands were still clenched on the wheel. Her whole body was shaking. There was black hair in her mouth. She realised she was leaning right on top of Barbie, who was straining to take her full weight.

"We're alive!" She heard Hurst yell nearby.

"And we're going to be dead if you don't shut up and get out!" Arabina snapped.

Margot turned around. The ship was boiling hot and thick black smoke was pouring out. She needed to get outside; she could feel herself losing consciousness. Around her, the group scrambled towards the exit. Barbie grabbed her hand, making sure she went with him.

"Sunglasses!" She heard a cold voice call. Margot shoved her hands deep into her pockets, looking for the pair Damien had given her and awkwardly put them on her face. When she got to the door, Barbie was already helping Hurst and Arabina outside.

"Give me your arm," Damien's smooth voice whispered, close to her ear. She was reluctant but held it out, letting him put it over his shoulder as he helped her down. The ship was leaning so hard to one side, that it was hardly a jump to get to the ground below. Margot hated to admit it, even to herself, but she was grateful of Damien's support. Without him, she would have collapsed. However, it still didn't change the fact that she shrugged him off as soon as her feet touched the ground.

"Thanks for that," she said sarcastically, removing her arm from his shoulder. Margot couldn't help it, being stubborn was in her nature and she was too proud and headstrong to accept help; especially, when it came from him.

"Get back everyone," Damien said, "This is going to attract a lot of unwanted attention."

"It's also going to explode," Barbie added.

Damien slapped a pale hand on his forehead. He had been trying to keep them all calm.

"Trees," shouted Arabina, pointing to the undergrowth at the opposite end of the field. Margot looked at her; she was no longer in her tall, Latino form. She had once again transformed into the blonde woman from before. Damien and Barbie looked up at the sky and nodded. Arabina was right; they needed to get undercover and fast.

Without a further word or thought, they turned tail and ran from the wreckage. Margot looked behind her; the front of the ship was ablaze. She stared at the flames; as they danced in the air, accompanied by the thick black smoke, which pirouetted towards the open sky.

"Don't look back," Barbie said, as he limped alongside her. She nodded in agreement, her face bearing a determined frown, her eyes transfixed on their next destination.

They reached the trees and dived into the wild bushes. Margot was thankful that the small woodland area curved down into a large ditch, it was perfect for that kind of situation. Once everyone was hidden; Margot and Barbie pushed Hurst back up. He was the smallest and the only one able to fit underneath the bushes.

"Hey, careful," he squeaked, as Barbie placed a hand in an area he hadn't been aiming for.

"Oh. Sorry," he said. It was a good job Margot was at hand, as Hurst began sliding back down the bank. Arabina gave an evil laugh. Margot saw Damien glance at her and thought that just for a second she had seen a look of worry in his eyes.

There was the sound of beating wings coming from all directions. They fell silent.

"There's loads of them!" Hurst hissed, trying to be as quiet as possible. "They're gathering round the ship."

Loud screeches filled the air. Margot bit her lip ring hard and grabbed her ears, trying to muffle out the terrible sound. It was like nothing she had ever heard before. It was so painful, so ear piercing and unholy. It sounded like the end of the world, like every soul on Earth being destroyed. (She wasn't sure what that would sound like, but she imagined it would be close.) It was torture; it was like every creature in the world was crying out in pain.

And then it stopped. Everything began to feel normal as the last traces of the awful sound faded away.

"They were screeching," Hurst whispered.

"We- know," Arabina said through gritted teeth. "Just tell us the things we can't see, or hear."

Margot glanced at the rest; they weren't as affected as she had been. The screeching didn't bother them at all. Was there something wrong with her? She had been scared, since her trip to Haszear that she'd been getting weaker. What if she was?

"They're calling their master." Damien said with a pensive expression. Margot's eyes widened.

"She's not coming," Hurst said, squinting at the group of Brontangus. Margot wished she could see what was going on. The 'going into hiding' thing never worked out well for her. "They're just staring at the sky and she's not coming. Oh wait; someone's coming though, wait, I can't see who-" Hurst sounded like he was straining himself to try and see. "It could be the dark rider."

"The who?" Margot asked.

"SHHH!" Damien and Arabina hushed her together.

"No... it's definitely not him, they're wearing a white cloak, can't see their face, hood's still up," Hurst tried to push himself up higher. "He's talking to them, but I can't-" Arabina clicked her fingers and his large ears grew to twice their size. He looked very similar to one of Margot's old test subjects in an experiment at school. It wasn't her fault that she had managed to seriously deform his face, it was a complete accident. Of course it didn't help that he used to bully her.

Hurst turned around to shower his leader in compliments, "Oh, thank you my Queen."

"Hurst," Damien snapped.

"Yes right," he said, resuming his original position. "Search, he's saying something about a search. Oh wait I've got it, 'search the area thoroughly, leave no stone unturned, get- I can't work it out, something about head or a hive. Head or a hive, that doesn't even make sense?" Hurst had failed to notice no one was listening to him. They were looking anxiously at one another. Except Barbie, of course, his blank expression remained.

"They're coming for us," he croaked.

"Come on," Damien said, moving further into the trees. Barbie grabbed Hurst and they followed. Above them they could hear more wings beating overhead, moving towards the wreckage.

Damien stopped; the wooded area reached a steep slope. He glared down the bank. The trees dispersed further down the slope and at the very bottom the soil turned to sand.

"It leads to one of the beaches," he said and kept his voice low. "We're on the very outskirts. Hardly anyone inhabits this area."

Margot glanced down at the golden sands below, it reminded her of Bequia.

"We're doomed!" Hurst shouted. He dropped to his knees and began to pray.

"Not quite," Margot's face broke into a smile. She pointed beyond the trees.

In the distance, where the bay ended, high above the beach sat a huge building. Although it was a little way back from the cliff edge; the top of the hotel was visible. Damien grinned menacingly. "Well, we'd better get going then."

*

Jade sat on his bed, cleaning his purple goggles. He was immersed in complete darkness, only the smallest ray of light between the curtains was visible. It sent a few small rays across the floor in front of his feet. As usual, Jade was thinking too hard. It was a typical trait of his. He was a notorious over-analyser. His friends found it hilarious, but most people he met attributed it to him being crazy. It had never really bothered him until recently.

He didn't want people to think he was mad. He wanted, more than anything, for them to believe him. His opinion had been changed again. He knew more than he had ever done before. Why was he the only human there who remembered Earth? A lot of questions were still unanswered in his mind. He knew what to do. It wasn't going to be easy, but he was sure it was the right thing… or was it? He didn't know any more. What he did know, was that if he didn't get some proper company soon, he really was going to go mad. The only thing he'd been able to talk to openly was his Jonovicator. And although he may have created a female character in an application he'd designed called 'lonely friend'. (In case periods of long isolation arose.) The only thing it could say was 'How are you?' and 'Good'.

He picked it up, opened it out and flicked it to the application to see if it'd made any progress. It hadn't.

"I think I'm going crazy," he sighed at the holographic woman smiling back at him.

"Good," she replied in the most positive voice known to man.

"No, no it's not good really!" He said and tossed the Jonovocator aside.

"Oh Margot," he put his head in his hands, "I can't do this without you."

"Good!" The woman replied.

"It's not good!" He sighed, "I'm going to deactivate you."

"Good!"

Jade felt a sudden burst of anger, but before he could act on it he was distracted. The room was cold, *really* cold. He felt woozy. Jade's eyes widened, he had felt the same once before. *Oh no.* He grabbed onto the side of the bed, his body swayed and he fell to the floor. The room dissolved before his eyes. Everything was fading, until all he could see was black.

He sat in the darkness, wondering what was happening. Where was he? All was silent.

"OHHH GOD!"

Jade jumped so high in the air that he thought his head would crash into the ceiling. In the distance someone was screaming, crying out in pain. "OHH GOD PLEASE; PLEASE! NO MORE!"

Jade panicked. He wanted to help the person, but had no idea where they were. His head was running in circles. Jade tried to get to his feet, was unable to move, his body was a dead weight. He felt a strange sensation, warm liquid running down his neck, but when he was at last able to move, nothing was there.

Then there were other voices coming from all around him. At first, they were talking so loud he found it hard to hear what they were saying, but then, one became more prominent than the rest. He heard a female scream and scream until it was only her voice he could hear.

"I'm going to kill him. I'm going to kill him for what he's done!" She yelled. "Wait until the world knows what he's done! That back stabbing, evil…"

Her voice faded and other voices took over. They were crying so loud, he was scared his eardrums would burst. He wanted it to stop!

Jade opened his eyes. He was lying on the floor of his hotel room.

"What's happening to me?" He whispered, staring at his shaking hands. There was a loud banging sound coming from the door. Jade recoiled, screaming.

"Jade! Jade is everything alright?" Reenie called from the other side. He sighed, wiping his brow. It was only her, he thought, laughing at his nervous reaction.

"Jade," she said. "There was a girl screaming!"

"That would have been me," He said and cringed, banging his head hard on the floor.

"Oh," she said in a surprised tone. Jade scrambled to the door to open it before she walked away.

"Hey," he said, more confident and provocative than he'd hoped, he leaned on the door frame, panting. Reenie smiled at him suspiciously, raising her eyebrows as she accepted the wave of his hand to invite her to sit on the bed.

"Are you sure there's nothing you want to tell me?" she said, laughing at his posturing.

"No, no," he said, still a little out of breath.

"Look," she said. "I don't know what sort of shit you're into, but could you at least try and keep it down?"

Jade felt his cheeks flush bright red. He couldn't deny that he found Reenie really attractive. He had done since he'd met her. Nor could he deny the fact that if she asked him out or made with a move on him; he wouldn't decline.

In fact, ever since he fell into Izsafar, he thought their relationship had been going quite well. She had thought him to be relatively normal... although after the evening's events she thought he had some bizarre fetish that he liked to carry out on himself. Jade sighed, he couldn't win.

"No! It's not like *that*, not that I'm boring when it comes to- oh never mind, I'm going for a walk," he said. He made his way to the door and grabbed his goggles.

"Oh, okay then," he heard her call after him. "But open your bloody curtains for once!"

Jade wasn't listening; he dashed down the blue corridor and got into the nearest lift, pressing the button for ground floor.

Jade rushed into the reception, not quite sure where he was going. He was still in shock, still panicking. The room was so bright. Light streamed in through the windows. He shielded his eyes, before putting his goggles on. Jade cringed; he had never liked the sunlight.

He sighed, that was much better. He looked towards the pool through the large windows on the right. Something caught his eye; at the reception desk were more people. Another family, he suspected. It was a strange sight to see family check in. Most people arrived alone. It must be a really popular one, he thought, trying to get a good look without being too obvious. It was no good, the couple had turned away. All that stood out about them was their bright blonde hair. For a moment, he thought one of them had been Margot. Then there was the small child. But he was fully covered up and wearing a large baseball cap over his face.

"Excuse me." A deep, croaky voice came from nearby. Jade turned round, to see a large hotel trolley at his feet. He moved out of the way.

"Oh sorry- sir, erm sir- lady, yes lady." He said, giving the hotel maid a double-take. For the first time in a long time, he had to look up to meet their eye level. However, the height of the person wasn't what perplexed Jade, or the fact that he'd never seen a maid in the building, it was more what gender they were. He stared long and hard as the maid moved past him and down the corridor he had just come from; still pushing the enormous trolley.

Jade raised his eyebrows. Well that was… strange. He didn't question it and continued to pace round the hotel trying to think of an answer. When nothing came, Jade decided it was time to return to his room.

"Am I going insane?" He sighed and ran his hands through his dreadlocks as he moved up one of the empty corridors.

"No, you twat."

Jade jumped. He turned around, looking for the person that had replied to him. It was female, he was sure it was female. The corridor was empty. *No, no it couldn't be.* Right in front of him was the trolley the strange maid had been pushing earlier. He took a step closer to it, gingerly holding out his hand.

"Hello?" He said, getting on his knees to inspect it further. "Hello? Can you hear me?"

"Oh, because that looks *perfectly* sane Jade Wilde." A sarcastic voice answered him.

Jade stopped what he was doing. The voice hadn't come from the trolley. Still on his hands and knees, he turned to look behind him… and there she stood. Jade's face broke into a wide grin.

Her black clothes were torn, her face bruised and hair a complete mess. She was covered in dust and dirt, but he didn't care. She was here.

"Margot?" He said, looking up at the woman who stood over him. "But where- how… it's really you?"

"Yes, Jade," she said pulling him to his feet. "It's really me." Jade didn't say a thing; he just threw his arms around her. Margot, was not ready for that sort of greeting, was almost knocked backwards.

"I thought you were dead, I thought you were dead!" He said, squeezing her hard.

"Jade, dude! Circulation, man! Chill!" She said, trying to back away. He finally pulled away and was downcast by her comment.

"It's good to see you too, man," she said, trying to hide the fact that if given the chance, she'd still be hugging him.

"What are you-"

"No time for questions," she said in a whisper. "Dangerous forces about."

"Well, where did you come from? When I looked no one was-"

Margot pointed to the left, a door was wide open. It was the utility room if the abundance of cleaning products was any clue. Jade felt like slapping himself in the face, it seemed so obvious, and there he was, talking to trolleys.

"Right, my room then," he said, in a serious tone. Jade glanced down the corridor. It was empty. Most of the guests were outside enjoying the weather. He turned and made his way down the corridor.

"Wait! I'm not on my own," Margot hissed, beckoning him to stop. She waited for a moment, stared into the cleaner's room and stage-whispered: "Barbie! Get out here!"

Jade expected to see a beautiful young woman emerge, he recoiled as the tall transvestite from earlier stuck his head round the door.

"Ahh," Jade said with a nervous smile. "Hello again."

They didn't waste any more time; Jade rushed them through endless corridors, up staircases and away from the lifts. Normally the journey to his room was a short one but he didn't want to risk being seen by anybody. Margot was in danger and if they were caught... he didn't want to think about the consequences.

"Right," Jade said at last. "This is my room, number one, one, five."

The door was ajar. Reenie always shut it on her way out. Something wasn't right. Margot raised her eyebrows.

"Keep quiet, everyone," Jade whispered. "I'll go first."

He pushed the door wide open and crept inside. Margot followed. Jade bent his knees, trying to stay low to the ground which, when you're tall, is difficult. Barbie didn't even attempt it and stood outside the door.

Jade's gaze flicked around the dark room, searching the shadows. Margot tapped him on the back, pointing to the bathroom. The light was on. People were speaking in hushed voices. Jade's eyes widened. *Who was in his room?* Next to him Margot took a deep breath.

"What," he mouthed.

Margot pointed to the bed. If they hadn't been in that situation the gesture would've seemed rather sexual. Margot's gesture confirmed Jade's worse fears.

On the opposite side of the room, a figure was sitting on the bed, staring at the unopened curtains. Margot wished she could see who it was, but Jade's room was so dark, it was hard to see anything.

"On the count of three," Jade mouthed, giving Margot the thumbs up. It was at that point, she realised what was going on. Jade, however, didn't.

"No!" She mouthed in return, waving her arms about.

"Now?" He mouthed back. "Okay!"

Before she could grab him it was too late.

Jade charged at the figure. He ran and dived on the bed. It all seemed to be going well until the figure turned and flipped Jade so violently over its shoulder that Margot feared he would crash through the floor. She cringed as he hit the floor with a bang. *This is going to get messy.* Margot prepared herself. She raised her hand, getting ready to strike. Any excuse to hit the man and she'd take it. She'd just pretend she was as clueless as her best friend.

"That won't be necessary, Margot," a smooth, cold voice spoke to her.

"How does he know your name?" There was fear in Jade's voice. "Strike Margot, whilst you can!"

But Margot wasn't going to do anything of the sort.

"You are a terrible lip–reader, Jade Wilde," the figure looked down at him.

"Hi Damien," Margot said, she flicked the light switch.

"You!" Jade spat as he writhed in pain on the floor. He glared at Damien, pure hatred in his eyes.

"Interesting place you've got here," Damien said. He took a wander around the room, there were objects slung over the chair, covering the table and over the majority of the floor space. Jade didn't reply. He watched the vampire and loathed every step he took.

Barbie rushed inside and closed the door behind him. "I look a complete mess, human," he said to Margot. He was standing in front of Jade's dressing table mirror.

"Me too," Margot sighed, she realised what an absolute state she looked. Since embarking on the journey, her looks had been the last thing on her mind. But because she was surrounded by other humans - other *normal* humans - in an everyday environment, she felt the pressure of social conventions once again. Her hair stuck out in all directions and her face wasn't half as pale as it usually was, it was smeared with dirt and grime. Margot sighed again. She looked at the others; they were all in the same state. Barbie's long black hair draped over his face, he looked worn out, whilst Damien's clothes were filthy.

Jade tapped his fingers; he was still on the floor. "Margot who are these– ARGHH!" He screamed as a small red man crawled from underneath the bed.

"It is rather messy in here," Hurst said, dusting himself down then lying on a pile of clothes.

"Indeed," Damien said.

Jade, was embarrassed and he got to his feet.

"Oh, don't be offended dude," Margot said. "Hurst loves messy shit; it's like a demon trait or something."

But Jade wasn't listening. If he had been, he would have jumped at the word 'Demon.' Instead, he scurried around the room, trying to pick up and salvage anything he could for fear they might sift through his things. He was right.

"I never understood why your race needed so many items; especially so much pointless technology." Damien was unimpressed. He picked up bits and pieces from the dresser. His gaze shifted to a small round object, he picked it up, examining it closely with a suspicion.

"I'll take that, thank you." Jade said, snatching the Jonovicator from Damien's grasp. It added to the growing pile of stuff in his arms. "It is, after all, just another pointless object."

Hurst and Barbie shared a different attitude, they skipped around Jade's room, impressed (as impressed as Barbie could be, he used many monotone 'wow's) with all the possessions that Jade had.

"Barbie, what's this?" Hurst asked. He held up a remote control.

"That turns on the picture box and changes the channels," Barbie said, gesturing to Jade's television.

"Wow! And what are these?" Hurst squeaked in reply. He moved to a pile of clothes that Jade hadn't yet managed to pick up. Hurst stretched a pair of boxers in his hands.

"I'll take those, if you don't mind," Jade said.

Margot started laughing. "Jade, chill, we have bigger things to worry about than your dirty underwear! Now if you'll just sit down, I'll explain."

The sound of the shower turning on caught their attention. Jade sighed, he had forgotten about the light in the bathroom.

"What now?" He said, rushing to the door.

"I wouldn't-" Damien began to warn him, but it was too late.

There was a scream, lots of apologies and an array of Spanish expletives. Margot's eyes widened as the lights began to flicker.

"Mistress, are you okay?" Hurst asked, as he also ran through the bathroom door.

"You can get out as well!" Arabina screamed. There was a loud bang, and Hurst and Jade shot out of the bathroom. Margot and Damien glanced at each other, hiding their smiles as Jade collapsed.

"Right, okay, everyone stop! Stop! Margot, who are these people? Why do they keep using the word 'human' and how the hell do they know my name?"

Hurst took in a short breath on the word 'hell'. Damien smirked and folded his arms as he sat on the bed. Margot could feel him watching her every expression. She was under pressure, wondering if Jade had lived up to the vampire's expectations.

"Okay Jade, just shut up and listen…"

With help from the others, Margot told Jade her experiences. She told him of Izsafar and Silvia, and about the danger they were in. He said nothing; he sat on the end of the bed, his head in his hands.

"So, let me get this straight," he said. It was taking every ounce of his brain to retain everything he had just heard. "You broke into Izsafar?"

"Yes."

"Sabotaged the carnival?"

"Yes… well technically it wasn't me-"

"Stole a ship?"

"Yes."

"Blew up an angel?"

"Brontangus! And yes, well okay that wasn't really our fault-"

And now you're on the run?"

"Yes exactly!"

"Margot… *Are you crazy?*"

"Well if you say it like that it sounds bad." Margot said. "But if you-"

"How did you guys even find me?" He said, he rubbed his temples and stared at the floor. Margot felt guilty; once again she had dragged him into her own problems.

"I assure you, it wasn't deliberate," Damien said in his usual cold manner. "When I saw you earlier in the reception, I decided to say we were relatives. The hotel was full, it was our only option."

Jade felt insignificant. He thought Margot had come looking for him. But it was pure coincidence that she happened to stumble upon his whereabouts. He was hurt, offended. Jade had risked everything to find her. He could have stayed on the Earth and started again, but *no*; he was once again the subject of another crazy scheme created by Margot Grant.

"No it's okay, I get it," he said. He went to the window. "I understand how this works now. Of course I'll help. I am after all just a pawn in all of this."

"Jade, come on man." Margot said. She got up and went to his side.

He turned away, shrugging her off. "It's always about Margot Grant. She's always in the spotlight, she knows what's happening and doesn't care if the rest of us are left to suffer alone in the dark." Jade's voice broke a little with emotion.

"Jade," Margot pleaded. "It wasn't like that."

"Get the popcorn, Barbie, Arabina quick, you're missing it," Damien mocked as Arabina walked out of the bathroom, a towel covering her body. Something told Margot that Damien was really enjoying the display of human emotion.

"It doesn't take long to replace me, does it?" Jade said, glaring at Damien, who was still smirking. "Is that all I am to you? *Disposable*. Someone you can toss aside and pick up when you need them again?"

Margot cringed. For the first time, she tried to empathise with Jade. It must look pretty bad from where he was standing.

"Look," she said in a soothing tone. "Jade please listen to me, it's been really hard, okay dude? If you'll just-"

There was a knock on the door.

"Oi, Jade you in there?" Reenie called. "I'm worried about you!"

"Hide," Damien said quietly. Margot's heart leapt, *Reenie was ok*. She wanted to meet her, talk to her again, but Damien beckoned her under the bed along with him.

"But I know her!" Margot hissed.

"It doesn't matter," he whispered. "We can't trust anyone. We must keep the people who know about us to the absolute minimum."

"One moment," Jade said. Barbie somehow managed to squeeze himself into the wardrobe, whilst Hurst buried himself in the pile of clothes that Jade had just attempted to clear away. Arabina rushed back into the bathroom and slammed the door.

"So, what's happening?" Reenie asked, bouncing happily into the room.

"Not much, just tidying," Jade said kicking the pile of clothes Hurst was buried under. There was the sound of a faint 'ouch'. Reenie glared at the pile for a moment but chose to ignore it.

"Don't, don't sit over there," Jade said, as Reenie made her way to the small chair next to the wardrobe.

"Okay," she said and gave a little laugh. "So, where do you want me?"

Jade could think of so many positions, as he sat her on the edge of his bed. She smiled at him, her many piercings sparkling in the unnatural light.

"So glad you've finally heard of the term 'light switch'," she said and smiled up at him. Jade returned it with one of his own. He couldn't help glancing down at her body. Her bare arms, covered in vibrant tattoos. She was wearing tight fitting black clothes again. They suited her slim figure. Jade couldn't help himself in moving closer to her. "I'm worried about you," she put her hand on his leg. Margot was feeling extremely awkward. Hers and Damien's heads were mere inches away. Margot listened, was Reenie trying to come on to Jade? She was angry. So angry that she wanted to burst through the bed and tear the room to pieces.

"Look, I'm okay, everything is perfectly fine," he said, looking about the room just to check.

"Jade?" Reenie said. Margot could see her legs moving closer to his.

"I think I'm going to vomit," Margot whispered to Damien.

Reenie leaned closer. Jade was beginning to feel awkward too. He'd been waiting for a moment like it ever since he'd met her but at that moment he wished for anything but. However, something seemed to be distracting Reenie, she pulled away, staring at the bathroom door.

He followed her eyes, swearing under his breath. Water was streaming from under the door and soaking the carpeted floor.

"Ahh," he began, trying to think of an explanation. His mind was blank. Reenie approached the door, pausing just outside. Suddenly it sprung open and Arabina stepped into the room, still in her blonde human form.

"Who is this?" Reenie said; her hands on her hips. Margot had to suppress her laughter.

"Hi, I'm Evie, I live up the hall," Arabina said, trying to hide her Spanish accent. It wasn't working, she sounded like a bad English impersonator. "Thanks for the shower, Jade."

Reenie raised her eyebrows.

"Jade just let me use his as mine is broken, but now erm… I think his is broken too." She looked down at the flood. Reenie folded her arms, she wasn't impressed.

"Glad you enjoyed it," Jade said.

There was a long pause; a long, awkward pause. Normally having two girls in his room would feel a bit like Christmas, but not under the circumstances.

"Well," Arabina said, unsure of what to do next. It was clear Reenie was waiting for her to leave and it would seem suspicious if she didn't. "I'll be going then." She said, moving to the end of the room. Margot felt Damien jolt. It was dangerous for her to leave and he knew it.

"Right then, bye," Jade said. He closed the door behind her. It wasn't long before Reenie took her leave. Jade sat on the bed and sighed, wiping the new sweat from his brow. Barbie fell from the wardrobe, whilst the others climbed out of their hiding places.

"We have to go after her," Damien was serious. Margot could see he was trying hard to keep his calm persona. "Jade Wilde, you are one of the biggest idiots I've ever met."

"I didn't ask for this!" Jade raised his voice.

"Enough," Barbie said. "That is not going to help anyone."

Jade and Damien glared at each other. Margot felt almost relieved that it wasn't her and the vampire for a change.

"You're right I'm, I'm sorry," Jade said. He lowered his voice and tried to calm himself down. Neither he nor Damien broke their glare.

"I've, I've got a plan. I'll go find her and bring help." He opened the door. "Wait here."

"Jade, hurry back," Margot called after him. "I'm sorry."

"I'm sorry too, Margot," Jade said, closing the door. He pulled out a key, and made sure it was locked. "I don't want to do this, but, she's right, you've gone too far this time."

Chapter 11

The Hotel Massacre

"He's been gone for too long," Damien said. He stood in front of the window, arms folded. It was a pointless thing to do; the curtains hadn't been opened since they'd arrived. But he stood motionless for half an hour, as though waiting for something extraordinary to happen. "I'm going to go and find Arabina."

"No! He'll come back," Margot said. She sat on the bed staring at her hands. Hurst mimicked her. His were trembling. He didn't speak. Margot had a feeling he was too worried to move.

Barbie on the other hand, was oblivious. He sat at Jade's dresser, mumbling to himself and re-applying his make-up. Margot went over to him; he didn't acknowledge her.

"Barbie?" Margot leaned on the back of his chair; watching him as he applied powder to his pale cheeks. She smiled, she had been right. He looked very beautiful. "Why don't you try something different for a change? You know dude, like, green might-"

"No." He said. "No, it has to be like this. It's how she-"

He looked up, there was shouting outside.

"What is it?" Margot said. She lowered her voice. Her fists clenched, preparing for danger. Without warning, Damien threw open the curtains. The others recoiled, covering their eyes. Margot had forgotten how bright it was outside, she felt like a bat that had dwelt too long in its cave.

"We're safe behind the glass," he said, turning to them. "Ahh..."

"What's wrong?" Margot asked, approaching the window, but Damien quickly pulled the curtains shut. He rushed around the room, picking up odd bits and pieces.

"Okay everyone; grab what you can, we're leaving." He added under his breath: "That dirty little rat."

Margot had a feeling she knew who he was talking about. She pulled back the edge of one of the curtains, it was worse than she imagined.

Hundreds of Brontangus surrounded the hotel, screeching. They swarmed and gathered like storm clouds. Margot looked down at the guests by the pool, who, instead of lounging care-free, were screaming in terror, trying to find cover from the ungodly creatures that surrounded them. Her focus shifted to the fields and beaches beyond the hotel. She uttered expletives under her breath as she watched in disbelief. She saw in the distance, a myriad of white-hooded figures advanced on the hotel. They were countless in number. Margot had no idea who they were, but she had a feeling they were on the side of the creatures.

She met Damien's cold gaze. They stared at each other; they didn't have a chance.

"What's all the- ARGH!" Hurst was screaming, he had opened the curtains and shut them again in one movement. "Damien! White riders! Silvia's army!"

Damien kept his eyes fixed on Margot. They were trapped. Even if they did escape the hotel, what then? They'd just have to keep on running. The mission was hopeless.

A voice called out on the intercom.

"Could we ask that all residents please return to their rooms calmly and safely whilst we carry out a thorough search of the hotel, for your safety. Do not panic. You are not in any danger. We repeat; please do not panic."

"Don't panic?!" Hurst squeaked. "DON'T PANIC. We've been ratted out! It's *her* fault. She said we could trust him!" Hurst pointed a long red finger at Margot

Barbie glanced at Hurst.

"My fault? My fucking fault?" Margot' rage was rising "Without my judgement, we'd have already been caught!"

"Enough!" Damien snapped. "There will be time for blame later; right now I suggest someone comes up with a plan - and quickly."

He went to the door and twisted the handle. "It's locked."

*

Arabina skipped down the corridor, laughing to herself as she explored the hotel. She loved causing chaos, especially for humans. Upsetting that girl, ruining Jade's chance of a potential relationship, it had given her a much needed boost. She felt alive again. After all, she couldn't help it; it was hereditary, in her blood.

The sound of doors opening from the opposite end of the corridor echoed. A woman bolted past her, her curly brown hair bounced in front of her red face. She was breathing heavily, just managing to retain enough air to scream "Run!" Arabina stared as the woman, drenched in sweat, ran to the next staircase.

"Stupid, stupid, stupid," she laughed. "There's a lift," she called after the woman, "You don't have to run! You -"

Arabina listened. There was screaming coming from outside. *What was going on?* Before she had time to question the events; she heard a faint rumbling from the staircase. The hotel vibrated. The screams increased in volume. She stood in the middle of the corridor, waiting. A calm, female voice belonging to the lift spoke: "Floor 6. Doors opening." *Ping.*

A crowd burst from the lift. Stairway doors swung open and hordes of frantic people tried to cram themselves through the doors at the same time. Arabina was pushed and shoved along as humans fled. People were beginning to trample one another. The crowds grew to such density that weaker individuals were pressed down to the floor with little hope of surfacing again. Unsure what was going on, Arabina forced her way through the crowds to the end of the corridor. She pressed her face against the large window at the end.

"Oh shit."

For the first time since arriving, she panicked. She also understood why it was so difficult for people to find their way about the hotel. Wherever she had been in the building, it all looked the same. Every corridor had the same blue patterned carpet. Every room had the same essential furnishings. There were no distinguishing features. There were no paintings on the walls nor did many guests own personal items. Individuality had been wiped out of every inch of the surroundings. She was lost.

Arabina wasn't sure how many times she'd been up and down in the lifts, nor how many different corridors she'd walked along. She didn't know the number of Jade's room. Something was sucking the life out of her, making her forget. She felt like she didn't want to be found at least, not by Damien.

She climbed more stairs. The next floor was full of more screaming, frantic people and the same sense of panic. She was dizzy and nauseous but continued to run, despite it. She was losing power, being drained of energy. Arabina came to a gradual stop, clinging to a wall to steady herself as humans flurried by her. She watched amidst the chaos. She staggered back and forth, barely keeping her feet. Her head was spinning and she could hear a strange buzzing. Then, someone grabbed her.

Arabina didn't have time to comprehend what was happening as she was dragged forward and pulled into a room.

"They'll be coming soon," said the figure, placing Arabina on the bed before checking around the room. Arabina shook her head, trying to figure out what had happened. She was in yet another hotel room. The question was; whose? At first, she thought it was Jade's, but as the room came into focus, she noticed distinct differences. Instead of clothes and technical items flung in every corner, the room was spotless. The layout was identical, though bare of any feeling of homeliness. The beige bed Arabina sat on was made and looked as though she was the first person that had ever lain upon it. The tables were bare; the wardrobe was open, but empty. There were no personal belongings in sight. The figure stood by the door, peering out into the hallway.

"I think we're okay," she said, turning back to Arabina.

"Lucy?" She could just about make out the woman's ghostly white skin in the darkness. Her long black hair flowed behind her; however it looked a little more dishevelled.

"Hello," her red lips curved in a smile.

Arabina sat up. It was a strange coincidence. However, to say she was unhappy about it would be a lie.

"Lucy, what are you doing here?" Arabina asked, cringing at her own accent.

"Living here," the other woman replied, as though it was obvious.

Arabina took a second glance around the room. *That's debatable.*

The mystery of Lucy's character intrigued her. It made Lucy more attractive. Arabina could feel her human pulse racing as she moved towards her. She didn't want to leave…

"So," Lucy began.

Arabina shook her head, she had to leave. Being helped by the human was embarrassing enough, but not finding the rest of her comrades was worse. If she didn't get back to them, she feared she would be in deep trouble. She got up to leave.

"Well thanks," Arabina said, desperately trying to hide her accent. "I'm gonna leave now, it seems a lot less loco outside."

She pulled the door open, but Lucy slammed it shut again and leaned against it.

"No." She said in a stern voice. "Stay here." It was a command, not an offer.

It was getting harder for Arabina to stay in character. She hated being told what to do, especially by a human. She felt her anger building. Arabina knew she could so easily kill Lucy or just use brute force to open the door. She could feel her powers returning to her, she was regaining her strength by the second. Arabina looked down; if she wasn't careful her eyes were going to start glowing red. It would be so easy, so easy just to toss her aside.

"You're a relative?"

"What?" The question knocked Arabina back.

"Of Professor Wilde, I saw you and your family check in earlier."

Arabina's spirits dropped. For some reason, she wanted to tell her the truth… but she wouldn't.

"So what if I am?" Her reply was cold.

"They're coming for him," Lucy lowered her voice. "I heard them downstairs."

Lucy moved closer: "Evie, they're going to his room. I don't know why. They're looking for people."

Their faces were inches apart. Lucy's soft voice was tantalising in Arabina's ears. Her eyes widened. The others were in danger.

*

"Kick it, Barbie! Come on dude, get that stiletto in there!" Margot shouted, trying to jeer him on. Barbie ran at the door, hoping that somehow it might just give way.

"It's no good," Damien said. "These doors will have enchantments on them." He sat on the bed, staring at the wall. Margot looked around for some way out, anything that would help them, she was frustrated.

"Nothing, nothing, nothing!" She yelled, throwing objects everywhere.

"Calm down, Margot," Damien said. "There is just no way out. That's that."

"You give up way too easily, man," Margot said. She ripped clothes out of Jade's drawers and tossed them behind her. On reaching the last shirt, she paused in mid-fling when she found a collection of small, orange balls. They were only a little bigger than marbles. They had been left to roll around the bottom of the drawer.

"What the fuck?" She muttered to herself, picking one up and examining it closer. "Why the hell does Jade have a draw full of mini bath bombs?" She shrugged, and resumed exploring the drawer.

A loud bang behind her made Margot turn around to look. Hurst had climbed up Barbie's back in terror, even Damien had jumped. The wall adjacent to Barbie contained a small smoking hole. Margot shot Damien a look of disbelief. "Did I do that?!"

They surrounded the drawer, each picking up the strange balls to throw them at the wall. They demolished it piece by piece until they had made a Hurst-sized hole.

"That'll do," said Damien, wafting his hand through the smoke. It was so thick Margot could barely see where his voice was coming from. "Hurst first."

The Demon stepped through the hole without hesitation.

"Right, Margot, you next"

"Let me in, let me in!" Hurst screamed, scrambling back through the hole. He leapt over the bed and quivered in the corner of the room.

"What?" Damien snapped.

"White Rider! In the hallway!" Hurst hissed.

Margot and Damien looked at each other with trepidation. A strange, glowing light had appeared on the other side. Through the smoke, they could see the bottom of a luminescent white robe. It was stationary, waiting, floating.

"Damien?" Margot whispered. She could hear the fear in her own voice.

"Get back!" Damien shouted, grabbing her around the waist and thrusting her back onto the bed with him. The wall with the hole crumbled before them and a blinding light flooded the room. The figure made its way over to them, Margot gritted her teeth. *This is it.*

Without warning, Damien charged at the White Rider; teeth bared. He bit hard into its side. It happened so quickly that Margot only saw brisk, white flashes in the darkness. She grabbed a handful of orange balls from the drawer and threw them at the hooded creature. Hurst quivered, rocking back and forth with his hands over his ears as the balls exploded above his head.

It was hard to tell if Damien was winning or losing. She was scared her intervention had made matters worse. The two fighters crashed about the room, making a tremendous noise as they laid into one another. The wardrobe collapsed, the mirror smashed, the bed was in pieces. An almighty crash shook the room as Damien was hurled against the wall. His feet lifted off the ground as a white hand gripped his throat. He was out of breath, choking. Margot was transfixed; with no clue how to help or what to do. She looked at Damien's face. *Run. Run!* He mouthed to her in desperation but in her frenzied state, there was no way she was going to do that.

"Sorry about this," said Barbie, hitting the figure hard over the head with a chair. The chair fell to pieces around Damien and the White Rider. It was dazed for a few seconds, but didn't loosen its grip. Watching Barbie had given Margot an idea.

The White Rider turned on the transvestite, lashing out at him with its free arm. Barbie's long arms grappled with it when a vase flew across the room, hitting the creature straight in the face.

"Hey, dick! Over here!" Margot shouted. She threw every object she could find. Hurst crawled under the broken remnants of the bed, passing her pieces of it. The group's efforts became too much for the creature, with Damien still in its grasp, it began to spin. Margot, Barbie and Hurst shielded their eyes from the dazzling light that emanated from the spinning creature.

"Sunglasses!" Margot ordered. They obeyed. It didn't help much, but it was a start. "Keep attacking!" Margot yelled. The figure turned towards her. It stopped spinning, but had begun to release bursts of white light from beneath its cloak. Margot dodged them; she rolled back and forth beside the bed. She was corned, and the figure loomed over her. There really was no way out.

Margot braced herself. The creature was no longer interested in Damien, it let him go and he collapsed in a heap on the floor. Margot stared at his motionless figure and felt a deep rage flaring inside her. Two hard hands appeared from behind the Rider and grabbed hold of its neck. Barbie was taller than the creature; he lifted it off the ground. It was getting weaker in his strong grip and the white light dimmed.

There was a loud crack and the creature dropped lifeless next to Damien. Margot looked at Hurst; he stood beside her and Barbie, looking down at the two bodies.

For one horrible moment, no one moved. Margot stared at Barbie, her face full of dread.

"Is he?" She said, looking down at Damien's limp body.

Barbie shrugged.

"Barbie," Margot voice's was just higher than a whisper as she kicked the hooded figure, "You, you broke its neck."

"What do we do now?" Hurst asked. The sound of screaming started up again, outside the room. It was a complete contrast to the room, which emanated nothing but silence. Death gave an eerie atmosphere, but Margot felt calm, and then remembered Damien on the floor.

She looked to his body and flinched as he coughed and struggled for breath. Damien clambered to his hands and knees before getting to his feet. It took some time to steady himself.

"Right," he said, breathing deeply as he dusted himself down. "They'll be upon us soon. We must leave." The three of them stared at him, unable to move.

"Damien are you-" Barbie began.

"Yes, I'm fine. Now come on!"

After taking one last look at the strange creature, Margot slipped through the hole in the wall, following the others. That floor was silent. Nothing moved.

"Plan?" Margot turned to Damien.

"Take Hurst and Barbie, hide. I will find Arabina."

Hurst was disgruntled over not being allowed to find his queen.

"Now, wait a moment," Margot said. It was too late. Damien was already bounding down the corridor. Two hooded figures burst from the room opposite 115, blocking their path.

"Hide!" Damien yelled as he ran round the corner.

Barbie grabbed Hurst and with Margot following, he sprinted in the opposite direction. Margot didn't look back, she didn't want to know if it was still following them or not. They ran up a flight of stairs to the next floor. The corridors were still full of panicking residents.

"Any idea?" Margot panted as they edged through the corridor clogged with humans. "All these bloody places look the fucking same."

Another white figure appeared at the opposite end of the corridor. Barbie and Margot darted in the opposite direction, crashing into the aimless, screaming bodies. They turned at the end of the hall, with the huge windows at the back of the hotel to their right. The White Rider was gaining on them. Every hallway, corridor and staircase was a replica of the previous. Margot had no idea how far they'd come. She just knew they had to keep running. Then something caught her eye.

"The lift!" She yelled, pointing to the end of the next corridor. Barbie understood her intentions.

"Hurst, open the doors. We can't afford to wait." He hurled Hurst through the air.

Hurst squealed as he landed in front of their escape route. Margot realised that Barbie was a lot stronger than she had imagined.

"Press it, now!" She screamed. The White Rider was gaining; it had picked up speed. The doors still hadn't opened. Margot clenched her fists as she tried to run faster. It was no use. She *really* needed to get into shape. Even Barbie was overtaking her.

"They're not opening!" Hurst screamed, frantically jumping, trying to press the button again.

"Keep trying!" Margot screamed, as she got closer, then she realised: "*Hurst!* That's a no smoking sign! The arrows! On the left!"

She could feel her muscles burning as she forced the last of her energies into action. Margot couldn't keep it up for much longer. She shut her eyes tight and opened her mouth; it was a look of agony. Then, unable to lift her feet any more, she crashed to the carpeted floor.

The White Rider advanced. Its feet left the ground and it floated above her. Seeing the figure overhead somehow unleashed new waves of adrenalin. She had a renewed desire to fight. Margot kicked her feet in the air. She managed to hit it in the chest and it ricocheted off the adjacent wall. Overall the struggle was useless. It returned, angrier than before.

"Get back." Barbie said. Margot didn't know whether he was talking to it or her.

"The doors are open!" Hurst said.

"Hurst!" Margot yelled, out of breath as she tried to push the creature away from her. "This really isn't a good time right now, dude!"

Barbie launched himself at the figure. He hit it so hard it was stunned for a moment. Taking advantage of the situation, Margot scrambled to her feet.

"Quickly, they're closing!" Hurst screamed, trying to keep the doors open with his tiny arms. The gap was closing fast.

Taking Barbie's arm, Margot sprinted towards the lift; the creature was up and gaining on them.

"Nearly there-"Margot strained. Her fingers outstretched towards the door. She was only meters away…

"Come on," Barbie said, holding the doors open, just long enough for her to clamber inside. He followed, letting them close behind him.

Margot slumped against the wall. Her heart was beating frantically.

"We made it." She laughed. "Oh god we made it! Thank fuck for that!"

"No Margot, thank God!" Hurst corrected her. Barbie shrugged.

"What now?" the transvestite asked as the lift ascended floor by floor. Barbie's hunched posture amused Margot; he stood like a candy cane to fit himself in the lift. They were clearly not built for people of his height.

The lift stopped moving. With a ping, the doors opened.

"Close the doors," Margot whispered. Outside, many more white figures lingered in the corridor. They hadn't noticed them. They continued to float back and forth. She watched as they searched each room, checking every door on the top floor. Although still unnoticed, Margot knew if they stuck around any longer, they'd attract attention.

"Hurst," she hissed at the demon. "What?" Hurst turned and saw them. "ARGHHH!"

Every White Rider turned to face them.

"Close the fucking doors, then!" Margot screamed as the creatures closed in on them. Once again, they escaped capture because of Barbie pressing buttons. The doors met, but the lift was going nowhere.

"Why isn't it working?!" Margot shouted, hitting the down button again. There was a loud bang and the whole lift shook. Hurst fell backwards.

"Margot, they know, they know!" He squeaked, getting to his feet.

"They're trying to get inside," Barbie said as the banging continued. The lift shook again and again. Margot knew it wouldn't be long before those *things* achieved their goal. *There's got to be a way out* she thought, pacing back and forth. *There's got to be a way out!*

"I really wish there was more room in here," Barbie complained.

"Barbie, not now!" Margot snapped. "I'm trying to think." She didn't bother looking at him, as the lift continued to rock back and forth.

"But human," he said. "Look at this. Now really, they haven't crafted this object very well."

"Barbie what are you-" Margot turned to see the transvestite lifting an air vent on the ceiling.

"See," he continued. "I tap it a few times with my head and it just comes off."

"Barbie, you are a genius!"

With great difficultly, the three of them clambered through the trapdoor of the shaking lift and onto its unstable roof. Margot thought she had underestimated the transvestite. Looking around the gloom, Hurst spotted a door, not too far up from where they were standing. They knew it was their only chance of reaching safety.

*

The hotel was flooded with Silvia's followers. There was no way in, and there was no way out. The hooded figures hovered across every corridor, searching every room and as Arabina sat in the darkness, she couldn't help thinking that it wouldn't be long before Silvia herself, joined the party. Lucy remained plastered against the door.

"Just let me go," Arabina said, falling back on the bed. Lucy ignored her, looking out of the spy hole.

"Stay here," she said.

"Wait! Where are you going?" Arabina rushed towards the door.

"Look," Lucy turned to her. "If I don't come back, you need to hide, do you hear me? Hide and make sure they won't be able to find you. They've already searched this room, they probably won't come back. I don't know what they want, but I think I've got a good idea." She threw open the door and disappeared. Arabina smiled, she liked the girl's attitude. But it didn't mean she was going to listen to a word of what she was saying. She pulled open the drawers to see if there was anything that could help her. They were empty. The wardrobe, however, harboured something that could be of use. Arabina's lips curved into a menacing smile and it wasn't long before she too, fled the room.

*

Margot stepped into the dark room.

"Where are we?" she whispered.

"Supply room," Barbie said. Margot nodded and reached for her night vision sunglasses. Barbie was right; they were surrounded by rows of boxes, piled to the ceiling. She looked around, it was a huge room. It was like a haunted warehouse. Whatever the room was, it was clear that it wasn't open to the public. It had a dilapidated and abandoned look about it, a stark contrast to the pristine public areas. Margot could see rafters supporting the structure of the building. She didn't like it; it looked like it was ready to collapse.

They crept through the gloom. With every step, Margot grew more tense, imagining a new surprise was about to take her out. Her fists clenched tight but she wasn't conscious of clenching them. It didn't feel like they were in the same building, the world outside was so far away. Margot heard movement, at the opposite end of the room, a door opened.

She couldn't see what had come through. She couldn't hear it. But she knew for sure that whatever was there was dangerous. She could sense it; the atmosphere had changed. Barbie and Hurst pulled her away.

"We can hear you," a ghostly voice called from the shadows.

Barbie's heels were clicking along the floor. She turned her head, there was no one there.

"No one move," she whispered. "Take them off!"

"We will find you," the voice called out again, but it sounded closer.

"Hurry," she whispered to Barbie.

"They're buckles," Barbie replied.

A cold gust of wind swept past her face. Margot stared at Hurst, he was terrified.

"I can sense you," the voice seemed to be coming from all around them.

Great, there were more of them. She stared into the distance, glowing white figures lit up the darkened room.

"Done," Barbie said standing up. The silence was broken. Loud screeching could be heard from all around.

"Run!" Margot yelled.

They set off, twisting and turning past obstacles. She didn't know what her plan was any more. She was helpless and exhausted and surely soon, there wouldn't be anywhere left to run.

Without warning, Barbie stopped dead.

180

"We need to leave, what are you doing?" Margot hissed. But he didn't answer, instead he pointed to a pile of boxes leading up to the rafters. Hurst nodded.

Struggling, they made their way to the top and clambered onto the high beams. Margot looked down at the glowing figures moving between the aisles of boxes.

"We need a plan," Hurst squeaked.

Margot thought of the only plan she could. "Could we jump out of the top floor window?"

"No."

"Okay, okay I know this sounds crazy but could we just kill ourselves?"

"Margot," Hurst said, in a voice that made him sound like an annoyed school teacher.

"I'm just saying guys we really don't have a-" She stopped talking and listened.

Something was moving beneath them. Her whole body turned cold. Next to her, Hurst's body was rigid. The demon leaned close to her, his mouth trembling as he put it to her ear: "The Dark Rider."

Margot frowned, *who was that guy?* She looked down. They had climbed a lot higher than she'd thought; her night visions didn't reach to the floor. Margot could feel herself swaying atop the boxes; she must try to keep her balance. She had to hold out a little longer. Hurst reached over to her, pointing a finger to where he was staring. She strained her eyes, searching for what Hurst could see. In the darkness, there was a figure, barely visible to the human eye and it was definitely not human. Its long, black cloak covered its head and body. Although it may have looked similar to the rest of them, Margot knew it was a lot more dangerous given Hurst's whole new realm of fear. Before she knew it, Margot joined him. All warmth was dissipated, leaving behind an icy atmosphere. Despite her attempt to fight it, she was frozen with fear. She knew she should look away and do something, but it was hopeless. She couldn't stop staring. The figure wasn't moving. It didn't walk around with the rest of the creatures, it stood perfectly still. Margot held her breath. One sudden move and they would all be done for.

"I can sense you," grumbled the voice. Next to her she felt Barbie rummaging, she nudged him to keep still. Standing on the rafters wasn't an ideal option; they looked like they had seen better days. Margot was paranoid just holding onto them. Below them, a White Rider glided towards the black one.

"They're not here, sir." Its voice was only just above a whisper.

"Move out," the Dark Rider's voice echoed off every wall. Margot wanted to laugh as the two Riders moved towards the door. Barbie continued to quiver. Balance obviously wasn't his forte, Margot thought, as she watched him cling to the beam.

Barbie lost his footing. He knocked a large box from the top of the pile. Margot screwed her eyes together as the object tumbled as if in slow motion to the ground, spilling its contents over the floor. The Rider turned. They were done for. It scanned the room until it was staring directly at them through its hooded darkness. She could feel its piercing stare burn into her eyes. *Oh god, it could see them.* Margot watched as it took a few steps forward. However, before it had chance to go further, one of the white figures approached and whispered something Margot couldn't catch. Taking one last look, it turned and left the room, slamming the door hard.

Too scared to move; the three sat in silence. Only after a considerable time did they make their way back down to the floor. Margot had never concentrated so hard on anything in her life. It was a true test of endurance. All that mattered was staying alive.

"What just happened?" she whispered.

"I don't care," Hurst replied, dropping to his knees. "Just thank *God* that we're still alive."

And for the first time, Margot did.

After a wait in the darkness, they went back across the gigantic store room. Margot opened the same door the Black Rider had gone through with great trepidation; they went through it and down the quiet staircase. Margot had no idea what to expect any more. She shivered; they were on one of the main stairways of the hotel.

Barbie pointed to the first door they came to. It led to the hotel's upper hallway. They went through it.

Her eyes were dazzled by the bright light. She reached for the sunglasses given to her by Damien. When Margot opened her eyes again, all she could see was the aftermath of chaos. Windows were broken, doors hung off their frames with single hinges, and the remnants of people's lives were scattered across the corridor. Nothing moved; the only sound Margot could hear was the ticking of a clock lying on the hallway floor.

The remains of the carnage were strewn along the upper hallway. Debris spilled onto every level. Dead bodies littered the floor, making Margot nauseous. What made it worse was that all the death was because of them. The guilt weighed heavy on her. The only thing that gave her hope was the fact that many White Riders were also lying face down in the rubble. She glanced out of the window; the Brontangus were distant dots in the sky. The living had fled. Deep down, Margot felt that it was right she hadn't run with them. But she felt every bit of life had been taken away from her. She felt like a wild, free horse, tamed. Silvia had broken her.

"Human," Barbie said in his monotone voice. "We need to search for Damien and Arabina."

She shook her head and snapped out of her trance. "Okay." She'd never tell them anything was wrong, the internal struggle was her own to bear and bear it she would. It was strange to watch the other two when it came to the death surrounding them. Hurst skipped and jumped over bodies, whistling happily to himself, relieved the immediate danger was over. He looked like a holiday maker, the way he adjusted his sunglasses over his beady eyes.

The transvestite, like Margot expected, had no physical reaction. However, on closer inspection she saw his grip tighten as his eyes darted from one body to the next. It must have taken him a lot of effort to resist temptation.

"There's nothing here!" She shouted, kicking the debris beneath her feet. She was frustrated, but the frustration was making the fear that the next time they were reunited with Damien and Arabina, it could well be in another world.

"I wouldn't be too sure of that," a smooth voice replied behind her.

"Damien," Hurst called. Margot turned to see the vampire leaning at the end of the corridor, arms folded, and his distinct smirk still prominent.

"Where the hell have you been?" Margot yelled as the vampire made his way over.

"Oh, you know, just relaxing, having a coffee, what did you think?" Margot glanced at his neck; there were heavy bruises where the creature's hands had been. She frowned, not wanting to feel sorry for him, not wanting to make the same mistake. Damien hitched up the collar of his trench coat. It was clear he didn't want to make it open to public inspection. "Let's keep searching." He said.

"Hey muchachos!" A familiar Spanish accent called. Arabina peered out from behind a door. She had disposed of her disguise and was wearing her red dress and dark skin once more.

"Oh, your majesty!" Hurst squeaked. "You're alive."

He looked like an over excited puppy about to wet itself.

"Of course," Arabina replied, making her way over to them. She tutted and kicked a dead body. "Humans can't keep anything nice can they? Must admit though, I am impressed with the current decorations."

Damien stepped forward. "Arabina, did you not hear the announcement?"

"Of course," she replied. "It said not to panic."

"She does have a point," Barbie said.

Damien chose not to reply; her humour wasn't needed.

"We're leaving," he said.

"But Jade-" Margot mentioned the person on everyone else's minds.

"Professor Wilde nearly got you killed." Damien walked away, the others followed suit.

"No! Jade wouldn't do that!" She stood rigid. "He was brain washed; they all are!"

"Margot," Damien said, "He's not like the rest; the light does not affect him. He made his choice."

Margot didn't respond. She wouldn't believe it, she refused to believe it. She ran her fingers through her white hair. How did Damien know if Jade had been taken in by the light or not; he didn't. There was still hope; she'd keep telling herself that. But deep down, Margot knew that Damien was probably right. She followed them down the stairs, not bothering to keep up her guard. Margot knew she had to snap out of her funk, she had to focus, but she couldn't help it. Jade was implanted in her mind. He felt like an addiction, her personal drug.

Margot looked around; they were in the reception on the ground floor. There was nowhere else to go but outside, there was nothing left for them inside the hotel.   Like everywhere else, the hotel lobby had been destroyed. Margot's heart leapt as she glanced at a hooded figure, lying directly in front of her feet.

"Sunglasses," Damien ordered. There was a hint of warning to his voice that Margot hadn't heard before. She had a strong suspicion he was more worried than he was letting on.

"What now?" Hurst asked.

Damien gave one of his grave smiles in return, "We leave of course, Hurst. There is no other option available."

The tiny Demon shivered in response.

"Damien," Barbie said, staring into the distance through the broken window, "We have three choices; take our chances through the trees, travel to the towns via the lakes, or I could try and find another ship."

"I think it's time we follow the lakes," the vampire replied.

"The lakes?" Arabina said.

"What else do you propose we do, sit here and wait to rot?" Damien asked; his eyes blazed in anger.

Margot smiled, if Barbie could grin, the use of the word 'rot' would have lit his face up. "Of course, if you'd rather wait here-" She began and was cut off by Damien, who implored that the group *move out* in a tone which was much sharper than usual.

"Not you," the vampire said, looking at Margot and Barbie. "I want a word, if you please."

He strolled back to the foyer, beckoning them to follow. Margot had a funny suspicion she knew what it was about. "Just to let you know what happened back in the bedroom was an extremely rare occurrence for me." Damien said and Margot snorted.

Damien chose to ignore it. "As you are both fully aware, I am perfectly capable of fighting my own battles, especially against this." He looked down at the hooded creature, dead on the floor. Margot couldn't believe what he was telling them. *He's ungrateful that we saved his life? Could vampires even die in the first place?* She opened her mouth, ready to protest, but he silenced her.

"Thank you, without you; I'd mostly probably be critically injured by now." His words were brief, his tone was cold, but Margot and Barbie couldn't help but stare at each other as he strolled away.

"Well that was… unexpected," Margot was stumped for words.

"I know," Barbie agreed. "I am in complete shock."

She laughed at his unintentional sarcasm.

"What was *that* thing?" Margot glanced down at a body lying metres away from her. She strolled over, kneeling down at the figure's side. If she could only turn it over, see what was underneath one of the strange creature's hoods. Barbie watched her from a distance.

"Don't touch that," a smooth voice spoke in Margot's ear. She turned around, to see the vampire standing over her.

"Damien, this could help," she said, staring at the body again. He lowered his pale hand and grabbed hold of Margot's. Damien's fingers felt like icicles.

"It will help no one, it will only make things worse," he said. He let go and walked away. "Arabina, you need to transform so we can leave."

Satan's daughter was nowhere in sight.

"Your majesty?" Hurst called. There was no reply. The hotel was silent. Margot and Damien exchanged looks of concern. Damien didn't need to say anything; they had already begun searching.

"She's out here," Barbie called from outside. The three of them rushed to the pool area. Margot tensed, the outside was just as bad as inside the hotel. Every sun bed had been upturned. The bar, once full of people and their laughter and the clinking of glasses, had collapsed, taking people under with it. Margot couldn't help but think of Frank. The atmosphere outside the hotel had a haunted essence about it. Perhaps because there, the dead count was even higher. The entrance was piled with bodies; the outcome of unsuccessful escape attempts. The pool had turned red and two females in bikinis floated in stillness and silence on its surface.

"I can't do it," Arabina was slumped against the wall with her head in her hands. She screamed in frustration. "Something's fucking wrong! My powers, they don't want to work!"

It was hard to feel sorry for Arabina. For Margot in particular, it was near impossible. However, she did feel a slight twinge of sympathy on that particular occasion - at least, enough not to mock her situation. She guessed the rest of the group were thinking the same thing as they kept their mouths shut too. If Arabina's powers weren't working, they were all in trouble.

"Just wear this for now," Damien said and threw her a dark green cloak. "I took it earlier from some human's wardrobe."

He bent down and pulled her to her feet. "We can't afford to waste time."

"Let's go," Margot sighed, dusting off her leather jacket. She knew they had awoken something that could never be put back to rest. A war had begun. Tension had been building between Silvia and Arabina for years. It wasn't about Earth anymore; it was so much more than that. Finally, Margot was starting to see things from another perspective. She took one last glance at the hotel then she walked out into the trees, leaving the two floating bodies to slowly sink to the bottom of the red pool.

Chapter 12

The Innocent Traitor

Everything inside the walls of the castle was still. Nothing dared move. In the west wing of the castle sat a very confused Jade Wilde. His gaze was transfixed upon the red sky, which glared through the small arch window. Small flakes of ice and snow drifted through the air and settled on the castle grounds. Jade took his goggles off to clean the lenses. She wasn't there yet. She'd be late, he had a gut feeling.

It gave him just enough time.

"Day four, or it could be five... oh I don't know, all these days seem the same to me," he muttered into his Jonovicator. "I'm not sure if I've done the right thing. I was just trying to help, but something seems seriously wrong here. Now I have no idea where any of them are... Reenie... Margot..."

He stared into the distance. "Something must be-"

Footsteps echoed. Jade panicked and thrust his Jonovicator back into the pocket of his trench coat. The door opened and the small room filled with bright light. Jade screwed up his eyes, reaching for his goggles before he even dared to look at the angel. Silvia's hair and multi layered dress floated as though she was standing on a gravity free zone back on earth.

"Jade," her voice came from everywhere apart from her mouth. It bounced off the walls, the trees outside, even the clouds. "You have served me well, but Margot was not found."

"No," he whispered. "No, no, no, no, she was there! She isn't..."

He couldn't bear to say the word.

"No, Professor, she's alive. But she's causing chaos. Her, and her interesting set of friends."

Jade put his head in his hands. "I can't believe she would hang around with those people, after all you told me. It's dangerous, it's crazy-"

"You will re-join your friend Reenie in the town of Kious and continue your search," she said and leaned closer. Her hair and dress still flowed as if it was caught in a breeze.

"I just I – I just want her to be safe, I just -" Jade stammered, unable to finish his sentence.

"Love, it is a natural thing, Professor Wilde." The angel spoke in a calm, reassuring tone.

Jade's cheeks flushed. "I never said anything about-"

"I know; it's hard, but remember why you are doing this, it is for the greater good of humanity, I promise you. You will see Margot again." She shone too bright for Jade to see the reassuring smile spread across her face. It was like staring at a megawatt light.

Silvia walked away, unsure of whether she was trying to convince him or herself. How genuine had she come across? The humans; they were so different to many of the other creatures she had encountered. Their minds were so complex. How could such powerless beings have such powerful emotions? How could they feel so strong, so passionate about matters they had very little knowledge of? It was chaotic, animalistic almost… or maybe it was simply just human.

Love - she remembered that feeling. What a strange, immature, involuntary reaction and yet, humans deemed it one of the most beautiful emotions in life, it gave them a reason to live and fight to be alive. She shuddered, it must not distract her. Silvia knew she had to tread carefully around that human. He was not like the rest. He was not affected by the light of Izsafar. She had pondered on that for a long time. Why? Why him, in particular? Better scientists than Jade had fallen into its mesmerising clutches.

No, love wasn't a bad thing. She had done it for love. She loved all creatures and she would help them all - whatever it took. Silvia reached the bottom of the stairs in time to meet her other visitor. She walked back to the great hall.

His long robes, flowed down to the cold ground, his hood draped over his face - The Dark Rider. She didn't need to see his face to feel his piercing glare. The darkness within him filled the room. It was easy for her to tell he was from elsewhere. She approached him, he didn't bow. He refused to bow. The Dark Rider was the only servant that didn't.

"You asked to see me," he said.

"Yes, you have failed me," Silvia circled him. He wasn't intimidated. "You let them go, after *he* caused all that trouble. We need to move quickly. Professor Wilde isn't stupid, he won't believe us forever."

"He seems like an idiot to me."

"But still, do we really want to take that risk?"

He nodded in reply. Silvia continued.

"How do you catch a criminal in a land of criminals?" For a few moments it was almost as though she was talking to herself. "How can they sin when I give people free rein?"

"No idea, my lady. When is the next batch ready to come down? You must not forget your duties; these people seem to be distracting you."

Silvia was taken aback. "Soon, very soon." She replied.

"And Margot Grant?"

"Will be caught and condemned to death, along with the others. Get searching; do not let me down. You know the penalty and after all I have done for you…"

He laughed. The angel was bemused. *Was he being sarcastic?*

"Of course," he replied. "I will see to it they are brought here."

"Alive," Silvia added as he turned to leave.

"Of course," he replied. "You must have some fun too."

The door slammed.

*

"… and then there's the matter of how we can actually breathe, dude. I mean like, on Earth we have oxygen and shit. But this, this right here is *fucked up*, I mean, am I breathing oxygen right now or something else?" Margot turned to Barbie and passed him a cigarette.

They lay on their backs amongst the tall trees. They had been there for hours, waiting for Damien and Hurst's return. She looked into the bright, burning light filling the sky. It was so temping to take her glasses off; she wondered if Barbie felt the same. In the distance they could hear voices, ships on the move, people living their new, regulated lives. They were outside the town of Kious. There it sat, meters away from them across the tranquil river.

"…and gravity!" Margot continued, "I don't get how that works here either, man! It's like the basic fundamental scientific knowledge, how come I don't feel different from being on Earth?"

Barbie didn't answer. He lay back in the grass, smoking and at peace.

"…well you must have some regulations on gravity, or how else would we be staying on the ground or not be being crushed into it? Man, your zone set up may be weird or something. Artificial perhaps."

"What are you talking about?" A cold voice asked. Margot sat up to see Damien and Hurst approaching.

"Oh, you know." She smiled at the vampire. "Just science, something you seem to hate."

Damien turned his gaze skyward, exasperated. "Typical human; you have to 'know' everything." He grinned, and took out his own packet of cigarettes. At least the hotel had been good for something. "Whatever happened to a bit of mystery?"

He turned to her: "You understand of course, I'm talking about keeping your head down and your nose *out*."

It was Margot's turn to give the exasperated look. She was no stranger to keeping a low profile, just very bad at it. "I'm sorry 'mystery man', but just because you're a technophobe and hate any developing race," Margot jumped to her feet, trying to do a bad impression of the vampire.

"Oh no, look it's a toaster," she dropped to her knees. "Whatever will I do?! Oh, you humans, heating bread with your *science*!"

Damien glared at her.

"She has a point," Barbie said, getting to his feet.

"Ha! Even Barbie agrees!"

Damien ignored the comment and turned away. Margot smirked, it was the first time she'd been able to silence him.

"On a more serious note," Damien said, staring at the town across the river. "We have managed to find a place to stay. Around the back of the houses there's a run-down barn. It doesn't seem to be in use, it should be easy to keep a low profile there."

After the last time, Margot wasn't so convinced, but agreed anyway. She turned to the pale blue sky; not one Brontangus had been seen since the hotel incident. That unnerved them all. Silvia was up to something.

"We're wasting time," Barbie said, following the albino's gaze.

"One moment, I shall fetch Arabina and then we'll move out, prepare yourselves, bring what objects you have." Damien went back into the trees. Margot followed, he needed a hand.

She lay curled up underneath a dying tree, fast asleep in the green cloak. It was probably the only dying tree in the whole of Izsafar and it didn't take a genius to work out what power had killed it. The longer Arabina had laid again its trunk, the more the tree turned black, with its leaves shedding by the second. Margot was starting to realise the sheer power of the woman... demon. *Demon-woman?* She still didn't quite know how to define her.

There was something unnerving watching Satan's daughter sleep. Seeing evil at peace was like watching a politician doing the hula (equipped with full dress and coconut bra); the two just didn't go together. But Margot didn't think Arabina was evil; she didn't think any of them were. Sure, she didn't agree with some of their ways - most of their ways - but did that make them wrong?

Damien bent down and nudged her. He was a lot gentler with her than on the day of the fire. At least Margot thought so, until-

"Get up, we don't have all day," the vampire almost yelled close to her ear.

"*Alright already*," Arabina moaned, rolling onto the grass and stretching. Even though she tried to regain her usual stature; the fire in her voice half-simmered. Arabina was weak.

"She can lean on me," Barbie's voice croaked behind Margot.

"Very well," Damien said, turning away and heading back to the opening in the trees. Hurst ran past the vampire, arms wide open as he rushed to Arabina's side. "Don't even think about it." Damien said to him. The demon bowed his head, and walked away.

At last, the group emerged from the trees. Before them, a quaint wooden bridge sat on the river banks. The light beat down with fervent intensity without the trees. There was no breeze.

"Damien, how do you know this place is safe?" Margot asked, standing at the foot of the bridge.

"Silvia groups her victims very carefully. She makes sure they are placed in their usual environment within their usual social groups."

"What do you mean?"

"I mean when she brings humans to Izsafar she doesn't just drop them off anywhere. She arranges them into different towns and villages. Simple idea, but clever. Put it this way, when she created this group, I think she selected every human that evolution forgot."

Margot raised her eyebrows. However, once across the bridge and at the entrance of the town, she understood what he meant.

She felt like she had been transported hundreds of years into the past as they made their way onto the quiet streets. The land of Izsafar was a strange place. One moment she was in a metropolitan haven, the next she was in an apparent rural dead-zone.

Although, still containing much plant life, it was far more disparate; it was barren in comparison to the other side of the river. They'd left the humidity of the luscious greenery and entered a much more arid atmosphere. The trees, the grass, even the air felt starved of moisture. Dust blew about as Margot kicked the mustard coloured ground. It took her a while to realise they were standing on one of the main roads of the town. Where was the concrete, but more to the point, where were the people? She glanced at the rest of the group, who were looking in all directions, lost.

Dilapidated houses stood in dishevelled rows on either side of her. Some of them looked like the next gentle breeze would send them tumbling to the ground, piece by broken piece. Still the group walked, unsure of where Damien and Hurst were leading them.

Margot asked: "Damien, where the fuck-"

Margot stopped mid-sentence. From the sky came the familiar sound of beating wings. It was them.

"Quickly," Damien called, leading them through a door. Margot and the rest of the group followed. She wasn't sure where they were going, the only prominent feature about the building, was the fact that it was more stable than the rest, though still in the same pitiful state of repair.

Barbie slammed the door once he had pulled Arabina inside. The group ignored their surroundings and kept their eyes fixed on the sky through a broken window frame. Amidst the blue, two Brontangus circled the air.

"That was close," Margot said.

It was at that moment, she realised they weren't alone. The smell of cigarettes and alcohol was emanating from somewhere in the room. The sound of a smashing glass pierced the thick atmosphere.

"Now looky here," a thick American accent said. "Are you going to buy anything or just stand in the doorway all day?"

"Just act casual," Damien muttered.

"Oh god, hillbillies. Why did it have to be hillbillies?" Margot said. "It's gonna be 'Deliverance' all over again!"

The group scanned their surroundings; they were in a saloon full of people. The bar had fallen silent. Every face in the crowded bar looked in their direction. However, they weren't the faces Margot had expected to see.

Apart from the barman, who looked like he'd just been imported from a cattle farm in the depths of the American South, it was one of the most diverse gatherings of people she had ever seen. People in heavily-adorned military uniforms sat with the very stereotypical elite and pristine-suited business men. She also noticed a few of the women who wore what could barely be categorised as clothing.

"Well?" The barman said. "You're goldarn losing me business here."

He turned to the customers: "All right, stop your staring; it's just a bunch of weirdoes."

A few people let out awkward coughs before going back to their drinks.

"A bunch of what?" Margot's anger was sparked once again. She was sure if Arabina had been well, she'd react with flagrant objection. Barbie nudged her hard. The albino then realised the humans had never seen demons or vampires before.

"Sure," she said. "Sure I'll take a drink." And before anyone could stop her, she was on her way to the bar.

As Margot approached the bar, she heard a multitude of accents, from the most refined enunciations to the thickest of non-standard dialects. She saw what she believed to be the full spectrum of human skin colour and a sliding gendered scale from manly men to manly women and vice-versa. Trust alcohol to be the binding agent in human bonding in other worlds.

"Right then," Margot leaned on the sticky wooden surface of the bar. "I want one of those."

She pointed at a liquid in a long bottle with a twisted neck. It caught her attention because steam was furling from the open bottle. "Ooh and that, and that for my friend, Barbie."

She paused and turned back to the worried group. Arabina was leaning on Barbie; Margot didn't think she would be drinking anything. Meanwhile, Hurst trembled; he was petrified amongst the sea of humans. She sighed; he was going to need a double at least. Next, she turned to the vampire.

"Surprise me," Damien said with a disgusted look on his face. Margot shrugged. She lit a cigarette as she made her extensive order. Her excuse being that she was in a new place, she had to experience their culture.

"And just exactly how do you propose we pay?" Damien asked; he came to lean on the bar next to her. Margot had not thought about that, with so many people, what currency did they use? Back on Earth, they used cyber-notes; nothing was paid for with physical objects any more. It just didn't work; too much theft.

The barman smiled. He reached under the table and produced a small lime green pot, just bigger than a shot glass. The pot was sealed at the top, apart from a small hole in the centre, in which the barman inserted a long clear tube with a small black and yellow device on the end of it.

"There you go," he said, pushing the object towards her.

"What the hell?" Margot said, to the amusement of some of the customers. Damien nudged her hard in the side. *Low profile, low profile*, she repeated in her mind.

"She's new here," Damien said to the suspicious looking barman.

"Ohh!" The man winked at him, to his displeasure. "Phew," he said laughing and wiping his brow. "I thought you were one of them goldarn rebels they're searching for. Or a weirdo."

Margot sniggered with him. "Dude, that's a good one!" It was a defining moment.

"It's simple," the man continued: "All you godda do, is take this tube here, put it on your forehead and we'll take some of your thoughts. They'll go into this pot and I'll empty it out with the rest. Don't worry, it won't take long and it'll ping when it's done."

"Huh?"

"You know, just take some of your thoughts..." he hesitated, trying to find the right words. "Your brain... thoughts? Oh, I don't know what the right words are."

He leaned closer. "To be honest, I ain't got no idea, what this stuff is."

The man laughed again. Damien threw an icy stare in Margot's direction. She laughed nervously. "Okay dude, how about you just... put it on my tab?"

Twenty minutes later...

"We shouldn't drink these." Damien said, staring towards the opposite side of the room. He was an amusing contrast to the intoxicated people that surrounded him. They had chosen the only table available and much to their displeasure, it was right in the centre of the room.

"Aw, come on, dude," Margot said, staring at the vast selection of drinks that had been placed before her. Although she didn't appear to be, Margot was smart and intuitive. She felt she knew the people in the town were no threat and after finding out how people paid for things, understood a lot more why people were so detached.

"One;" Damien said. "We don't know if Silvia has drugged them. Two; these drinks are a lot stronger than drinks on Earth and three; this is most unwise when trying to keep a low profile."

"What? We're blending in well!" Margot protested. "Look at what everyone else is doing!"

But before Damien had chance to reply, an unexpected voice spoke out.

"Tell me something," Hurst said, leaning forward in his chair. "Why do you drink?"

Margot looked around, before answering. She looked at all the people who laughed and joked around her and she felt strange. Why *did* she drink? The people were acting like idiots. It was fun, she told herself. But *was* it? Was it really fun, waking up and puking all morning or finding yourself in bed with some random guy, or worse, in some random guy's house? Or waking up to find your purse had been stolen or you spent all the wages you earned that week because you'd been so drunk you'd lost any form of judgement?

Was it really fun or just a waste of time?

"Let me explain this to you bluntly," Damien turned to the demon. "Humans are quite a stupid race. Many do it as a pointless activity, to fill their time so they feel they are using their time wisely in society and deluding themselves in to how much fun they're having. However, Hurst, this is but one example. There are of course, as Margot will tell you, many more brilliant reasons for this self-destructive hobby. For instance, some find they can't handle their own pitiful existence, therefore feel the need to intoxicate themselves in order to, how they say, 'numb the pain'."

He turned to Margot with a smug grin on his face. "But then you see, this is where addiction raises its dark head and they realise that something is most terribly wrong, that something is missing from their lives. And so they give up, having some pointless epiphany regarding the need for something more meaningful in their lives - and that is where religion swoops in to take its victims."

"Oh," Hurst squeaked. He lowered his head and studied the drink in front of him. Margot thought he might bite after the comment on religion, but she had a feeling he didn't want to challenge the vampire.

"It's not always like that," she said with a sigh. "We don't all do it, Hurst. Some of us do it for the enjoyment and know when to limit ourselves before it ever gets to that point. This guy," she nudged the vampire. "Is generalising."

"Oh, Margot," Damien shook his head. "Why are you humans all so pretentious? Why do you constantly feel that you're individual and special? You are all the same, parasites, crawling on the skin of your worthless planet. The Universe is one of the most pointless realms I know. The humans are so stupid, fighting their own race, in order to gain what, power over another, for another to take that power from them? Let me tell you now; there is nothing special or different about you, you were not born to be a star, nor change the world. You were born with one purpose; to live and reproduce and instead, your species chooses to destroy."

Damien's words were cutting. He didn't really mean it, she told herself. He was trying to wind her up, that's how it worked. She pursed her lips. It was a reaction he was looking for, that was all, and she wasn't going to give it to him.

"Damien," Barbie said. "I rather like humans, I find their company pleasurable."

"That's because they're dead by the time they get to you." Damien said. His bitter tone came through even though he kept the smirk fixed upon his face. He was patronising at times, patronising in the extreme. But it was clear the vampire didn't want to linger on the subject.

"These drinks are safe, they're from the same distributor supplying The Halo and Harp, all alcohol comes from the Under World, therefore it's all fine. I just didn't want you to intoxicate yourself, but frankly, I've given up." Damien leaned back into his chair.

Margot stared back at him. She knew why he had done it. He was trying to test her, trying to see if she would resist her old careless ways; behaviour that she had once performed almost every night on earth. *Well, fuck him.* She was going to do what she wanted.

"Cheers," she raised her glass. Screw the low profile; it was time to have some fun.

*

A few miles down the river, it was a different story. There was no loud laughter or intoxicated fun. Instead, two figures dressed in long brown cloaks were making their way up stream, following the river bank. There was an aggressive and forceful air about their movement, an undertone of pressing importance. As they reached the next town, they descended into the river, wading through its cool waters before climbing out again when they were alone. One was tall, whilst the other was much shorter and agile. It was impossible to tell their gender or race, their hoods covered their features. The only thing clear was that they were in a hurry, as they stole through the long grass.

There was nothing stealthy about Jade Wilde.

He tripped over the hem of his cloak and fell back into the water.

"Jade!" Reenie stage whispered. She pulled off her hood and ran to the waterside where he was splashing about.

"I'm okay!" He said, gasping for breath as he hauled himself onto the bank.

"Inconspicuous, Jade" Reenie shook her head. "We need to keep this low-key!"

She leaned over to grab his hand. Jade stumbled further up the bank. He stood up, wrung out his dreadlocks and cloak and looked into the distance. All was quiet as the strong light beat down. They were surrounded by dense countryside. Vast stretches of trees and hills filled the horizon. It was hard to believe how close they were to the next town.

"I don't understand this place." Jade adjusted his goggles. "It changes faster than a woman changes her outfits."

Reenie smiled: "That's a bit of a generalisation."

"You're right, sorry."

"Come on, only two more villages to go. How are you so sure anyway, how do you know this isn't going to be another dead end?"

"I never said I was positive, but it's the closest village to the last attack, it does make sense if you think about it."

Reenie nodded, it was a reasonable answer. She lifted her hood back up over her face.

"Reenie," Jade called. He hadn't moved.

"What is it Jade? We need to hurry!"

"Do you think this is right?" He looked at her, trying to appeal to the softer side he had met on the cliff top. She looked down at the ground and removed her hood then she sat on the side of the steep river bank.

"There is no other choice," she said. "We are doing the right thing Jade, I know it."

Jade wasn't so convinced with her answer.

"Reenie I-"

"What is it with you and her?" She turned on him. "You've been obsessing over her since we got here! That's why we ended up on this fucking mission in the first place."

She took a breath, trying to calm herself down. "Don't you get it? She left you, she doesn't care! She wouldn't give two shits if you were dead." Reenie said. She realised the impact of her words and put her hands to her mouth: "Jade, I'm sorry, I didn't-"

"Let's keep going." He stood up. He didn't look at her as he lifted his hood to cover his face.

"Jade," Reenie said. "I didn't mean it, I know you miss-"

"Don't even say her name," Jade snapped. He could hear his voice going hoarse. His throat tightened, making it hard to breathe. He tried to keep calm.

"Can we just drop it, *please?*" Jade's voice was low, barely higher than a whisper.

"Okay," Reenie replied in a soft voice. "Okay, we'll keep going, it can't be long now."

They set off again downstream.

Jade was thankful she had decided to let the subject go; he was ready to burst into tears every time somebody mentioned her name.

*

Margot was warming to the bar. Despite the people's major lack of brain cells, they were quite amusing and helped to take her mind off the negative surroundings. She also thought it was the perfect way to annoy Damien. Margot glanced over at the vampire; he returned it with a signature sneer. He was perched on a bar stool by the open fire at the end of the room. Margot didn't understand how he did it. No matter what he did, he always looked the essence of cool. She shook her head and turned away.

Hurst had volunteered to look after Arabina who was coming to. They had put her on a shoddy green sofa at the end of the room on which she was attempting to sit upright.

"Mistress, oh my Queen, you should rest," Hurst squeaked, he became more alarmed every time Arabina tried to sit up.

"Hurst," she snapped: "Will you just shut up?!"

Meanwhile, Barbie was standing with a group of the most masculine men in the bar, some with huge bellies, wearing football shirts brandishing team names Margot had never heard of, and probably neither had they. The others in the group were gym enthusiasts from their bulging muscles, constrained by their tight sleeves.

It was an absurd contrast. She laughed as the transvestite cast his sullen face down at the group as they attempted to tell jokes.

"And then," a short bald man continued, leaning on Barbie for support. "And then, 'e says, the bird wasn't even mine in the first place!"

There was a roar of laugher then every face was focused on Barbie's. "Oh she's a weird one, aint she?"

Oh god, Margot thought, still watching, *these people really were stupid.* Something caught her eye. Someone distracted her - she couldn't believe it - sitting only a few meters away was the president of the United States of America.

Before Margot had time to think, she clambered over tables. She yelled: "Mr President! Oh God! Mr President!"

The world leader looked around, confused. "Oh," he murmured, his pale eyes stared at her. Margot took a step backwards. He looked empty, devoid of personality. Though it was clearly him, he didn't quite match up to the person that had been projected in the media. He was wearing a very formal and expensive black suit, which appeared to have been his only attire for some time, given its tattered edges. His hair, once a handsome dark brown, was projecting in all directions and had etches of grey amidst the original colour.

"Mr President?" Margot repeated, although there was a hint of anxiety in her voice.

The people at his table were similar; the other men also appeared to have dressed for a formal event. As she looked harder, she realised they had no distinguishing features. They sat, together; smoking, drinking and laughing vacuously at endless anecdotes and comments. As Margot neared table, they turned and looked, not with suspicion, but confusion.

"And what can I do for you, ma'am?" He asked; his drink shook in his hand. The stupid grin on his face made Margot uncomfortable. He was clueless.

"Just wanted to say," Margot thought quickly. "That erm, well like, yeah good job with everything and stuff."

But as she backed away, she was lost for words. Perplexed, the President turned back to the other men and continued his meaningless conversation.

"It's not extremely attractive is it?" A smooth voice whispered in Margot's ear.

"Oh shut up, Damien!" Margot snapped, putting another cigarette in her mouth. The vampire faced her. He grinned to reveal his canines. Margot had to look away. He was right; the people were in a complete mess. They had been reduced to husks.

"Damien," she said, after the striking realisation. "How come every place we've been to here is like a bar? I've not seen a school, a fire station or anything yet; just hotels, bars or clubs."

"That's because they're some of the few things available to you humans." Damien said. "Now really, Margot, haven't you figured it out yet? Silvia is not trying to create free thinkers. Many of the people she has taken wouldn't want to be that in the first place. This seems to be a meaningless human culture that satisfies every person in Izsafar. And let's face it, shall we? People here don't need to work or create, they don't need to do anything, all they have to do is exist and existence becomes extremely boring something to fill the time."

Margot didn't reply. She didn't know what to say. After a long life of drinking and intoxicating herself, had she really just been wasting all her time? She thought of Jade, he never wasted his time. He put every minute to good use. She wished she'd have done the same.

Before Margot had time to continue pondering, there was the sound of a smash.

"Look out," Damien said, diving on Margot and pulling her to the ground. A bar stool hurtled past where her head had been. It flew straight into the window. The pub fell silent. Margot looked up, Damien was directly on top of her, and despite his sunglasses she could see his cold blue eyes staring at her red ones. That moment lasted an eternity.

The silence became a roar of shouting. Out of nowhere, people were turning on each other; throwing punches, picking up stools and yelling obscenities.

Margot regained her wits. "What the hell, man? Get off of me!" She shouted. She pushed the vampire off her and scrambled to her feet.

"A thank you would have been nice," Damien said, springing up beside her. They stood and watched the unruly crowd of people.

"What is it? What's going on?" Margot scanned the room, looking for the disturbance. There didn't appear to be one.

"Nothing," Damien replied. "They've obviously just had a drunken disagreement." A glass smashed on the wall next to where he was standing.

Margot raised her eyebrows. "Idiots."

"So, are you sharing the same brainwaves as me at the moment?" He asked, turning to her with his usual grin. She smiled in return.

"Split up, get the others, get the fuck out whilst doing some extremely stupid shit in the process?"

Damien nodded.

"Hell yeah!"

They ran in separate directions, looking for the rest of the group.

"Godda go!" Margot grabbed Barbie's hand, trying to yank him backwards. He wasn't hard to find, the transvestite had positioned himself in the middle of the room. He was the only person standing stationary within the chaos.

"But your tab-" Barbie began.

"That's not important right now!" Margot yelled, dodging more airborne pint glasses.

Barbie nodded. They went to find the rest of them.

It wasn't easy especially when the punters were doing their utmost to not only destroy the building, but each other in the process. Margot and Barbie made their way past drunkards engaged in full-blown fist fights before finding Damien and Hurst lifting Arabina up from the sofa. She shook them off, insisting she could walk by herself. Margot bit her lip ring in frustration; it was not the time to argue. The brawl was going to draw attention and that was last thing they wanted.

"Guys! Hurry the fuck up, seriously!" She shouted at them and to her surprise, they listened.

"Margot's right," Damien agreed. "Let's go!"

Margot's right? Margot's right? Is he on drugs? It was not a phrase she expected come from the vampire's mouth. She smiled to herself and followed them to the door.

The barman was standing on a table, brandishing something that looked very much like a rifle.

"Now looky here!" He shouted at the crowd, hoping they would stop. They didn't. His plan wasn't working. He loaded the rifle and cocked the trigger. "OI!" He shouted, pointing the gun at the door.

"Damien, he's got a gun," Hurst hissed.

"Really?" Damien uttered with acidic sarcasm.

The group crept to the door. Despite their efforts, crouched over, moving slowly, it was pointless, everyone could see them.

There was a crack and a boom as the barman fired.

"GO, GO, GO!" Arabina screamed. They sprinted out of the door away from the chaos inside. The bartender was unable to fire the gun again. He had underestimated the force of the recoil and it had blown him backwards, he was launched off the table. He landed in a heap, disappearing into the mire of inebriated calamity. His customers exploited the opportunity; they helped themselves to the untended bar.

"Fucking hell, that was close," Margot said. She leaned on a nearby building. Most of the group, unaccustomed to exercise were mimicking her. Hurst collapsed in front of them.

"Hurst, get up," Arabina snapped, she was annoyed at the small demon. He jumped to his feet and almost knocked Arabina over. Satan's daughter screamed out in anger, uttering innumerable, indecipherable curses.

"Shush!" Damien and Margot said together. She glared at the building they were standing behind. For the first time, Margot felt almost safe in the shade of the barn like the danger couldn't get to her when she was out of the glaring sunlight. However, she wasn't prepared to stick around to test the theory.

"Damien what are you doing?" She hissed at the vampire who was heading to the other end of the barn.

He kept close to the wall, as he got to the end and peered around the other side.

"Just as I thought," he said, strolling back to the group. "Deserted, yes, this is definitely the place."

"And where exactly *are* we?" Margot asked, folding her arms. They must be pretty close to the edge of town, apart from a few houses in the distance; all she could see ahead was more dense countryside.

"At this moment in time," he said. "It's the safest place we can be." He disappeared around the corner at the other end of the barn.

Margot shrugged at Barbie; he replied with a *'don't look at me'* sort of head shake. After checking the coast was clear, she and the others followed.

Their surroundings were so quiet, that Margot could still hear the brawling in the distance. She wondered where the rest of the town's residents were. *Why is this place so deserted?* As she entered the large, open doorway, there was a distinctive smell emanating from the inside. It was dingy, dimly lit by the light leaking through the cracks in the planks that held the barn together - just.

On the floor, a thick layer of straw crunched with every movement. That filled her with paranoia and began to sober her up. They were all austere once again; each of them on red alert. Well, almost all, Arabina skipped into the barn with reckless abandon. She was in one of her *up* moods.

"Great place, Damien!" She said, dancing towards the back of the room. "I'm very impressed I have to say."

The others weren't as keen. "Come on," Damien beckoned, ignoring Arabina. Without realising it, Margot stood still. It was hard not be suspicious of the vampire's intentions. *How was he so sure this place was safe?* Something was wrong and Margot sensed it was something to do with that smell. Once inside, the others didn't seem as worried, they strolled through the room, following their leader to the dark area at the back. It was clear that the change in light was a relief to them. After all, it was the first time they'd spent so long in the sun.

There was no more time to linger; she put her hand over her nose. That awful smell was getting stronger.

"Damien, what the hell is that?"

But the vampire didn't need to answer her question. In the middle of the floor, a body lay face down. It was hard to make out the finer details in the dim light, but upon further inspection, she could tell that it was a man, or at least had been. It didn't take any more investigation to know that he was dead. She approached the body and bent down by its side. It was sodden with blood. The victim had been murdered; his throat was ripped out, the straw under and around him was saturated in scarlet and brown where it had started to congeal in the heat. Across from her, Barbie knelt down. She glared at him; the smell must be like a 'welcome home' present. He bent close to the corpse, peering at its features. Margot shivered to think how close he was to the body, but then it dawned on her, she was the same distance away. Death didn't seem to bother her so much anymore; not after all that had happened. She remembered how aghast and disgusted she'd been when she had hidden from the transvestite behind one of his corpses. In that moment, she was numbed. There was nothing distinctive about the man; she didn't know him, why should she care?

She stood up, taking her mind off those disturbing thoughts. She was starting to think like Damien. *Damien.* It didn't take a genius to work out it was no accident.

"What did you do?" She turned on the vampire.

"Oh really Margot, are our morals getting involved again?"

"You killed him," she said.

"He wasn't as willing to rent the premises as I expected," Damien replied, shrugging as though nothing had happened.

"He did nothing wrong."

"But he would have," Damien argued. "What did you want me to do? Let him rat us out to Silvia? When it comes down to it, it's every creature for themselves."

"They'll find him."

"I am not an idiot, Margot, I thought about what I was doing. As you notice, thanks to certain tools used by me, he looks like he has been here for weeks."

"Yes he does." The albino replied, gripping her nose tighter. She continued walking; she stepped over the corpse and sat on the hay bales at the back of the barn.

Arabina had regained her energy levels and jumped to her feet. "Alright muchachos," she said, with too much enthusiasm. "We've made it this far, now is the time to attack!"

The group gave their response of complete silence. They stared at her, unimpressed. All except Hurst, he thought it fitting to jump up and down, clapping his hands and cheering. Barbie pushed him off his hay bale and he fell to the floor.

"You can't be serious?!" Margot said.

"Bitch, did I stutter?" Arabina yelled.

"What the fuck, man!" Margot tried to keep her voice as low as possible as she approached Satan's daughter. Looking round at the others, she said: "She's crazy!"

No one spoke. Margot became increasingly frustrated. Would no one stand up to Arabina? Just because she had power, she felt she could make unreasonable and impossible demands.

Just when the albino thought she was the only one who saw sense, a cold voice broke the tension.

"And just what exactly do you propose we do?" Damien asked, leaning against a haystack in the corner: "Your highness?" He added with sarcasm.

Arabina paced back and forth. It was hard to tell whether she was deep in thought or trying to contain her anger.

"Simple," she said. "We fight. We bring my army!"

"How? We cannot attempt another fight over the border now, can we?" Damien contradicted her. Margot was sure the vampire was loving the power he had then.

"Hurst will go, he is small." She shrugged.

The Demon, who was dusting straw off his clothes, winced.

Damien let out a cruel laugh. "Hurst? Hurst couldn't lead anything."

Margot thought that was a little harsh. She glanced at the little demon. He didn't look up, nor did he protest.

"Oh come on, how bad can they be?" Arabina continued

"The Dark Rider's with them." Hurst said, looking up at last.

"Yo guys," Margot knew it wasn't the right moment, but she was tired of being confused. "Sorry to interrupt your little bitch fest, but who the hell *is* the Dark Rider?!"

Damien looked at her as though she was the biggest idiot in Haszear.

"We saw him, Margot," Barbie said. "We saw him." His voice echoed through the barn.

Margot remembered that cold voice. That sense of fear, of hopelessness she felt. She had heard Hurst mention him a couple of times but had never made the connection. If that man had made Arabina fall silent, he must be bad news.

"And another thing," Margot continued, much to the disgruntlement of

Damien. "Why is he even called the Dark Rider? He doesn't even have a ship, what can he ride? Nothing!" She shook her head at the stupidity of it all.

Damien turned to her. "For your information Margot, he is called the Dark Rider as he's the only one of Arabina's people who has changed over to Silvia's side. And legend has it his feet have never once touched the earth of Izsafar, as he doesn't belong there. He is the most feared and hated creature in the whole of Haszear."

"All right!" Margot raised her voice. "Jesus Damien, I was only asking, why do you always put a downer on shit?"

She was sure she saw Hurst and Arabina stifle a laugh as the vampire walked back to the other side of the room, muttering '*humans*' with derision under his breath. She had to admit, no one could annoy him like she could. However, under the surface, she was worried. Although able to crack jokes on the outside, Margot knew they were in serious danger. The only person who was oblivious to their peril was Arabina.

"Let's face it," the vampire said. He stepped out of the darkness to where the light was thinly cast. "You do not have a clue what you're doing do you? Not one single clue."

"Now that you mention it," Arabina began. "I think Margot had the right idea, let's just drift off, back to the pub." The bitterness in her voice told Margot she was probably just doing that to annoy Damien. But as she skipped off back to the entrance, Margot was unsure.

"You just don't understand do you?" Damien kept his voice calm, but he was beginning to sound more patronising by the second. "This is all a game to you, isn't it? Your people need you Arabina, you should return, not to lead them to war."

"Don't tell me how to lead my people, Damien!" She screamed in return. She had stopped skipping and was stomping towards the vampire. Her eyes were blazing.

"You're a fool for taking this situation so casually." Damien's voice was deadly serious. "She knows we're here, there's no turning back now. Silvia will never stop hunting you. You have condemned us to death."

No one spoke. For a few moments, they were all as expressionless as Barbie. Margot had never heard Damien say anything like that before and hearing it out loud made it real.

Damien went back into his corner and collapsed on a hay bale, facing away from the group. Arabina went the opposite way, to the barn door, whilst Hurst followed her lead, not daring to get too close to her. Margot glanced to Barbie for support; he was looking at her. He stood up and went to her side in silence. He grabbed her shoulders, staring straight into her eyes and then Margot knew what she must do. To anyone else, the glare would have looked the same as any other Barbie had ever given, but Margot knew; knew, that deep down they were on the same wavelength. She understood him and he her. She nodded, pulling away from his side. Barbie was right, it was up to her. Up to her, to get them back up on their feet. Up to her to think of a plan. Up to her to lead them back out into the light.

She looked around at them. It was time. "Right! Listen up guys, girls," she glanced at Barbie. "Or whatever. I never wanted any of this, but I've got to deal with it. But that's just it; it's not about getting what we want but wisely using what's given to us." She paused for dramatic effect. "Arabina. You are stupid, but Damien, so are you. We can't run away from our problems any more, all we've been doing since we got here, is running. We can't let Silvia win. She has destroyed our homes, our friends and it would be wrong to walk away just because it's harder than we thought. At the same time, dudes, we can't just go into this blind."

Margot was surprised to see that everyone was staring her intently. In her head, she wanted to dance around and say 'fuck yeah', but she decided to relish the moment in private and hold her expression in keeping with her words to give the full effect. "You guys are the weirdest bunch of people I think I've ever met and by god, I've never been in so many near-death situations in such a short space of time."

She then added, laughing to herself: "And to think, my Mum thought my friends on earth were bad influences." Margot looked at their confused faces. "The point is, in a strange way, we're a team. And if we don't do something, no one else will. Just imagine how powerful Silvia will be after this. If her position is restored then what happens? We are in one of the most powerful worlds of Narcatoe after all."

Damien grinned at her, Hurst applauded while Barbie pulled her off the hay bale into a rib crushing hug. Arabina did not turn around.

"I have to say, Margot," Damien said as he stepped forward once Margot had broken away from Barbie's grip. "I am impressed. Despite glorifying everything like a cheesy comic book, which was extremely unnecessary, you do have a point, but no plan. So we are back to square one again."

Margot groaned; she knew he would say something like that. Once again, Damien had to ruin any spirit anyone else had.

"However," he continued, much to her surprise. "That will come later."

Arabina turned around, and walked up to the albino. Margot was scared she was going to get a punch in the face, but instead the tall woman took her hands, she spoke soft and slow in her strong Spanish accent: "You are right."

And for the first time ever, Margot agreed with her.

Chapter 13

'There's a light.'

Despite coming to a decision, the hours rolled on as the group sat in the barn, trying to think of a way out.

"Oh, where are the undead at a time like this!?" Arabina said. "They eat enough brains for all of us!"

Margot had to admit, she wished she'd had a plan when she suggested staying in Izsafar, she glanced over at Barbie who was standing at the edge of the barn, looking out into the light.

"Still clear?" she asked.

Barbie turned, lifted his arm in the air and saluted. Margot smiled, at least one thing was going to plan. She then turned to Damien, who had retracted back to his corner, thinking hard. Margot knew there was something he was unhappy about, although what it was, she couldn't make it out. He had disliked her from day one; maybe it was the fact of the added power she had gained in those few minutes back when everyone was paying attention? For the first time since she arrived, they had listened to her and, if she was being honest, it felt good.

"Why won't you just let me use my powers?" Arabina asked, sounding like a spoiled child.

"Because, we don't know if they'll have the same effect as last time," Damien answered in his usual stern way.

Margot tried to block it out, she had to focus. She zipped up her leather jacket; it was getting cold in the barn. *Who had she met here? Who could help them?*

"That's it!" She jumped up. Her sudden movement surprised Hurst and he hid behind a hay bale, scared they were under attack.

Wolf. Why hadn't it occurred to her earlier? Wolf and his boat. He was travelling this way. They had to get to the river. She explained her plan to the others but they didn't seem convinced.

"How can we trust him?" Damien asked.

"If human trusts him," Barbie said from his lookout post. "Then that's good enough for me."

Margot beamed at him, whilst Damien gave his usual exasperated glare.

"That's all very noble, Barbie, but how can we trust him? Why is he not affected by this place and why would he want to come here of all places? It's too risky."

"I see your point, Damien," said Arabina, looking out into space. "But we really don't have any other options and if he does turn out to be bad, we can always just kill him."

Margot appreciated the irony in their casual approach to murder whilst accusing Wolf of being the bad guy.

"That is a good point," the vampire said, glancing down at the dead body. Hurst, who was standing by Arabina's feet, gripped his cross. Something told Margot the idea of more killings was causing moral conflict within him. *Demon Christian*, she shook her head just thinking about it, and how backwards the world was.

"So, should we take a walk to the river?" The vampire said, straightening his trench coat.

"Run," Barbie said in his usual monotone voice.

"Oh, but Barbie," Damien said and grinned. "I've just had lunch."

"No, run now," Barbie repeated, hurrying away from the door. It took a moment for the group to realise Barbie was serious.

Outside, it was no longer quiet. Margot froze in horror, listening to the blood curdling screams and shouts beyond the barn door.

"What is going on?" Damien asked, sounding more annoyed than worried.

"Fire," Barbie said, backing away from the door and returning to Margot's side. "The buildings are burning; they must know we're here."

Damien turned to Arabina; a look of dread filled her eyes. Together they ran to the door, and peered outside.

"He's not joking," Arabina called back to them. "It looks like half the town is burning."

She leaned out further, trying to get a better look. Suddenly, Damien yanked her back inside the barn. Before she could protest, he said: "There are figures in the middle of the street. Looks like Silvia has invited friends."

He walked away from the door and began examining the barn, picking up anything that could be useful.

"What do we do now?" Hurst squeaked in panic. The demon dropped to his knees, falling into deep prayer.

Arabina turned to answer him. "We fight!"

"We run like hell!" Margot said, she turned to Damien: "The river; Wolf's boat has got to be there." She thought back to the few boats they had passed earlier that day that were moored up. Why didn't she think to check?

Barbie nodded and to her surprise, so did Damien. "Put the cloak on," he said, throwing it to Arabina. "And make sure to keep the hood up."

They scattered around the barn, collecting belongings. Once they had taken all they could find, they crept to the back of the barn. It was their motive to stay as far away from the main stretch of the village as possible. Margot turned to look at the carnage before following the others. From where she stood, it looked like the whole town was alight. The climate didn't help; it couldn't have taken much to set the town ablaze. Amongst the masses of terrorised human beings, she could see Silvia's hooded army motionless and hushed within the chaos. She glared at them. It made her sick to see their white cloaks, burning as bright as the flames that surrounded them. Was Silvia so desperate to find them that she'd burn her own cities, destroy her own towns? Was it really worth losing all those innocent lives for – for nothing? Just as she was about to run, something caught her eye. Not all of them were wearing white, there were a few more figures, dressed in brown and those guys didn't seem nearly as content amongst the flames.

Margot could dwell on the subject no more; Barbie was beckoning her to follow them. She hurried on.

"Right," Damien spoke in a low voice once they were all together. "The only way we can get to the boats is by going back where we came from. So let's stick to the backstreets and- Arabina… where are you going?"

But it was too late. Arabina ran from the group and headed straight into the blazing streets. She raised her hand to her head to stop her hood from flying off as she charged between the burning buildings, straight into the centre of town. Across the other side of the street, a pale woman, dressed all in black was helping someone out of a burning building. Arabina's body shrank and her skin turned pale while she transformed back into her human disguise.

She screamed as a sharp pain hit her in the chest. She was hurting all over, she was becoming weak. *What was happening to her?*

She decided to ignore it as best she could and keep moving.

"Lucy," she gasped. The woman helped an old woman down the stairs and into the street. "What are you doing here?"

Lucy turned, shocked to hear Evie's voice. "Evie! How did you get here?"

"Don't play dumb!" Arabina snapped. "Are you following me?!"

"Following you?" Lucy asked. "Evie there's more important things to worry about; the town is on fire, do me a favour and help these people!"

"How did you get here?" Arabina didn't know whether to jump for joy or be suspicious.

"If you must know, this is one of the closest towns to the city and after our last run in, I thought it would be best to leave; you know what with the whole massacre and everything." She looked at Evie like she was an imbecile.

"Well, are, are you okay?" Arabina asked. The words slipped out of her mouth before she could stop herself. She felt powerless around the woman. She wasn't strong minded Arabina, but weaker, softer Evie. It was a strange feeling. "I'm sorry," she said, before giving Lucy a chance to answer. "But it does seem kinda suspicious, seeing you again."

"Oh yes," Lucy replied sarcastically. "I'm really suspicious, running through town like I'm being followed instead of actually helping innocent people."

Arabina lowered her head. "Good point."

Behind them, someone screamed.

"Well, got to go," Lucy said, glancing at a house across the road. "And before you ask, yes, I'll see you again, don't you worry your little blonde head. Just try and be a little less selfish next time."

She smiled at Arabina's blank expression.

Arabina had just remembered that her hair was blonde. She'd been half tempted to yell at the woman 'Are you blind?' She was glad she hadn't.

"Sure," she said with a little smile as Lucy ran off into the next building. Arabina sighed, what was it about that girl? She looked around. After talking to Lucy she had forgotten she was in a burning town surrounded by Silvia's army without any sign of the group.

"Oh shit."

"Find Arabina!" Damien yelled as they hid at the back of a burning building.

"I can't see her anywhere," Barbie said, sweeping his eyes across the buildings. Hurst, who was standing on his shoulders, also shook his head.

"Then we have no choice," Damien said. "We will have to venture into the centre of town."

"Wait," Margot said, before the vampire could say anything else. "Let's split up, we'll look too suspicious otherwise."

Damien nodded. "I'll look after Hurst, you and Barbie go together and stay close to the edge of the town, I am unsure whether these people know what we look like." He looked from Barbie to Margot, making sure they understood him.

"We'll meet you in the woods across the bridge from the town." Margot replied. It was a daunting thought to split up, but it had to be done. Who knew when the Brontangus would arrive, or whether Silvia would make a special journey down there? Hurst, was down from Barbie's shoulders, clasped his long red fingers over the bottom of the vampire's trench coat.

"Let's go, Hurst," Damien said and he ran towards the town. It was clear Hurst hadn't expected the sudden start. Holding onto the coat, he was jerked off his feet. Margot couldn't help but laugh as he squeaked, his beady eyes widening as he was dragged along. Barbie stared at her and she stopped. She looked further into the distance and knew that she and Barbie must follow suit. As Damien sprinted away with Hurst struggling to keep up, it dawned on Margot that it might be the last time she saw them. She bit her lip ring as she did in times of stress and looked at the inferno in front of them.

"Come on, Barbie," she sighed, handing him a self-lighting cigarette, she put one in her mouth. "Let's go."

The lump in Margot's throat grew as she and Barbie entered the town. It was hard to stay close to the buildings when each one was on fire, but somehow she and Barbie managed it.

"I can't see her anywhere!" She called back to him. The town was so full of smoke and fire it was hard to see anything at all. In front of her, white figures were gliding in and out of flaming houses. Margot was uneasy; if they didn't leave soon they were sure to be spotted. It was getting far too risky.

Arabina stood transfixed. There was no point in running. The fire itself calmed her, reminded her of home. However, the fact was that she was stranded. She looked around to find some sign that the group were still there. They wouldn't leave her, surely? A mechanical screech came from the sky, followed by the sound of mechanical wings.

Above her, four Brontangus circled overhead, scanning the ground. Before she knew what was happening, one let out a huge shriek and hurtled towards her. Arabina screamed, diving for cover underneath the wooden decking of a burning house. But the creature wasn't fazed. It was out of control and determined to catch its prey. Swooping down, intent on its target; it crashed head-first through the house. The wooden building collapsed around it, caging the beast within its walls. Behind her, Arabina could hear the house collapsing just above the decking.

"Damien!" Hurst screeched, pointing at the newly destroyed building. They came to a halt amidst the pandemonium, staring at the destruction. "You don't think…" the demon couldn't complete his sentence.

"One way to find out," Damien said, charging towards the house. The nearer they got, the clearer it was that the burning, collapsed building encasing the thrashing Brontangus was impenetrable. The vampire knew that soon it would collapse. "Hurst!" He yelled, watching the demon quiver on the spot behind him. "We have to go, she could be in there!"

Hurst nodded and followed the vampire towards the house.

One thought ran through Arabina's mind - she had to get out. Behind her the building collapsed in on itself in stages. The Brontangus struggled to escape and the sound of crowds screaming again spurred her on. Arabina crawled towards the underbelly of the stairs. There, she knew she could slip out through the gap. The floor above her had lowered; she could feel it falling in behind her, almost close enough to trap her feet underneath the rubble. There wasn't much time. She was almost there, as she dragged her body along the ground. Pretending to be human was much more difficult than she'd first imagined. Above her she could hear the wood creaking and groaning with the added weight. *Almost there*, she told herself. Around her, the porch finally began to cave in, piece by burning piece. *Not far to go*. Arabina screamed with frustration as she tried to pull her body from underneath the floor. She had reached the end, all she had to do was squeeze out, but it was so difficult. The gap was closing in as more of the building above fell. She was exhausted. She didn't have the strength or the energy. She was going to be crushed.

Just when all seemed lost, a cold pale hand reached in and grabbed hers. Arabina grinned as the hand yanked her out of the debris. She made it with seconds to spare. Arabina laughed as she heard the rest of the building collapse behind her.

"I thought you'd never find me," she gasped at her rescuer.

"So did we," said a cold voice. Arabina froze, above them stood a tall glowing figure, in a long white hooded cloak.

Margot and Barbie dashed through the door of a corner shop. They had been spotted. A bell tinkled above them as they entered. They scanned the room. It was empty. The contents of the store were littered across the floor, like someone had burst through to make a hasty escape. The shop was tiny; Margot stared at the counter that sat behind the cramped shelves. Perfect, she thought, dashing to the edge of the room.

"Quickly," Margot said, diving over the small counter. "I don't think it saw us come in here!"

It was a dangerous move to enter the building; it was burning from the outside in. Margot didn't know how long it would be before the blaze entered the store. Barbie, however, was occupied by other things. He limped towards her, checking what the shelves had to offer on the way.

"Do you think I'd be able to find marshmallows?" He asked.

Margot raised her head up from her hiding place. "How can you think of marshmallow at a time like this?"

"I just thought of human sweets, I've not had any in quite a while." He shrugged.

"Dude! Not the time," she couldn't believe he would stop to consider it. The small bell rang again. Margot screamed, as a member of Silvia's army glided into the shop and clobbered Barbie on the back of the head.

The transvestite dropped to the floor with a thud and there he lay, motionless.

"Right, now you're fucking in for it!" Margot yelled, gritting her teeth hard. "Leave him alone!" She screamed and jumped from behind the counter; she ran at the figure trying to pick Barbie's body up. Delving her hands deep into her pockets, she pulled out a handful of the small orange balls from earlier and launched them at the creature. They exploded, throwing it backwards. Using its moment to her advantage, she looked around for more things to throw. The shelf next to her was piled with cans of baked beans.

"They'll do." Margot shrugged, she grabbed as many as she could and launched them at the creature as it tried to get to its feet. "Ha!" She exclaimed, hitting it directly on the head with her third throw. She threw another, but it missed and hit Barbie, who was still on the floor.

"Ouch," he moaned. Her heart leapt; at least he was alive.

"Sorry, dude!" Margot called, and threw another tin.

The effect didn't last as long as she'd hoped for. Whatever the thing was, it wasn't going down that easily. The figure reached into its cloak and pulled out a small black device. From where she was standing, it looked like a small television remote. *Why was the thing just standing there? Why had it stopped fighting back?* A terrible thought struck Margot. "Barbie!" She screamed. "Run! Run into the house!"

The figure's finger hit a red button on the control in its hand. The device unleashed a thick, grey smoke. Margot turned and sprinted for the door behind the counter, screaming as the whole room became engulfed. Next to her, she felt Barbie grab her around the waist, pushing her in front of him. Something felt different about the smoke; it was thicker and clung to her skin. At first, she thought it would knock them both out, but she was wrong. Once Barbie was through, she slammed the door.

"It's not following!" Margot said in confusion as she and Barbie barricaded the entrance with boxes. They were in the store room.

"Human, it's no good." Barbie stopped what he was doing. "I've seen that smoke before. It is no ordinary smoke; it chases people and encases them, bringing them back to its master."

Margot chewed at her lip ring, smoke was filtering through the cracks under the door. "We need to get out!"

She wasn't sure if it was her sense of panic or the actual room itself, but it was getting hotter. Margot looked around for a way out. The storeroom was tiny and cluttered, filled to the brim with useless household objects, ready to go on sale for the payment of people's thoughts. She was surrounded by kettles, fans, ice cube trays and by the looks of it, a lot of out-of-date food. Margot cried out in anger as she rummaged through them, they were no use.

Barbie was trying to cover all the gaps where smoke was seeping in. He thrust a collection of designer bath towels under the door. "I can't hold it back much longer."

Margot searched in desperation. "God, Barbie, anyone would think we were losing air." She stopped what she was doing. There had to be another way out. Although the room was barely lit, Margot was sure there was a window. She scanned the wall, thinking about what was behind the clutter, how the room was structured. She scrambled over a pile of dusty boxes. She had noticed a curtain hanging down on the left hand side of the room. The bottom part of its faded red material was agitated by a breeze. She beamed; a doorway. It must lead to the stairs.

"Barbie, I've found it!" Margot cried, as she scrambled to the curtain, pulling it back. "Oh... shit!"

Her eyes widened with terror as she glanced upwards. It led to a stairway, a blazing stairway. There was no way they'd be able to climb those steps and live.

"Change of plan," she shouted to Barbie, who found it near impossible to keep smoke at bay. The smoke was weaving through the miniscule gaps, tangling around his legs and trying to pull him to the floor. It was a viscous substance and Barbie struggled to fight it off. His body was being consumed and he sank to the floor. *She had to do something.*

What could combat smoke? She looked around at the equipment. Nothing there but the kettles and... fans. *Wind! That was it!* The smoke had filled half the room. Barbie was nowhere in sight. Margot tore open the boxes of fans. She hoped they were battery powered. She felt a sharp tug at her feet and she fell to the floor. The smoke had morphed into small hands; it grabbed her legs and pulled her back towards Barbie.

"No!" She screamed, holding on to the box, as she was pulled across the floor on her stomach. She pulled the box along with her. She refused to let go of it, refused to give up hope. *If I could only... just... grab one.* Margot strained her arms, pulling the box towards her. She was up to her knees in the thick smoke, and it overwhelmed her lower body.

She yanked the box to her chest and pulled out a small fan. With one touch, it whirred. Margot turned onto her side and aimed it at the smoke. It worked! She felt like cheering as it cleared from her feet and calves. Margot reached into the box, getting hold of another one for her other hand. Looking like a household, low budget version of *Lara Croft*, she ran towards where Barbie had been. As the smoke cleared, the transvestite gulped in air.

"Thanks," he said, getting to his feet.

"Barbie," Margot said as she spun around on the spot to deflect the smoke from all angles. "Get two fans, and then stand back to back with me."

He obeyed.

"We need to get out through the window; it's the only way dude. Okay," she said, feeling his back on hers, (or to be more precise, a good length of his legs as he was so tall). "And walk!"

They stayed close, guarding themselves at every angle. Margot was fearful at one point, fingers of smoke got so close she thought they would lash out and rip her body to shreds. With great difficulty, they clambered over the boxes, back towards the small window.

"Okay, just hold them off for one minute." She said. She turned to find something large to throw. The fire was at the foot of the stairs; they didn't have much time. Next to her sat an old chair, she grabbed it and launched it at the window. It made only a tiny crack, they needed something more. Margot grabbed a tool box from the side. After prising it open, she pulled out a hammer. She turned to the window, smashing at it again and again.

"That will do!" She turned to Barbie: "Barbie, go!"

"No," he said. "You first, if I let go, we're both done for."

There was no time to argue. Margot lifted her body up and out through the window, falling head first on the dry grass on the other side. She picked herself up to assist Barbie.

He was having great difficulty. The smoke had wrapped around his legs again, trying to pull him back in as he tried to squeeze through the tiny gap, he wasn't as small as Margot. He was well and truly stuck.

"Leave me, human." He said, clinging to the window frame. "Go on and find Damien."

"No!" Margot screamed. She had to get him out. There were no tools out there she could use to make the gap wider.

Margot jumped in the air, baring her fists at the window. She smashed through it with both hands. She screamed in agony as glass shards and blood splatters flew through the air and down her hand. Margot continued thrashing at the window until Barbie could slip through.

"Hold on!" She yelled, grabbing him under the arms. She pulled with her remaining strength, tearing him from the window. Barbie made it through to land on top of Margot. They collapsed in a heap on the grass.

That one moment seemed to last an eternity. Instead of moving Barbie, she let him lie there on her and embraced him. He was a lot warmer than she had expected, not cold like Damien, but more human. Sometimes Margot forgot just how real a person he was.

"We're alive!" She said with a nervous laugh, still clinging to him.

"We're alive." He repeated, with his usual lack of enthusiasm.

Margot burst into laughter, "Oh, Barbie, nothing ever changes your depressing mood does it?"

He didn't reply. And in that one eternal moment, Barbie was the closest person to her in the world.

*

Arabina was hoisted to her feet. She looked down at her hands; they were brown. *How could they be brown?* She had transformed had she not? She couldn't feel her hair, as both her wrists were held by White Riders standing on either side of her. *This is it*, she thought, as her feet were dragged across the ground. *There is no way out this time.* She had been caught out of her own stupidity and there was no one there to help.

"Call down one of the Brontangus," said the shorter of her captors. "They can deliver her back to our master."

Arabina didn't struggle. She saw no point in it.

She heard one of them gasp and she was dropped to the ground. The other let out a piercing scream. Turning to face the commotion, Arabina saw Damien's hands gripping the neck of one figure and Hurst attempting to bite the ankles of the other. The vampire looked at her, signalling for her to help them. She jumped to her feet and punched Hurst's opponent full in the chest. It fell back to the floor. There was a horrible crunch; she stepped on its head under the hood. On the ground where the creature lay, a dark red liquid oozed into the dust.

"Okay," said Damien, throwing the other to one side. "Let's leave."

There were no disagreements and they ran, leaving behind the dusty roads and carnage. They headed to the bridge. They weren't alone; many of the locals tried to cross to safety too. The nearer they got to the edge of town, the harder it was to move.

"Some of them are following us!" Hurst screamed, looking back.

"Don't look back!" Damien shouted. "Keep moving; we're almost there."

But their progress didn't last long, the crowds slowed them down. They tried to weave in and out of the hordes of people. Damien looked at the line of boats moored up by the river, many were leaving. He hoped, for Margot's sake, that Wolf was still here. He scanned them, wondering which one would be his. Damien stopped. Through one of the windows in a small wooden boat, a man was waving, beckoning him to go inside. Damien didn't move. They'd made it to the river bank, but they were nowhere near the bridge. Was it a trick or worth following? He glanced behind them, Hurst was right; the White Riders were getting closer. If they waited, they'd risk being seen. Damien nodded at the man. Then, holding Arabina round the waist, he guided them to where the boat was. They followed without question, making their way down the river bank so they had a clear spot to make a jump.

"Throw me the little one!" The man yelled to Damien as he ran up onto the deck.

"Damien," Hurst squeaked as the vampire picked him up. "Now Damien, you don't have to, you don't have TO- ARGH!" The demon was hurled through the air and into Wolf's arms.

"Okay," Damien looked at Arabina, still clutching her tightly. "Get ready." They leapt and landed on the wooden deck. Damien's sunglasses fell from his face and he had to grab for them, as he shielded his eyes. He turned to Arabina, lying next to him, panting heavily.

"Cast off, lad!" Wolf yelled to a younger boy standing behind a great, wooden wheel. He stared at the town as he put Hurst on the floor. "Quickly, the others are downstairs, get below deck, all of yeh, now."

*

"Well, what a mess this has turned out to be." Wolf said, searching around the small galley for cups. The boat was a lot bigger than Margot imagined, it was like stepping into an underwater mansion. Although it looked small, she hadn't realised how many levels there were or how deep the river was; they were three floors down.

"I have to hand it to you lass," Wolf looked at her. "When I thought you were going to find your friends, I didn't think it would turn into a rescue mission."

He shook his head in disbelief. "You've got guts, I'll tell you that."

He looked across at her 'friends'. The group were sitting around a small table, just off the galley; all except Damien, who sat in the darkest corner. What Margot liked was that it was lit by candles covered with yellow stained lampshades that hung from the walls.

"We're more like acquaintances - or forced business partners to be more accurate," Damien said. "Who are you?"

"A friend," Wolf replied.

Damien wasn't convinced; he went into the galley to have a closer look. However, there wasn't a lot of room and Margot, who was moving to sit at a bar stool, knocked into him.

She yelped and grasped her hand, it was throbbing. Margot realised it was the first time she'd given it any thought. After the activities of earlier, her mind had been preoccupied, but everything had calmed down and she realised the full extent of her injury.

"You're hurt," the vampire said, fixing his distant gaze on her.

"It's nothing," said Margot, keeping her hand in her leather jacket. She hadn't taken it out of her pocket since they had escaped through the window.

"Margot, you know my species, I can smell it. That is most definitely *something*." He turned to Wolf. "Excuse me, despite applauding your unwanted hospitality, my colleagues and I need to discuss a private matter."

"I get the hint," Wolf said. He turned to the rest of the group: "You all must be tired, there are beds downstairs when you have finished."

He was obviously unsure whether to leave Margot alone whilst injured. "He's right," he said. "That will need to be seen to, there's a first aid kit on board; I'll go and find it."

She nodded.

"Show me your hand," Damien demanded once Wolf had closed the door.

"No," she said. Margot didn't trust him with blood - especially hers.

"Margot," he said. "Stop being stubborn, if I wanted your blood, I could take it quite easily."

Begrudgingly, Margot took her hand out of her pocket. Hurst gasped and so did she. Her hand was dripping; her knuckles were bleeding from where she had punched the window.

"Right," said Damien, not looking at it. Although he appeared calm, Margot could tell he was struggling with the sight. Taking her arm, he led her to the sink and turned on the tap. "Wash it off and then I'll pick the glass out."

Damien being kind? This definitely is a development. "How did this happen?" He said, with his usual coldness. *Okay, so maybe change takes time.*

"She saved my life," Barbie said. The group looked at him. "She could have left me, but she saved my life."

Margot smiled at him and he stared back. It was nice to know that he cared.

"Well Barbie, that's extremely touching, but right now we have more important matters to discuss and Margot, despite trying to play the hero, you should think about your own welfare, we can't win this war if we go around and stupidly injure ourselves now can we?"

Margot's anger had once again been fanned by Damien, but she decided to hold her tongue.

"I believe we need a plan," said Arabina. She had been quiet after the attack. "Margot is," she paused as though something was stuck in her throat. "Right. But we should work together as a group and not go charging about as though we're against each other, or we can't do this."

Margot was in shock. *What was happening to these people? Did they all get hit on the head or were they actually starting to see sense?* She decided not to say anything, knowing Arabina and her manic fluctuations; her good mood may not last long.

"Well, thank you for pointing out the obvious Arabina," Damien replied. "Where would we be without your noble judgement?"

She growled with frustration and mumbled about his disrespect, to which he smirked in response.

Margot knew it wasn't in their nature to do to anything that wasn't for their own personal gain. She remembered what Damien had said the first day she'd met him *'I'm only doing this because I owe Barbie a favour.'* Although Arabina was mad at the state of her lands, actually getting her to act upon and to stick to it was a different feat. She had a short attention span, so Margot knew whatever they were planning, they had to do it, and do it quickly. However, making a world older than hers change its ways was not an easy task.

"Guys!" Margot said. "This isn't helping." She tried to think of a way that she could make them focus on the pressing issues. Getting Arabina to shut up would be a start.

The door opened and Wolf strolled back into the room.

"Take it," said Damien. It took Margot a while to realise he was talking to Wolf. Damien was holding her hand under the tap, picking out the remaining pieces of glass. Margot could feel his hand tremble, although he tried his best to hide it. *It must be hard dealing with blood when you're a vampire.*

"With pleasure," Wolf replied, taking Margot's hand and applying pressure to the wounds. She had to admit she found it all degrading.

"I know what you're trying to do," Wolf said.

"Oh, do you now?" Damien said. "And what would that be?"

Wolf didn't look at him, but continued to bandage Margot's hand. "You're trying to take down a very powerful system and there are only five of you, who don't seem to know what you're doing. At the moment, you don't stand much of a chance."

"Nice to know that privacy still exists," Damien said, lighting a cigarette.

"I can help you," Wolf continued.

"Although," he said, finishing up with Margot's hand. "I think it would be best if we went a bit further down the vessel. Don't know who may be listenin' near the surface."

He got up and walked to the stairs that led to deeper floors. Margot and the rest followed.

"How can we trust you?" Damien asked. He hadn't moved from his spot.

"Well, judging by what Margot told me last time, I think I should be the one that's worried. Don't you?"

Damien glared at him, before following him downstairs.

*

After descending two more flights of stairs, Wolf opened a door, to reveal an all but bare room. The main feature was a large table in the middle. The table, like the ship, was old and worn, much like the person who owned them.

"Right," said Wolf, sitting at the top end of the table. "Take a seat."

Everyone but the vampire sat down. Margot looked around, apart from the small window and a half empty bookshelf; the room didn't really have much to offer. Wolf placed a small, square device on the table, not unlike the one used by the army member in the shop. When he pressed the button, it wasn't smoke that was omitted, but peaceful music.

"Right, now don't think I'm stealing your thunder, Damien, this is your call, I'm only here to help," he said in a kind tone. Margot couldn't help but smirk; it was funny how the guy picked up on things.

"Okay, we know that Silvia uses mind draining powers through people's purchases, the use of the Brontangus to remove humans and we are also aware of the light factor." He tapped his pocket, with his sunglasses in. "However, there are still a few things we are blank about, like where does the angel reside, how does she completely zombify these people-"

"And who the army are!" Margot blurted out.

"Yes, Margot," Damien said with forced patience. "That too. So, what do you suggest we do now?"

"Couldn't we just move my army over here?" Arabina said, for the hundredth time.

"How? How can we get them over the East side of the Torgeerian mountain range? And it could kill thousands of humans if they did get here." Damian said.

"Maybe we should let this human talk." Barbie said and pointed at Wolf.

Wolf smiled at Barbie before speaking. "Firstly, you don't have near enough information to start acting, you need to know this enemy inside out before you even think about doing anything. Secondly, Silvia operates with a mix of mind power and hi-tech gadgets from what I've seen. Maybe this means that she's not got as much power as we think, no one in Haszear uses human technology."

"That is a good point," Damien said.

"I'm sure I recognise that device," Margot turned to Barbie. "You know, when that dude tried to smoke us out. It reminded me of something. Yeah, I know I've seen something like that before."

"Impossible," Damien spoke just higher than a whisper.

"Listen," Wolf said, leaning back in his chair. "I've been living on these seas a long time. I know the ins and outs of this place and I ain't never seen people like you try to take it down. I have to admit, I respect what yeh doing."

"And your point is?" Damien asked.

"My point is: I know where everything is; I can take you wherever you need to go when the time comes. My other point is: you're closer to cracking this than I've ever been. We're just missing one important element."

He looked into the distance then snapped back out of his trance. "I don't think we'll discover that now, though. You're tired. There are beds in the rooms above us. I'll take you there."

"If you don't mind," said Damien, "I'd rather go back up to the top deck."

"And risk being seen?" Wolf said. "I don't think so, besides Damien, you're probably one of the only ones here that can offer proper protection to Arabina so you will stay with her."

Damien nodded.

"But, I would like you to join me upstairs in the galley."

Margot raised her eyebrows. *Why did Wolf want to talk to Damien separately? Surely they were all in this together.* Damien gave a menacing grin. "As you wish."

Ten minutes later Margot and Barbie were sitting on beds in their room. She looked out of the small window, out into the clear, blue and endless sea. Like the land, it was devoid of any natural wonder. Margot didn't know how long they'd been travelling, or where they were, but she had a funny feeling that Wolf was keen to head towards open waters. What was it about the water? It was a very odd rule for people not to be able to set foot in it. She thought back to the river, the water was so deep there, especially if Wolf could steer his secret monstrosity of a ship through without it hitting the bottom.

Margot slumped against the wall. "Oh Barbie, what the hell have we got ourselves into?"

Barbie shrugged, lying back on his bed. "I don't know, human, and all this because I made you a cup of tea." Margot thought back to when she'd met him, it seemed like years ago.

"Barbie, why didn't the smoke follow us out of the window?"

"I think it is mind-powered, human," Barbie said. "And the army member did not know we'd escaped. It seems very dangerous what Silvia is doing, mixing technology and magic. No person has attempted this before."

"Hmm." Margot jumped on her bed and lay back. She thought of Arabina and Hurst above them and how quiet she had been, something wasn't right. She was just tired, perhaps.

"Barbie, thanks for looking out for me, dude. When this is all over, you can come and stay with me back on Earth."

As always, Barbie's expression didn't change, but she knew he was grateful. "And you can stay at my house."

"Ermm thanks." Margot wasn't so sure about the offer after the last time.

She glanced upwards again, restless. "How about I go make you a cup of tea? It's my turn."

"Okay human," Barbie rolled over, he wasn't far from sleep.

Unsure of what she was doing, she crept back up the darkened stairs towards the galley. She wanted to know what Damien and Wolf were talking about. There was a light coming from the galley doorway and as Margot moved towards it, she could hear voices.

"... are we on the same wavelength?" She heard Wolf ask.

"Of course," Damien said. Margot didn't dare move closer, the door was ajar and she would risk being seen.

"People like you and I play a dangerous game, lad," Wolf continued. "I just hope you know where you'll stand when the time comes."

"I'll bear it in mind," the vampire's sarcastic reply was par for the course.

"Damien, these people look up to you, I just hope you'll fill them in on every detail before this fight breaks out, because trust me, soon, it will."

"They have sufficient information, thank you." Damien said. "Do you think mooring us in the North is a good idea?"

"The jungles are the emptiest part of Izsafar and besides the lad's been sailing all day, he needs his rest." Wolf paused. "And you never answered me fully..."

But before Margot could hear Damien's reply something caught her attention. A faint banging was coming from higher up in the ship. Deep in conversation, the other two hadn't noticed it. She was about to ignore it when it started again. Something was going on up there. Margot crept past the door and up the next flight of stairs, making sure every lamp was off. She reached into her pocket and pulled out her night vision sunglasses, she slipped them on. She listened in the doorway of the next floor. Silence. She waited for something, anything, but nothing made a sound. Just as Margot was about to turn around to go back downstairs, she heard an absurd scream from above.

This is it, she thought. She ran up the stairs. When she got to the door it was open. The room was pitch black inside. It was Wolf's office, the Captain's room. It contained his books, desk, maps and documents. Inside, she could make out the outline of the book shelves. A hooded figure ran across the room. Margot ran after it.

Knowing it hadn't seen her; she picked up a poker from the fireside and swung it hard at the back of its head. The figure was different to the rest: It was wearing dark colours; it also wasn't floating. It didn't have the ethereal eeriness surrounding it that filled her with dread. Margot turned on the lamps. She turned back to the creature. It was trying to get to its feet.

It moaned. Margot braced herself with the poker, it was taller than she was, but she reckoned she could handle it.

"Bring it on, you bastard!" She shouted, running at it and hitting it with all her might, but it didn't fight back. Instead the creature tried to block her attack as best it could.

"Ouch, Margot, stop it!" It shouted.

"What?" Margot said, the wind taken from her sails. "How do you know my name?"

"Margot, it's me." The figure lifted up its hands and pulled back its hood. It was Jade.

"Oh," she dropped her weapon, a small contrite smile on her lips.

"See," Jade smiled back. "I knew I'd find you!"

Margot's smile dropped.

"I FUCKING HATE YOU!" Margot screamed launching herself at him once again. "YOU BASTARD! YOU UTTER BASTARD! HOW COULD YOU, HOW COULD YOU?"

It was not the response Jade was hoping for.

"Ahh, Mr Wilde," Damien said, as he and Wolf stepped through the doorway. "So nice of you to join us."

Chapter 14

The Meeting

"Margot, lass," Wolf said in an attempt to soothe her. "Now just calm down."

Margot's red eyes were burning with anger as she stepped away from Jade. Finally she averted her gaze.

"Do what you want with him!" She shouted at Damien and Wolf. "I don't care! Drink his blood if you like, or drown him!"

She stormed past them in the doorway, still ranting. "Just keep him away from me! I don't want anything to do with him!"

Jade was left standing in his usual awkward manner, in front of the two men. "Women hey?" He grinned nervously.

Margot stormed down the steps and back into hers and Barbie's room, slamming the door. Barbie was perched on the edge of the bed, aware of the commotion upstairs. She glanced at him before facing the wall and letting out an almighty scream.

"Did you stew the tea?" Barbie asked in a guileless voice.

"Worse," Margot gritted her teeth. "Professor Wilde has decided to grace us with his presence."

"What are you going to do?"

She shrugged. Margot tried to hold back the hot tears that were welling up. She wanted to pass it off for anger, pure rage, because she was Margot Grant and Margot Grant didn't cry. She didn't know what to think, what to feel or say. Her mind was full of so many emotions relating to Jade, it was hard to contain them all. On one hand, she wanted to rip his face off and beat him to a pulp, but on the other, she wanted to embrace him and never let him go.

The boat may have been large, but due to the silence on board, sound travelled far. Upstairs, the two of them could hear a struggle, the knocking over of objects and the sound of footfalls on the stairs.

"Margot," Damien walked in without knocking. Margot was offended, like he'd interrupted a private moment.

"What, Damien?" she snapped.

"He wants to talk to you." Damien looked at his nails. Margot narrowed her eyes at his reaction; she guessed he felt he was above the petty situation; like a teacher dealing with a fight between two misbehaving children.

"Look," he sighed. "We need him to talk, he may have information and we could use it against her."

"But we can't trust him," she said, her voice getting higher. "You said it yourself Damien! And after what he's done! I thought you of all people-"

"Oh Margot," Damien said. "You judge situations far too quickly. Something seems different about this one. I do not believe for one moment that he was sent by Silvia. Now meet me and Wolf in the galley in ten minutes and please do try and stay calm. Trust me; you will need some of the few brain cells you own, so bursting them all is a bad idea."

He gave an insincere smile before closing the door behind him. Margot looked out of the window at the endless blue. She felt an arm around her shoulders; the transvestite was trying to comfort her. Margot looked up at him.

Barbie's dark eyes stared into hers. "Human, it will be okay."

But that was too far for her. He'd gone past her comfort zone, breached the barriers she'd built around herself and, though she showed no sign of pain to the outside world, he knew that she felt it. It was that that made all the difference to her. It had never happened before. She wanted to cry with him, she wanted to share the emotions that she'd hidden for so long. But she was scared and embarrassed by the knowledge and therefore Margot did what Margot did best.

She stood up and moved away from him.

Trying to keep her voice steady, she said: "You know; it's really hard to take the word or judgement of a necrophiliac transvestite seriously, especially when he never shows any sign of emotion and uses the same monotone voice for every sentence!" She rushed out of the room and slammed the door.

"Oh dear," Barbie sighed. "Something tells me the human's a bit upset."

Margot walked towards the galley, she regretted what she had just done. *Ah well*, she told herself, *I'm here to save the Earth, not make friends.* She took a deep breath as she stepped into galley. The room was quiet after the commotion. As Margot entered, she saw Damien leaning on the counter, staring at the table and chairs at the opposite end of the room. There, tied to one of the chairs, was Professor Jade Wilde. Margot had a feeling that knowing Jade, he *would* have gone quietly. He wasn't gagged, but he didn't make a sound. He glared at Damien, only shifting his gaze when Margot looked at him. She made sure she didn't stare too long, not wanting to catch his eye. She couldn't bear staring into his eyes. Wolf sat in the corner behind Jade, watching him. "Okay, you have your wish, Professor; now will you indulge in conversation with us?" Damien was impatient.

"Margot," Jade pleaded. "Please, you have to understand. This is not what it looks like, if you could just listen to me, you'll know."

Margot didn't look at him; instead she focused all her attention on the smoke rising from Damien's cigarette, watching how it danced and furled into the air.

"Professor Wilde," she said, pacing. "Who sent you?"

"Margot, what has gotten into you?"

She ignored the comment, continuing her questions. "So, you think after trying to kill us once you'd do it again? Follow Silvia's ruling?"

"Wow, if I knew you were going to be like this I would never have bothered following you from Earth in the first place." Jade sighed. "She's right, you lot really are evil, I just didn't want to believe it."

Although the comment was said to himself, Margot couldn't ignore it. She flung herself at his chair, gripping his shoulders. "How dare you!" She said through gritted teeth. "You're the evil one, not me. You're the one killing innocent people. You're the one not stopping the monstrosity that is Izsafar. You, not me! All I'm trying to do is help!"

"But I don't want to hurt anyone!" Jade said, offended. Then he said more quietly: Everything I've done has been for you."

"You and your little friends set the town on fire!"

"Well now, that was an accident!" Jade said.

"So it *was* you! You were so desperate to hunt us down you burnt the town!"

"Not exactly," Jade said. "I erm, well it's quite embarrassing, but I leaned too close to the fire in the pub and set my cloak alight. Then I couldn't seem to stop running around when they advised me to." He could feel his cheeks starting to burn.

Behind her, Margot heard Damien laugh quietly. "Right," she continued. "But you hurt people! Tonight, that woman's scream, I heard it just moments before I found you!"

"Actually, that, erm… that scream was me."

"Why did you scream then, you were the one breaking in!"

"Because, I almost knocked his Earth globe over! It looked so expensive; do you know how much those things cost?"

It wasn't the reply she was hoping for. It was getting harder to interrogate him. Although she didn't want to admit it, Jade would be Jade and no matter how much she tried, she couldn't help but remember that fact.

Trying to appear unaffected, Margot continued. "How did you find us?"

Jade didn't reply.

"I said HOW DID YOU FIND US?"

"Margot," Jade spoke in a quiet voice. "What you are doing is wrong, don't you realise that?"

Before Margot could reply, Damien stepped in between them. "Before this pointless conversation goes any further I think it's time that someone takes the exasperating task of filling Professor Wilde in on the facts."

Margot finally broke eye contact and turned to Damien. "You're right," she said. "But it won't change anything."

Jade stared at the floor.

With Margot's lack of cooperation, Damien took up the task. There was a horrible tension between him and Jade as they sat face to face. Damien was happy to have power, he thrived on it. But as Margot sat with Wolf in the corner, she was sure it was something more. She watched as the expression on Jade's face changed from shock, to sadness, to guilt. He screamed to protest but no words left his mouth, as he writhed with anger, knowing that he'd had so much wrong done to him. He'd been through so many emotions, he reminded Margot of a human mood ring by the time Damien had finished his speech.

For a while, the room was silent and Jade dropped his gaze to the floor again.

"What are we going to do?" He asked in a whisper, still not daring to look them in the eye.

"*We* are going to do nothing," Damien corrected him. "You are going to leave, either this boat or this world. Which one, I haven't quite decided yet."

Jade looked up. "I can help you!" He shouted. "I want to help you! Don't you understand, I'm not a bad person! Everything I did, everything-" But Jade couldn't finish his sentence.

"That's enough!" Wolf cut in before Damien could taunt Jade any further. "Like it or not, Damien, we need him. You said it yourself; we need someone on the inside."

Damien leaned back in his chair and folded his arms.

"I don't care if it hurts your ego, Damien. Leave the poor lad alone for once, can't you seen he's been through enough without you givin' him a hard time?"

Although Damien wasn't impressed, he didn't protest. Wolf leaned towards Jade, undoing the ties around his arms and body.

"Thanks," Jade said, taking off his cloak. Margot stared as he did so. His clothes, although worn and dirty, were still the same old clothes he always wore. His trench coat and flamboyant shirt remained intact. It almost assured her in a way, that he was the same person he had always been.

"Right," said Wolf, looking round at them. "I think Damien and I should go and wake the others. You two stay here, put the kettle on. I think we could all do with a nice cup of tea."

*

The sound of the kettle broke the silence as they stood in the galley, arranging cups. Every now and then Jade would glance over at Margot to see if there was any chance of her making eye contact with him. Margot's stern face remained fixed on the task in front of her.

"Margot, I'm sorry, I didn't realise-"

"Save it," she said.

Suddenly, he threw a cup on the floor, smashing it.

"Jade!" Margot yelled, looking at him for the first time.

"You know what, Margot?" he said, hoping she wouldn't pick up on his dramatic statement. "I risked everything for you. I didn't have to come to Izsafar, I chose to, to find you and even when I thought Silvia was going to do the right thing, I disobeyed her orders to follow you here. In fact, you are the only reason I'm here now!"

"Are you going to pick that up?"

"I've not finished. Oh, okay fine, but I can still make a valid point from down here," he said dropping to his knees. "So I am sorry if I did wrong, but let me tell you it wasn't intentional, you're not exactly the do-gooder here. Everything I've done has been for you, I wasted some of the best years of my life, sacrificing my time to find aid for the earth, because you didn't want to and where has it got me? Nowhere, that's where. I'm still un-respected and uncared for."

Margot felt a pang of guilt in her chest and she turned away.

"Oh Margot," Jade said as he clambered to his feet, throwing the empty cup in the bin. "I didn't mean to upset you."

He went awkwardly behind her, longing to put his arms around her. However, before he had the chance the door opened.

"Am I spoiling something sentimental?" Damien asked. He helped a dozy Arabina to the nearest chair.

"Wow, Damien, I'm surprised you understand the word." Margot snapped.

"Hello," the transvestite greeted Damien in his usual banal manner. Margot tried hard not to snigger at Damien's reaction. Wolf was the last to enter, closing the door behind him. He signalled to Margot to turn the radio on. It was so many centuries old; it wasn't surprising that she struggled with the task and tried to turn on the microwave next to it. He sighed.

"Okay, everyone," Damien said. "We all know what we're here for. Professor Wilde here seems to be the missing piece of our puzzle. So, what is the location of Silvia's lair?"

Jade shook his head. "I don't know," he said. Damien raised his eyebrows. "Honestly! I know what it looks like; I just never remember how I get there. I leave with the Brontangus, and then I'm there outside the castle."

"Brilliant," Damien said. "And I suppose you have no idea of her plans, her intentions, where she modifies her humans? Anything of use at all, Professor?"

"Look, when I was there, she kept me in the castle, in a tower, away from everyone else. She just gave me tasks to do up there, and I did them."

"Extraordinary," Damien said. "Well, as fulfilling and exciting as your tale is, we really don't have time to listen to it at the moment."

Barbie leaned forward on the table towards Damien.

"Damien, Wolf has a point. Maybe Mr Wilde should keep going to Silvia's base and gain information for us."

A flicker of surprise flashed across Damien's face. Barbie never made suggestions.

"I agree," said Arabina, rubbing her eyes. "He's our only way into that bitch's lair."

"Very well, Professor, you'd better become an accomplished actor overnight or our plan is foiled."

Jade nodded, he leaned on the side of the work surface. However, his hand slipped and he fell into a heap on the floor. Margot cringed.

"Fantastic," Damien closed his eyes in exasperation. "What do we do in the meantime?" Hurst squeaked, his nose the only thing visible from behind the kitchen table.

Damien shrugged. "Well, since your leader is finally starting to gain some control over her people, why don't you quiz her?"

Arabina glared at him, her eyes turning red. "Everything we can to bring that bitch down." She said through gritted teeth, not breaking eye contact with Damien.

"Professor Wilde," Wolf said. "You never did answer Margot earlier, how did you find us?"

Jade gulped and looked at Margot. "It works," he said.

"Jade, what the fuck are you talking about?" She snarled.

"'Face'," Jade sounded as if he was out of breath. "It works, I know, I've been seeing things, using it. It's so strange Margot, but it works, well done!"

"That explains why the light hasn't affected you," she replied. "That explains it." She closed her eyes. Margot stood so still Jade thought she was going to faint. Margot was never that quiet.

Suddenly she jumped in the air. "IT WORKS!" She screamed, knocking several empty cups off the work surface and cringing as they smashed on the floor.

"How did it happen? Can you control it? What does it feel like? How long does it last?" Jade was having questions thrown at him so fast that he couldn't make out what she had said.

"Margot," Damien said. "Excuse me for interrupting, but would you please care to elaborate on what you are talking about?"

Jade grinned and said: "Margot, invented something most extraordinary and when used properly, it could help us save the world."

"Without the clichés, if you please." Damien's patience was wearing thin.

"Margot," Jade spoke with exaggerated care. "Made a drug, that makes the person who takes it hallucinate visions of the future."

Wolf stood up from his chair, whilst Hurst slipped off his.

"What?" Arabina said, wearing the same frown as Damien. "Impossible! A human can't create something like that! That's the work of magic!"

"Well, looks like I did," said Margot, leaning back and pulling out a cigarette.

"It's still a bit rusty," Jade said. "The effects haven't actually worn off and it can be unpredictable when I have them, but it does work."

"What are the side effects?" Damien asked.

"Well, hallucinations getting confused with reality I suppose, I mean," he turned to Margot. "I saw you fall off a cliff."

"I did!" Margot shouted in her excitement. "Or, well, was pushed."

She sneered at Damien. "Jade this is great! Where are the rest of them?"

"Well…" Jade looked down at his feet. "They may be back at the hotel, with the rest of my inventions."

"Bollocks!"

"We're not going back there for some stupid high," Damien said.

Wolf, who was still on his feet, approached the vampire. "That *stupid high* may be the answer to everything." He looked at the rest of the group in turn. "Time for you all to sleep I think, looks like we have a lot of work in a few hours time."

∗

When Margot woke, she thought she was dreaming that Jade was alongside her.

She stared at his face as he slept, he looked worn out, exhausted. The lines on his face had deepened; much liked the bags around his eyes. Margot didn't want to imagine what he'd been through. The thought sent shivers down her spine. They were both old before their time.

Margot got out of bed and went to the window. Staring out into the clear blue water, as always, was a desolate affair.

"Brought you tea," a croaky voice said behind her. Margot jumped, she had been so busy staring at Jade she had failed to notice Barbie's absence from the room.

"Thanks," she said, accepting the mug. Margot shook her head. "Barbie look, about what I said, I-"

"Forget it, it's fine," Barbie said. "I am obviously undeveloped when it comes to emotions." He turned and limped out of the room. Margot sighed, rubbing her eyes. She wasn't sure if he had been offended or not. Leaving Jade to sleep, she crept up the stairs to see who was awake. She found Damien first, he watched over Arabina as she slept; a frown on his face. Hurst lay curled up on the floor a few metres away. Margot entered the room, and went towards his chair by the window.

"I'd advise you not to go above deck; the Brontangus seem to be regrouping. It's their time for collecting humans again." He said to her, not taking his eyes off Arabina.

"I'll bear it in mind," Margot said turning around.

"Damien," she paused in the door way. "Can't we just be civil with each other? I mean I know we don't like each other, but for the sake of the guys."

"Of course," Damien said in the irritating smug way he had. "As soon as you control your emotions and stop having unpredictable rampages."

Margot could feel her blood boiling. "You always have to dig at something don't you?" She said, raising her voice.

"For goodness sake, Margot, we can't get anything done unless you keep a hold of your anger," he snapped back.

"You never complain at Arabina's unpredictable rampages." She said through gritted teeth.

"Yes, well you are not the king of the underworld's daughter now, are you?"

Margot didn't reply, she wouldn't ask again. As she slammed the door she heard him shout: "Meeting, I suggest you wake Professor Wilde soon."

Margot stormed off, not noticing the boy standing right in front of her. She walked into him and the cups of tea he was carrying spilled.

"Sorry dude," she said, bending down to pick them up. She frowned as she got to her feet. Who was the boy? She stared hard, taking in his features.

Suddenly, Wolf appeared behind him. "Allow me to introduce my boy,

Eric." He gave with a wide grin. Margot remembered hearing his name as she'd been pulled onto the ship; and only vaguely remembered seeing him.

The son was very different from his father. Unlike Wolf, who had a wide and stocky build, Eric was tall and thin; lanky even. Margot wouldn't have thought the two were related at all. Eric smiled awkwardly at her as she extended her hand to him.

"Nice to meet you," Margot didn't smile as she spoke. "I'm going to wake Jade."

"Ok lass," Wolf said as she walked away. "The galley in half an hour please."

Her heart pounded as she re-entered the room where Jade lay. He was still asleep. Margot walked over and shook him gently. When there was no response, she shook him hard.

"Oi! Wake the hell up!"

"I am awake," he groaned, rolling out of bed. "Why can't you be subtle like normal people?" Jade stretched and sat up.

"We've got a meeting in a moment," she told him.

"Great, so I can be ridiculed and we can come up with no solution."

Margot sat on the edge of his bed, a stern look on her face. "Jade Wilde after everything you've done, are you just going to give up? You're a good person and together we will find an answer. You've never failed me yet." Her face broke into a smile.

"You're a good person too, Margot," he smiled back.

She shook her head, letting her white hair fall in front of her face.

"I'm not," she muttered. She went back to the window. "I'm selfish, Jade, I'm not like you. But I'm going to change; I've learnt things since I've been here, dude, amazing things."

"Margot, I don't want it to be the same when we go back."

"No, me neither! I don't even know *if* we'll be going back."

"I don't think you understand my point, when we go back I want it to be different between you and-"

There was a loud splash in the water nearby.

"What the-" Margot yelled. "Jade, hold on tight."

"Why?"

The ship rolled, throwing Jade back against the wall. He felt his Jonovicator slip from his pocket and he dived to retrieve it. Just as the ship was beginning to steady, there was another violent surge and pitched and rolled again. Upstairs, Margot could hear the sound of smashing crockery and she gripped onto the window frame for dear life, pots and pans fell from the sides and glass shattered. Something large in the water caught her eye.

"Something's in the water!" she shouted as she waited for the froth to clear so she could get a better view. Her eyes widened. "Oh fucking hell! Jade, you're not going to believe this!" As the ship settled again, she threw herself away from the window and crashed into the wall. Jade ran to the window, taking her place.

"Oh dear!" His mouth dropped open.

"Can you see them?" Margot asked, leaning forward.

"Yes."

"The guys aren't gonna believe this."

*

"…so dude, I was holding onto the window waiting to see what this thing was and then I saw them." Every eye was fixed on her.

"It was two Brontangus and they just kept swimming down. It's like they weren't gonna stop. And that's not all; they were taking piles of humans with them. All tied up like a bunch of balloons." She shivered.

"But no one's allowed in the water," Arabina shook her head. "It is the first rule of Izsafar."

"Exactly," Damien said. He had his back turned to Margot. "That makes sense."

"What?" Arabina asked, annoyed.

"Her lair is underneath Izsafar. Just stop and think for a moment. The Professor described a castle like no other, in a stormy sky, which looked almost red through the tiny gaps where the clouds parted. She couldn't put it in the skies of the Over World; the angels would see her work and stop her, but not this way. This way she is invisible, a ghost of Izsafar." Damien paused again, creating his own dramatic suspense. "My friends, Silvia is wiser than I gave her credit for, her lair can be found beneath our very own floating island."

"Of course," Wolf stared out into the distance. "The skies of the underworld. Why didn't I think of it before?"

"The sneaky bitch!" Arabina shouted, banging her fist down hard on the table. "How dare she pollute my father's realm with her… goodness!"

Barbie looked around at the group. "What's a balloon?"

"Well Professor, looks like it's up to you." Wolf walked over to Jade, patting him on the back. Jade winced; like Margot, he was also in shock. He had missed the wall, gone through the door and down two flights of stairs though.

"Okay," Jade nodded, hiding his pain and increasing fear. "What do you want me to do?"

"Infiltrate," Damien said. "You will go to Silvia, tell her anything you need to so she believes you are on her side. Act like an extremist for all I care and then once you have earned her trust, steal her secrets. Find out what she's doing and how she is doing it."

"Look, erm, Damien I've always been the thinker, Margot is the practical one." He said.

"You wanted to help," Damien returned to his original position near the window. "And in all honestly Mr Wilde, I have my doubts whether you'll be able to pull this task off, but unfortunately we don't have a line of bumbling idiots to choose from."

"Damien!" Wolf shouted. "Shut up."

"Right," Damien ignored him. "We'll start preparing now. Hurst, get the Professor some food supplies and Wolf, we need to make it look like he hasn't boarded this ship."

People began shuffling from their seats.

"Wait!" Jade shouted over the scraping of chairs. "How do I get there? I can't dive *that* deep!"

"Brontangus." Damien replied.

"I told you, the Brontangus take me there. I missed the one I was meant to meet yesterday."

Well, can't you just hitch a lift with another one?" Arabina shrugged.

"They're under very strict ruling as part of their punishment. They can only do what they're told to. It isn't like thumbing a ride, Arabina!"

Damien thought for a moment. "This could be an issue. We don't know how safe the location is for humans, on approach anyway…"

Damien's words trailed off, Jade could feel himself going into vision state once again. The ship was fading…

Like back at the hotel, he couldn't see anything. His vision was pitch-black. Piercing screams filled his ears. *Who was that? It was a woman, definitely a woman's voice.* Then she too was fading… *Come back*, he wanted to scream, *I can help you.*

When his eyes opened, he realised his own voice had taken over from hers. Jade was lying on his back in Wolf's galley. Margot's face was above him, the others stood back.

"Jade, what did you see?" She asked, passing him a damp towel. He could feel the cold sweat running down his face. It took a while to regain his wits - and his voice.

"There's something wrong," he said. "Recently I've not seen anything, just heard this scream, this woman's scream. Is that normal?"

Margot didn't answer his question, "Come on Jade," she said, "Let's go get your stuff ready."

Chapter 15

The Second Descent

Jade Wilde felt a pain in his heart. No sooner had he found Margot than he had to say goodbye again. He stepped on deck, into the light, his legs quivering. Soon it would be time for the Brontangus to return, to take the humans, and he would unwillingly follow.

"You know the plan, Professor," Damien said, looking out over the side of the ship.

"Yes, unfortunately," he said.

Damien turned to him. "I have a lot of respect for you." He held out his hand, Jade took it.

"Thanks Damien." He forced a smile which the vampire didn't return.

"That doesn't mean I have any fondness towards you. Just keep your eye on the task at hand."

"There isn't much time; we'll be reaching the shore soon. Make your goodbyes short." Damien turned and walked past Margot as she emerged from below deck. He disappeared down the stairs she'd just come up. She frowned as he passed.

"He's a douche," Margot said to Jade. "You get used to it after a while."

"I realised," Jade said. "So," he began, unsure of what to say.

"So," she replied. "Are you ready?"

"Margot, am I ever ready?" He sighed.

"You'll be fine, dude, you're smart."

"But you-" he said, stuttering.

"Jade," she interrupted. "Times are changing. You can do anything you want, you just never believe in yourself. Cheesy, I know." She shrugged in an attempt to disguise the sentiment.

"Woah, what's happened to Margot Grant?"

"She's still here, she's just learned to stop being a dick to the people she cares about."

Although they were silent, they knew they were thinking the same thing; it could be the last time they would ever stand face to face.

There was an awkward pause. She moved closer to him, he edged closer to her. Their eyes were fixed upon each other; the burning red meeting the brown. Jade bowed his head until their faces were inches apart. It was the perfect moment, the perfect setting had it been watched from behind a camera by a production team.

"Margot," he whispered softly.

"Yes, Jade."

"You're... you're actually standing on my foot."

"Oh, right, shit, sorry dude," she said, looking down and stepping backward.

Anything that could have been romantic ceased to be.

"We're pulling into the harbour," Wolf called. "Everyone below deck; Jade, brace yourself."

With one final look at Margot, Jade turned to face the new surroundings. Hidden behind the trees was a village. He stared at its small wooden dock; his destination.

"They'll be here soon lad," Wolf said, patting him on the shoulder. "You'll be fine."

Jade nodded in response. He couldn't form an answer, his mouth was dry. His words lost. A horrific scream could be heard in the distant skies. They were fast approaching.

"Wolf, we can't linger," Damien's sharp voice was more piercing to Jade than the Brontangus.

Wolf nodded. "Okay," he looked at Jade. "Remember, if you start feeling strange make sure to wear your goggles. Who knows what the skies of Under World have to offer."

There was a bump as the ship collided with the side of the dock. Wolf glanced at his son, who had ducked down behind the wheel.

"Eric!"

"I expect to see you in two human days." Damien said; looking down as Jade scrambled over the side.

He didn't look back, he didn't say goodbye, just stared into the distance.

His eyes fixed on his destination. Jade's legs trembled as he walked. He wasn't cut out for it; he wasn't cut out for anything. He was Jade Wilde, a thinker. That's what he did; he thought, never acted. But what was science without action? What was the point in philosophy without a reaction to the debate? He adjusted his goggles as he stepped onto the land. It was time.

The village was quiet. The shacks were almost bare amongst the density of the trees. Jade looked around. He could hear whispers from the depths of the forest. Jade gulped. He saw fires still burning, baskets knocked over on the ground, tools and items scattered. He bent down and picked up a soup ladle lying near a bowl that had been tipped over. It was still wet. The more he saw, the more it worried him. Someone had been eager to leave.

Jade thought he was being watched. The bushes seemed to have eyes everywhere. He listened harder. Jade dropped the soup ladle. It fell to the floor with a clatter. He winced, not wanting to attract attention to himself.

"Pssst," a voice whispered.

Jade jumped, and looked around. There was no one there. The place was as dead as it had been since he arrived. Maybe he was too late? Maybe the Brontangus had already been and taken what they needed, and he; the so called hero, had failed yet again. He sighed.

"Pssst."

Jade jumped again. He hadn't imagined it that time.

"Hello?" He called out. And then something caught his eye.

A girl, close to one of the houses, was reaching out her hand from the thick undergrowth, beckoning him forward. She was so dark; it was understandable how he had missed her before. Her enchanting skin blended in with her environment. He tried to find her face behind the vast array of leaves; it was paralysed with an expression of pure horror. *Was this a trap?* There was no time to find out. Jade ran to her, weaving in and out of the trees.

"What's wrong? What's happening here?"

At first, she could not speak; only fix her horrified gaze upon his. She grabbed his shoulders, pulling him towards her until their faces were inches apart. He could feel her arms shaking. Their faces were so close he could see in detail the bloodshot veins staining the whiteness of her eyes. Something had traumatised her. Her gaze was fixed on him for a moment longer and then she yanked his ear towards her mouth.

"Run."

The word was so quiet it was almost as if the wind had carried it.

And then suddenly, she released his ear and he watched as she sprinted off into the depth of the forest and out of sight.

"Wait!" He shouted after her, but it was too late. She disappeared like a shadow.

Before Jade knew what was happening, he heard the familiar sound of beating wings. The wings belonged to no bird. He could hear the unsettled rustling of the trees around him. Whispers were coming from every direction. It was as if the forest was conscious. At last it all made sense; the villagers hadn't been taken; they were hiding.

Piercing squawks filled the air. Jade had no time to run; a Brontangus dived into the trees in front of him, missing him by mere metres. The forest erupted with screams. People ran in all directions. He saw the same men that had run past him seconds before, tossed into the air. The creatures dived from the sky, searching for their human prey like starving birds hungry for every last worm.

Jade thought it might be a good time to run. He sprinted through the masses, like he was in the depths of a war zone. Around him, people were being torn apart as they dived for cover. There had to be some way of getting to Silvia's castle without being caught. The idea hit him hard.

Without having time to take account of his actions; he sprinted towards the main section of the village, making sure he was in full view of everyone.

"Brontangus!" He yelled at the sky. "I am an official member of Silvia's army! I requested your assistance." He stopped and thought; that was way too nice. "No, I *demand* your assistance to take me to her castle!"

It was a bold move and Jade had no confidence that it would work. To his surprise, one of the hooded creatures turned, hovering in the air for a moment in apparent contemplation.

"Well, that was easier than I imagined," Jade muttered, dusting off his hands. Suddenly the Brontangus swooped down from the sky, heading straight towards him.

"That's right," Jade almost sang the words. The expression on his face changed when he realised the creature wasn't slowing down. That's when he knew, it didn't matter; humans were all the same to them. Jade gulped. "Oh god."

The Brontangus launched itself at him; its underbelly, inches from the ground. He rolled out of the way, barely missed by the creature's outstretched palm. He turned in the dust, not wanting to look back. Jade was pulled backwards. His feet left the ground and his body flipped over in the air. Jade looked up, his coat was caught on one of the creatures wings. He was thrown about with every beat of the wing. Jade gritted his teeth, knowing he could fall hundreds of metres through the air and smash to the ground at any second. His body tensed as he waited for the creature to dive back down to the ground. It didn't. It was moving towards the sea. They had what they'd come for. It was time to head back to base. Jade closed his eyes. He heard one last screech before they plunged into the sea.

*

"You don't know what that drug is doing to him." Damien said.

"Well, as far as I know, it does what I intended it to do and that's good enough for me." Margot said.

"Yes Margot, we've established that, but at what price?"

Margot turned to him: "Okay I admit it. I've got no idea what that blackness is. It's strange, this drug is a hallucinogen. A vision should be accompanying whatever else is going on."

"Well, let's just hope nothing drastic happens to Professor Wilde." Damien said.

Margot knew that behind his sunglasses, he was staring at her. She didn't reply. She didn't want to admit it. *What if he was right? What if something was happening to Jade, something awful?*

She followed Damien back down into the bowels of the ship. There, deep below the surface of the sea, the others were waiting around the table, waiting to discuss their plan.

Wolf stood up as they entered. "Has the descent ended?"

"We believe so," Damien replied. "Now, what is our plan?"

"It's simple," Arabina said. "We fight fire with fire!" Margot had forgotten how powerful Arabina was. The rest and recuperation had certainly recharged her batteries; she was as feisty as she'd been when they first met. The weak woman Margot had seen being carried across Izsafar was like a myth, a distant memory.

"Please elaborate," Damien sighed, bringing her back to reality. "I'm sure if abstract words alone were enough to defeat her, she'd have been dead long ago if she'd listened to your logic."

Hurst shot him an evil glare over the table, which didn't go unnoticed by Wolf.

"Come on, now," he said holding his hands up. "We're not 'ere to fight."

"Oh, but we are," Damien grinned.

"Arabina's got a point," Barbie said, getting to his feet. "Until we know what's going on down there, we can't do anything, but we can prepare. Silvia is using technology from the human world. We have humans, why not use them?" he gestured a long hand to Margot and Wolf.

"Interesting," Damien tapped his finger tips together.

"And," Barbie added. "Humans have already said Silvia is behind the times of the Universe. Our technology could be greater. Something they haven't got."

"Yes Barbie, but don't forget they have very powerful magic and who knows what tools Silvia's army are using. Just because things are limited in Izsafar, doesn't mean it's the same in her castle. You explained what happened earlier with the grey smoke. Magical creatures were never meant to touch such technology, it's dangerous. I speculate she's combining mind-power and weapons."

Margot's head was spinning. "Okay, she said, so let's just get a few things straight. Silvia is using our shit, to what level we don't know, mixing it with magic."

The scientist in her found the last word hard to utter. "And somehow combining it with mind control? This is so trippy."

"And it's about to get even more *trippy*," Damien replied.

If there was a list of words that should never have appeared in his vocabulary and that was definitely one of them.

"Margot, what science do you specialise in?" Damien asked.

"Well," she said, rattled by the question. "Mainly chemical research and drug development, I also know a lot about mechanics from my Dad."

"Yes, yes, we don't want a life story," he interrupted. "What I want to know is, can you conduct and power electricity?"

Margot burst into laughter. "Damien, when was the last time you set foot on the earth? No one uses that anymore! The elements needed to generate it ran out before I was born!"

To save Damien embarrassment, Barbie added: "They either use parts of stars collected through robotic devices or certain elements of the earth."

"Then what do they use here?" The vampire asked. Margot smirked despite his calm exterior she could still detect a sense of irritability towards her.

"I don't know," Wolf said. "But if we're going to build anything, I think we'd better go and find out."

*

Jade gasped as he surfaced. He thought the descent would never end. It was so peaceful down in the depths of the sea. For a moment he wished he could stay there forever, away from all the chaos and hardships that had beset his life. It was so easy at that moment to relinquish himself of all responsibility and worry...

There was a loud crash which brought him back to reality. Jade screamed. He was engulfed under a sky of dark storm clouds. Jade shuddered as they thundered with lightning flashing all around him. *This is not safe.* The clouds dominated the air. There was no clearing, no sky in sight, but still the Brontangus pushed on, plunging further through the treacherous skies, they descended.

"Turn back," Jade screamed, as a flash of lightning speared one of the unconscious humans. At the angle at which he hung, it was hard to see what was going on; he was still being jerked in all directions. He had no control. "WE'RE GOING TO DIE!" The words came out of his mouth before he could stop them. His comment didn't go unnoticed.

Jade felt a stone hand seize him around the torso, crushing his chest. As he gasped for breath, it yanked him from its wing. He cringed as he heard his trench coat rip down the middle. Where was Silvia's lair? They had just travelled through Izsafar; surely there was nowhere else to go? Then, as Jade tried to compose himself, he remembered the conversation they'd had on Wolf's ship.

This must be... the skies of the Under World.

A gap amidst the endless storm appeared. The Brontangus aimed straight for it, miles below them. More of the clouds began to subside. Instead of the constant, perfect blue he had witnessed when on Izsafar, the sky was a burning red. He could feel the temperature rise the further down they went. It was a dry heat.

And there, in the heat, was the castle and its exquisite grounds, in suspended animation.

At first Jade couldn't do anything but stare at it, that same beautiful castle that he had taken comfort in, was home to a killer; a killer that would trap and extract every human mind that existed. It didn't seem conceivable. The closer they flew, the looser the grip around him became, until there was no grip at all. Before he knew where he was, Jade had fallen in a heap outside the front doors.

For a moment he couldn't move. He kept his face pressed to the grey rock. It was so smooth, although not soothing in any way. He didn't want to think how high he'd fallen.

There was a creak as one of the doors opened. Jade stared at the ground; he couldn't bring himself to look up. His whole body was seared with pain.

"Ah, Professor Wilde, so nice of you to drop in." It was a familiar ghostly voice. "Jade Wilde, please rise."

Jade didn't have any choice in the matter; his body lifted into the air, as Silvia raised one of her glowing hands, levitating him above the ground.

"You are late," she said, dropping him with a gentle thud. Her voice was only higher than a whisper but so powerful. It seemed to be coming from all around him, deep in his mind. He winced as he hit the ground, but managed to remain standing.

"I see you've discovered my secret. The entrance through the water was my own idea, to stop humans venturing where they should not go and seeing what they should not see. Even the shallowest of pools, are as deep as the one you have just travelled through today. The restriction keeps my castle hidden, it was my only option. They do not favour me in the higher areas of the sky and I could not have my beautiful castle seen in Izsafar, so this was the only option."

Jade was more apprehensive by the minute; he glanced around before replying. They were alone and yet he felt more vulnerable than he would have done had a million Brontangus been surrounding him.

Erm," he began, not sure how to reply to the comment. He then remembered about staying in character, but if he agreed with everything, surely it would look far too suspicious. "That's all well and good, but surely you can't say it's a human paradise and not let them experience the beauty of the sea. We humans love the sea and nature."

"They have their artificial pools."

"Yes, but surely you must have-"

"If humans were so fond of nature, they wouldn't destroy it!" Silvia snapped. Her voice surrounded him and shouted so loud he was sure his ears would bleed.

"I'm sorry," she said in a whisper.

After a long pause, she continued: "So, Jade Wilde," she circled him, flying in and around him, like a ballet dancer of the air. Her dress lengthened and flowed and soon all he could see was pure white. He wasn't sure what was happening. He was disorientated, confused.

Jade could still hear her voice, but it came more from within, penetrating his ears from the inside out. "I am sorry Jade," she said. "But an external force like you cannot know the secrets of this land and what I am doing. You found her didn't you? You found her, and now you know."

It suddenly clicked in his mind what was happening. He had to change her idea of him and he had to change it fast.

"Yes I found her!" He found himself struggling to breathe for the first time. Silvia spun round him, her long robes suffocating him.

"I found her and you know what? I hate Margot Grant, I want Margot Grant dead! I want her dead, you hear me!" Jade couldn't believe the words that had come from his mouth; he hadn't meant to say them.

Silvia stopped and hovered above him. He could feel himself breathe again.

"You hate her?" She asked, surprised at the statement.

Jade took in a great gasp of air.

"But Mr Wilde, your whole intention here-"

"Well I was wrong, wasn't I? You were right about them and her, they know what you're doing but they're no threat. I'm sorry I didn't return, I was following her, but I lost her trail. She wants to take down this whole operation, but we can't let her. These humans need help." Jade frowned as he spoke, dropping his voice by a few octaves to try and make himself sound manlier. If Margot had seen him doing it, she'd have said he was a fool.

"I see," Silvia replied. She sounded unconvinced.

"All I want to do is good," Jade said, almost pleading. "I see now, that her ways aren't right. You shouldn't have lied to me Silvia. That was wrong, but I understand why. Like the Earth people, you thought I wouldn't understand you, but I do. They didn't understand my ways either, they said I was crazy, but I'm not and neither are you."

If that phrase didn't do it, he didn't know what else would.

"Maybe I have misjudged you, Professor." She spoke in measured tones, as she looked him up and down. "I will give you the opportunity to join us, join me. But, if I find you are deceiving me-"

Jade screamed as Silvia raised her hands to levitate him over the edge of her castle grounds. He was suspended high in the skies of the Under World with no ground to break his fall. He looked at the angel; she walked to the edge of her kingdom to get a better view of his helplessness. Jade looked down. He couldn't see any ground beneath him, only red mist and sand storms clashing in the hot, turbulent air. The sky felt barren, empty, like a desert too large for any man to traverse. It felt hotter down there, he thought, as his feet dangled.

"It's a long way down." Silvia said, bringing him back from the edge and placing him on the ground. Jade tried to stifle his fear; when he thought he'd gained leverage, she shot him back down again.

"Follow me," Silvia commanded, as the two huge doors creaked open. He gulped, that was it. He was going inside.

*

"This isn't a good idea."

"It will be fine."

"Dude, I'm telling you, we shouldn't be back here." Margot had second thoughts about the mission.

"Damien said the plan was okay and so did Wolf." Barbie tried to reassure her.

"I don't see why *they* couldn't have come here."

"Damien and Arabina are nearby."

Margot shrugged and leaned on the wall. Barbie stood next to her. They looked odd in their many different layers of clothing. She was wearing Damien's black trench coat and a scarf around her face; complete with large sunglasses to top it off. Barbie, due to his size, had to choose from Wolf's array of fancy dress. Margot glanced at him, in his green poncho and large Mexican hat. It was less of a disguise and more of a *look at me, I'm here* outfit.

"We look like weird drug dealers, standing here." She sighed.

"Well, I think we fit in well, human," He said.

"Yeah," she mumbled, "in an asylum."

Arabina wasn't allowed to change; Damien's orders. He'd been paranoid after the last time she tried to use her magic. She shouldn't be there at all, but she was. It annoyed Margot; Arabina was just a constant distraction for them. She stared at the road in front of them, watched as the occasional ship flew back and forth as she stood in the shade. They were on the outskirts of the city of Izsafar, a place where Margot had vowed she would never return.

"This is stupid," she hissed. "They're never going to believe it."

"All we have to do is what he told us then we get to go back to the jungle."

"Fine," she said. Margot saw a small, blue ship coming down the distant road. "What about that one? It used to be a good model."

"Human," Barbie said in warning. "We wait for the signal."

Margot nodded. She turned, looking up behind her at the grey building on the opposite side of the road. There, in one of the building's many large windows stood a figure. On the fifteenth floor, Damien stared out of the window, waiting, his eyes fixed on the ground.

"We haven't got much time." He mumbled to himself. It was difficult waiting for the road to empty; even the outskirts were hard to clear. Soon, people would be going back to their houses and hotels and it would be the perfect time to strike. However, the longer they waited, the closer it got to the Brontangus' time to come out and play.

"Are you going to hurry up?" Arabina whined. "I'm bored."

"We'd better abort the whole thing then." He turned to her. "You chose this path Arabina, now you must follow it."

Margot looked at her watch. It was a pointless action, but something she would have done at home. "He's taking his time. If he's not careful, we're all going to be done for." Margot looked into the distance, figures danced in the sky. They were near and heading their way.

Damien's grip tightened around the object in his hand.

"Are you going to throw it?" Arabina snapped. Damien ignored her, despite the eerie quiet of the street there was still the occasional pedestrian or the buzz of a passing ship.

"Arabina, will you kindly shut up? You're not making my task any easier." He sighed, returned to his original position and tried to regain focus.

"What's so fucking difficult?" She asked, getting off the bed and picking up an object from the dresser.

"All you have to do; is choose a ship, like that one." Arabina pointed to a green ship moving slowly down the street towards the building. "Wait until about... now, and then just throw something, like this."

Damien tensed. Before he had chance to stop her, she launched one of Jade's small orange balls out of the window and into the path of the ship below. There was a sudden explosion as the front of the ship fell apart, landing on the street below.

"Jesus!" Margot gasped. "What's he playing at? He was only meant to cause a dent! Not blow the whole fucking thing up!"

Barbie looked down the road. "We've got more problems than that right now."

Margot followed his gaze; in the distance another ship was approaching.

"Let's just stick to the plan," she said, staring at the smoke rising from the ship in front of them. "Come on!"

Margot ran up to the side door.

"Human," Barbie said, catching up to her. "Remember what these people have been put on Izsafar for. We don't know how safe they are."

Margot stared at him, after what she'd been through, dealing with a few humans was sure to be the least of her worries. The door opened. Smoke poured out, followed by a choking, elderly couple. Margot felt herself cringe; it was the same couple that had almost driven into her with their flying dodgem at the fair.

"OH GOD!" The chubby woman yelled in an American accent. Her blonde ringlets fell gracefully in front of her face as she clambered out of her vessel, trying to return her straw hat to its original position on her head. "Charles, Charles, where are you?"

"I'm here," the old man replied as he jumped down from the ship seconds after her. He adjusted his baggy, tan shorts over his stick-thin legs; they couldn't have looked more ridiculous. Margot tried not to laugh at his choice of beige outfit, with his baggy tucked in shirt, socks, sandals and red baseball cap.

"Oh god!" The woman turned, flinging her arms around her husband and giving him an unwanted embrace.

"Are you alright?" Margot asked, doing her best to try and sound concerned. It took a while for the woman to register her presence.

"Honey," the man said, raising his voice and trying to pull away from his wife. "Are you going to talk to this nice lady?" He was thankful for an excuse for her to let go of him.

"For god's sake, Charles," his wife said, pulling away from him. "Will you just give me a moment? I'm in shock!"

Margot and Barbie exchanged glances. Margot felt more awkward, the longer it went on. Finally, the woman turned to her. "Oh, yes honey! We're okay. But our ship! It's as though something just fell out of the sky!"

Margot glanced at the window where Damien was standing. She looked at the woman, "Well me and my friend here know a thing or two about ships and we don't mind taking a-"

"Oh, a Mexican!" The woman said excitedly, turning her full attention to Barbie. "And in classic attire too! You never see Mexicans wear ponchos and sombreros! Quick Charles, get the camera!"

*

"What are they doing?" Damien glared down at the scene below him.

"I think they're taking photos." Arabina laughed as the woman, began striking an array of poses around Barbie.

"They're supposed to be looking at the engine!" He tried to keep his composure.

"Oh don't worry," Arabina laughed. "I'm sure they'll get to that after the souvenir shots." Her smile dropped as she looked back down the street. "There's another ship!" She said, running back to the dresser to fetch another object. "Don't worry muchacho, I'll sort it!"

"Arabina, NO!"

*

"...thanks for that sweetheart," the woman said, smiling at Barbie. "It must be really hard farming pigs all day...ARGH!" She let out another ear-piercing scream. Margot, who had lost interest in the conversation, turned just in time to see Barbie collapse to the floor. Next to his head, she saw the stone that Damien was originally meant to throw. Blood stained the top of his hat. She wanted to punch somebody. Margot glanced up at the hotel window, and made a gesture. Just when she thought things couldn't get any worse, she saw another ship approaching. Margot ran to Barbie's side and knelt down, shaking him in a desperate attempt to try and wake him. The new ship came to a halt and the door opened.

"I saw the explosion, is everyone alright?" A gruff voice called out to the group. Margot recognised that voice. She knew she must keep her head down. There was a pause and then the tone changed. "What's going on here? Why is there a dead Mexican?"

Margot risked a glance in the direction of the voice and regretted it. A tall, well-built bald man was making his way over to the scene. The woman ran up to him telling her story. "Oh god…" Her words were echoes in the back of Margot's mind. At that moment, her thoughts were drowning out her surroundings. Her eyes filled with tears behind her sunglasses. Everything was moving in slow motion; nothing mattered any more. She was defeated, hurt, betrayed. The man behind her was someone she'd known all her life; her father.

"Get out of the way, girl." A hand pushed her backwards, forcing her back into the present. He knelt down to examine Barbie for himself. Margot snapped back into action. He couldn't know who she was, it would ruin everything. She smiled sadly to herself; plans always went well until human emotions were involved. She must remember who she was: Margot Grant, the woman with no weaknesses. She took a deep breath, it didn't matter, he didn't recognise her and she watched him check Barbie's pulse.

"He's all right," he said getting to his feet. "Now, do you want me to have a look at your engine?"

"I'll check it too," Margot was on her feet before they had time to answer. It was the only way to get the information they needed. Time was running out, the Brontangus would soon be upon them. Without that piece of information, they didn't stand a chance against Silvia.

"Fine." Her father spat.

Margot watched him as he opened what was left of the bonnet. He still had the same strength, the same mischievous manner that she once knew, but something about him was different. More wrinkles had formed around his eyes, more lines on his forehead, he was old, tired, worn by the passing of time. She knew Izsafar would have drained him, stolen his thoughts, but something told her it was more to do with the lifestyle choices made in his past, rather than moving to Izsafar which had caused his haggard appearance.

"Right," he mumbled as he leaned over. Although almost completely destroyed, the engine still lit up, flashing an array of different colours just from his touch.

"Extraordinary, isn't it?" There was warmth in his voice that Margot only heard when he talked about mechanics. Lost in his own world, he was captivated by the technology. She smiled; it was nice to see that side of him. Margot looked back to the engine and pulled down her sunglasses to get a better look. It was way more complicated than she'd imagined. Although the area it took up in the vessel was small, it had so many buttons, cogs, knobs, tubes and wires that she was unable to focus on it all at once.

"Well, as far as I can see," her father turned to her. "The explosion had nothing to do with the engine. Strange."

He frowned, staring at a bronze pot set at the back of the engine. Margot followed his gaze; it was something she'd never noticed before, due to the complexity of the equipment. The pot was oddly primitive compared to everything else; it was circular and smooth, with a strange round grate sticking out to the front of the ship.

"Best just check the fuel," he muttered. He lifted up the lid to see inside. Margot stayed close. She had a feeling the pot's contents would contain all the answers they needed.

Peering inside, she saw a strange, swirling liquid. It was like nothing she'd seen before. It was thick and white and at first, resembled something she'd rather not mention. She stared harder and the contents of the bowl changed. It grew more transparent and shapes appeared, human shapes; memories.

Margot tried to muffle a gasp as he dipped his finger in and watched as the liquid dripped like honey back into the bowl. The images of the bowl changed. She saw a small girl, with white blonde hair and a pale face; a couple argued in the background. Margot's heart raced.

"Will you stop looking over my shoulder like that?" Her father yelled, slamming down the lid and glaring at her. "Fucking hell, you're just like my bloody dau-"

He stopped himself before the word left his mouth. It was a comparison, not an accusation, but still too close for comfort. "Who are you anyway?"

The hairs rose on Margot's neck as her father looked her up and down for the first time.

"A friend," she replied in a quiet voice.

"You're lying," his eyes narrowed. "I have no friends, not anymore." He walked away, leaving her by the ship's side.

"Come on," he yelled at the couple. "I'll fix your ship back in town, we've only got half an hour till the curfew."

Margot watched in silence as her father attached the ships together, and drove away without a second glance at her. She felt numb as he disappeared into the distance. They turned a corner and he was gone; that would probably be the last time she'd ever see him. Next to her, Barbie murmured as he came to.

"Well?" She heard Damien ask as he and Arabina rushed towards her. "What was it?"

"Mind power," she replied quietly, not taking her eyes off the street.

"Someone you knew?" Damien asked.

"Yes," she whispered. "It was my father."

*

As Jade walked through the castle he was unable to look away from the grand décor embedded into the walls. Silvia took him on a circuitous route through the building. He knew the reason for it. She didn't want him to know his way around. Jade followed her past the throne, through a door into one of many vast corridors. A grand, red carpet covered the floor and lead the way through the house. Jade could feel his palms sweating.

What if she knew? What if she knew of his plan?

He took in a deep breath, trying to calm himself. He was in too deep to lose his nerve. Silvia lead him through another door, until they were outside again, walking along an undercover walkway. Like the inside of the castle, it was also a shade of cream. Jade gazed beyond the stone pillars to a beautiful garden in the centre of the castle grounds. He was unable to take his eyes of the immaculately cut grass and the range of exotic flowers. Even in the skies of hell, it looked like the perfect summer's day. If any religious person had seen it, they'd have thought it to be their heaven. It was ironic, it was anything but that.

The thing that caught Jade's attention was not the nature of hell but what lay in the centre of it. Before him, stood a bandstand, featuring a circular structure at its centre. It was the only indication that it was not man-made. Its structure was old and delicate and dovetailed neatly into itself, forming an ostentatious pattern. He stared at its grand gold, green and red. There was something special about it all. For some reason, Jade was overcome by a sense of belonging. He felt the need to go out and bask in the light, stand on the bandstand.

"That," Silvia said. "Is the heart of the castle. I thought it rather nice to have a garden in the centre of the castle grounds, wouldn't you agree?"

He nodded his head as they stepped back inside.

"Unfortunately," Silvia continued. "Reenie was unable to join us today."

Jade gulped.

"You mean, you killed her?" He asked.

"No," the angel laughed. "She just wasn't able to make it today, she has work to do."

Jade felt his cheeks turning red as he carried on following her down the ornate corridors.

They reached the end of the walkway. A hooded figure guarded the doorway to the next room.

"Professor," Silvia gestured to the creature. "Meet the leader of the White Riders; he's going to take you through your training."

*

On the bottom floor of Wolf's boat, Barbie lay underneath a green ship. He'd been there for a good few hours; tampering with the engine and replacing parts. Soon, it would fly again. The couple decided that it was no longer of any use to them and left it behind. Waste not want not, it didn't take long for them to steal it. It wasn't part of the plan, but no one had noticed. It was funny, Barbie thought, how they lost interest in things that were broken.

Hurst wandered in carrying a cup of tea. The room was bigger than any he had seen on Wolf's ship. Wolf called it the loading bay, a place where he stored large objects and imported new items. It reminded Barbie of an empty, white warehouse, something that was out of context on a ship like that.

"They still haven't returned," Hurst squeaked anxiously.

"They needed to go to the scrap yard," Barbie replied and continued to work.

"Yes, well I don't like it," Hurst paced up and down next to Barbie. The transvestite let out a deep sigh and crawled out from beneath the ship.

"They needed parts for weaponry. Arabina will be safe, don't worry."

"She shouldn't have gone!" Hurst wailed. The demon was almost hysterical. "If anything-"

"Hurst you know we've passed the stage where status actually means anything. There's only a few of us over here, we must all pull our weight. You know Arabina, she may make stupid decisions sometimes, but she loves her land, she won't stand back whilst it gets destroyed."

For a moment, the demon looked as though he was going to get angry. Instead, he closed his black beady eyes and fell silent, then stared at the ground, maudlin.

"I'm scared, too." To the average person, Barbie's monotone voice may not have sounded reassuring. But it was the very thing Hurst needed to hear. "We're the heroes now," Barbie said. "It's time to stop being a coward."

He turned away from Hurst. "This is a nightmare."

"Oh no," Hurst squeaked with terror. "I knew it wouldn't fly, what will we tell the others?"

"I was talking about the stains on my skirt," Barbie said. He looked down at his outfit and sighed again. "These will never wash out; I know I'm wearing black, but the grease."

Hurst shook his head in disbelief, they were on the brink of war and Barbie was worrying about his clothes. Hurst stepped closer to get a better look at the ship, which, when you're only a few feet tall, is a lot harder than it seems. Much to his embarrassment, Barbie had to pick him up to show him the work on the engine. The transvestite had been busy; most things underneath the bonnet had been replaced with bits and pieces the others had brought back from multiple trips to the scrap yard.

The yard on the outskirts of the Westside of the city was huge. The vast wasteland was piled high with mountains of waste, always deserted, even by the Brontangus and White Riders. Despite that, Wolf believed they should enter with caution. The group had gone there disguised as a waste disposal team, using a stolen loading ship in order to move about the landscape undetected. Gathering the waste and producing the weapons wasn't the problem. Getting something to power them with was.

Although the engine was full of fuel, everything that Margot had made so far wasn't. They hadn't considered how to obtain what she had seen in the brown pot, but there was no way she would empty her own thoughts in there.

Barbie put Hurst back on the ground and reached for the tea that the demon had brought for him. As he did something caught Hurst's eye where Barbie had been working. Whilst the transvestite was preoccupied, Hurst studied his tools. He reached down and picked up a black and white photograph of a woman.

He spoke gently, his words filled with sorrow. "Faith, after all this time? Don't, don't you think-"

"No," Barbie said, taking the photo from the demon's hand. "She's just a human. She is unimportant to me." He turned his back on the demon.

Hurst narrowed his eyes and raised his voice. "She was not just a human and you know it! I suppose Margot Grant is just a human too?" The demon waited a moment. "You don't have to sound like the others in our world; you don't have to sound like Damien. Despite how undeveloped their world may be, they are still creatures just like us."

Barbie remained silent, his back turned.

"I said a prayer of faith last night," Hurst said. "I always do."

"That won't make her any less dead." Despite his words, there was still no emotion in Barbie's voice. He turned around, staring Hurst in the face. "Tell me, Hurst, why do you believe in that human religion when you know full well that it is most probably based on our world? Damien was right; it's because of people like you and me that this war started in the first place. We're one of the most developed worlds in the whole of Narcatoe. We shouldn't be travelling around greeting the others."

"Humans may be undeveloped in terms of technology, but they have more love and emotion and faith than any creature I've ever met. Just because we're one of the most intelligent dimensions doesn't mean we know *everything*. We don't know how we got here, why rule out a God?" Hurst got closer still to the transvestite and stared him straight in the face. "What gives us the right to be correct and them the burden to be wrong? That's what I don't understand. They're the most free thinking and passionate creatures I know, and as far as I'm concerned they're equal to species like us."

Barbie glared at him. It was the first time, he'd heard Hurst say something and actually sound sure of himself. Even the demon was astonished. He had to shake himself before he spoke again. "Barbie," he said gently. "I'm not saying forget her, but you need to let yourself be at peace."

"Don't you understand? I can never be at peace, I am not a free creature like you; I am cursed."

The door at the far end of the room opened, Margot entered. "Hey dudes, what did I miss?"

"Nothing," Barbie said as she went to inspect the spaceship.

"Barbie, I got you some cigarettes, okay so you have to light them yourself here, but still good, huh?" She threw him the packet and grinned at him.

Barbie nodded. There were three successive bangs from the other side of the room.

"Well, come on," Margot beckoned the two of them. "We haven't got all day, guys."

Shrugging, Barbie and Hurst followed her out of the room and watched as she bolted the door. Once secure, they looked through the window. Peering through, they saw a large door open at the opposite end of the room and water poured in, soon the room was flooded.

Barbie sighed. "I left my biscuits in there."

The water was not the only thing to enter the room; a square ship glided in through the door and parked next to the green one. The large door closed and small holes appeared all over the floor and walls of the room. They heard the whir of pumps as the water was forced out of the room. The doors of the white ship opened and three figures in white overalls and ski goggles jumped from the vessel.

"Right," Margot said. "Let's go." She unbolted the door and stepped into the room.

"I see you've been busy, Barbie." Damien grinned, as he, Wolf and Arabina pulled off their disguises.

"Going to check on my lad," Wolf said. "We'll be setting sail soon, not long before we're reunited with Jade."

Margot's heart leapt.

"I can't believe we have to wear these things," Arabina complained, unzipping her overalls to reveal her red dress.

"Margot, I think we've collected enough items for an extensive armoury once everything is put together." Damien said.

Margot followed him around to the rear of the white ship, where he pressed a button opening the doors of the ship. She waited until the electronic steps lowered before climbing up. It was dark; the only light was coming from outside. It was built like a 21st century articulated HGV, separated into two main compartments; a cab for the driver and a place to load the goods. It was bigger than any human vessel Margot had ever seen. She couldn't move for the vast array of objects they had retrieved.

Margot examined broken TV sets, light bulbs, kitchen rails, shopping trolleys and more. She smiled. It wasn't perfect but they would do with it what they could.

"So," Damien grinned at her. "Do you think this will be enough?"

Margot climbed back down the steps. "Prepare yourselves guys; we've got a hell of a load of work to do."

*

Once again, Jade was face down on the floor.

"Try it again," a cold voice said.

Jade sighed. He pulled himself to his feet. They were in a grand hall, with a high, painted ceiling made up of hundreds of years'-worth of architectural influence, finished off with a patterned, cream marble floor. The only downside was that it was one of the training grounds for Silvia's army. Around him were hundreds of white hooded figures involved in varying activities. While some trained in the centre of the room, others plotted on blackboards around the outskirts and tried out new inventions.

"How can you learn to use our inventions, if you can't perform a simple defence move out in the field of battle?" Jade's trainer snapped.

"I'm trying!" Jade replied, dusting himself down. "You, you just move too fast."

"Professor," the figure said. "I was standing still."

Jade blushed. "Yes well-" He didn't finish his sentence. He was distracted by the view, through the rows of arched windows in front of him. Behind the White Rider, the Brontangus glided past the castle window, carrying humans.

"Where are they taking them?" Jade asked the hooded figure.

It shook its head. "You're asking the wrong person, only Silvia and the Brontangus know that." It shivered. Jade was beginning to think the humans weren't the only ones to fear the stone creatures. Maybe he had misjudged them; maybe they weren't so bad after all. But Jade's train of thought was halted as he was slammed back onto the polished stone floor.

The creature sighed. "Try again." It said, pulling him to his feet.

Jade frowned, what were they?

"Right," it said. "It's obvious your fighting skills need work."

It turned around and chose something from a pile on the floor. "This is one of the many tools in the basic kit we are given. You will learn to use them all." The hooded creature handed him two flat objects. At first glance they looked like the soles of shoes. Jade saw they were much thinner and didn't bend like normal soles would.

"What do I do with them?" He asked, staring at the objects. There was something familiar about them, something that he was sure he had seen somewhere before.

"You put them beneath your feet. They are the reason we can levitate and fly. They also enable us to pass through the water without the help of the Brontangus."

Jade's face lit up as he placed the soles beneath his feet.

"I thought you could fly by magic." He said; shocked by what he was discovering.

"Then you thought wrong." The creature walked behind him. Jade gulped. "All our tools are controlled by the power of the mind; all you have to do is imagine your destination and concentrate on the theory of flying."

Jade shut his eyes, and screwed up his face as he concentrated. The creature's voice and noises from the hall faded away. He had to master it, if he did, imagine the benefits it would have for him and the team; for Margot.

The voice of the creature came back to him and it sounded way too distant for his liking.

"Mr Wilde. Mr Wilde can you hear me? PROFESSOR!"

Jade opened his eyes and gulped. He'd been concentrating so hard he hadn't realised he was floating so high, he could almost touch the painted ceiling.

"Oh god!" Jade screamed, trying not to panic. "This is not good! This is really not good!"

"Professor, it is important that you keep concentration or-"

But it was too late, Jade fell. He closed his eyes. He didn't want to see how close to the ground he was. Jade kept his eyes shut, bracing himself for the pain. When he didn't hit the ground for some time, he was confused. Was there something on the weird soles that enabled him not to feel pain? He opened his eyes and winced, he was suspended in mid-air. It didn't take long to work out how it had happened, because there, at the end of the room stood Silvia; her white glow cascaded over the hooded creatures, her long hair floating around her. Jade cringed, he felt stupid.

"Everyone, stop what you're doing." She didn't open her mouth, her voice echoed in the heads of those in the room.

And stop they did. The room fell silent as she advanced. "Where is Jade Wilde?"

They pointed to Jade, suspended in the air.

"Hey Silvia," he waved, gritting his teeth in a fake smile. "What's up?" Acting casual probably wasn't the best course of action. And anyway, it was extremely hard to pretend everything was normal when he was suspended metres above the floor.

"Meet me in the main room, Professor, we have much to discus and there is someone I am anxious for you to meet."

Jade nodded.

Silvia turned to the hooded creature training him. "You will take him."

She clicked her fingers as she turned away and Jade dropped to the floor.

A thought occurred to him as he was led through the corridors of the castle; it was a thought he knew he probably shouldn't voice, a thought that probably wasn't even relevant, but if he was interested in sneaking around the castle and obtaining certain information, it may well be in his best interest to speak up.

"Where do the Brontangus sleep?"

"Sleep!" The creature leading him was shocked. "They never sleep. It is part of their torture. You must remember Professor; they are the scum of all eighty one dimensions. They do not deserve sleep."

Jade frowned. "But surely, they're trapped in those stone bodies? They were other creatures or beings before they became Brontangus?"

"Of course," the hooded creature said. "What is wrong, Professor?"

Jade wasn't sure if he should say, wasn't sure if it was important. The thought had been eating away at him since he'd arrived at Izsafar. It was a moment he couldn't forget. He remembered back to that fateful day when the Brontangus disappeared right in front of him and became that horrific ball of ghostly mist rushing around him.

"When I first came to Izsafar the Brontangus that brought me dissolved into the Earth or disappeared or something." He remembered it, and shuddered before he spoke again. "And then this strange white spirit appeared."

"That's impossible." The creature snapped. "You know of the mind-power this place has over humans, you must have been mistaken."

"But what if I-"

"You were!" The creature shouted. "You must have been!"

He didn't continue with the conversation, they had reached their destination. No sound came from the room they were about to enter.

Jade didn't like the quiet that filled the castle; it made him uneasy, as though someone was plotting something awful, right under his nose. The room was no exception. The only thing that was different was the large throne at the opposite end of the room. He guessed it was where Silvia spent most of her time when she had company.

"Come and stand before me." The voice was just louder than a whisper in the back of his mind. He moved further into the room.

"This is where I leave you." The hooded creature stepped back and left them alone. Only... they weren't alone. As Jade went towards Silvia, he noticed another figure, leaning on the back of her throne. The Black Rider.

Jade gulped, he had never come face to face with the man before. Or hood to face as the case may be. Margot had warned him, they all had. He was going to have to converse with the guy.

"Professor," the Rider moved from behind the throne and as he approached, he held out a black-gloved hand. "I have heard much about you."

Jade gave an awkward grin and shook it. "Hello, Mr Rider, sir."

Jade thought how stupid that must have sounded.

"Professor," Silvia turned her head towards him. "The Rider has something for you."

Jade nodded and held out his hand and the Rider dropped a small object into his palm. On first glance it looked like a compass in a ball. The arrow pointed up and down as well as around. Jade examined it.

"Interesting," he muttered. On his touch the arrow went berserk, spinning in all directions.

"We are giving you the task you always wanted," Silvia said. "That object will lead you straight towards Margot Grant, if you want it to."

Jade turned to the Rider. "Why don't you use it?" he asked. "I'm sure you're a better fighter than me and well... just generally better."

"Because," the Rider said. "It was made so that it would work for humans and humans alone. I cannot use it."

"Where did you get it from?" Jade frowned.

"That is not important."

"Professor," Silvia interrupted. "It works via human mind power, imagine your deepest desire is to find Margot and it will point out the way. We will let you sleep and then you will go on a test run. You'll find her and find out what her plans are and how the group are developing. It should be easy. You already have her trust. If you are successful then I guarantee the next time you visit the surface, Grant won't be breathing when you return."

"Okay," Jade nodded. His heart pounded in his chest as he turned to walk back to the training room, then he turned back. "Silvia, does everything here work on human mind power?"

Silvia smiled. "Of course."

"And you store it in the castle?"

"In the centre," the Dark Rider replied. "Izsafar wouldn't be able to function without it."

"Okay," Jade replied. "Just so I know how to fuel my ship if I choose to use one."

And it was at that very moment that a horrific plan formed in the back of Jade's mind. The Dark Rider had confirmed it. He knew exactly where to go and it started with the castle's garden.

Chapter 16

The Last Goodbye

It wasn't a dark and stormy night that Jade Wilde decided to put his plan into action. It wasn't even that quiet, which, if you asked Jade, seemed a rather unfitting setting for what he was about to do. He couldn't help it, his mind loved to romanticise situations and it was the only thing that gave him the courage to carry out the task. He was standing in the same corridor that Silvia had led him down during his first visit to the castle. Before him, lay the beautiful garden. He stared at it in awe. Everything had been manicured and organised to perfection. The grass was golf course length, the flowers ranged through every colour, size and species he could imagine - and were arranged into neat patterns of squares and spirals in their beds. It wasn't the aesthetics that interested Jade. In the centre of the garden stood the band stand, and if the Dark Rider was correct, that was his ticket to victory.

Jade had to be sure he wasn't being watched. Silvia could be anywhere. He looked right, he looked left and then right again, just in case. Jade smirked. It was like crossing the road all over again. He glanced up, checking the sky was clear; it was filled with the cries of distant Brontangus. He ducked back and shook his head. *What am I doing?* They were on the same team, or at least, they were supposed to be.

"Okay," he said. He clenched his teeth and pulled down his goggles. "Let's go."

Jade sprinted towards the garden, jumped between the stone pillars of the castle and landed on the grass.

Before his eyes, the castle grounds expanded, the beautiful flowers grew tall and tangled, more bushes and trees rose from the ground, blocking his view. In minutes the whole garden had transformed into a wild jungle. *It must be some sort of defence system*, he told himself, wondering if others outside the garden could see what he could. He brushed past the bushes in front of him and stepped deeper into the wilderness and tried to get a glimpse of the bandstand.

"Oh great," Jade sighed, as he got a clear view. There was a maze of thick bushes and trees; they looked taller than the castle itself. At the top of a hill in the distance, the bandstand stood. Through the bleak maze, it stood out, gleaming in the one ray of sunlight that shone down on the landscape.

"It's never simple, is it?" Jade said to himself. He dashed through the trees and out of sight.

Much to his surprise, it didn't take him long to reach the centre. Then again, with the compass in his hand, he felt he'd cheated. He smiled as he put the invention back in his pocket and took out his Jonovicator. As he climbed the hill, he took pictures and notes. It had been hard to do whilst at the castle, but Jade wasn't stupid, he'd been using it to record everything since he'd set foot in that small village in the jungle. Jade smiled to himself, he couldn't wait to show Margot. He felt uneasy as he climbed the hill. Something was wrong. Although the landscape was deserted, Jade was sure he could hear voices. Since he entered the maze he had been sure he'd heard whispering, laughing, crying. It was almost as if the garden itself was alive. Jade waited on the stone path. He turned around to glare back at the maze. All seemed well, all seemed quiet. The only movement he could see was in the sky. He watched for a moment as a group of Brontangus flew up high into the storm clouds. He didn't feel like he was in the castle gardens any more. The castle was in sight. Jade knew he mustn't dawdle; he turned back and continued on his quest up the hill.

After a further ten minutes, the bandstand was in sight. He almost laughed out loud as he collapsed on its bottom step to catch his breath. It was just as beautiful as he remembered; intricate engraving decorated the stone work, just like the castle walls. It had a different feel, more alive, more colourful; not the same atmosphere of melancholy, but a sense of hope, a feeling of happiness rooted in the structure of the small building. Jade got to his feet and looked inside. It was empty apart from a small stone well in the middle of the floor. Jade frowned; *what a strange place for a well.* As he looked closer, he saw a glow coming from the inside. The Dark Rider had been right; he was in the right place.

There wasn't time to see if it was a trap. He went to the well and looked over the edge. To his surprise the well wasn't dark at all, it was silver. A long way down, but Jade never expected to see the bottom. It begged the question of what was down there. He leant further over, and his fingertips touched the jelly like liquid that filled the well.

Jade screamed and pulled his hand away. His fingers were burning. It was not water. Jade looked at the liquid, it was changing, forming shapes, patterns, turning white.

That had to be it.

He reached into his trench coat and pulled out his Jonovicator and a small test tube. Another piece of equipment that Silvia's army owned. The hooded trainer told him it would hold as much liquid as he liked; all he had to do was hold it over the substance he wanted to collect. Carefully, Jade took the edge of the bottle in his hand and hung it over the well. It started sucking up the strange liquid. He gathered a substantial amount, and took more 3d photos with his Jonovicator then he placed both objects in his pocket.

"Who's the man? I am!" He sang, and did a jerky victory dance. He couldn't help it; he had never done anything like that in his life. All that was left was to get back.

Jade froze; he could hear voices, real ones. And they were heading his way. Unsure of what to do, he ducked down behind one of the bandstand's walls.

"… well I'm starting to question where your loyalty lies," Silvia's voice rang out.

Jade swore under his breath: "This is not good."

"I'm afraid I don't understand," the Dark Rider said.

Jade felt like slapping himself; out of all the people in the castle, they were the two he'd rather avoid. He was too scared to glance up, but he was sure by the sound of their voices that they were heading straight towards him.

"You have been absent more than usual recently, don't deny it. I know you wish to spend time with her, but I promised you no harm would come to her."

"Excuse me, Silvia, but I am doing what I said I would, I can be of more use on the surface. You of all people should know that."

There was a long pause before Silvia spoke again. "Very well, but I have the Professor, I expect to see your hood down here more often."

"And how much use do you think he'll be?" The Rider asked. "He's just a human."

"I know," Silvia replied. "He may be as cold hearted as the rest of them but at least his cold heartedness has passion behind it. He has a big job in hand."

A loud screech filled the air as more Brontangus flew overhead.

"And what about *those* monstrosities?" the Dark Rider said in a bitter tone.

"Those 'monstrosities' as you like to call them, are the only things keeping my plan running smoothly. I do not believe the speculations about them, there is no way they'd have the power to rebel" Silvia said. "I have to admit, Arabina did scare me, but she is weakened and with Mr Wilde on our side, nothing will- oh hello."

Jade looked up to see the Dark Rider and Silvia looking down at him.

"Hello," he said, getting to his feet and brushing himself down.

"And what the hell do you think you're doing here?" The Dark Rider snapped.

"Well, I was going for a walk and then… well I stepped into the garden and got lost." Jade thought playing dumb was the best option.

"That doesn't explain why you were on the floor."

"Well I wasn't looking for a contact lens!" Jade replied sarcastically. He was sure that if he could see the Dark Rider's eyebrows, he'd be raising them in confusion, or disdain. When no one said anything, Jade thought it best to keep talking. "Look," he said. "You scared me, okay? I was lost out here and then I heard voices and yes, it scared me so I ran and hid."

"How gallant of you," the Dark Rider said.

"You know, Professor," Silvia cut in. "I do love this garden; it's perfect, you can easily get lost and have time to think. I often come here to get away."

She clapped her hands and when Jade turned around it had returned to normal. They stood in the bandstand amongst the beautiful vegetation.

"Just be more careful where you tread next time," Silvia said. "The things that are the most beautiful to look at, seem to be deadliest to the touch."

Professor Wilde nodded, took his things and went to prepare for his voyage to the surface of Izsafar.

*

Jade gasped for air as he climbed onto the nearest land he could find. The ascent was so strenuous; he vomited water as he climbed on the bank. *Never again*, he thought to himself. He knew why humans didn't travel below the sea. No way was that healthy. He thought descending was a problem, but he hadn't realised the half of it. After throwing up, Jade thought it would be a good idea to clean up before he met Margot, wherever she may be. The two human days were up and it was time to report back to the group. Jade sat up, he took deep breaths and wrung out his dreadlocks and trench coat before clambering to his feet. He wobbled as he tried to steady himself, he felt faint and the heaviness of his soaking clothes wasn't helping the situation. Jade glanced around at his surrounds for the first time; he was on a bank, next to a grey sea. It didn't seem like Izsafar at all, or at least not where humans would dwell. Jade's eyes widened as they came into focus. He was standing in the middle of a huge landfill.

Around him, hills of rubbish were piled high. All he could see was human debris. A large sewer pipe, meters away, was pouring a green substance into the river. Jade cringed, was it really Margot's location? Maybe the compass was wrong. He pulled it out of his pocket. It was flashing red. Jade sighed, that meant he was close to his destination. Nope, he was in the right place. He took a deep breath and turned to walk up the hill of rubbish.

It wasn't the most pleasant experience ever, but he thought it may help him have a clearer view of his surroundings. Once up there he hoped he'd be able to see the albino. At the top, he could see little more than he could before. Jade wiped the front of his goggles. In the distance there were sounds of ships and people. He was near the city. Jade sighed, he looked around for the second time; there was still no sign of *her*. It was seemed hopeless.

"Oi, you!" A voice came from behind him. Jade jumped.

"Don't move! Hands up in the air."

Jade froze.

"I said; hands up in the air. Where I can see them."

He felt something hard at the back of his head and heard the hammer as it was cocked back. His heart was pounding as he lifted his hands in the air. But Jade Wilde just wasn't scared any more.

"Fuck you!" He shouted. He turned around and punched the gun out of the person's hand. That would have looked impressive, had he not slipped and fallen half way down the hill, pulling things after him that no decent person would want to speak of.

"Jade!" The voice shouted. "Jade, it's me Margot."

She ran down to him. "I was only fucking with you. It's not loaded." She laughed as he tried to find his footing in the mounds of rotting food and diapers he had landed in.

"Oh," Jade said as he resurfaced. He stared at her white outfit. Margot removed the hood, but kept her goggles on as she gave him a hand getting him to his feet.

"Pretty cool, huh?" Margot said examining the gun she had fashioned. Jade glanced at it, as he dusted off the remnants of waste from his trench coat. It wasn't bad for saying she'd made it out of second hand parts. Yes, admittedly, it looked like a deformed hairdryer, but at that moment in time, Jade decided it was best not to complain.

"I think I landed in someone's bin." He said, looking down at his boots, which were buried.

"Don't worry, there are things much worse than that round here, trust me."

Margot said, dusting him off. She moved her hand away as fast as possible and shook it.

"On the plus side," she said. "You showed some balls. I've never seen you act like that before."

"Well, you know," Jade said, trying not to look too pleased with himself: "When the going gets tough and all that."

She smiled, and not to gloat or mock him. It was a warm smile; one he rarely received from her. He smiled back. Despite being covered in rubbish, the moment was one to savour. It was also very brief and cut short by a pretty pissed off vampire.

"Oh that's so mature, Margot," Damien said, walking over the embankment towards them with Arabina at his side. Jade didn't recognise them at first due to their disguises, his gut instinct was to lash out and to try and attack again.

"Hmm, the Professor seems rather skittish today," Damien sneered, turning to Margot.

"I *am* here Damien," Jade said, trying not to raise his voice. The vampire shifted his gaze.

"Did you get the information?"

"Not all of it."

Damien exhaled in disappointment.

"I've got something better; fuel for your weapons."

Damien stared at him, intrigued. Jade tried not to look too smug in return. For once he felt cool.

"Right, we need to get back to the ship." Damien said, as he walked past Jade without another glance. "Interesting choice of accessory, Mr Wilde, it's always good to know we're working with a human sanitary bin."

"What?" Jade mouthed to Margot. She looked at him and tried to stifle a grin.

"You've got a stray tampon on your shoulder."

"Oh for god's sake!"

It didn't matter what miracles Jade Wilde performed, one thing was for sure, he'd never change.

They approached the ship with caution. The others zipped up their jump suits, leaving Jade the only one in normal clothing. Well, what he would call normal anyway. It was almost too easy, as Damien led them through the mounds of rubbish. Jade looked around, he was on edge, expecting to see Silvia's army or a Brontangus in the sky at any moment. However, he saw nothing.

"We're almost there," Damien called. "Just around this last-"

He turned the corner. In front of the ship a bunch of Silvia's army were awaiting them.

"What do we do now?" Margot asked through gritted teeth. They were outnumbered with a ratio of two to three.

"The only thing we can," said Damien, rubbing his hands together. "I do like a challenge."

"Well, alright," Margot said. She pulled her homespun gun from her pocket and fired at the nearest member of Silvia's army. A blue beam blasted from the end of the gun and penetrated the creature's chest. It was thrown so far back it crashed into the bottom of the rubbish hill behind it and caused an avalanche, submerging it.

"Well, that's one down," she shrugged.

"Margot!" Jade yelled as he and the others dropped to the floor. "You told me that thing wasn't loaded!"

"Well it wasn't really; I just emptied some fuel from the ship for a trial run."

"I'd love this conversation to continue," Damien yelled at them. "But currently we have more pressing matters to deal with."

He was right, that shot signalled the start of the fight. Silvia's henchmen flew at the group; the first two grabbed Damien and threw him to the ground, leaving one each for the rest of them. Jade watched as Margot and Arabina tried to avoid being targeted. They knew there was no point in fighting them, they were too strong.

"Jade," Margot yelled, picking up a dustbin lid and using it to deflect the red rays being shot at her. "Look out!"

She was a fraction of a second too late, as Jade turned he was hit in the face and knocked to the ground. He lay there for a moment; blood trickled down his face. He looked up as army members hovered over him, waiting to strike. He could hear Arabina and Margot screaming. *What was happening to them; to her?* Jade was so angry, so full of hate and that was when it came to him. Everything seemed to speed up in his mind; he saw a vision, a vision of the immediate future. Getting up, the creature would attack him from the same angle as before, knocking him back to the ground. Once down, it would break his legs.

Jade gasped as his mind flashed back into the present. He may still be on the floor but he possessed the advantage. He knew what was going to happen.

Then something else came to Jade; he had been given the same tools as the army. Instead of getting to his feet, he waved goodbye at the Brontangus, stuck out his legs and shot backwards across the ground. Jade hadn't removed the soles from his feet.

"Haha!" He yelled as he shot into the air. Reaching into his pocket, he pulled out a pair of white gloves, matching the army members. The figure flew at him, but Jade was ready. He knew it was aiming for the right side of his body, so he dived to the left, grabbed its arm and flung it half way across the junk yard.

Below him, he heard Margot: "What the fuck is going on?"

"Yes! Super strength!" He yelled and zoomed towards the rest of the group.

Jade flew behind Arabina's attacker, who hadn't noticed what had happened. Jade picked him up and threw him into the distance to join his friend.

"Thanks," Arabina panted. "Now let's go kick some more ass." She picked up a steel bar from the floor and charged at Damien's attackers. The vampire was motionless. Arabina hit one of the creatures over the head. It didn't quite happen like she had envisaged. The White Rider turned on her.

"Ermm, okay, that didn't knock you out like I thought it would!" She said, backing away. "Jade, Jaaaade, JADE!"

"I'm on it!" Jade said, swooping down to grab the figure. He wasn't so lucky on that attack, Damien's second assailant grabbed Jade around the ankles as he leapt into the air.

"Oh no you don't!" Arabina screamed, she lifted her arms and conjured two boulders out of the air. They landed on its feet. The creature screeched, thrusting its head back and letting go of Jade's ankles. It raised its hands to the air in agony.

"Thanks," Jade gasped, disposing of the one he was carrying, he watched the other crawl away.

Arabina doubled up in agony as Jade and Margot dealt with the last one.

"Arabina!" Damien yelled, picking himself up off the floor. His hood had been ripped off and his forehead was bleeding but aside from the blood, he looked just as beaten and bruised as the rest of them.

"I'm okay, Damien." she said, trying to straighten up.

"You weren't supposed to do that."

"It was an emergency!" She snapped at him.

Jade landed back on the ground. He couldn't help grinning. Maybe he wasn't as weak as he thought, or as useless. He'd achieved something he'd always wanted to do. He felt different, but not as though he'd changed as such, but more as though he'd developed, grown.

"Jade," Margot yelled. "That was awesome!" She ran over to the others. "Did you guys see him?"

"One question," Damien turned to Jade: "How did you do that?"

"I was using the tools Silvia's recruits are given when they join, or whatever they do. Every one of them has a set." Jade said, taking off his gloves.

"Okay," Damien leaned forward. "Let's just get back to the ship." He put his arm around Arabina to support her and they made their way to the misshapen ship door.

"Evie? Evie you out here?" A voice called from the other side of the hill.

"Oh, what is it now?" Damien groaned. His fingers were inches away from the handle.

"Evieeeeeee?" The voice called again.

Damien dropped his hand. "Friend of yours, I'm guessing?" He said, looking at Arabina who was dancing on the spot. Over the hill, another person dressed in a white walked over the hill. Damien's eyes narrowed.

"Erm, just give me one second." Arabina said, bounding over to Lucy.

"Lucy," she said, remembering not to remove her hood.

"I *knew* it was your voice," Lucy grinned, taking her goggles and hood off to reveal her long black hair and pale features.

"What are you doing here?" Arabina said as Damien approached them.

"Oh, here we go again," Lucy looked skyward. "I'm sorry that I came across from the village where I last saw you, which is coincidently two miles from here." She paused, waiting for an explosive reaction. "Oh come off it, Evie! Do you really think I'm following you? I'm getting supplies before that bloody voice thing gets involved, people need help. A village has just burned down and I can't find a fucking thing and I really don't fancy giving away any more brain cells." She winked. Arabina knew they both had the same level of understanding.

"I like you, Lucy," she said. "You're rebellious, that's kinda hot."

Lucy smiled cheekily. "Babe, you flatter me." She took a step closer to her, putting her hand on the back of her head.

"Hello," Damien interrupted. "And who are you?"

"Oh," said Lucy, taking a step back. "Well hello, I'm Evie's friend, Lucy."

"Hmmm," he raised his eyebrows. "Of course."

"What the fuck are you guys doing, anyway?" She said folding her arms. "How come every time you see me I have to explain myself, hey?" Her lips curled into a perfect smile.

"I think we should leave, *Evie* come on." Damien turned his back and Arabina followed.

"Watch over her for me," Lucy called to Damien. Then she zipped her hood up and went in the opposite direction. Damien watched her go, his eyes still narrowed, whereas Arabina's lowered with mild anguish.

"You're going to get us caught, if you're not careful." He sighed. They returned to the others.

"Wow," Margot said kicking an empty can over to Jade. "We really do get rid of a lot of shit. I mean look at some of this stuff. I bet the person that dumped that here only wore it like once." She pointed to a dirty woollen jumper.

Jade looked at her. "Awful, isn't it? Are we really going to try and save the human race after all the chaos they've caused? Maybe we're better off just letting the earth rot."

"Humans are selfish, careless creatures," Damien said, examining his nails.

"Shut up Damien, because you're really not selfish at all," Margot snapped. The speech at the Halo and Harp flooded back to her. *A favour.*

She looked back at Jade. "Someone once told me we're fighting choice, which is something every species, no matter how much they suck, deserves." She glanced at Damien. "I wonder what happened to that person."

He ignored the comment. He opened the ship's door. Margot folded her arms.

"Sometimes," she said through gritted teeth. "I think of the most horrific ways of him dying just to make it bearable to stand next to him."

Jade laughed, "I bet my thoughts beat yours right now."

Margot turned to him, raising her eyebrows. "I think I'm a lot less innocent than you, Mr Wilde."

Jade burst into laughter. "I think I beat *you* in that department," he said rolling up his sleeve. She laughed back and hit him on the arm.

"Hey guys!" Arabina called.

"What is it now?" Damien asked from inside the ship. Jade and Margot went round the back to find their leader staring out into the distance.

"The land," she said, pointing towards the city. "It's fading."

She was right. Far out in the distance, patches of sky were flashing from black to blue, the light wasn't as bright. The buildings were losing height. Something was wrong with Izsafar. It looked almost holographic. Margot looked down at the ground in front of her; it seemed to be melting away.

"What's going on?" Arabina said.

Jade gulped, he had a strange feeling he knew the cause and it lay in his pocket.

*

"...there seems to be something about the well, I think it holds more than just human thoughts, I have a strange feeling that whatever lies down there is a massive part of what we're missing out on," Jade said pacing in front of the group gathered around Wolf's table. He'd been pacing for almost forty five minutes; explaining his endeavours in Silvia's castle with the help from the holographs he'd managed to capture on the Jonovicator.

Wolf smiled and clapped his hands, "Well done, Jade. I'm impressed. And

Silvia definitely has no more followers?"

"She has a lot," Jade admitted. "But they're all White Riders and Brontangus, apart from the Dark Rider. Oh and one more thing, they mentioned something about the Brontangus rebelling or something."

"Did Silvia believe it?" Wolf asked. "Because that doesn't seem likely."

"The Dark Rider suggested it," Jade answered.

"I suspect they're all getting pretty paranoid down there and after what you saw, it does worry me. Change is coming very soon, mark my words. We must all be prepared to fight."

"I think what happened today was my fault," Jade said. "I stole human thoughts from the well to power your weapons."

"Yes, we know, Jade." Margot said. "And we're grateful."

"No, I don't think you understand. I took a noticeable amount."

"How much did you take?"

"Almost half the capacity of the well," Jade laughed. It was a very nervous laugh. He pulled out the test-tube sized bottle in his coat.

"It's all in here, don't worry," he said as he watched their mouths drop. "It expands inside, depending on the contents it holds."

For a while, no one said anything. They were too astonished. Before anyone got a chance to speak. 'The Voice' made another announcement to her residents.

"May I ask all residents of Izsafar to return to their homes immediately. This is not a test. Please return now."

As Silvia's speech ended, the group regained their focus. Margot rubbed her head, her brow furrowed.

"I hate that!" Arabina yelled. "It's like she's in my head!"

"She's scared." Damien said. He got up and went to a window. He stood for a long time, pondering the situation.

"That's it," he said. "If the whole of Izsafar runs on mind power, maybe it can't exist without it; maybe those thoughts are maintaining the image of the human paradise. Whereas if we use them against her, it'll begin to disappear, Izsafar will disappear."

He turned around to address the group. "She's mad, she's vulnerable, now is the time to strike, Professor. You have to go back down there, it's critical. Earn her trust, god knows how, and try and get below the well, see if you can steal more. Whilst the rest of us will-"

"What?" Margot said, and got to her feet. "*Now?* But Damien, he just got back!"

"And now he needs to leave," Damien snapped. "Don't you get it, Margot? Because he took so much energy, the whole balance of Izsafar has been disturbed. We could win this."

"No!" Margot yelled slamming her hands on the table with such force it made Barbie jump. "We stick together!"

"He's right Margot," Jade said. "We actually have a chance of doing this."

"But we still have no army!" Margot shouted. "Just a shit load of moles!"

"That never stopped you and Arabina wanting to come here!" Damien said.

"But we don't know her next move, it's too-"

"I think I can solve that." Jade looked at Margot. "You see, I never got chance to tell you but I can control Face, I knew the moves the army members were going to make before they hit me. I changed my future."

"Then it's settled," Wolf said. "Jade will go back."

He walked over to him, resting his hand on Jade's shoulder. Jade nodded, he knew what he must do. It was time to fight mind power with mind power. He looked around at the group, and closed his eyes.

The vision was difficult. Silvia wasn't stupid; she was prepared for it. She had put up multiple defence systems, making it a lot harder for Jade to try and spy on her future, but he strained harder. He was determined to know her plans. A sharp pain surged through his head and he doubled up. When he opened his eyes, he was floating through the skies of Izsafar, through the huge doors of the castle and into Silvia's front room. There she stood, with the Dark Rider. Jade couldn't make them out clearly; he could only distinguish their outlines. When they spoke, their voices were distorted and echoed; making it difficult for him to catch what they were saying.

"Get the Brontangus, bring more humans," Silvia yelled. "Izsafar needs their thoughts urgently."

"And do you still not question he is behind it?" He heard the Dark Rider say. "If you only show me where you take the humans, I can assist you, Silvia."

"And what makes you think that I should tell you all my thoughts?" She snapped at him. "You know full well *everyone* is a suspect, even you, Rider."

The vision of the room grew fuzzy. Jade's body throbbed, he couldn't take any more.

"Jade?" He heard Margot's voice. "Jade! Are you okay?"

Jade opened his eyes. He was leaning over the table, supported by Barbie on one side and Margot on the other.

"Yes. I'm fine. She knows someone's touched the pool, but she won't tell the Rider who she thinks it is," he said pulling away from them. "It appears no one knows where the humans are kept. But I reckon I have a good idea."

He fell silent, trembling. Jade's eyes suddenly rolled into the back of his head and he jerked. His breathing was laboured. His fists clenched upon the table. Barbie took hold and lowered him to the floor before he did any more damage.

Arabina asked: "What's happening? Is he having another vision?"

Margot's eyebrows flickered in response only her eyes were wide. It didn't look like she was listening to the question at all. Her attention, like everyone else's, was focused on Jade.

He let out a scream and sat bolt upright. For a moment, his eyes were filled with fear.

He then turned to them and Margot watched as all the worry in his face disappeared as quickly as it had arrived. He was hiding something.

"Sorry," he said, getting to his feet. "Thanks, Barbie." The transvestite passed him a glass of water. The room was filled with an awkward silence.

"My mind's hurting. Nothing to worry about," he said, trying to reassure them, to reassure her.

"Jade, what did you see?" Margot asked gently.

"Nothing," he said, placing the empty glass on the side.

"Tell me for fuck's sake, tell me what you saw!"

"I didn't see anything Margot, I didn't see anything okay?" Jade turned around, staring her straight in the face.

"Stop lying!" Margot screamed.

"I'm going to get ready for the descent," he said calmly, ignoring her comment. Jade walked out of the room.

"Yes," Damien said. "I think, I shall go and check a few things."

Arabina's looked as though a violent thunder raged within. "Just wait one moment!" She shouted following him out the room. He continued walking down the stairs and into the room they were sharing. Arabina followed and closed the door behind her.

"Why do you have to be such a dick?" She screamed at Damien.

"Oh, I do apologise, so now *I'm* the bad guy for doing exactly what you wanted... *again?*" Damien watched her.

"You know what could happen to him!"

"Yes," he said.

"And you don't care? How can you do that? How can you put Margot through that, after she came all this way for him?"

"Since when did you ever care about Margot Grant?" He raised his voice. Arabina was confounded by his comment; she'd never really seen him angry before.

"Arabina, all I've ever done is what you want! When you wanted to go into hiding in the chapel, who told not a soul of your whereabouts? Me! Even when your people needed their leader, I said nothing. You were the one that told us to go to Izsafar and I went, even though I believed it was a disastrous plan. You were the one who blew up that couple's ship. And who had to deal with the repercussions? Me. Would you like me to go on?" In his eyes, intensity burned such as she'd never seen before. "And I have never questioned *any* of your actions, but for some reason, when I try and create some sort of order, when I try to actually solve the problem, you seem to think it's a great idea to piss all over my plans. Well, not this time."

She grabbed a vase from the side and smashed it on the floor. "He will die!"

"Margot knew the risks of coming over here!"

"But Jade didn't!"

"It's his choice, Arabina! Sacrifices must be made! For the sake of Haszear"

"Only when you're not the one making them!" She took a step closer to him, furious. "You only think about yourself!"

He turned away from her, walking to the window. "If you knew what I had sacrificed for you…"

"Oh, why thanks, Damien," her voice was full of sarcasm. "What did you do? Go down to Silvia's lair and risk being murdered for me? Why, you shouldn't have! You know, I'm so lucky; it's so nice to know that you're the most loyal follower I have. I must tell my people to be more like you!"

"Oh trust me, Arabina, I am loyal to you, I always will be." He turned to her. "Even after everything you've put me through, I still follow you, which I must say is more than most, but I will never respect you as a leader. You're a selfish, immature, spoilt little girl, so now's the time to grow up."

Arabina's eyes widened, they were no longer full of hate. She was upset. Damien however, was furious. He clenched his fists, staring her in the face. A tense silence filled the room as they glared at each other. Arabina burst into tears as Damien passed her and slammed the door behind him. Wolf was outside. Damien glared at him as he went up the stairs.

"Maybe Damien," he called after him. "You're the one that needs to do some growing up."

*

Margot, Barbie and Hurst sat in the galley.

"Here," said Barbie, handing them cups of tea. "According to humans, this drink solves problems."

Margot laughed, she wasn't sure if he was being serious. She heard footsteps on stairs and watched as Damien strolled past the doorway and up to the top deck.

"Oh dear," Hurst said. "That didn't look like it went well."

Margot frowned. "I'm going to find Jade."

Margot went down the stairs to the room that she and Barbie had first stayed in on the day of the fire. As she passed the first bedroom, she could hear muffled voices from behind the door. She wondered what Arabina and Wolf were discussing. Margot reached the door to her room and pushed it open to find Jade organising his equipment on one of the beds.

"Hey," he said as she came in and sat opposite him.

"I'm sorry I yelled at you," she said and looked down at her hands.

"It's okay," Jade smiled at her. "If I was you, I would have yelled at me too."

Margot frowned. "Riiight." She looked at his kit. They excited her, she wanted to go over and examine them; try out the tools, the weapons, but it didn't seem appropriate.

"You can come over and try them out." Jade wasn't even looking at her. He didn't need to, he knew her too well.

"It's funny," she said, picking up the soles. "That they're using this stuff at all. I thought they'd be, well you know, magical like her."

"Yeah, me too, it's curious, I keep wondering what species they are."

Margot shrugged. "Beats me. It is funny though, after the hotel massacre, I almost removed one of their hoods, but Damien told me not to. He said something about me not liking what I would see."

Jade frowned. "Strange." He shook his head. "Anyway Margot, if one of these things, creatures-"

"White Riders,"

"Whatever they are, if they attack you, just disarm them of weapons, okay? The gloves give them their strength, the soles of their shoes can be pulled off and their coats do something too. They also have a range of other devices I'm still trying to work out."

"Right." Margot watched as Jade demonstrated what he'd learned and explained what each item did. It was important, she knew. It would help her.

"Jade," she said picking up the compass. "What does this do?"

Jade stared at the object in her hands; the compass was flashing red and pointing at him. He smiled.

Suddenly the ship shook. They grabbed hold of the bed to keep upright. A picture fell, smashing onto the floor. Jade gasped as all the items on the bed scattered.

"What's going on?" He said, getting on his hands and knees to salvage the objects.

"I don't know," Margot said, rushing to the window. The sea was no longer peaceful and calm. It raged. Change was definitely upon them. The door burst open and in walked Wolf.

"Galley. Now."

Margot could feel an awful tension as she got to the galley. No one was speaking. The group sat in silence expect Damien, who was absent.

"Something strange is happening to Izsafar," Wolf said. "Clearly the situation is much worse than we thought. I've just been out on deck and it's like the whole of the land is moving and disappearing. We're going to have to act now." He turned to Jade. "I want you to go down and gather the rest of your things, Hurst you too."

Hurst looked as though he was going to faint. "Why me?" He squeaked.

"We need someone to cross over the Torgeerian mountain range, back to Manhaden to gather an army."

"But, but, but-"

"I'll take you to the South West side. With the land in crisis, she's less likely to notice you leave, I reckon now is our only chance. Silvia's land is falling into disarray, she's not going to sit back and watch. I don't want to imagine what she'll do to the humans on the surface."

Hurst quivered. Margot sighed; Wolf must not know him very well. *How could he be so confident he'd complete the job?* The demon was the biggest coward she knew.

"The rest of us will gather weapons and head to the city."

She, Barbie and Arabina, who hadn't looked up throughout the conversation, nodded.

"Professor, you know what you need to find out. Get the location and report back. Once we know that, we'll be able to see if we can get them out. We'll be able to finish this. "

"Wait," Arabina looked up. "There's no real plan here."

"We can't do anything until the Professor goes down there."

Jade nodded.

"Come on, Hurst," Jade turned to the demon. "Let's go get ready."

Margot waited until they'd left the room to ask the question that had been bothering her.

"Where's Damien?" She muttered to Wolf, watching as Arabina clenched her fists at the mention of his name.

He shrugged, running his hand through his beard. "I'm guessing the vampire is cooling down."

Margot raised her eyebrows. "*Damien* got angry? Mr 'I'm so cool'?"

"Everyone's capable of losing their temper," Wolf said, glancing at Arabina, who had returned to staring at the floor.

"Well, come on then," Barbie said. "Damien or no Damien, we have work to do."

*

Margot felt like she had fallen into a distorted dream and in a way, she supposed she had. The artificial paradise that was Izsafar was falling apart. She thought back to her original goal; to find Jade. Oh, how she had changed. How time had changed. It was strange to think, in terms of Earth time, last week she had no idea Izsafar even existed.

Everything had changed.

There was no going back to how things were.

None of it had been her intention, but she knew she had no choice. Margot lit a cigarette as she walked down the stairs. The smoke billowed to the ceiling. She wished she could slow down time. Things were moving too quickly. Life was just moving too quickly.

Margot passed Wolf on the stairs. "Ten minutes until Jade goes, Eric's almost got us to the destination." His words echoed in the back of her mind. It was like she was underwater, trying to surface. She didn't feel completely conscious as she stepped into the room where Jade Wilde was packing. The day's events seemed like a fairy tale. Any moment she would wake up to find Jade lying beside her in Bequia. They had never really left Earth, it was all an awful nightmare caused by 'Face'.

He turned round as she opened the door. And that was when it hit her. It really may be the last time she would ever see him. Margot reached in her pocket and pulled out her sunglasses, rushing to put them over her eyes.

"Got everything?" She asked.

"Just about," he said, not looking at her. "I think it should be enough."

Jade straightened his trench coat. There were no words between them. It was the quietest they'd been. Margot sat on the bed, staring at the wall. A minute lasted a thousand years.

"Well," Jade said. "I'd best be leaving." There was a sign of hesitance as he went towards the door. Margot nodded as he passed, twirling her thumbs. His hand was on the door knob, she watched as he opened it. *It was now or never.* She sprang to her feet.

"Jade," Margot looked at him, her sunglasses hiding the tears in her eyes. "You can't go back down there."

He turned back, confused and shocked. "What are you talking about?"

"That day, that day at the bar back on Earth," she tried to collect her words. "You can't Jade; it's too dangerous now, you could- I could… lose you, for good." She started to shake.

After all these years, Margot Grant was being emotional? Jade was shocked. He looked at her sadly. He put her hands on his shoulders and pulled her close to him.

"Oh, Margot," he said with a tone of sorrow in his voice. "You were never going to lose me, not after I spent all this time trying to find you."

She held him tighter, silent tears falling down her face. "Please don't go," she whispered. Margot ran her hands through his long black dreads and moved her palm gently across his face. She couldn't believe it was the first time she was doing it. The brown eyes met the red and between them, flowed a shared understanding, a longing that overwhelmed them.

"There are so many things I should have said," Jade began.

"I know," Margot said, smiling at him sadly. "I know, Jade." She laid her head on his chest.

"Hey," he said, putting his hand under her chin. "Hey, look at me. I'm here now, with you." She forced a smile as he continued. "And when this is all over, we can go home."

"Jade, we can never go home, not now."

Jade sighed, she was right, they knew too much. What would happen to them in the end wasn't something he wanted to think about. He wanted it to last forever, he wanted to stay right there with her and live in that moment. The chaos outside didn't matter, nor the war, the room felt like the centre of every world.

"Time is short," Margot whispered. "Now what were you going to say?"

"That I-"

The door opened and in walked Damien. "Professor, we need to move now." He stopped for a moment, studying the scene in front of him. "Oh, sorry. Did I interrupt? How rude. It's just that we have a potential war to attend to."

Jade took a last look at Margot and left the room, leaving her alone.

His tears were hidden behind his purple goggles as he followed the vampire up the stairs.

"Nice to see you've decided to return, Damien," he said, trying to sound casual as they walked to the top deck. The vampire turned around and smiled before opening the door. The light hit them hard as they stepped out into the open. It wasn't as bright as Jade expected it to be. Something had changed. They were moored by a quiet river bank, surrounded by overgrown grass. The tall, slender trees were in bloom and stretched high into the foreign-looking sky. It was almost too perfect. Romantic, some would say. The land was deserted; there wasn't a Brontangus in sight. Jade knew why they had chosen the spot. It was uninhabited. He could leave the ship unnoticed. The chaos hadn't reached there yet. He wished he could have stayed. He felt so very peaceful. Jade wondered if it would be the last time he'd feel at peace. He didn't look back at Wolf or Damien; it wasn't their faces that he wanted to remember, and without a second thought, Jade dived into the deep water.

Damien went back down the stairs and into the room where Margot still stood. She was motionless, facing the wall.

"Margot," Damien said. "You know what these black visions mean don't you?"

Margot didn't look at him, she nodded her head.

"Yes," Damien sighed. "I was afraid of that and sadly, I think so does he."

*

Jade Wilde fell from the stormy clouds to the gates of Silvia's castle. The skies of Under World were more violent. Jade could feel change in the air. It didn't seem so quiet; lightning forked above his head and he watched as hordes of Brontangus flew high above him. He didn't mind, he embraced the storm. Jade put a smile on his face as he entered the castle. He knew he had to get back to the well. It was the only way he'd be able to find out what was going on.

Jade paced through the castle, his eyes fixed on the garden. It may change again, it may take him an age to find the middle, but he would find it. He wouldn't give up until Silvia was stopped. Margot was right, every creature deserved choice.

The castle was empty. He expected to see Silvia, a Rider or at least a guard, but in that moment, he felt like the only person in existence. He was almost there. The garden was once again meters away. He was about to leap onto the grass when-

"Jade," a voice called from behind him. Jade stopped dead in his tracks. He knew who it was.

"Yes," he replied, scrunching up his eyes. Jade turned to see Silvia standing at the entrance of the corridor.

"What are you doing?"

"Erm I was just-" Jade couldn't think of an excuse in time.

"Follow me," said the angel. She turned and went back where she'd come. Jade followed. *She has to know*, he thought as they walked back into the throne room. He wondered what she would do. He imagined her blackmailing him, torturing him, even killing him. Jade gulped. He was done for.

"Professor," she said. "We're on the brink of war; I'm going to have to move a few things forward."

Jade frowned. It was not what he expected. "Someone has stolen a lot of human thoughts... are you not even going to *question* me about it?"

Silvia laughed. "Professor, everyone is a suspect. But right now we have more pressing matters, a rebellion is upon us. Looks like you'll be killing Margot sooner than you thought."

Jade laughed nervously. "Oh, brilliant."

Silvia tapped the sides of the chair three times and stood up. She took a step away. The chair began to shake and Jade watched in awe as it moved backwards to reveal a set of steps beneath where it had sat.

"My most guarded entrance," Silvia said. She smiled, turned round and descended into the darkness. With a hint of hesitation, Jade took a deep breath, and followed her.

It was bleak and dismal. The passageway had barely enough space to move in and Jade had to crouch low to ensure he didn't bang his head on the damp stone roof. Without Silvia's glow, it would be pitch-black. That was the only thing he thought he'd ever be thankful for when it came to the angel. He used the light to get a look at his surroundings as he put his hands on the cold walls to stop himself slipping on the slimy stairs. The walls were covered in strange markings, which were more prominent the further they travelled.

They walked deeper into the darkness. The light of Silvia's castle was long gone. Jade's nerves were knotting in his stomach. All he could hear was the resonance of their footsteps as they echoed off the cave walls, and the dripping of what he hoped was water. He was getting hotter, despite the atmosphere getting colder.

"Silvia?" He called out. "Silvia, where are we going?"

"Oh, don't worry Professor, you'll see." Her words bounced off the walls. She was enjoying herself. What was she going to show him? So many questions ran through his mind, it was hard to focus.

"Quickly, Mr Wilde." Silvia picked up the pace. The temperature was rising and the ceiling lowering; sweat formed on Jade's forehead. He was slipping across the floor as he tried to keep up with her through the twists and turns. He began to panic. Where the hell was she taking him? Would it be the end of Jade Wilde? Suddenly, she disappeared.

"Oh god." He whispered and stopped.

Jade couldn't move. He felt caged in, paralysed. *This is it, I am going to die. There was no doubt about it.* He pulled down his goggles, the night vision wasn't working. Perfect timing. *Think Jade, think. What would Margot do? Well, probably kick and punch everything, until she found a way out... okay, bad example.* A thought occurred to him, the sunglasses from the lab! He reached into the pocket of his trench coat, grasping desperately for them.

"Aha!" He said, pulling them out. His action was a little too enthusiastic, and the glasses flew out of his hand and he heard them fall further down the steps.

"Note to self," he said to the Jonovicator, which was still recording in his pocket. "In future, always prepare for being trapped in an angel's castle. However rare these situations may be." He got to his knees, leaning forward into the darkness to try and find the glasses he'd accidentally tossed away. Jade traced his hands along the steps in front of him. The stone felt thick and slimy, like a rock covered in seaweed. Then he felt something small and hard, almost like a claw. There were a few of them on the floor. He thought nothing more of it as he raised the sunglasses to his face.

"There you are-"

Jade froze as a bloodcurdling scream echoed through the tunnel.

It echoed all the way down the passageway. He couldn't tell where it came from. He sprang into action. He wasn't sure whether it was a blessing or a curse that they worked. Jade looked down at what he held in his hand, they weren't claws at all, they were fingernails; human fingernails. He screamed and scrambled to his feet, hitting his head on the ceiling. Jade looked around him, the walls were dripping with blood. The floor was coated with it. It was all over his hands, it was what he'd been slipping on. He staggered back in shock, trying to cover his mouth with his shaking hands. It all made sense, they weren't markings on the walls, they were scratches; attempts at freedom and he was trapped like all the others.

"If you're going to kill me," he yelled. "You might as well go ahead and do it!" He tried to get to his feet, but fell forward. The floor disappeared and he plummeted into nothingness.

Chapter 17

The Empty Stitches of Eternity

At best, people were difficult to motivate once they decide on a particular mindset; teenagers especially. Those living in the city of Izsafar were no exception, and no matter how Margot Grant and her unlikely team struggled to gain their attention, they didn't listen.

"People of Izsafar," she yelled into the chaotic street. "You need to listen to us! You are in grave danger! We need to rebel against the voice!"

No one cared. People panicked as the buildings crashed to the ground around them. Izsafar was fading and no one knew what to do.

"This is stupid," Margot turned to Barbie. "They're not listening to me; they just keep running around and screaming."

Barbie shrugged. "Human, they're scared. Maybe we should get Arabina and Damien to do it and we should stay with Wolf on the ship?"

"No! They have to listen!" Margot turned back to the crowd. "Guys I really think-"

An egg hit her in the face, and someone in the distance yelled: "Fuck your revolution we're going to die!"

"Fuck you!" She screamed. Crowds ran, heading to the outskirts. Not that it would help, they couldn't escape it. It was everywhere.

"Nice choice of makeup," Damien said, appearing by her side.

"Piss off, Damien," she said, wiping her sunglasses. "Where are they?"

"Trust me," he said, moving out of the way of a family. "It won't take long, they'll be here and they'll try to collect every human they can get their hands on. Something tells me, this time, they'll be coming for us as well."

Margot frowned. "Why are they all panicking now?" She asked; staring at the hordes running like ants on an anthill smothered with honey. "I thought they'd still be doped up."

"The effects are wearing off, what with Izsafar fading," Damien said. "I've got a plan, I'll be back later."

"You can't just leave!" Margot called after him as he disappeared into the crowd.

"I'll return," he called back. "Just promise me, if anything dreadful occurs, you'll think about your own safety first."

And just like that, he was gone.

"Ha," Margot muttered to herself. "You're one to talk about my safety when it was you who tried to kill me!"

A horrible cry filled the air. Margot dived to the ground, covering her ears. Many people did the same.

"Human!" Barbie yelled. "The Brontangus, they're here!"

*

"Sorry about leaving you there, Professor, but you were awfully slow and I had some business I needed to attend to."

Jade opened his eyes; he was laying on yet another bright white floor. It was blinding. He grumbled and looked up to see the angel standing above him.

"Get to your feet." She ordered.

Jade stood up, trying to get a better look around him. His vision was hazy; it was hard to see with the blinding lights dazzling him. He could make out rows of operating tables, —occupied by dead humans. White Riders scurried back and forth, returning to their allotted tables.

"Is this a laboratory?"

"Yes, Professor." If Silvia wasn't so dazzling, he was sure he'd see her lips curl into a twisted smile.

"What am I doing here?" His vision was coming back into focus. The more he saw, the more apprehensive and nauseous he felt. All around him, humans were being cut open, examined, parts of them being inserted into tubes and conical flasks. The clean walls were lined with miles of shelving, full of samples, charts and graphs. They were too far away for Jade to make out.

"You'll find out soon enough," Silvia said. "I'll explain everything to you, don't worry Professor, if I wanted to kill you I would have done it when I first met you. We have a rebellion that may actually be successful. I need all the help I can get; I've decided it's time to start revealing my secrets to those I trust. I can trust you, can't I Professor?"

There was an awkward pause before he answered.

"Of course you can." Jade smiled. Lying through his teeth was something he was beginning to get used to.

"Brilliant. Now, if you care to follow me."

Silvia went towards a glass door at the opposite end of the room, forcing Jade to pass by the masses of experiments. He covered his nose to keep from gagging as he passed. It was horrific to see humans operated on so clinically, being treated like bacteria. He watched as the figures cut them up and pulled them apart, piece by piece. In the end, he had to quicken his pace, focus on Silvia's floating hair. Anything was better than seeing his own kind being destroyed, no matter how much of a disappointing race he thought them to be.

Behind the glass door was another large room, it contained rows of tables full of weapons.

"This is where I study human technology." Silvia said. "I like to see how destructive it is."

"But you're an angel, you have magic, you don't know about experiments! How did this all happen?"

"Well. Yes Professor, I have had some help, don't you worry all shall be explained. Ah," she said and looked in front of them. "I see they are conducting a trial run."

Jade's eyes widened as he saw a woman being chained to the wall in the middle of the room.

"Of course," Silvia said. "Some of them can be a bit uncooperative; the effects of Izsafar seem to wear off once they come down here."

"No! Get off of me!" The woman screamed as the chains were tightened around her legs. Jade stared helplessly as a short, fat White Rider placed a tiny object on the floor. A beam of blue light shot from it straight towards the woman. She exploded. Pieces of her body flew across the room, splattering the target wall behind her in blood. Jade could feel himself shaking, he wanted to vomit. A fine mist of blood floated through the air.

"The power of the mind!" The fat White Rider exclaimed. He turned to Silvia: "Boss, the new weapons will soon be ready to use and they won't even need to be hand-held."

"It just goes to show," Silvia said. "You can do anything if you put your mind to it."

Jade was speechless. *How could a life be so disposable?*

That room was noisier than the others. All around him clanks and bangs were heard as new devices were being tested.

"Shall we continue, Professor?" Silvia asked, walking on. But Jade didn't know if he could move, once again he was frozen to the spot in that awful place. How could she be so casual about what had happened? She was a monster. He forced himself to take a few paces forward.

"Any questions so far?" She asked.

"Y-y- yes," he stuttered. Then something caught his eye. "Wait, what is that?"

In the centre of the room there was a large bronze pot. If Jade had been with Margot the day she and her father examined that engine, he would have known it was very similar. Jade stared at its strange blue markings. They looked like hieroglyphs, or runes. Whatever they were, they seemed to be the forms of an archaic language.

"That," Silvia turned to him. "Is the heart of Izsafar. Without that, everything you have seen would be a figment of your imagination."

It was the most horrific tour Jade had ever been on. The ugly truth of Izsafar had finally been revealed and it disgusted him. She took him deep into the dark prison cells, where she kept her victims. She led him down endless corridors, leading to rooms full of newspapers, research and documents on every resident that set foot on Izsafar. But the worst, Silvia saved until last.

The prisoners called it 'The Room', there was no grand title needed. It was on a separate floor. Jade hated to imagine why. According to Silvia, it was the last room humans entered before they returned to the Earth. The final step of their journey. Any human that entered the room would never be the same again. He had heard whispers and gasps as he passed people as they walked to the steps. He continued to follow Silvia, shaking with every step he took down the winding spiral staircase. The corridor that led to The Room did not seem terrifying at all. Like the rest of Silvia's castle; like many of the other areas, it was white, though it had an element of grandeur. Jade stared at the glass chandelier above his head as he approached the entrance. There were large paintings on the wall, portraits of humans from long ago, humans that Jade recognised from history lessons. And then there was the music. A sweet, enchanting, peaceful chorus drifted down the passageway towards them. It didn't seem like he was in the same place at all.

"This, Professor," Silvia said as they approached the end of the room. "Is the most important room in the whole castle." She led him through another glass door which led into the most exquisite room he'd ever seen.

It looked like a medieval banqueting hall but there were some features that didn't quite add up. The hall looked almost holy; stone carvings of angels curved round the stone pillars that surrounded the long table in the centre of the room. Jade stared at the vast array of food on the table. There were all sorts of items, from bowls of grapes to full roast chickens, all served on golden plates with golden goblets to match. It looked like a feast for royals. Jade walked round the table, tracing his hands over the grand red and gold chairs. He noticed a light shining on the table, a light that wasn't coming from the candelabra. He looked up to see a beautiful stained glass window emitting what could only be artificial light. The picture was of an angel, similar in appearance to Silvia, only Jade believed the painted angel to be a lot older. The ceiling surrounding it was similar to the castle above, with paintings and intricate decor. At the far end of the room was a small stage with an old dance floor in front of it, awaiting a crowd. Jade felt lonely in that room, it was like standing on a ghost ship.

"But I don't understand," he said.

"Professor, this is not the room I was speaking about," she pointed to a red door, opposite to the one through which they had entered. "*That* is the room."

"Then what is this place?" Jade asked.

"This is the waiting room, despite what Margot and her gang may think of me, I am not a complete monster." She crossed the room towards the red door. "Come, Mr Wilde."

Well, it was what he'd been waiting to see. Jade ambled across the room, his heart pounding, his palms sweating. Maybe it was full of army members, with weapons, or a large brainwashing device. It could be a torture room, filled with more remains of past victims which, like him, had once clung to the hope of escaping.

Silvia paused outside the door. "Please, Professor, I believe you should do the honours."

Jade gulped. "Of course." He curled his fingers around the handle and pushed it down.

At first, he thought he was in the wrong room. He was disappointed as he stepped inside. It was plain, white and empty, aside from one object; a wooden chair, the same shade of red as the door. As Silvia closed the door, the room him didn't seem like a room any longer. He was floating in nothingness, drifting between the pathways of eternity.

Despite the door and chair remaining in their positions, Jade felt as though they had hurtled miles away. He couldn't see the walls any more, everything was white; everything was meaningless.

"But there's nothing here." He said, sitting on the chair. "No weapons, no magic. Nothing. How can this be the room in which humans are changed permanently? How can this be the final step of modification?" He put his head in his hands, trying to grasp the concept.

"Professor, this is the closest thing to nothingness you will ever see in your small life, it's enough to drive a person to insanity."

"So that's what you do, just leave them in here until you break them?"

"Not exactly," she said, stepping away from the door. "I will go in with my chosen patient and search deep into their thoughts. The whiteness that surrounds us is soon full of their memories. My job is to reveal to them their crimes, their sins. I replay them again and again until they beg, plead for a chance to redeem themselves and when they do, which they always do, I take away every single bad trait about them, wipe the slate clean, give them chance to start afresh. Then and only then can they leave Izsafar and return to the Universe to live a new, carefree life."

Jade was speechless.

"They choose to change themselves to become a better person," she said.

"Patients," Jade said to himself. He stood up, glaring at her. "Patients? You make it sound like they're ill!"

"They *are* ill. They are infected with greed, selfishness - horrible sins."

"You don't give them a choice though, you force them to choose! Forcing someone is not a choice."

"They had a choice; life gave them the choice to do good, to have the freedom, to create, to share and they chose to throw it all away. Look at them Professor, they're monsters."

"The only monster I see is you."

He ran to the door fled into the waiting room. What Jade had seen down there made him feel more sick than any fairground ride. He collapsed to his knees as the angel once again closed the door.

"Why did you show me that?" He stammered. He didn't know what else to say. There was nothing in his vocabulary that could describe what he was feeling. Sometimes, nothing was uglier than the truth.

*

Margot dived for cover as the army swarmed the city. Rushing down an alleyway between two tall buildings, she pulled out her gun and pointed it at a White Rider. The blue beam hit it and it flew backwards, crashing into a sky scraper. Barbie had the same idea and he rushed to her side and checked the coast was clear.

"Where's Damien?" She yelled. It was so hard to be heard over all the noise on the street. The army had been there a while, trying, like the Brontangus, to police the humans, to restore order. It wasn't working. They couldn't be calmed, not any more.

War had broken out.

It was no typical war. The humans were not rebelling; they were lashing out in confusion. They were doing what humankind does best; destroying everything, until they found an answer, however useless or irrelevant it may be in the grand scheme.

"He's not back yet. Oh if we could only calm them," Barbie said, staring out at the blood-stained streets. "Maybe Silvia's people will stop."

"I doubt it," Margot frowned, she stared in the same direction as Barbie, her hands embraced the gun she'd fashioned. There was no chance of returning to Wolf's boat. She looked for the others. They were nowhere in sight.

"Human!" Barbie yelled. Margot felt a blow to the back of head and was knocked flat as a White Rider descended upon her.

*

Two figures strolled into the waiting room, both white, both hooded and cloaked.

"Jade," Silvia said as they approached. "Don't you understand why I have shown you all this?"

"I understand a lot of things, but not this." Jade said, getting to his feet. He recognised one of the White Riders as being the short fat figure he'd seen earlier; the one who had tested the weapon on that woman. They stood in silence, at the flanks of their master.

"You soon will," Silvia continued. "There's just one last thing I have to show you."

*

Margot heard a crash as Barbie threw the figure into a group of dustbins behind them.

"Here," he held out his hand and pulled her to her feet.

"Barbie, duck!" She shouted. The transvestite bowed his head just in time to miss the dustbin that was flung at him. It hit the wall, spraying rubbish everywhere. The figure was back on its feet.

"Without its weapons it's worthless," Margot said. "We need to disarm it." She took her gun out, trying to steady her aim.

*

"Why are there army members here?" Jade frowned, taking a step back.

"You see, Jade Wilde," Silvia said. "You are one of the most intelligent humans I've ever met, but sometimes you can be so stupid it's unbelievable.

284

Your problem seems to be that you always ask the wrong questions."

Jade wasn't quite sure where her speech was going. "What?"

"That's exactly it!" Silvia's glow seemed to get brighter and her voice echoed off every wall. "*What* instead of why."

"Silvia," Jade said, taking a few more steps back. "I'm afraid I don't understand what you mean."

Silvia glided in circles around the two immobile army members. "Oh I think you do Professor. Questions such as, what are behind the hoods of these mysterious figures, what do they look like... what are they?" "Deep down, I think you may already know the answer."

*

Margot Grant was flung against the wall again. It was becoming such a frequent occurrence she feared it would soon become a hobby. The figure hovered in the air above her. The gun she carried was jolted from her hand to clatter onto the ground. It caught its eye and it flew towards it.

"Not this time," Barbie said, diving on top of it when it was inches from the ground. They brawled; resembling a spinning yin-yang ball as they rolled about the floor.

"Shoot now, Margot," Barbie commanded. Margot was frozen to the spot; she didn't want to hit Barbie.

"Just do it." He spoke before she had time to answer. Margot pulled the trigger and the same blue blast hit both Barbie and the army member. They shot back to the end of the alley at full force and collapsed in a pile on the floor.

"Barbie!" Margot screamed, running down the alley towards him.

"I'm okay," Barbie said weakly, pulling away from the creature. "Not sure if he is though. I think it's knocked out." They stared at the creature; it was slumped against the wall, looking a lot less mighty than before.

"We should disarm it." Margot said. She stood over the White Rider and pulled off its gloves.

She gasped and fell back in shock. Barbie, who had only just got to his feet, grabbed her before she hit the floor.

"What's wrong?"

"It, it has... human hands."

*

"You!" Jade said as the figures pulled back their hoods.

"Professor, allow me to introduce Doctor Clarke, leader of the U.A.S and our newest member; Reenie."

Clarke's face curved into a smile, he looked exactly the same as he had when Jade had first met him; smug, in control. Reenie however, looked quite the opposite, her face was paler and she seemed to quiver with discontent as she stared at him. He turned away, unable to look her in the eye. Jade's fists tightened; all that time, he'd been taken for a fool, tricked. How had he not seen it before? How had it taken him so long to realise?

"But, how? Me, Margot, the U.A.S; we built weapons to fight against Silvia."

"No, Jade, you and your friends built weapons for Silvia. We had to make sure the rebels were being put to good use, not being disruptive." His face twisted into an ugly smile. "But the scientists soon came round to our way of thinking. This is the only way to purify the world, stop the wars."

Jade didn't believe a word of it. Clarke wasn't like Silvia; there was no meaning behind what he said. He had no morals. Morals seemed only to develop once he'd decided on the most profitable outcome. Yes, there was definitely a reason why he was doing it, but Jade knew he'd have to dig a little deeper.

"So, Professor," Silvia said, breaking the intense stare between them. "What do you think?"

"About what?" Jade asked, losing all sense of who had the status in the room.

"This has been your initiation ceremony." The angel produced a white cloak from behind her dress. "This can be yours if you want it to be. Join us Professor, help us change your world and the human race once and for all."

*

"Oh God, Barbie," Margot said, leaning on his shoulders as she tried to stay upright. "These are members of the U.A.S."

She reached out, pulling back the hood of the White Rider. "I helped these people! I thought they were on our side!"

Barbie knelt down next to the human, examining him closely, running his hands over his face. "This doesn't make any sense," he looked up at Margot. "You're killing your own kind."

Margot screamed in anger, she punched the wall hard. She watched as the blood ran down her knuckles. "She's got us destroying ourselves." She banged her head on the wall then turned to face him. "We've got to find the rest of the guys, Barbie. They have to know."

They turned and faced the entrance of the alleyway. Out in the street, people rushed past the alley, screaming and yelling; some with weapons, some fighting, whilst some were just looking for a safe place to hide. She could see fire and refuse covering the once perfect streets. The alleyway was almost like a parallel world, a cinema screen, airing a violent film. The madness didn't seem scant metres away.

"Come on," she said taking Barbie's hand. "We've got a job to do."

They walked slowly into the chaos.

*

Jade couldn't play along any more. He stared from Silvia to Clarke to the terrified Reenie. Their eyes met for the second time and he saw something he never thought he'd see in her. He saw himself, or at least what he used to be. Once, Jade would have done exactly what she did, quiver like a coward and watch as their world was destroyed; too terrified to speak out, too sensible to start a revolution. But Jade wasn't that person any more.

Maybe once he'd held a defeatist attitude, a passive role in the narrative of his life but Jade had changed.

"I will never join you!" He yelled. "This is a horror show, this place is awful Silvia, I expected better. It's like a concentration camp!" He picked up a knife and stabbed it into the wooden table.

"We're helping the human population." Silvia spoke slowly.

"You're destroying them!"

"By creating world peace? By helping them survive? By making your stupid little world a better place? I have to say I'm surprised at you Professor, you're extremely ungrateful. I thought that was what you and Margot always wanted, the very reason for you building the ship. To stop the wars, create a peaceful way of living."

"Silvia, this isn't living. What you're doing to these people isn't helping them to live, it's lobotomising them! This takes away the whole point of their lives. We're only humans, we're meant to make mistakes, lovely, beautiful mistakes. It's what makes us ourselves, no matter how terrible our choices may be!" He paused before adding, "I'd rather be dead than live like they do!"

Reenie gasped. The other two were silent. Jade half expected a comment such as 'that could be arranged', but instead, he got nothing.

"Right then," he said, a little confused by their silence. "You can fuck your proposal and while you're at it you can go fuck yourself as well. We will win this war Silvia, I don't know when, I don't know how, but you will never get away with this."

And after that dramatic speech, he ran out of the room.

They stood stock still and for a moment it was silent once again.

"My lady," Clarke hissed, interrupting the peace. "He knows everything there is to know, what do we do?"

"Do not panic," Silvia replied. "I have to say I was hoping for a more co-operative reaction, but this still plays nicely into our hands."

"But he will tell them everything!"

"Exactly," Silvia said, staring at the glass door through which Jade had just departed. "He will lead us straight to Margot and the rest of the rebellion. Follow him and kill them all. I shall be close behind you with the Dark Rider. It's time everything was returned to order."

"And the surface itself?"

"Once they're dead, we'll have no problem restoring Izsafar to its original glory. Now go."

*

Jade ran back up the stairs, darting through the rooms and corridors, passing the hideous experiments, the suffering.

"Come on!" He yelled at the soles. Jade jumped in the air and used them to lift himself off the ground. He looked up; the ceiling of the operating room had a small opening in it. It looked like a haunted loft entrance, the sort found in really old houses. Jade smiled, impressed that he'd found the way to the surface. It was just as he thought; Silvia had made the entrance awkward on purpose so that only U.A.S members and higher beings were able to gain easy access and besides, he couldn't bear the thought of retracing his steps through that bloody staircase.

It all made sense; how Silvia's weapons were so complex, how she knew so much about humans, why Jade's sunglasses worked but his goggles didn't. So many things were clicking into place. Jade pulled the compass from his pocket; he had to get to Margot before she did, for if not, she would surely kill them all.

*

"ARABINA!" Margot yelled. She saw the demon running from a Brontangus. Margot picked up an exploding ball and threw it off to one side to distract its gaze. It hit the building near her and she had to run to dodge the shards of glass.

"What is it?" Arabina screamed, running towards her and Barbie.

"We need to leave!" Margot shouted.

"We can't, the Brontangus are guarding every possible escape route"

Margot looked back to where they'd come from. The stone creatures stood in the middle of the road. "Right," she said. "There's a canal in the centre of the city, I bet Wolf will be there. He's not stupid."

"It's our best chance," Barbie shrugged.

"Wait," Arabina said. "Where's Hurst?"

Suddenly the demon came flying through the air towards them. He screamed as Barbie caught him.

"Hurst, that was not a clever thing to do," Barbie said, putting him on the floor.

"They used me as ammo to throw at the army!" Hurst yelled.

They ran down the main road, into the heart of the city. Weapons blazing, they dodged the deafening explosions around them. Barbie and Margot took the lead, shooting anyone that got in the way, protecting the other two from falling buildings and attackers. Their plan was working, as they moved further into the city.

"We're almost there!" Margot shouted. "I can see the canal."

The stretch of water was coming into view; it split the city in two. Margot looked down at the water; there was no way to cross apart from the bridge in the centre. She looked at the boats that were parked on either side.

He could be anywhere.

"Okay guys, looks like this is going to be-"

"Human look out," Barbie said, he grabbed her around the waist and threw her to the floor.

She heard a loud crash close by as a ship crashed to the ground.

"Oh god," Margot whispered. She had no idea who was inside, nor did she want to stay to find out. She turned to face Barbie, who lay next to her. "This is madness."

He nodded in reply. Above them more Brontangus screeched through the sky, whilst the humans screamed on the earth.

And then she heard a voice; a voice that stood out from all the others. It pierced through the piles of demolished buildings, the smoke and fire on the streets; it stood out from the pain, the blood the torture. On the opposite side of the canal, Jade Wilde was running towards her.

"MARGOT! MARGOT GRANT!" He yelled, emerging from the smoke.

"JADE! I'M HERE OVER HERE!" She screamed, her face breaking into an uncontainable grin. They were almost in the centre of the city. If she ran towards him they were sure to meet on the bridge.

Margot was just about to climb over the ship and break into a sprint when

Barbie grabbed hold of her shoulder.

"Human no, look." He said, pointing.

Her smile faded. Jade wasn't the only one to emerge from the smoke. Behind him, two other figures appeared from the chaos - the figures of Silvia and the Dark Rider.

The fighting in the centre of the city ceased. Everyone's eyes were focused on Jade Wilde. Despite knowing who was behind him, he refused to stop running.

"Margot," he screamed. "I have to tell you something!"

"Stay where you are," Barbie said.

"Kill him." Silvia's command echoed throughout the city.

"NO!" Margot screamed as the Dark Rider left the angel's side and flew towards Jade. Jade stopped running and turned. He had reached the small bridge and there he stood, watching and waiting for the wrath of the Rider. He knew after that command there was no way he could win. There was nowhere to run, nowhere to hide and for once he was glad of it. Jade Wilde wasn't scared any more. He was thankful; thankful that he'd had the time to do what he needed to achieve. There could be no greater gift in life.

"Bring it on!" Jade screamed and closed his eyes.

There was the sound of a blade ringing and Jade Wilde collapsed dead on the ground.

"NOOOOOO!" Margot screamed. "Jade! Jade!" She left the ship's crash site and ran to the bridge where Jade lay bleeding. Behind her, she heard the distant voices of her friends telling her to stay where she was. They sounded so unimportant.

Margot couldn't turn back; she had to get to him.

"Human," Barbie's voice began to fade into the background. "Leave him."

But Margot couldn't.

She ran through the violent streets; where humans still fought and fell. Everything seemed to be happening in slow motion again. Margot could feel the hope draining from her body the closer she got. The whole point in what they were doing, all the faith they had of defeating Silvia was lost forever. Margot had lost her reason for being there. All hope of winning the war had resided in one human being and that human would never move again.

She didn't care what became of her; if she lived or died.

"Get away from him!" She screamed at the Dark Rider as she approached the bridge. To her surprise, he backed off, retreated to his leader. Margot threw herself over Jade Wilde, hugging his body, crying into his chest. There was something peaceful about the way the blood dripped from his neck, the way his smile curved. She looked into his eyes, those eyes that would never look at her again; those all-knowing windows to the soul. *He had known. He had known all along.*

Margot forgot the outside world, she forgot the war. The only person that mattered was the one she'd never speak to again.

Jade Wilde, her best friend, was dead. And with his life, her life followed. She was dead inside.

Once again, Margot Grant was completely alone in the world.

Chapter 18

'For Margot'

There are two types of people in the world; those who live for themselves and those who live and sacrifice their lives for others. It was at that moment Margot Grant realised who Jade Wilde had been and what she ought to have been all along. As she lay on his motionless chest, she knew that the ones we consider good; the knights in shining armour that reside in our long forgotten dreams, are those who die way too early. He was gone; never to move or laugh or love again.

She couldn't get up, she didn't want to. She lay on his body as still as him. She wanted to lie there for all eternity. The war around her was a distant dream, all that was real had been taken from her.

"Human, let go of him." Barbie's arms reached around her as he tried to lift her to her feet. "We have to leave."

"No," she replied through gritted teeth. "I want to stay here."

"If we stay, we all die."

His words hit her like a hammer. The world around Margot finally came back into focus. She got to her feet, staring bitterly into the distance. The Dark Rider and his master were preparing to take flight.

"Find Arabina!" She heard her call. "The others aren't going anywhere."

Margot's eyes burned. She wanted to kill them both.

The albino clambered to her feet. "I have seen the devil today!" She yelled at Silvia. "And he is your artificial God!"

Silvia turned back towards her, before bursting into a horrible fit of laugher. "Oh Margot, Margot, Margot you are blinded by your rage. You see this is where you are wrong. I have to say I am shocked, I would have thought by now you realised that I have never been a part of your human religion."

"No, Silvia," Margot walked to the end of the bridge. "*You're* wrong. You have become everything that qualifies for a religion; only you're more than that, you're an extremist dictator! Silvia, you are controlling and vindictive you have been put in charge to keep us in line."

She had to pause; the words got lodged in her throat. "And in doing so you have created exactly what you set out to prevent, you have also killed-" She couldn't finish her sentence.

Silvia came closer towards her, the Dark Rider at her side. Margot could feel Barbie's hand on her shoulder, tightening his grip.

"Poor, weak Jade Wilde," Silvia, said crossing the battle field.

Margot threw her head back in hysterical laughter. "Weak?"

"I'm afraid I don't understand, Miss Grant."

"Sorry, it was just that he had you fooled until the very end. He never wanted to kill me at all. You see, Jade wasn't working for you, he was on our side. Shame how that little detail slipped past you! He did this! All of it." She held her arms out to the destruction around her.

"You hold a valid point, Miss Grant."

Margot gasped, Silvia's words no longer came from her mouth, but the depth of Margot's mind. She wanted to talk directly to her. Barbie could hear her too, he grasped his head.

They watched as the angel backed further into to the distance and the Dark Rider advanced.

"However," the angel continued. "We all have our little secrets. Do you think that I did not expect this? Did you think that you were the only one with a spy on the inside?" The Dark Rider advanced further towards them. Margot distinctly heard her whisper: 'Show them'. She had a feeling the command was not for them. The Dark Rider stopped metres away and slowly removed his hood.

"Damien?"

The vampire's pale face stared back at her - the face of a murderer. Margot turned to Barbie, she had a feeling he was thinking the same thing. *How could he do this?* They'd been taken for fools; deceived throughout the whole operation.

"I changed my mind!" Silvia's voice boomed. It was so loud that it shook every building still standing.

"Kill them, kill them all, but bring Arabina to the castle, alive." The air surrounding her filled with white smoke and she was gone.

Like a swarm of bees, Damien and the U.A.S members flew at them.

Margot watched as they stormed towards the bridge.

"Not today, bitches!" Arabina screamed jumping in front of them.

"Where the hell did you come from?"

"Never mind that now, we're got bigger problems! Me and- oh god, where's Hurst? HURST?"

Margot followed Arabina's eyes to see Hurst running between the masses; running in the opposite direction.

"HURST, YOU COWARD!" She screamed as he disappeared amongst the crowd. She turned back to the others. "I guess it's just us."

The army was closing in, the leader of the group just metres away. All hope seemed lost. If it was the end, Margot was happy to say that she had tried.

"If we die-"

"Who said anything about dying?" Arabina snapped at her as she raised her arms to the sky.

"Arabina," Margot frowned. "I highly doubt that a Mexican wave will-"

Barbie nudged her. "Look."

Margot stared at the water, it was rising from the river; rising around them. It spun fast to make a perfect circle around the group. Margot looked up; it reached high into the clouds as it spun like a liquid tornado.

"Give us your best shot!" Arabina screamed. The U.A.S charged towards them. Margot and Barbie braced themselves. As soon as the White Riders tried to breach the water they were taken by the current and were carried up into the distance. She had created a barrier and it worked.

"You want a fight?" Arabina screamed; she turned back to Barbie and Margot. "Brace yourselves to run, Wolf's ship is close."

Margot looked down stream towards the silent vessel, untouched by the chaos surrounding it.

"Arabina," she said. "What are you gonna do?"

Arabina laughed hysterically. Margot felt the ground shake beneath her feet. She looked at Barbie; it couldn't be good. The skyscrapers around the bridge began to sway.

"You think you can defeat me this easily? Well try this on for size!"

It was as though every person surrounding them had frozen in time. The hooded figures stopped fighting and turned to the buildings. There was a few seconds of silence before everything came crashing down.

Fighting became an insignificant feat. Margot watched as the army fled.

"Retreat!" One yelled: "Back to the castle!"

Arabina continued to laugh as she lowered her arms, the spiral sea that had once protected them shot across the city, flooding the streets. Margot watched as it carried away humans and destroyed the buildings with its brute force. Had it really come to this? She turned to look for Arabina but she was nowhere in sight.

"Come on," Barbie said, grabbing her hand and leading her through the carnage. She nodded, pulling out her gun and firing it at any U.A.S member that got in their way.

"Human, we need to get back to the ship."

"But where's Arabina?"

Barbie didn't reply.

Margot screamed, grabbing the transvestite and throwing him aside as a large chunk of rubble crashed down at their side. The water and dirt had mixed to create a sludge that smothered the streets. Barbie lay face down in the mess. Margot had to pull hard to try and get him to his feet. Then her eyes caught sight of something. In the distance, Damien was fleeing from the city, flying high towards the north east of Izsafar. Margot glared as his figure became smaller.

"I'm going to kill you." She muttered through gritted teeth.

"Human?" Barbie said, finding his balance again. The albino was pulled from her trance.

"We're almost there," she took his hand and they ran to the ship. There wasn't much time; if they remained there any longer, the whole city would be destroyed. She could make out a figure standing on the deck. Wolf was waving his hands, beckoning them to come faster. Margot heard an ear piercing squawk behind her. It could only mean one thing. The Brontangus were following.

"Faster Barbie!" She screamed as it dived towards them. Its aim was unsuccessful so it banked high into the sky, ready for a second attempt. The ship was so close. *If I can make it ... just a little further...*

Margot leaped onto the deck, pulling Barbie with her. They collapsed on the floor, closing their eyes and panting. They had made it. They were safe.

"Margot, move!" Wolf screamed.

She opened her eyes to see the Brontangus flying towards the ship at full speed. She sprung to her feet, grabbing Barbie by the arm.

"In here!" Wolf yelled, opening the ship's door. Margot and Barbie dived inside just as the Brontangus hit the deck, shaking the vessel. It reached its hand towards the entrance but Wolf was quicker and slammed it hard. The Brontangus let out an ear piercing scream and flew away into the sky.

"Right," said Wolf catching his breath. "Where is everyone?"

Margot and Barbie looked at each other.

"Hurst?" Wolf asked.

"He fled," Barbie replied.

"And Arabina?"

"We don't know," Barbie looked down. "We lost her in the mayhem. There's a high chance that she didn't make it."

Wolf rubbed his forehead. "I refuse to believe she's dead. Not yet anyway." There was an awkward pause.

"Jade's dead." Margot spoke before he asked the question. "Damien killed him, I saw it."

"Damien?"

"He's the Dark Rider," Barbie said. They went down the stairs towards the galley. "He's been working for Silvia all along. We were taken for fools."

"Yeah," said Margot, lifting up her head. "And you know what? I'm gonna kill him. I'm going to murder Damien." Her words were cold and calm.

"But Margot," Wolf said. "We don't even know where he-"

"Yes we do!" Margot raised her voice. She pulled out the compass from her leather pocket. "This will lead us to him." She placed the compass in his hand. "It'll glow red when he's near."

Wolf stared at her. "Margot-"

She turned her back on them. "You know as well as I do, with the Dark Rider out of the way we'll have more of a chance of breaking into the castle."

"Do you not think we should wait?" Wolf asked. Margot turned round.

"For what? For Izsafar to repair itself? For all our work to go to waste?" she said. "There's a high chance we're all gonna die anyway. Let's go out in style. You must want the same, as the point of that compass hasn't moved at all." She walked from the room.

Wolf had a strange feeling it had nothing to do with Izsafar or Silvia; it was to avenge the death of a friend. He sighed; everything had gone way too far. He looked down at the compass, it was pointing North East; he cringed, it was pointing towards the snowy blizzards and icy shores of Izsafar. It was the coldest place the angel had created; where the snow was thick and icebergs hid from the view of oblivious sailors. It was a bleak and dangerous place, one that he tried to avoid at all costs.

"Well?" Barbie asked. He had been sitting at the kitchen table in silence.

"We're going to find Damien," Wolf sighed. "You'd better go check on Margot."

Barbie nodded and left the room.

Margot was right; Wolf was interested in finding Damien, but not for the same motives as her. He went upstairs, shouting commands to his son to cast off. Wolf sighed again as he stared back at the burning city that once was thought of as a paradise. The thought of leaving the Queen of the island behind sickened him.

"Wherever she is, if she still breathes, let's hope somebody will find her and bring her no harm, if not, all hope is truly lost."

*

Arabina opened her eyes. The bright sky shone through her sunglasses and she covered her squinting eyes with her hand. She was pale, meaning she had changed back to her original human form. That was good; safer at least. She sat up slowly; the earth swayed around her as she did. She was weak, dizzy. Arabina shook her head, waiting for her eyes to focus. She was shocked at what she saw. The city was a waste land; so many buildings were half standing, others had collapsed into the road. Arabina got to her feet, the city was burning. The riverbank had burst, the bridge had been destroyed. She was on top of a mound of rock, once a building. She must have grabbed it as she was swept away by the current. She walked to the edge, jumping down onto the sludge swathed road.

The city was silent. Not a living soul remained. She was alone. They had left her. She protected them and they had left - and Damien - she didn't even want to think about what he'd done. *Traitors, the lot of them.* They had abandoned her on the blood-stained streets after she had saved them all. Arabina sat down on the rocks and sobbed into her hands. There was no hope, not any more.

"Evie?" A voice called behind her.

Arabina looked up.

"Oh god, it is you!" Lucy ran towards her, embracing her. Arabina didn't speak, just smiled.

"I heard what happened in the city and I thought you'd have gone there so I came to try and find you. I've been helping with the survivors. There's not many." Embarrassed by her affection, she backed away.

Arabina stood up, but didn't face her. "You, you came back for me?"

"I do care you know, after saving you the last god knows how many times."

Arabina's lips curled into a wider smile.

"You're lucky you weren't killed," Lucy said. The two women did not face each other. Instead, they looked out into the distance, staring at the destruction.

"The angel has managed to control the destruction for a few more hours and then, who knows what will happen. Those guys really did create war."

Arabina turned to her. "We have to go into hiding. She'll want every human she can get."

"Or better still," Lucy said, interlinking her fingers with Arabina's. "We could run from here Evie, over the Togeerian Mountains to freedom. Run away with me."

Arabina smiled. "It's great but-"

"But what? Don't you trust me?"

"You're right," Arabina turned to her, taking both her hands. "There's nothing here for us." She took one last look at the city, at where Wolf's ship had been. "Let's go."

*

Margot sat on the bottom step of the stairs, staring at the picture she had taken from Jade's ship. She'd kept it close to her, leaving it in the pocket of her coat. She didn't think a photo could mean so much to her. She looked at Jade's face. He was laughing. Margot remembered the days when they used to laugh. *Before all this.* She thought she would never laugh again.

"Human?" She turned to see Barbie at the top of the steps.

"Yes, Barbie, what is it?" Her tone was harsh.

"Do you want to talk about it?" He came and sat beside her. Margot got to her feet.

"There is nothing to talk about." She crumpled the photo. "Everyone dies, life is a cycle."

"I don't think you mean that. He was a good friend."

"I don't have friends, Barbie!" She raised her voice. "Margot Grant has never had 'friends', if you want to be the best, you can't afford to become attached. Emotions are a weakness. Yes, there are my fellow colleagues and people like you but-"

"Jade was your friend."

"I need to prepare for going to meet Damien," she said, trying to walk past him on the stairs. Barbie blocked her passage.

"Margot."

"What would you know about it?" She yelled, scrunching the picture more.

"I'm sorry, Margot."

"Don't talk to me," she replied. "You don't get it do you? You're not sorry, you're not anything, just the same monotone reply again and again and again, you don't feel anything! How would you even know what it's like?"

She dropped to the steps, put her hands over her face and closed her eyes. "I'm sorry."

"I do know what it's like."

Margot raised her head.

"I used to go to Earth all the time. It was my favourite place in the whole of the eighty one worlds to visit. The people there were so passionate, so complex. I would go there for Earth years, just living amongst the people. And then one day, I met a beautiful girl. I fell in love, for the first time. And more

298

amazing, she loved me." He paused, reminiscing. "I told her everything, about here and she agreed to come back with me, to live with me here."

Margot frowned. "But Barbie where you live-"

"It didn't always look that way," he said. "We bought the house under Arabina's rule and lived happily in the dark. Until the angels found out; they came down from the Over World, they took her and killed her." He stared out into space. "I was empty, I didn't know what to do, but it didn't end there. I had broken the law of Haszear. I had taken a human there to live; you have to understand, being one of the most powerful worlds, that was seen as a disgrace. They couldn't decide on a punishment for me. I begged for death, but they wouldn't kill me. I didn't want to live, not without her. I felt so terrible that I didn't want to feel anything anymore. So I asked as a punishment if they would take my emotions from me, allowing me never to love or have to grieve again. They agreed, but it was a trick."

Margot's eyes widened.

"They took away my right to display emotions, but not the feelings themselves. I never seem happy or sad, but I feel. I feel like you or anyone else. So don't try and hide when you feel terrible, because I know, human." Barbie sighed. "They said they buried her on the island. I searched and searched but never found her grave."

"So when I saw you in the graveyard..."

"I was looking for her. I am cursed; I can only love the dead."

She put her hand on his shoulder.

"The angels here are not the ones you read about in human stories, remember that human. All creatures that hold power are dangerous."

"Oh Barbie," Margot said, pulling the transvestite in for a hug. "I lied earlier, you are my friend; you always have been."

The ship shook.

"We're approaching Damien's location," Wolf called down to them.

"Okay," Margot called back. "I'm ready."

The windows of the ship were thick with ice as they approached the freezing shores of Izsafar. Wolf had only ventured so far once before and had vowed never to do it again. His hands shook on the wheel as he steered the ship through the heavy snow. His son looked at the treacherous mountains that loomed on either side of them. One avalanche; and they'd all be killed. Sweat dripped from his brow, judging by the state of Izsafar at the moment, that was a strong possibility.

"Sir I'm not sure-"

"Take the helm lad," Wolf said. "He's close."

Margot stood in the room in which she and Jade had slept in, looking at herself in the mirror. Wolf had given her a thick, black trench coat to wear over her clothes with black leather gloves to match. Her sturdy boots were able to take the snow and ice; she hoped she wouldn't have to climb too far.

"You'll be needing this," Barbie said, passing her an odd looking gun.

"So the human legends about vampires aren't true," she said taking it. "No wooden stake and all that."

"This gun has reinforced wooden bullets, aim straight for the heart."

Margot frowned at him.

"Yes, believe it or not, humanity did get something right for once, but this is almost one thousand human years on, do you think we're going to use wooden stakes?"

"Good point."

They walked up the steps to where Wolf was waiting.

"Sunglasses," he said to Margot. She nodded, sliding them over her face. Wolf put his hand on her shoulder. "We will wait for you here, Izsafar is crumbling. You must be as quick as you can."

Margot nodded, taking the glowing compass from his hand. She opened the door and the two men followed her onto the deck. Margot turned round, trying to take everything in. It looked like drained the colour had drained from the world. Everywhere she turned, all she could see was towering, falling, ever-reaching white. It didn't feel like they were anywhere near the city, or any sort of civilization. The ship was covered in snow; her feet crunched as she walked to the edge of the deck. Wolf's son moored them as close to the icy shores as possible. She climbed onto the side, holding on to the rope securing the sail. How could somewhere so beautiful hide something so evil?

"We stop here," Wolf said, walking with her and Barbie. "Damien isn't too far from here. I expect he's taken to the mountains."

"Thanks Wolf," Margot said. She turned to Barbie: "I'll be back as soon as this has been dealt with."

Barbie stared at her. "The difference between me and you is that you have the chance to start again, mourn by all means but don't waste your life grieving for the dead."

"I have to do this." She smiled sadly and jumped from the ship onto the bright white landscape.

Margot walked through the wilderness, keeping Jade's compass close to hand. It was pointing towards the highest mountain. The mountain looked like it could stretch all the way out of Izsafar and into the Over World. She looked up at its colossal height, disappearing into the hazy sky. As she lifted her gaze, she saw movement. Margot saw him; a lonely black figure, stark against the snow on the mountain side. Her heart raced and she quickened her pace towards him.

It had been a tough climb, but the compass was burning her hand. He was close. Margot pulled herself over another rock and the ground levelled out. She was finally able to pause for breath. Margot's heart burnt with anger. Hatred was the only thing forcing her up the mountainside. She turned to see how far she'd climbed and there, standing on the very edge of the cliff, was Damien.

His heavy black cloak snapped like a flag in the raging winds and he looked out towards the landscape of the desolate world. He belonged there, amongst the cold wilderness. Margot pulled out her gun and crept towards him, her finger on the trigger. Adrenaline rushed through her body as she closed in. She was ready; the whole operation would be easier than she thought. Then she realised something was wrong. He stood as silent as the snow, as motionless as the mountain. She stopped. Had he seen her? Did he know she was there? Margot thought she surely couldn't risk it, but she was too close to turn back. She charged towards him at full speed.

He turned just before she struck, but to her surprise didn't retaliate. Margot hit him round the head at full force with the gun and he dropped to the icy ground. She kicked him in the side, punched his face, stamped on his body. He didn't move. He lay in the snow, taking every blow with a devilish smile on his face. Margot backed away; the punishment just wasn't satisfactory.

"This is not how it's supposed to be!" She yelled as Damien picked himself up.

"What did you expect, an epic battle to the death?" He asked. "Return to the ship Margot, leave me, there is nothing for you here." Damien turned away from her, back to his original position, a little more beaten than before.

Why wasn't he fighting back? She couldn't let her morals get in the way. She had a job to do and she would damn well not leave until it was complete. Too much was at stake.

"I can't do that," Margot said, pointing the gun at him.

"Fine."

The vampire came at her too fast for her to react. He was as quick as lightning. He prised the gun from her hand and threw it off the cliff. She was defenceless and he moved so fast she couldn't see him.

"Show yourself!" She screamed, looking around. Damien was nowhere to be seen. Many people would have given up at that point, many people would have turned back, but Margot Grant was determined to keep going for the sake of her friend.

"I'm not leaving!" She shouted. And she didn't.

She stayed true to her word. It felt like she'd been there for hours. Margot sighed, sitting down on the cold, hard ground. The compass burned and she jumped. She took it out of her pocket to find it was spinning wildly. Margot frowned, what did that mean?

"Didn't I tell you to go away?" A smooth voice behind her asked.

Margot stood up and turned. There he was; his pointed face as hard and cold as the mountainside. His pale blue eyes froze the fire from her angry gaze as they glared at one another.

"I came here to kill you." She said simply.

"Well you must have had a change of heart," Damien said. "I know you Margot Grant. If you were going to kill someone you'd have already gone ahead and done it."

She glared at him. "Just looking at you fills me with pure hatred."

"Emotion should not rule our heads."

"You know what, Damien," Margot said, backing away. "I thought I was a really selfish, heartless bitch. I honestly did, and I didn't think I could find anyone else worse than me, but congratu-fucking-lations, you take the gold." She applauded.

"Do you think I feel nothing?" Damien yelled; his voice breaking as he turned away from her.

Margot stopped smiling. That was something she'd never seen before. There was something more to the situation, something strange that she had no way to understand at that moment. Damien wasn't his usual proud, obnoxious self. He looked like he was hurting, suffering. It confused her. She no longer felt anger, she felt sorrow. Margot tried to shake off the thoughts. His act was getting to her. She mustn't be fooled, that... *creature* was a killer. But as Margot stared, she felt the pain that flooded his melting heart.

"Leave me." Damien said.

"Damien?" She asked, walking to his side. Neither of them could bear to face one another.

"I don't understand. What's going on?" She wasn't sure what to think any more. The whole situation didn't make any sense.

"Oh Margot," Damien snapped. "Don't you understand?"

"Obviously not."

"I did it for her." Damien's body grew tense as he spoke. Emotions weren't his strong point. "Arabina."

"Arabina?"

"When Silvia first fell, she was going to kill Arabina." he said, having trouble processing his words. "I couldn't let that happen, so I went to the angel and asked for her to spare Arabina's life."

As Margot listened, she was sure Damien was under-exaggerating his actions.

"She did, but at a price. I'm sure you've guessed what that is." He sighed. "I tried to lead her away from our trail as soon as we got here, but there's only so much one can do."

It was beginning to make sense; Damien's mysterious disappearances, his vast knowledge of Izsafar, the reason for Margot not lifting the hood to reveal the U.A.S. He had known all along. She wasn't sure whether to be relieved or angry.

"That white flash Jade saw on the beach; that was you!" She said, thinking back to the day she had first shown him the building.

"Yes, I was arranging with Clarke when was best to move the weapons." He still hadn't turned to face her.

"And that's why he left 'Face', he thought it didn't work." Margot paused in thought for a moment. "You loved her."

Damien didn't reply.

"You loved Arabina."

"Leave me!" He raised his voice.

"No, Damien we have to go back, we have to stop this."

"Oh give it up, Margot; you know we can change nothing."

But Margot couldn't give up, not after all they'd done. "We *have* to try!" She yelled. "You know, I used to be like you. I used to hate the world because I thought the world was harsh to me."

"Oh, how similar we are," Damien replied sarcastically.

"But what I learned," Margot ignored him. "Is that it never stops, Damien. It never stops. You can hate everything and everyone around you, constantly wishing for a better life or you can appreciate what you have and build on it."

"What's the point? After she... after he... how can you even stand here after..." His words faltered. Damien lowered his head and Margot felt something towards him that she dare not admit. Slowly, she moved her pale hand towards his.

"This sadness," he struggled to speak. "It never ends does it?"

Margot shook her head. "No," she whispered.

Margot could feel the hatred that drove her to come on her quest melting from her heart. She had been driven, like him, by blind passion and as she gained clarity, the more complicated things appeared. Once again, Margot questioned her morals. Nothing was simply black or white; there was no good or evil, right or wrong, only existence. The snow around her was no longer treacherous, but beautiful. It was so pure, untarnished by the feet of men. Margot knew she would never be the same again: something had changed in her, something that most human beings never experience. She had lost everything; but she had gained something that she could never learn from a textbook, experiment or great philosopher - the appreciation of existence. Despite her grief, she felt okay. It was the most okay she had been in years.

She remained by Damien's side; neither faced the other. They stared out beyond the icy wilderness to the non-existent horizon, hoping for a new dawn.

*

"Evie? Evie?" A distant voice echoed in the background.

Arabina could feel herself falling away from the earth. Her mind was disintegrating. Her body was collapsing. She was weak, too weak to carry on. Damien had told her not to use her magic, he had told her and she had not listened. Arabina never listened to anyone and she was paying for it.

She would die. Her reign would come to an end on the very force that she had set out to destroy. On the very land that was eating her own world like a virus; spreading from the inside. It was fitting really; that good should conquer evil, that the angel should slay the demon. Arabina tried to get to her feet. She wasn't sure if she was still in her human form or not. Her sense of feeling was disappearing, much like her sight. What would become of her? Would they rejoice in her name and sing her songs in banqueting halls? Or would she be as easily forgotten as the dirt on a dusty mountain trail? Who would remember the devil's daughter?

Arabina smiled throughout her whole body. It wasn't a nice pleasant smile, but a cynical, twisted one. If that had been her last act of destruction, then it had been a good one. It didn't matter that she hadn't completed her goal; what was most important was that she had tried to.

*

Margot didn't expect that sort of treatment, especially from someone who had not only tried to kill her but had murdered her best friend. Yet, there she sat, side by side with him in the snow, her hand intertwined with his. They did not need to look or speak to each other. They did not need to voice their emotions; they were not those sorts of people. Margot and Damien had reached an understanding that never had to be spoken. It just was. They had formed a connection with the darkest of roots; the one was just as lonely as the other.

"Margot," Damien said, finally turning to her. "I have something for you. I took this from Jade's pocket."

Margot's eyes grew wider as he placed the Jonovicator into her hand.

"I was unsure what it did; however he wouldn't let me touch it when we visited his hotel room so that must mean something. I was going to deliver it to Silvia, but I don't believe that will be necessary."

"Damien!" Margot exclaimed, "Do you know what this means?"

"No," Damien said.

"It's like Jade's personal journal, he documents everything in here. There may be information-"

"- to destroy Izsafar." Damien finished.

Margot smiled that was it, their ticket to freedom.

She sat for a moment, staring at Jade's device. It stung her heart to think he would never hold it again.

"Right," Margot said, concentrating hard. "Now if I can just remember…"

Damien watched as she twisted the two sides of the Jonovicator and pulled the circle apart to reveal the large, flat screen.

"That's incredible," Damien said, not even pretending to be unimpressed. Margot clicked on folders, searching for anything that might be of use. She soon found what she was looking for. There were reams and reams of holographic pictures of the castle, notes on the U.A.S's gadgets and records taken from when Silvia had shown Jade around her underground laboratory.

"This is it," Margot said, listening to a clip of Silvia's voice.

"Margot," Damien said. "I think this folder is for you." Margot frowned, following his finger to a small black folder at the top of the page. There, in fierce red writing underneath it, were the words 'For Margot'. Margot tapped it. She cringed, hoping it wasn't something embarrassing. Inside were various other folders, all labelled things like 'maps' and 'plans'. The thing that caught her attention was right at the very top. A video recording called 'Play Me First'.

"Better do what the guy wants," she said, clicking it. A hologram rose from the screen. It wasn't a hologram of the castle, but of Jade Wilde himself.

He was panting. "Margot, there's not much time; they're after me, Silvia and the Riders. They're U.A.S members Margot, don't trust them." He looked behind. "I'm guessing if you're listening to this, I have failed to get to you on time, but I've known my fate all along so I had time to prepare. In the folders below is everything I discovered about Izsafar and 'Face'. They're all important, so read my notes well. I found where Silvia takes the humans, but have only had time to draw a quick map for you. There are audio files in which I have tried to describe it for you. It won't be long until Izsafar crumbles, but only if you do exactly what I tell you. And oh," he paused. "Sorry almost forgot something, look out for the Brontangus; I don't think they're as loyal to Silvia as we all think. Okay, glad that's sorted."

He took a deep intake of breath. "Now, go back to the hotel as soon as you can it's very important, go to the top floor, the storeroom. I've hidden your whole stash of 'Face' there. I'm sorry Margot, I kept taking it, it was the only way I could study its qualities." There were sounds of footsteps in the background. "There's no time to explain, just go to the hotel as soon as possible. I love you. Always have, always will."

She wanted to pause that part of the message, keep it forever just to prove that it was real. Margot stared at his face, her eyes filling with tears once more. There was her love, the man that had sacrificed everything for her and asked for nothing in return. If only she had said something on that beach, maybe things would be different. She knew it would stay with her for the rest of her life. Margot heard shouting. Jade ran.

"Godda go!"

The hologram disappeared. Margot stared down at the ship, she knew what to do.

There was rumble from the top of the mountain.

"What is that?" Margot, said.

Damien jumped to his feet. "Izsafar is becoming unstable again." He stared to the top of the mountain. "Avalanche!"

"We need to get back to the ship!" Margot said. The ground beneath her feet vibrated. She turned to see the ice and rock falling towards them.

"Come on!" She yelled at the vampire, but Damien wouldn't move.

"I said, leave me."

The rocks and ice were picking up speed.

"I'll never make it down in time by myself!"

She watched as they crashed towards them.

"Damien," Margot yelled. "We can't do this without you!"

The vampire nodded. He ran straight at her, picking her up.

"It's right above us!" Margot shouted. Damien looked around; if they had stayed there another second they'd be buried. He dived off the side of the mountain.

Margot kept her eyes shut tight. When she opened them, the avalanche was inches away as they flew. She jolted forward as Damien landed further down the side of the mountain and ran. They were on a vertical slope, speeding towards the snow at the bottom.

"It's gaining," Margot yelled, looking behind his shoulder.

"I know, I don't usually carry weight, or I'd be faster."

"Hey!"

"Margot; now is really not the time."

He was right; they hadn't far to go, the hill flattened out as they reached the bottom. All that was left to contend with was the maze of frozen ferns before them. They were harder to dodge when travelling at speed. Damien jinked left and right, with Margot, the unhelpful back seat driver shouting directions. Snow was miniature ice shards, pelting them, making it harder for him to see. He was picking up speed but unsure of where he was meant to be running. Suddenly, Damien caught his trench coat on the branch of a tree; his body jerked backward, launching Margot into the air.

"Margot!" Damien shouted, getting to his feet.

It was useless; all he could see was white. He stared at the trees waiting to be consumed by the snow.

"Barbie!" Wolf called, from the back of the ship. "Can you see them?"

The transvestite was at the opposite end, wishing he had telescopic vision.

"Not any more, no," he replied. "Wolf you better come over here."

"Which side of the mountain did Margot climb?" He asked, gazing at the avalanche. It was no use, even if they did try to find her; they'd never make it there in time.

"She'll be okay," Barbie said. Neither of them took their eyes off the mountain. Suddenly there was a crash and the whole of the left side caved in on itself. Rocks fell from the summit, unsettling its icy structure. It looked like liquid as it cascaded down the mountain side, picking up speed as the ice gathered in a river of rock and snow. Wolf stared up at the sky, letting the snow fall onto his face; hoping, praying for her life to be spared. He and Barbie did not need to speak; they were thinking the same thing.

"Hey guys." A voice came from behind him.

Wolf's face broke into grin. Soaking wet and climbing over the side of the deck was Margot. She shook out her white hair, before pulling out a cigarette; something she hadn't done in a while.

"How did you escape?" Wolf exclaimed, almost beside himself.

"Well," Margot owned up. "I had a little help."

A pale hand came over the side of the vessel, making Wolf and Barbie jump. Damien pulled himself onto the deck, with a lot more grace than the albino. Barbie took a few paces forward, clenching his fists, but Wolf held his hand up as a signal to cease.

"Damien," he said walking up to the vampire and holding out his hand. "It's really good to see you, lad."

Damien begrudgingly shook it, his harsh eyes met with Wolf's kind ones.

"Margot and I have found something, we must set sail for the hotel, quickly," he said. Looking at the confused response, the vampire added: "We'll explain on the way."

Wolf nodded and shouted commands at his son. He looked back at the others.

"There's something I have to tell you as well. But don't worry," he winked kindly. "I'll explain on the way."

Margot and Damien frowned at one another. After all she had discovered surely there couldn't be anything else she had yet to find out?

Chapter 19

Final Confessions

Margot sat at Wolf's kitchen table. She had been waiting there for a while, waiting for him and his son to come downstairs. She tapped her fingers on the wood as she contemplated what it was that he had to tell them. In the last few hours, her world had been turned upside down. What else could go wrong? Barbie brought her a cup of tea. She smiled at him. Margot sighed, there'd be no way she'd be able to drink it. Her stomach was so twisted in knots she could hardly sit down, but she appreciated the warmth from the cup, giving life back to her frozen fingers.

"Can you stop that repetitive noise?" Damien said. The vampire turned from his position by the window.

Margot glared at him, slamming her hand so hard on the table that her tea shook. The vampire narrowed his eyes but resumed his stance. No one spoke, no one needed to. They were too deep in thought: Those they harboured alone, and those they shared. The door opened and in walked Wolf with his lanky son Eric following.

"It is time that I told you all the truth." Wolf paced with his arms behind his back.

Margot frowned; Wolf had been the only one she'd ever trusted right from the beginning. Was he just as bad as the rest of them? Had he been lying the whole time?

He stopped pacing and faced the group.

"Sir, are you sure about this?" Eric asked nervously.

Wolf ignored him. Serious and very calm, he uttered three words.

"I'm an angel."

The room fell silent. The only sound that could be heard was that of Barbie's mug, smashing on the floor.

"There'll be no need for that now." Wolf sighed as Barbie bent down to pick the pieces up off the floor. Margot watched as he stretched his arm out and the pieces flew out of the transvestite's hands and into the bin.

"I don't understand." Damien said.

Wolf looked at him; his eyes were pools of sadness. "I was sent by the angels to watch over Silvia. To make sure nothing got out of hand. Silvia has no idea that I'm here. She is not able to enter this vessel. I'm unsure if she can actually see it." He waited.

Margot noticed he was losing his working class accent. She was numb. Everything she thought she'd known had been wrong all along.

"I am merely a guardian of Silvia. I assure you, I have had no information on the angel's plans or whereabouts. My job is to stay here. This," he gestured to his 'son'. "Is not a relative of mine at all, but a young angel that I have been asked to train to deal with this sort of situation."

The boy's face turned red and he hid his embarrassment from the others in the room.

Margot got to her feet. "Did it not occur to you to tell us of this earlier?" She was so angry. If Wolf had been an angel all that time why didn't he just tell them? Stop Silvia from getting out of control? Help save Jade? Actually do his job rather than make them all suffer?

"Margot, calm yourself, lass." Wolf said.

"She has a point," Damien glared at Wolf. "It would have made our discoveries much quicker and helped us with defeating Silvia. Unless," he paused. "You've been on her side the whole time."

Barbie shook his head. "No, I don't believe it."

"If I told you, aided anyone, or involved myself in any plans, they would encase my soul in a Brontangus." Wolf said in the same calm tone.

Margot sat back down.

"Can they do that to an angel?" Damien asked.

Wolf nodded his head. "I'm afraid they can, I was selfish." He sighed. "I'm sorry."

"But Wolf-" Margot began.

"No Margot." He said. It was the first time he'd interrupted her. "I've made my choice and I will deal with my consequences. I have chosen to help you, I do not agree with the ways of my people. Much like Damien has rebelled against his dictator."

Damien frowned.

"Then you've got to go and tell them!" Margot said. "The humans are in danger! The angels need to know, they can stop Silvia! You need to leave, now!"

"And how would you return to the hotel unnoticed? And what would you do if you got there and it was a trap. It is a possibility Margot." he said before she could protest Jade's loyalty. "No, I will stay until you have done what Jade instructed and try to think of a course of action. Then I'll take off to the Over World." He ran his fingers through his beard, thinking.

It was a risky move, with Izsafar in its unstable state, if he stayed too long, half of the population may be destroyed. Nevertheless, Margot respected his motives. It was probably a better proposition than she could have come up with. Wolf was old and wise; he had lived for many decades longer than Margot and would continue long after she was gone. She took a deep breath and stared into his kind eyes. She still trusted him.

So they were in agreement; Wolf would take them to the hotel and then return to the Over World to warn his people.

"Okay," Margot nodded. "But take Barbie with you."

Wolf stared at her; even Damien looked surprised by her negotiations.

"I want you to take him, or no deal."

Wolf nodded and turned to Barbie. "Barbie, I want you to come with me and saying 'no' isn't an option."

The transvestite stared at Margot. She knew he was wondering why she was doing that to him. She also knew if he was able to display emotion his face would show an expression of pure horror. He would understand soon enough.

Margot smiled, maybe, just maybe there was some hope out there. She felt the strangest sensation; it was the first time she longed to be out of the light and surrounded by darkness.

*

When Arabina awoke, she was staring at the canopy of a grand four poster bed. She turned over, looking round the room. Wherever she was, it was ornate, something fit for a monarch. The room was huge. She stared at the opulence and the door that opened into the en-suite bathroom. It was hard to take everything in, her vision was blurry, and she felt weak. A pang of fear pierced her chest. She came to the sudden realisation that she had no idea where she was. She looked about the room for Lucy, but she was nowhere in sight. She glanced at her hands, they were still white. Arabina let out a sigh of relief; she was still disguised as a human.

Arabina got to her feet, but collapsed to the hard marble floor, unable to support her own weight. She was weaker than she thought. The devil's daughter didn't even have the energy to pull herself up from the bedroom floor. Damien was right. She grimaced, hating the fact that someone was more knowledgeable about herself than she was. The door, at the opposite end of the room creaked open.

"Evie!" Lucy exclaimed, running forwards to pick her up. "God, are you okay?"

"Yeah," Arabina replied weakly, as she sat back on the bed. Lucy put her arms round her to keep her upright.

"You know," she said, as Arabina leaned into her chest. "That is a very strong Spanish accent; I would never have taken you for Spanish when I first met you."

"Well," Arabina laughed, trying to think of an excuse. "I spent a lot of time over there."

Lucy smiled, lowering her head back down on the pillow.

"Okay," she whispered, and kissed her on the forehead. "You're weak. Rest now. There's some food on a tray by the bed if you get hungry." She got up and went towards the door.

"Lucy," Arabina said. "Where are we?"

"Somewhere safe." Lucy smiled at her.

Arabina raised her eyebrows.

"Don't worry," Lucy laughed. "It's a deserted hotel. We're going to be okay."

"Okay." She replied. Arabina wanted more than anything to believe Lucy's words but there was something deep down in her soul, a gut instinct, telling her that something was wrong.

*

Damien leaned against the side of the ship as it sailed towards the hotel. He gazed at the silent shores. In the distance, nothing moved; the villages were deserted, the countryside empty. What frightened the vampire most was the lack of movement in the sky, no Brontangus, no U.A.S; nothing. It was haunting. Something big was afoot; he could feel it growing closer as the temperature rose.

"Damien," Margot called, coming out onto the deck. "We're reaching our destination."

"I thought you were resting."

"Believe it or not, it's difficult to sleep," she said, looking around the ship. "Wow, talk about empty."

"It's unnerving," he said as he continued to stare at the landscape. "Everything's so quiet; it feels like we're the only living creatures in Izsafar."

"Well, technically, aren't you un-dead or something?"

Damien turned and scowled at her. Margot smirked. She realised it was the first time they had spoken alone since the mountain. Admittedly, it was a little awkward.

"There's a lot you have to learn, I thought even your small brain may have picked up the fact that I was made to be more than a vampire when I chose to play out this role." He glared at her, she was getting used to him not wearing sunglasses like the rest of them. He had had no need all along. It was an odd thought, to think that he had had to play two roles. She'd just been herself.

"Do you really have no idea what's going on?" She asked.

"Really," Damien said sarcastically. "Silvia rarely told her followers of her plans. It's only recently, now that times are dire, that she has started to reveal details."

Margot didn't reply, instead she did something rather odd. Putting her hand on her head she reached out for something to lean on. At first Damien thought she was going to faint but then he soon realised what had caused the involuntary reaction. *'Give it up'.* He heard a voice inside his head. Silvia's voice. *'You may have stopped my running of this operation for the moment, but don't be blinded by a fool's hope. Izsafar is being restored as I speak. Soon, your mark on this land will disappear like a footprint in the sand. You can never beat me. I will find you and I will kill you.'*

"We're here." Margot said, through gritted teeth. Damien looked around. They were in open water; the south west coast. He looked over at the cliff top. There, surround by thick greenery, was the hotel basking in the full glory of the sun.

The ship's door opened and out hurried Wolf and Barbie.

"She's not happy," Wolf said.

"Really?" Damien asked. "I thought she was practically jumping for joy with that speech."

"Damien, cut the sarcasm, we really don't have time," Wolf sighed and turned to Margot. "As soon as you leave the ship, she'll be able to track you. I won't be able to protect you."

Margot nodded. "Thanks Wolf, for everything."

Wolf gave his usual kind smile. "Anytime, my dear; now go."

"Thank you."

Barbie began to follow her. Margot raised her eyebrows at him.

"What are you doing?" She asked. "You're meant to stay here."

She didn't want anything preventing him from going to the Over World.

"Human," Barbie said. "Last time I let you go alone, you were almost crushed by half a mountain."

"Guy's got a point," she shrugged.

The journey, once on shore, was easier than they had anticipated. There were no Brontangus to look out for, no army to run from. Margot liked the new Izsafar. However, there was still part of her that wished the 'Dark Rider' actually rode something. Margot was sick and tired of walking everywhere. The only thing that gave her the stamina to continue was the fact that she'd have an amazing figure by the end of it all. She looked back at Barbie who was walking up the hill behind her. At least she didn't have to wear stilettos and carry a limp; that *must* be hard work.

Margot's heart beat faster as they got closer to their destination. She prepared herself for the reeking bodies, the bloodshed, the smashed windows the... newly planted flowers? *What is going on?* Instead of the slaughterhouse she remembered, the hotel looked almost brand new. There was no sign that the attack had ever happened; which in a way, made the scenario more eerie. She turned to Damien and Barbie who had stopped and were staring at the entrance.

"Do you think it's safe?" She paused for a moment. "Wait, let me rephrase that; do you think there's a less than 90 percent chance of us dying?"

"I'd say 89." Damien replied.

"Good enough for me," Barbie shrugged.

They proceeded to the French doors beside the pool area.

"Let me go first," Damien said. He put on his black cloak and pulled up his hood. It was a good plan. No one would dare cross the Dark Rider. No sooner had Damien walked into the reception than he returned.

"What's wrong?" Margot asked, from her hiding place in the nearby bushes.

"It's empty." He shrugged.

Margot and Barbie crawled out from the undergrowth.

"Well, where the hell is everyone?" She felt sick. "Surely she can't have taken every human... can she?"

"I would have thought most have gone into hiding after the demolition of the city." He turned back to the hotel. "At least I sincerely hope so, for their sakes. Soon the light will start taking effect again."

They crept inside, constantly looking over their shoulders to check they weren't being followed.

"She's already been here."

"Well, no shit, dumb ass." Margot said, trying to hide her fear.

Barbie would have worn an exasperated expression if it was possible as the two of them broke out into an argument. Things were back to normal; or as normal as they could get for a necrophiliac transvestite. He pressed the button for the lift. It had all been redecorated; scarlet and gold curtains hung from the windows. A new carpet had been laid and freshly cut flowers had been placed in bronze vases on every table. It almost looked too inviting.

"I have a bad feeling about this." Barbie said as they stood in the lift, rising up through the building's many floors.

"Okay," Damien said. "We get the drugs, we get out, simple."

"It'll be fine, Barbie," Margot tried to reassure him. She delved into her pocket to find her night vision sunglasses. The lift came to a halt. The group braced themselves as the metal doors creaked open to reveal the door to the gloomy storage room.

Nothing had changed since the last time they'd visited. The boxes were piled high to the ceiling, creating a cardboard maze. It was creepy. She zipped up her leather jacket as a cold breeze blew. It was almost like it had its own chilling atmosphere. Damien felt the same. He looked down a few of the aisles. For some reason, he was convinced they weren't alone.

"We should split up," Damien whispered, turning to the others. They'd already gone. Margot and Barbie were nowhere in sight. "Right," the vampire sighed. "Better start searching then."

Margot explored the storage maze. It was massive and she was unsure where to begin. It was all very well Jade telling them to come, but couldn't he have left a map or something? She picked up the box closest to her and ripped off the tape; toilet paper. She dropped it; she doubted they could defeat Sylvia with something people used to wipe their arse on. She smiled to herself, wondering if angels even went to the toilet. She bet they didn't. Something distracted her. The box she dropped had started to shake. The boxes behind it were shaking too. Margot made her way backwards. The boxes continued to shake and then from the darkness, a large creature sprang out from beneath them.

Margot didn't stay to see what it was; she sprinted down the aisle with it chasing her. As she ran she could hear growling, she turned to catch a glimpse of the creature's burning red eyes and enormous body. There was no way she could fight that thing!

"Guys!" Margot screamed as she ran. "*Something's here!*"

Without warning, something small dropped from the ceiling in the distance. Margot gasped as she saw watched it drop. It was heading towards Damien.

"I must be crazy," Margot groaned, changing direction and heading towards the vampire with the creature following.

Barbie heard a scream; he stopped and ran back towards the entrance. He paused at the sight before him. There in the blackness was Damien, struggling with a small creature that had latched itself onto his shoulders. He swung back and forth to try and prise it off. What frightened the transvestite more was what was in the distance; Margot and the great beast were running towards him.

"Don't panic, Damien," Barbie said, as he ran towards the vampire, trying to grab whatever it was that sat on him.

"Guys, a little help here?" Margot yelled as she got closer to them.

"We're – kind – of busy – right – now." Damien struggled to speak. He turned just in time to see the huge beast launch itself into the air. "Oh – great."

Margot collapsed on the ground and the beast landed on her. She turned her body to face its huge teeth and glaring eyes. It was going to tear her limb from limb.

Margot punched the creature hard in the jaw, confusing it long enough for her to pull out her gun and shoot it in the face. It slumped and slid, crashing into a pile of boxes.

"Move back!" Margot yelled as they began crashing to the ground, burying the creature. Toiletries and cutlery flew everywhere. Margot dodged knives and forks as she sprinted back to the group. Meanwhile, Barbie had managed to prise the little creature off Damien. It kicked and scratched at Barbie, but was too weak to break out of his tight grasp.

"What the hell was *that*?" Damien asked, as he brushed himself down.

Barbie pulled the small creature up to face him. "Hurst?"

Damien was about to say something, when another figure approached from the distance, yelling so loud that it echoed through the room.

"What te hell is goin' on in here?"

Barbie dropped the demon on the floor. "Frank?"

They stared, frozen to the spot as the blind man approached them.

"Barbie?" He shouted and he tripped over the cutlery on the floor. "Is that you?"

Barbie went towards him, taking his arm and guiding him towards the group.

"Where's ma dog?" He said as Barbie sat him down. Margot looked guiltily towards the pile of boxes. She realised that the savage beast was Frank's demon guide dog. She rushed over to dig out the animal from the mess. It broke free, shook itself and returned to its master.

It was one of the most awkward reunions. To Hurst; Damien was a backstabbing traitor who had gone against his own people and worse, his Queen. To Margot, Barbie and Damien; Hurst was a cowardly selfish being and Frank was very much dead. No party knew what to say to the other. They were all confused. For a moment, the group stared at one another. They had all come so far since first crossing the border. Everything was lost in translation.

"What's going on?" Margot asked.

"Ohhh," Frank groaned, he sat down on a nearby box. "She's still here is she? Bloody human, thought you'd have killed her off by now."

Margot frowned. He hadn't changed at all.

"Leave her be Frank," Damien said, much to everyone's surprise. "We're wasting time. We came here looking for – ouch!"

"Traitor!" Hurst squeaked, kicking the vampire hard in the leg. "STUPID-MURDERING- TRAITOR!" He screamed and punched Damien.

"Would you care to repeat that?" Damien bent down, smiling so that his canines were showing. Hurst quivered and retreated to the safety of Barbie's legs.

"It's easy for you to say that, you coward!" Margot yelled.

"Oi! That demon saved me life!" Frank stood up.

"He betrayed our Queen," Hurst said, pointing to Damien.

"Everyone just calm down," Barbie said. "Damien's right, we're wasting time. I think everyone has the wrong end of the stick."

"What?" Hurst squeaked.

"It's a human phrase." Barbie replied. "Now, would you kindly tell us what's going on Hurst."

"Not to a traitor!" Hurst spat.

"Oh for fuck's sake, Damien's no traitor, he was put under a spell by Silvia," Margot lied. "You know he'd never betray Arabina."

"Oh." Hurst said. "Oh Damien. I'm sorry!" He dropped to his knees.

"Get up." Damien said in his cold manner. "Look, I don't care about your cowardly excuses, what I do care about is something that should be in this room. We're looking for-"

"'Face'," Hurst finished.

"How do you-?" Damien began.

"I ran for a reason," Hurst explained. "It was all part of Jade's plan, he'd seen it all. He knew it was meant to play out like this."

"What are you talking about?" Margot said.

"When I went to help Jade pack, he told me things," Hurst said. "He knew he was going to die so he gave me tasks to do after his death. Firstly, he told me where to find the 'Face'. He knew it'd take you too long to find it, so I found it for you. However, that wasn't the only reason I came here."

Margot and Damien looked at each other, they were worried. They could hear voices, distant, like that of a far-off crowd.

"Silvia made a portal from Izsafar to Arabina's land in case she ever had to escape. Jade found it." Hurst pointed up to the ceiling. "It's a portal to the Halo and Harp. It brings you out through the storm at the top of the pub."

Barbie, Margot and Damien all stared at the ceiling, lost for words.

"I'm small so I could get through the crowds of the city unnoticed. I ran here and went back." The voices around them were growing louder. "Jade told me you'd return so I knew when to come back."

"Hurst, so what is going on?" Damien asked.

"Well, once our people knew what was going on over here, they wanted to help." Suddenly people and creatures emerged from every corner of the room. They popped out of nearby boxes, jumped from the ceiling and dropped from the rafters. Margot spun round on the spot. They were surrounded by Arabina's people. There were so many of them that some had to hover. Margot felt her heart lift as they chanted. They were there because of them; there to fight for their island, but more important, for the freedom of choice. She was moved by the act of bravery.

"Jade knew we'd never win this war alone." Hurst said. "And look, they helped me dig out Frank."

"We realised..." Damien replied sarcastically. "Did you do all of this Hurst?"

"Yes." Hurst said quietly.

"I'm impressed; you may have just saved us all." He turned to the crowd. "Go down to the main conference hall. We will discuss our plans for destroying Silvia there."

There was a mumble of voices, the crowd remained.

"Erm, Damien," Margot said. "They don't know the way."

"Of course," Damien said and turned back to the ground, "Hurst will direct you to the lifts and stairs. He looked at the small demon: "Make sure they've all got something to shield their eyes. Margot and I will go fetch Wolf from the ship. I think that trip to the Over World may be slightly delayed." He grinned devilishly, and lifted his hood.

"Why did you lie?" Damien asked as he and Margot walked back through the undergrowth.

Margot shrugged.

"Oh come on, stop playing childish games with me," he said as he brushed back another bush, which hit her in the face.

"Now you're being childish." Margot groaned. "You want the truth? Fine. One: Because even if I did tell the truth, you wouldn't admit it. And two: You seem to like to keep this 'I don't give a shit' selfish, cold attitude going. God forbid you should show emotion." Margot

realised how hypocritical she was.

Without warning, Damien stopped walking and turned to face her.

"Margot." He sighed, trying to find the right words to say to her. He placed his hand on her shoulder. It was obvious he wanted to say something to her. He wore a sad expression, the same one he had on the mountain. Margot knew it was a rare occasion but she couldn't stick around waiting when Silvia was growing more powerful by the minute.

"Wolf's ship is over there." She pointed to where the vessel was floating just off shore. Margot went past him, brushing off his hand. Deep down, part of her wished she hadn't.

"Let's go," Damien agreed. "Before the Brontangus are released back into the skies."

They walked out onto the beach towards the ship, unaware that they were being followed.

*

Nearby, amongst the undergrowth was Margot's old partner Reenie. She crouched low, watching as they boarded the ship. She had orders from Sylvia to keep an eye on them.

"Yes," she whispered: "Margot's here and she's not alone, it looks like she's…"

She's what? Silvia voice rang out inside her head. It was so loud Reenie staggered back, trying not to fall over.

"…with the Dark Rider."

*

If any holiday maker of Izsafar had stepped into that hotel, they would have found it odd that it was inhabited by the strangest of creatures. They'd probably turn tail and run screaming from the building. Barbie stared at a couple with green, peeling skin. Surprisingly, they didn't stand out at all amongst the array of colours. There were some creatures that looked half-human, half-octopus, and other various animals. Many were gothic in appearance, pale and dressed in a similar Victorian fashion to Damien. Although, due to his ability to resist the light; Damien was the only vampire in the group. Creatures flew back and forth from the ceiling, restless as they waited for Wolf's arrival. To people like Barbie and Hurst, it was an average gathering.

"Well, this is all rather strange," the transvestite said, sipping from a china tea cup.

"What is?" Hurst squeaked. "Oi!" He yelled as a headless man rolled his detached body part under a chair where a demonic woman was sitting. Her skirt was way too short for it to have been an accident. "Pick that up, now!"

The man shrugged, bending down to find himself in a lot of pain as the female in question kicked his head across the room.

"All of it," Barbie continued, as though it hadn't happened. "Working with angels and humans, fighting Silvia, making change." He looked out of one of the tall windows.

"I know," Hurst grabbed his cross. "It's all rather scary, going against even our own people."

"Yes," Barbie agreed. "But something tells me, it's the right thing to do."

Frank's dog ran to the door, barking madly as Wolf entered with Margot and Damien. They walked over to Hurst.

"Well done, lad," Wolf said smiling down at him. The demon beamed in return. "Right, what is the plan?"

"More importantly," Margot said, removing her sunglasses. "Where is my 'Face'?"

"Follow me," Hurst said, leading them towards a grand oak stage at the very end of the room. The crowds watched as they passed. Margot had the feeling a lot of talk had gone on in their homelands. She wondered what rumours were floating around. She wondered who believed in what they were doing and who came out of curiosity.

"Jade found two different types of 'Face'." Hurst said. He stopped at two small boxes stage left. "One is for long term and the other for short term usage."

They nodded. Margot bent down, picked up a bottle of pills and unscrewed the top. She poured the contents into her hand. She smiled as she watched the pupils of the small eye-shaped pills dance on their blue background. It'd been a long time.

"I'm sure I didn't make this many," Margot said, puzzled at the amount of 'Face' there was.

"You didn't," Hurst replied. "Jade studied your research; he developed it and made more."

"Score!" Margot said. She turned to look at Damien's serious expression. It was obvious he didn't share the same enthusiasm.

"So what did he want us to do with them?" She asked, realising that she knew the answer.

"Take them." Hurst replied. "Jade said that even if we can't use them to control our vision, he believes that if we all take them, through the developments he's made, we can use them to communicate, share thoughts."

"Like…telepathy?" Margot raised her eyebrows.

"This is ridiculous," Damien turned to walk away, but Wolf took his arm, preventing him from leaving. Margot had a feeling he didn't find it ridiculous at all. Her conclusion was that he didn't like the idea of people picking at his thoughts.

"Awesome!" She beamed. "This is what every scientist dreams of!"

"I warn you, Margot," Hurst said seriously. "Once you take these, you risk not being the same, ever again."

Margot's smile faded. She knew they were Jade's words. It saddened her to look back on what she had done to him. She knew she'd carry that guilt for the rest of her life.

"There's not enough time to learn how to use it, war is upon us." Damien was frustrated.

"We don't have a choice," Wolf said. "It may save our lives, us, Barbie and your friend Frank should all take one. We can use it to communicate if nothing else."

Damien didn't argue; he knew he had no choice.

"Right," Wolf turned to the crowd. "Are there any more chairs round here?"

"There's some behind the stage," Hurst said.

"Good, lad, that's very good, because we're going to call a meeting to order." He raised his arms and the chairs flew and arranged themselves into rows around the crowd.

Margot smiled and went to get Barbie. He was staring out of one of the long windows; his eyes fixed on something that she couldn't see. "Look," and pointed up.

Margot stared up to the sky and for the first time, she saw a cloud on the horizon. The light of Izsafar was fading.

If only Barbie had chosen a different window to stare out of, he may have seen Reenie lurking in the bushes of the hotel grounds. She crept forward, lifting herself up to the window to get a quick glance inside. Reenie was shocked at what she saw. She jumped down, and pressed her back against the building. She slid to the floor, her breathing laboured as she tried to collect her thoughts.

'Well?' Silvia's voice rang out in her head. 'What did you see?'

"There's an army of them," Reenie panted, staring into the distance. "They're... I don't think they're human."

'Who is leading them?'

"I'm not sure." Reenie stuttered. "There's a group, I couldn't see the main leader."

'Is Margot Grant present?'

"Y- yes," Reenie was shaking as she continued. "And so is he."

'Traitor!' Silvia yelled. Reenie grasped her head in pain. 'Return to base immediately. I am assembling the army. If they want a war, they shall have one.'

Chapter 20

Over and Under

The clicking of Damien's boots on the hardwood floor was the only thing that could be heard in the Grand Hall. His audience braced themselves as he walked to the front of the stage, ready to speak. He looked as if he was about to recite a song, or act out a soliloquy, by the way he stepped forward with an air of supreme confidence. Margot wished pure entertainment was the reason behind it, but what Damien had to say was no performance. Not that time. She stood close behind him, in line with Barbie, Frank, Hurst and Wolf, hoping that whatever his choice of words; they would work.

"Good day to you all," Damien said. His voice echoed across the room. "We are all gathered here today," (Margot held in her laughter.) "To defeat Silvia and send the island back into darkness." The crowd cheered most of them rose from their seats.

"Please settle down," Damien urged. If they were so easily excited, he hated to think what they'd be like when he revealed the plan. "We shall fight against the armies, while our friend," he gestured to the angel. "Wolf will inform his friends in the Over World of the situation we're in."

The crowd fell silent as Wolf stepped forward. He could see the fear on their faces as he approached Damien's side. Some backed their chairs away; some frowned, whilst some yelled Haszearian profanities.

"Forgive me, for offending you," Wolf spoke over them. "I swear it was not my intention." The crowd began to settle again, although many were unconvinced by his words. "Now, so far we've discovered these basic facts about Izsafar…"

*

The hall was quiet as Silvia floated up and down the rows of U.A.S. members. No one dared move, no one dared speak. The angel stared at the crowd as she made her way towards the throne. "Good," she said, stopping in front of it. "You're all here."

She scanned the room one last time. "Now Reenie here," she gestured to the front row. "Has informed me that the rebels have formed an army of creatures and they are coming to kill you. They will destroy us. They will burn down our town, our inventions, our revolution." Though the crowd was silent, the underlying tension was surfacing. They clenched their fists and held their breath as she rose, like a child's balloon.

"Therefore," Silvia continued. "We must kill them all. I warn you, these creatures are not like you and me, they have no morals - and neither does Margot Grant."

*

Wolf took a step back, a little uncomfortable as he finished his speech. The crowd had warmed to him the more he spoke, he was proud; almost accepted amongst the strange creatures.

"Thank you, Wolf," Damien nodded at him. Wolf returned the gesture. "Now, you understand what we're up against, you must understand how to deal with the problem. Our people do not understand human technology, but Margot Grant does." He gestured to the albino. Margot tightened her fists as all eyes in the room fell upon her. People began to whisper, though their whispers were audible. After meeting Damien and Arabina, she had come to the understanding that the creatures weren't gifted with discretion.

"So, that's the human Frank was telling us about." A woman with large horns and dark red hair whispered.

"Filthy, filthy; Damien knows the laws," another said.

"For all we know, she's a traitor like the rest."

"Step forward Margot," Damien said. "Step forward."

Margot forced herself to the front of the stage. The crowd rose to their feet in an uproar. They reminded Margot very much of fans at a human football match only much more rowdy. They screeched, booed, howled and cried as she came to Damien's side. Their insults grew from audible whispers to explicit hounding.

"Damien, you've lost your mind, first an angel, now this!"

"The light has made him soft!"

Margot turned to look back at Barbie; even Frank was booing.

"Down with te' human!" He yelled. The transvestite hit him hard on the head.

"Frank, you're on our side."

"Fine." Frank folded his arms.

Margot baulked, her legs faltered and her heart pounded. But Damien continued to gesture for her to move forward. She paused; only she could lead a rebellion that hated her guts.

Without warning, a black winged figure dived front the rafters heading straight towards her. Margot gasped, many members in the front row were also leaping towards the stage. The winged creature landed on the stage, stretching out its huge claws towards her. Margot knew she shouldn't fight back; these people had to trust her. So she stood there, watching, waiting to be torn apart.

Damien dived in front of her, spreading his arms out wide.

"You – will – not –touch – her." He whispered, baring his teeth. Margot turned to see the group had surrounded her. Suddenly the ground around them began to shake, the chandeliers in the room swayed.

I know you are here.' Silvia's voice hissed. It was everywhere. It slithered down the walls, soared to the ceiling; penetrated their minds. The crowd looked around for fear she was behind them. *'You will fall, you all will fall. You have no Queen and those that lead you are pathetic outcasts. There is no hope, this is your last chance, return to the darkness or die.'*

The room fell silent.

"Is this what you want?" Margot yelled. "To be tormented like this in your own land?" She lowered her voice. "I may be a human, but I am here to protect you. This war with Silvia is *bigger* than humanity."

Damien returned to her side: "And it is also more than just protecting Arabina's lands and our livelihoods."

"It is?" Frank mumbled.

"Yes," Damien glared at him. "It's about saving another world of people; the human race. Many of you may jeer; many of you may think they are worthless, due to their lack of intelligence and their small minds."

"Hey!" Margot said.

"But, and as much as it pains me to admit it" he said as he frowned and looked at the stage for a moment. Margot knew it was hard for him to admit defeat or swallow his pride. "If it weren't for a human, we'd still be letting Silvia take our lands with her mountains. That human is standing directly before you, so I suggest you treat her with a little more respect."

The creatures looked about each other and returned to their seats.

"I know it's not in our nature to work together, but we must. For if not, we're just as bad as she is." Damien smiled as the crowd began to cheer. Finally, they had won them over.

"However," he continued, once they had fallen silent. "I will not be the one to lead you."

Margot turned to the vampire in confusion. After all that he had said, he was turning his back on them? Would he not fight after all? Would he return to the angel? She looked at the others on stage. They shared the same expressions and she saw as she turned to face the crowd, that so did some of the audience. After a long pause, Damien continued.

"No," he said and gave his devilish grin. "It would not be right. I have always thought of myself more a rogue than a leader. Instead, Hurst will lead you."

Frank burst into laughter. "Yeah, as long as yer don't tread on 'im by accident!"

He wasn't alone, many people laughed and those that didn't laugh gasped or uttered disapproving grunts. Margot looked down at the demon. His beady eyes were as wide as they could stretch and his long red hands quivered as he grasped his cross in shock.

"Step forward, Hurst," Damien commanded. But the demon didn't move. "I said, step forward." Like Margot, Hurst slowly moved forward.

"Has he not led you this far?" Damien called out. "Has he not found the portal to Izsafar? Protected his Queen as best he could? Fought hard and well?"

No one dared reply.

"How dare you discriminate, when all you have done is stand by and watch your island destroyed? This demon is smaller than all of you, however in courage, he is a giant. He is already your leader; he became so the moment you decided to follow."

Wolf's face creased as he smiled. Margot was sure she saw the edges of a grin appearing on Damien's face as Hurst stepped in front of him to face the crowd.

"Okay," the demon squeaked, adjusting his circular glasses. "Let's go and, as Margot says; 'kick some ass'!"

The people of the darkness rose to their feet, cheering. Margot finally felt a confidence in those they had chosen to fight with.

"Alright, enough of that, he's not been crowned king," Damien said. "Now, go and prepare quickly, we have much to do and very little time." He turned to Margot. Although he tried to hide it, she could see traces of pride, disguised by his apparent annoyance.

*

"Where are the Brontangus?" Silvia demanded.

"They're not here yet, ma'am" Clarke said, approaching the stage. "And neither is-"

"Don't speak his name!" Her voice echoed about the silent hall. She began to float about the room again.

"We will push out the mountains; take the whole of this island for ourselves. Arabina's people will not stand a chance. Every rebel you see in your path, destroy them. The same goes for Margot Grant."

"Erm, excuse me?" Reenie was hesitant as she interrupted. "But what about the humans still hiding; the humans you brought here?"

"What about them?" Silvia replied in a patronising, sweet tone.

"Well, won't they, won't they die?" She asked.

"They most probably will."

"But, your majesty, they are innocent!"

"Innocent?" Silvia screeched, turning on the quivering woman. "Innocent?" She repeated as she thrust her glowing face closer to Reenie's.

Reenie trembled and dropped to the floor, shielding her eyes from the angel's blinding light.

"Let this be a lesson to you all," the angel's voice shook the room. "Those humans up there are – *not* – innocent. They are criminals, rogues, scum of society. That is the purpose for being here and if they die, so be it. The Earth and Izsafar shall be safer, peaceful places."

She looked to her silent audience: "To obtain perfection, sacrifices must be made. It is the only way we can reach the utopia we have dreamed of. This is for humanity's own good. I have worked too hard to help you humans to have it all taken away from me by a group of lowly individuals! Now go. Go to the surface. The army is based at the south west, in the hotel by the coast. Go, kill them all."

After a final glance at their leader, the U.A.S. rose from the ground and swarmed out of the double doors. Silvia smiled as she watched them go. Margot wouldn't have a chance.

*

The hotel was full of life. Everywhere Margot turned, she saw people rushing about, preparing weapons (which largely consisted of Arabina's army picking up anything dangerous-looking from the hotel, i.e. chairs and knives) and running to one another to be reminded of how best to attack their opponents. It was strange to Margot; the scene was almost cartoon-like as she sat on the steps of the stage fiddling with the Jonovicator. Maybe it was because of sheer exhaustion, or that she had just consumed 'Face'. It was like she was floating, lost in time. She understood why Jade had been wary of it. She got to her feet to help with the preparations. Margot looked at Damien, he was instructing a zombie female how best to disarm the U.A.S. She saw his eyes drift, his focus slip, it was obvious that he was feeling the same effects. Jade had modified the drug to such an extent that visions would only occur when the person chose to view them. For that, Margot was grateful, she was so out of it that focusing her mind was impossible. She didn't need to wear her sunglasses any more. It was the first time since being in Izsafar she'd actually been able to leave them off. It was liberating as the light stung her eyes.

"Everything is almost ready," Damien said as she approached.

"Good," Margot replied. "Any idea where we're going to attack?"

"Oh, trust me," Damien said in an ominous tone. "We won't be going anywhere, she'll be attacking us. Hurst has already directed people off to the south west and we have a few traps hidden in the hotel."

Margot grinned in approval. "Well dude, I'm pretty impressed."

"Good." The vampire smiled at her.

"Margot, Damien," Wolf called, as he and Barbie approached them from across the room. "We're going to leave in a few moments, we'll be taking the ship to get to the Over World, but I trust you already know this."

Margot looked from the transvestite to the angel. Barbie kept his head down, while Wolf tried to smile the best he could. She knew he felt bad about leaving them just before the heat of battle. She also knew it may be the last time they laid eyes upon one another. How many times did she have to feel like that? "Sure," she said.

"We'll return as soon as we can," Wolf said, trying to hide the sad look in his eyes. Hurst, taken a break from running around after his army, approached.

"Are you leaving already?" he squeaked.

Margot, drifted out of the conversation, letting her thoughts wander to the window. It was strange, to die on such a beautiful summer's day. To fight in the perfect fields, against the backdrop of the blue sea, just seemed completely mismatched. War was out of place in those aesthetically pleasing lands. Margot shook herself. She had to remember, it was not life. It was a replication of living, and the people needed to go home.

"Margot!" Damien shouted, snapping her back into reality.

"What?" She shouted back.

"Wolf was saying that we need to get to Silvia's castle once the fighting commences."

Margot nodded at Wolf, "Sure Wolf, sure." She felt guilty for zoning out. The ground shook.

"What's happenin'?" Frank yelled, as his dog tried to pull him towards the door. Margot gulped, Frank's dog leading him somewhere only meant one thing; danger.

She shifted her gaze back towards the window. There, moving their way across the fields of the south were hordes of white hooded figures.

"BATTLE STATIONS!" Hurst screamed, nodding at Wolf and Barbie, before running off to command his army.

"Go," Margot yelled. "Go now!"

Wolf nodded. "Come Barbie, to the ship."

Margot and Damien ran with them to the hotel entrance.

"It's all clear," Damien said, checking towards the beach. "The army's approaching from the fields. Leave before they rise from the water."

"Good luck to you all," Wolf said. "And well done."

"It's not over yet, Wolf," Margot glared at him.

Without warning, Barbie lifted her off the ground, embracing her.

"Goodbye Barbie." Margot said, gasping for air as he let her back down. With that, the angel and transvestite disappeared into the undergrowth and out of sight.

Margot turned to Damien. "Well I guess this is it."

"It is indeed." Damien replied.

Margot pulled out her gun and they rushed back into the hotel. Inside was a sea of panic. It was as though the whole army was stuck inside a hurricane as they darted about the foyer. In the centre, all she heard was the demon's voice yelling commands left right and centre.

"THEY'RE GETTING CLOSER! PREPARE TO MOVE FORWARD TO THE FIELD!"

Margot turned to look for Damien but he wasn't by her side any more. She scanned the creatures running towards the main entrance. *Where was he?*

"FASTER!" Hurst yelled, "THIS WOULDN'T HAVE HAPPENED IF THE LOOK-OUTS HAD DONE THEIR JOBS PROPERLY!" The demon paused. "WHERE ARE THE LOOK-OUTS?"

Two huge figures crashed through the window and landed at her feet. Margot frowned, staring at the unmoving creatures before her. Silence fell and everyone looked in her direction.

"What is it?" Hurst said quietly, making his way towards her.

Margot bent down to the two figures. "Your look-outs," she said, looking up as he approached. "They're both dead."

*

Barbie and Wolf rushed towards the ship. There was something very wrong. No one was on the beach, no one was sunbathing. They were alone as they stepped on the shore. They ran and hit the waves hard as they plunged into the water.

"Quickly," Wolf said, as he grabbed hold of the ladder to climb aboard. Barbie took a deep breath, pushing himself forward. He was tired and, although he could feel the adrenaline burning at the very core of his heart, his body couldn't act on it.

"Barbie, come on!" Wolf shouted, as he threw himself over the side. The transvestite was almost there, if he could just reach out his hand a little further... Barbie felt something grab his leg, before Wolf knew what was happening, he disappeared beneath the surface.

Barbie was dragged below the water. As he struggled, he saw three U.A.S. members wearing breathing apparatus. They had been waiting for them. He could feel his lungs exhaling the much needed air, as they pulled him deeper and deeper into the abyss. As he began to lose consciousness, he wondered what Margot would have done in that situation. The answer was simple: whatever it took. He felt for one of the guns she'd made and prayed it would work underwater. It was tucked neatly at the back of his skirt. Before the U.A.S. had time to act, Barbie blasted them off his legs and out of sight. The third wasn't going down without a fight. He grabbed him from behind, around the neck, choking Barbie until the gun slipped from his grasp. Everything around him began to fade; he could feel his body shutting down...

Wolf wrestled the U.A.S. off Barbie, snapping his neck with ease and watching as he began to float to the surface. He grabbed the transvestite's arms and pulled them around his shoulders as he dragged him to the ship.

"Start the ship up, lad!" Wolf yelled, throwing Barbie onto the deck.

"Yes sir!" The young angel replied, running to the bridge.

Wolf bent over the listless body sprawled on the deck.

"Come on, Barbie!" He said, shaking him. "Come on, Barbie, breathe! Breathe!"

The transvestite spluttered as air refilled his lungs.

"Oh, thank goodness," Wolf sighed with relief. "Right, we're going after them. Where's your gun?"

Barbie's hand made a feeble gesture to the sea. Wolf sprang to his feet.

"Faster lad, faster!" he called, running around the sides of the ship. Wolf

329

gulped hard as he leaned over the side. The crystal clear water revealed more hooded figures swimming towards the ship.

The ship rumbled as the engines kicked into action. They had only ever been used once, and that was a very long time ago.

"Faster!" He yelled, knowing it wouldn't make a damn bit of difference.

Suddenly the U.A.S. members leapt at the sides of the ship and began to climb. Wolf ran to the bridge and took control of the wheel, turning it hard. The boat lurched, throwing the hooded figures back into the water.

"Take off, into the sky!" Wolf demanded.

"But-" The young angel stuttered.

"Do it, or watch as this place burns!"

Quivering, the skinny boy reached behind the wheel, where a white button was implanted into the wood. It didn't look like it was part of the ship, it was out of place.

"Now!" Wolf yelled.

There was a louder rumble as the ship rose from the water and lifted into the skies of Izsafar. Wolf ran out onto the deck, to re-join Barbie who was leaning over the side looking at the fresh bodies floating on the sea's surface.

The angel stared down at his hands. What had he done?

*

"Hell yeah!" Margot yelled, watching as the ship disappeared out of sight. The battle was in full swing and she was right out in the fields of Izsafar, at the very heart of the action. Around her, shots were being fired. Technology and magic were in full flow, taking control of the battle, yet taking lives at the same time.

Margot watched as a set of U.A.S. members tried to follow the ship and were intercepted by winged creatures who wrestled them in mid-flight. They fell to the ground.

"You're a disgrace to your kind," a hooded figure yelled as he ran at Margot. Before he had chance to take out his weapon, she fired, sending him reeling backwards.

"Yeah, whatever." She shrugged.

"Margot, behind you!" Hurst yelled. Margot dived to the floor as a beam of red light shot towards her. She heard the sizzling of her hair as it caught some of the rays.

"Right, red light burns, got it." Margot said to herself as she jumped to her feet. Something caught her eye in the distance. Damien. She watched as he fought against a group of white hoods, taking to the skies to battle in the air. It must have been at least twenty to one and more were joining. He wasn't wearing his hood; she knew many of them just thought of him as a rebel leader. It was clear Silvia wanted all of them dead. Margot gasped as one shot a green beam at his chest and he spiralled out of the sky

"Get off of him!" She screamed, running towards them. Margot thought it would be the opportune moment to try out another of her inventions. She took out a small white Frisbee-like object from her pocket and threw it into the air. It exploded to form a net, catching the majority of white hoods in the air. She watched as they collapsed on others below. Margot smiled and ran to Damien's side. It was something she'd designed back on Earth. The net automatically became three times heavier than its prey upon contact, immobilising them.

"That's slightly old school for your great mind." Damien said sarcastically, as he lay on the ground.

"Shut up," Margot frowned, pulling him to his feet. "I thought you would run." She changed her tone.

"Not this time," Damien said, throwing her a pair of U.A.S. gloves.

"Fuck yeah." Margot smiled at him, putting them on. "Now what?"

"Now," Damien said. "We head towards the water."

Margot and Damien dodged through the crowd and headed for the cliff edge.

"We're losing," Margot shouted as she watched the U.A.S. snap a woman's neck like a biscuit. Damien turned, Silvia's army had advanced. They were minutes away from breaking into the hotel.

"No," the vampire said quietly. "Not yet." He took her hand and they pressed forward into the unknown.

Meanwhile, Hurst was doing the best he could to fight and lead. He scowled as two U.A.S. members laughed as they approached him.

"What's he going to do, bite our ankles?" One snarled.

The other shrugged, "It doesn't matter, grab him."

They ran at him. Hurst sighed, sliding under the legs of the first and climbing up and over the other.

"Ha ha!" He laughed as he pulled the hood over his face and began suffocating him.

"Gep him moff mi!" The man screamed in a panicked muffle. The other, shocked at what had just happened, didn't quite grasp the situation. He turned, just in time to see the man crashing to the floor in front of him, unconscious.

He screamed and ran from the demon.

Hurst smiled, clasping his hands. "Well, that went quite nicely."

He grabbed his head, it throbbed unbearably. All of a sudden he heard a faint voice in the back of his head. It was Damien.

'The hotel, the hotel, the hotel…'

Hurst turned to see U.A.S. members flooding the doors and windows of the building.

"THE HOTEL HAS BEEN BREACHED!" He screamed, looking around him, "FALL BACK! FALL BACK!"

The ground shook. Izsafar was becoming unstable once again.

*

Barbie's heart beat faster as Wolf's ship slowed down. Anyone who didn't know him wouldn't notice the change, but Wolf did know him, he knew him all too well and he could sense his nerves.

"It'll be fine," he said. "Just stay calm and I'll do all the talking."

They were standing in the darkened doorway, leading to the outside of the ship. They hadn't moved from the spot since the ascent to the angel's realm. Barbie stared at the door, knowing soon he would have to step back out onto the deck. The waiting was the worst part.

"I don't know why the Human made me come here." he said, staring at the wall.

"Because Margot Grant has more up her sleeve than she makes out," Wolf said. He patted Barbie on the shoulder. "Don't you worry, we'll be just fine."

"Sir!" Wolf's apprentice shouted from the bridge. "We've arrived at our destination!"

Barbie's hands tightened into fists as the ship juddered to a halt.

"Come on, lad," Wolf said, reaching for the door knob. "Let's go outside."

Light flooded into the ship as the angel pulled open the door. Hesitating, Barbie covered his eyes with his hand and stepped out onto the deck. The vessel was surrounded by a white mist that poured over the sides, and filled the deck. Barbie tried to move it out of his way, for fear of not being able to see where he was walking. As he looked over the edge, he saw it rising off the cloud. The water didn't seem liquid. It was more like gas and made Barbie wonder how the ship was staying afloat in the weird atmosphere. He looked around; in the distance, beyond the mist, he could make out the outline of a grey city. The buildings there were taller than any human skyscrapers and all so different in shape and size. They were too far away to be able to observe their intricacies

If it was the place where angels dwelled, it was bleak and lifeless. Everything was grey or white, there was no colour. Nothing had changed since the last time Barbie was there. It was worrying. Sometimes change can be bad, very bad. But when nothing has changed for so long, nothing has advanced for years and years, it makes you wonder the values of the people living there.

"I suppose we should head towards the city." Wolf pointed towards where Barbie was staring. In the distance, they could see small figures moving back and forth amongst the huge buildings; flying in and out of windows, travelling from place to place. Barbie shook at the sight of the angels, forcing himself to look away for a few seconds.

"It's perfectly alright, Barbie," Wolf said, but before he could continue, his words faltered. Barbie turned to see a triangular formation of angels hurtling towards the ship.

"Wolf," he began.

"Just stay calm," Wolf said, not taking his eyes off the group. He knew where they were heading. The angels looked like shooting stars the closer they came. They shot through the white sky, until slowing down to encircle Wolf and Barbie.

Barbie stood petrified. Six glowing angels, so bright it was impossible to make out their faces. The angels could have been anyone, even Silvia.

"Good day to you," Wolf said, advancing towards the white creature in front of him.

"Anthony wants to see you, Wolf," a deep voice said. "You're in a lot of trouble."

"Now please, we don't have time to waste, it is of great urgency-"

"You can tell that to the Court of Angels," the angel replied. "You have been summoned. I wouldn't delay; they aren't in the best of moods."

Wolf turned to Barbie. It wasn't supposed to be like that.

*

"Jesus Christ, Damien!" Margot gasped for breath as the vampire placed her on the marble floor outside the castle. "I never want to take that journey again."

The vampire wasn't listening to her comments; instead he was staring at the doors of the castle as he threw on his Dark Rider hood.

"This is strange," he said. "The place seems empty. Surely Silvia can't have sent all her army to go and fight?"

Margot stared at the castle. There was indeed something odd about its silent walls.

"Here, put this on," Damien threw her a white hood. She pulled it over her head.

"Now remember," he said. "Act casual and follow Jade's map. I'm the Dark

Rider; you're a member of the U.A.S. If anyone asks, we're here to get more supplies."

"Okay," Margot said. They approached the double doors. "Act casual and nothing can go wrong."

It was difficult to act casual when there was nothing casual to aspire to.

Margot pushed the door open the castle was deserted. As they walked down the ostentatious corridors, they were the only two souls in the building. Even as they walked towards the throne in Silvia's main greeting room, it was desolate.

There was no one for miles. It was like walking on a beach out of tourist season.

"This isn't right," Margot muttered, as they approached the angel's great chair.

Damien turned back towards the empty room. "She must have called all of them up to the front, she must have been confident we'd never get this far."

"Be realistic," Margot said.

Damien shrugged, he moved the chair. She helped. Together, with sheer force, they managed to unhinge it and threw it against the wall to reveal the dripping steps beneath.

"I guess this is it," Margot shrugged. "No turning back now." She held the Jonovicator in one hand, the compass in the other. They pointed in the same direction. Taking a deep breath, she walked down into the deep passage.

Damien took one last look around at the empty room before following her into the darkness.

*

Wolf and Barbie were led through the city of angels. Much to Barbie's inconvenience, the Over World was lacking when it came to floors. The city was engulfed by the same mist that had filled the top deck of the ship. They didn't need the ground since they flew everywhere. Needless to say, they didn't have many visitors. Wolf thought it was extremely rude to other visiting creatures. It made the buildings seem like outer shells. There was something un-homely about the whole idea. It angered him as he watched two of the angels put their hands around Barbie, lifting him into the air to take him to the court.

"What about the ship?" Wolf asked.

"You can leave it here." One said. "And you can remove yourself from that ugly human form, now. You do not need to disguise yourself here."

Wolf sighed, straightening his back as his large wings sprouted out of his back. Barbie's heart leaped as Wolf grew taller, paler, brighter.

"I'm ready," he said, his blue eyes focusing on Barbie. "Do you have to glow so brightly, you're scaring him."

Wolf knew angels. They were pretentious creatures, exuding unnecessary grandeur for show.

The others ignored his request and lifted Barbie into the air and headed for the grey city.

Wolf was worried as they entered its large black gates. He hated entering at the very bottom of the city. That was where the crime was, where the sickest and most wicked of angels resided. He stared at the bottom of the run-down grey buildings, hoping that they'd soon be out the other side. As he passed darkened windows, he heard whispers, even taunts. His name had spread fast; he hoped words of his actions had not. His breathing became a little more relaxed as he watched the angels take off into the air; flying high towards the summits of the buildings. That was where the rulers lived; where the higher angels dwelled Angels judge class and power by height.

As they rose, the buildings changed, they were wider, grander in scale. Some were engraved with ancient symbols, carved by the hands of time as they grew more magnificent by the human hours. Despite entering the home of angels, the weather was as cold and dreary as an English day in January. It was nothing like the place spoken of in the legends and folktales of Earth. There were no choirs, no harps, not a single song; just the sound of distant voices whispering in the cool breeze of the urban sky. There was nothing at all holy about that land.

There was one place that Wolf thought could perhaps restore some faith in the stories told by the people of the Universe. Its tall white walls stretched higher than any building in the angel city and were guarded by thick golden gates with more spell on them than any cared to imagine. As they got closer, the decorations carved into its sides became more apparent. Barbie stared at the stones, depicting crippled demonic creatures pleading or being tortured. Above them, angels with long scrolls and furious faces looked down from tables, pointing long disgusted fingers and stretching out their wings. Around those scenes laws were written in the ancient language of the sky. Those that were unlucky enough to be taken there would soon find out about the building's lack of floors and the drop they would be put before. Right ahead of them, was the almighty Court of Angels.

*

As Margot walked through Silvia's lair she was horrified by what she saw. She imagined Jade experiencing the same emotions. It was like walking on the very floor of Hell itself. She turned back to Damien who was looking down at a human, left half open on a laboratory table. How could it not affect him?

"They must have left in a hurry," he said. Margot's heart was churning with anger.

"FUCK!" She screamed punching down hard on the nearest examination table. There was a loud clang as objects fell to the floor.

"Margot!" Damien snapped: "Control yourself. You're going to give away our cover."

"This is bullshit. How can she do this? This is so fucking wrong! And how are you so calm? How do you expect me to be calm?" Her voice echoed through the empty white room.

"May I remind you our purpose for being here, or have you already forgotten?" Damien spoke through gritted teeth. Margot took a deep breath, trying to calm her breathing. "Now," the vampire's eyes shifted to the Jonovicator. "Find the map Jade gave you."

Margot opened the device, finding the virtual map. "Well," she said. "The cells and the collection of thoughts are in two separate directions."

Damien studied Jade's holographic guide. "Okay, I'll take the passage towards the prisoners."

"No," Margot said firmly. "I'll find them. You head towards the power source."

"Margot, are you sure?"

"They're my people," her tone was stern. "I should go to them."

"Okay," he said, striding away from her.

"How will I know where to meet you?" Margot called after him.

"Trust me." Damien smiled. "I'm beginning to understand the ways of 'Face'. I'll be in contact."

The doors slid open and he was gone. Margot took a deep breath and headed in the opposite direction.

The room wasn't empty for long. Seconds after they had departed; the passage from the throne opened again and in drifted a third figure. His fists clenched as his feet hit the marble floor. His breathing was hard, his eyes keen; a little too keen, like he had come with a particular purpose; or a fatal task to carry out. Doctor Clarke was briefed and ready, his mission programmed. Only one individual would leave the castle alive.

*

"Wolf Zacarius Flynn and erm," the angel double-checked the name on his

336

scroll: "Barbie."

He paused again, looking around to check he had said the correct name. When no one laughed, he continued. "You have been brought before the court of angels for treachery and diabolical behaviour...."

Anthony Gabriel was the last angel in the Over World that Wolf had wanted to encounter. He knew the angel would never listen and it appeared he was their judge. He wasn't young, but he was foolish. Power had twisted him over the years and he showed mercy for no one. Wolf glared at him. He was enjoying the endeavour. Wolf knew they hadn't got on for a long time, but it sickened him to think that he was using the excuse to persecute him.

Barbie stared at the sheer drop beneath his feet as the angel continued. Below them was nothing but clouds: clouds and mist; which wasn't helpful when you're a wingless creature and in need of a quick get-away. Barbie turned to see collections of angels seated on floating benches all the way to the bottom of the building. There must have been millions. Was it some sort of sporting event to them? He looked up to the huge platform before him where Gabriel, who possessed the brightest glow and angriest expression, leaned toward them. No wrong-doing, rule and regulation went unnoticed. It was the ultimate criminal justice system, in that there was no justice, not for those convicted; guilty or innocent.

Barbie's arms ached; his neck was stiff from looking up too high for too long. He gave up, letting his head drop again. There was no point fighting it. He was bound by chains and he hung from the arms of two angel guards, floating above him. Wolf was in the same situation, only in less pain. Despite them trying to chain his wings, he managed to hover with grace. Such an achievement could only be accomplished by someone like Wolf. Barbie had a feeling he was doing it out of pride rather than ease.

"I understand my sins," he spoke out. "But let Barbie go, he has done nothing wrong."

"As I understand," Anthony said with a slimy grin. "This isn't the first time that the she-male has entered this court."

His blue eyes pierced Barbie's dark ones. As he stared, he saw the past, saw what they had done to him, to *her*. He was looking through a time warp. He turned his head; he couldn't bear to look any longer. "Look, we can discuss this properly later?" Wolf's voice was rushed as he stared at the transvestite.

"So you can make a quick get-away? I think not!" Some angels lower down in the court jeered. They were scruffier than the rest, and grey like the gargoyles.

"This isn't about getting away, this is about the-"

"The safety of those who inhabit the island, we have already been informed on your beliefs Wolf, and the way we see it is that Izsafar is in safe hands."

"In the hands of a villain!" Wolf spat angrily. Some of the angels around him booed.

"May I remind you, you are chained in the same spot as she was. Why are you any different?"

"Because what I did, I did because I thought it was right." Wolf said with methodical calm.

"And did she not?" The angel laughed. If he was a judge on the planet Earth, he might as well have said: 'So did Hitler'. However, the creatures weren't from the Universe and had no idea who that man was.

"The court has nothing more to say to you, I have never seen such disgusting behaviour from an angel. Not only have you revealed your disguise to more than one creature, including a *human,* you have also revealed the secrets of Izsafar and Angel Operations. I have no choice but to throw you to the sky dungeons until we can think how to punish you; *both* of you." The room erupted with applause. He turned to the guards: "Take them away."

Wolf stared at the sea of happy faces swimming in their own twisted ecstasy as he was hauled from the room. He then imagined the screaming and crying crowds of human beings directly below them as that pointless event continued to take place. It was the ultimate waste of time.

And he wondered, just wondered, if it was even worth carrying on.

*

"Where are they?" Hurst said as he looked towards the gathering storm clouds.

"Fer the last time, I dunno!" Frank yelled in return.

"A storm's brewing," the demon said.

They were rushing towards the hotel, desperate to get inside. Hurst watched as its doors and windows were swamped by U.A.S. members. If they weren't careful it'd be too late. If the portal was breached, that'd be it. Not only would the light be invaded but so would the dark. There would be no freedom. Hurst shrugged; he didn't feel like a leader. He didn't feel like anything at all.

"Come on, Frank," he squeaked. "We've a long way to go."

They charged towards the building. As long as they were still breathing, there was hope.

*

Margot could feel the temperature rising as she walked down the staircase. She only had her sunglasses to see by. She had been plunged into darkness.

Something about the place unnerved her; it wasn't the dripping of blood down the walls, or the smell of decay, urine and vomit. It was the underlying sadness that she felt as she walked towards the human living quarters. She could feel it, embedded in every scratch in the wall, every step on the path. It was almost as if the building was alive with mourning. Margot put her hand on the wall, a sharp pain shot to her head. She felt a sudden loss of loved ones, insanity, and loneliness. Margot took her hand away. It was dangerous magic. It was uncertain to say if she'd have that knowledge without her drug. It made her wonder if-

Margot realised she was not alone. She didn't think she'd been alone for a while and she didn't need the 'Face' to sense it. She listened, as quiet footsteps pattered behind her and a pitiful attempt at shallow breathing echoed from the walls. It was time to keep moving.

She ran down the last spiral of steps until she got to another door. The stairs were similar to those at the entrance, but much filthier. Margot hesitated to push the door, in case the same thing happened. A wailing sound from beyond gave her the courage to do so. She opened it and froze as it slammed shut behind her. Margot's stomach lurched at the sight. There were chains, bars and cells, combined to form a monstrous reason for a revolution.

Cells were piled on top of one another. There was little space and there was no light. Margot paced down the rows, trying not to avert her eyes from the horror before her. She found humans there, lying in their cells. The question of whether they were breathing was another matter. To Margot, they weren't people anymore; they were just bodies, lots of bodies in the cells, adorning the walls. She heard wailing, the same wailing that had forced her to open the door in the first place.

There, in the very corner cell, amongst a pile of bodies, sat a little girl rocking back and forth, her arms around her knees. It was hard to see her expression behind her long dirty hair, but Margot knew she was paralysed with fear. She raised her head and looked at Margot. Her eyes were blank, stripped of all emotion. It was like staring into the eyes of a doll. Margot leaned forward, trying to open the cell. She was thrown back by an intense pain. Silvia had cursed the bars.

Margot lay face-down on the slimy floor. She turned sideways, to look at the girl. She rocked back and forth faster, muttering something under her breath. Margot stared at her, watching her mouth move, as she tried to make out the words.

"They're all dead," Margot whispered as she translated the words. Margot leapt to her feet, realising what the girl had just said.

"They're all dead." The girl stood up, facing Margot. Her voice got louder each time she spoke the words: "They're all dead! THEY'RE ALL DEAD!"

Margot ran back towards the door as the girl's screams echoed in the background. There were more cells, more prisoners, she told herself. Silvia couldn't have killed them all, Silvia wouldn't kill them all. She repeated these words over and over until she got to the door. Margot stopped dead in her tracks. It was wide open.

She reached for her gun from her back pocket. It was gone. She tried to keep calm as she searched her leather jacket. It was no use, she must have dropped it. She was alone, alone and defenceless.

"Looking for something?" A cold voice echoed in the darkness.

Margot tried to concentrate, to contact Damien. *Help*, she thought, *come quick*. Margot hoped her thoughts were strong enough for it to work.

"You're a traitor to your kind, Miss Grant," the voice rang out again.

"Come out, then!" She yelled, clenching her fists as she scanned the area. The corners of the room were too far for her glasses to make out.

"And might I add," Clarke continued: "An extremely bad scientist."

Suddenly Margot was thrown forward into a door, by a blow to the back of her head. She spun around, getting to her feet. Margot's vision was hazy, but that didn't stop her making out the hideous figure before her.

"This is almost too easy," Clarke said, making sure his gloves were pulled on securely.

The gloves, of course! She ran at Clarke, grabbed his collar and threw him against the metal bars. His cloak protected him. He grabbed her jacket and swung her round so they reversed positions. She screamed in agony as he pressed her face against the enchanted bars. Margot was tired, she had been at war too long, and Clarke was just starting out. She couldn't fight him and she knew if she did, she couldn't win.

"What do you want?" She panted and sank to the floor. She was at her wits' end. Margot could give no more.

"What is going on in here?" A sharp voice called out as a new figure stepped into the room. Margot squinted, trying to gain focus as the vampire entered the room. Clarke jumped, stepping back from where she lay.

"Nothing, sir," he said. "I found one of the rebels lurking down here."

"Ahhh," Damien said, leaning forward, pretending to examine Margot. "I see."

"I told you sir," Clarke nodded his head. "I found her! Me!"

"Yes, yes you did," Damien said in a patronising tone. "However, this is not how Silvia treats her humans; she'll think you've joined the traitors."

"And no one takes orders from a traitor, do they Rider?" As Clarke spoke, he spun round, throwing a strange powder into Damien's hood.

"Come on Margot," he said, pulling her to her feet. "I think we need to return you to your proper place."

"Damien!" Margot yelled, as she was dragged by her collar from the room. Black smoke was coming out of the vampire's hood, as he struggled for breath.

Clarke slammed the door and dragged Margot up the stairs. She struggled as he floated back up the spiral staircase. It was no use, his grip was too strong but she never stopped. They had reached the throne room. *Where is he taking me?*

"The so called 'great' Margot Grant, taken down by one scientist, you're losing your touch."

He pulled her outside, to the castle ground. Margot stared at the edge where the marbled flooring ended. She knew where she was going. Clarke pulled her to face him as they approached the edge. She felt the hot breeze from the skies of the Underworld as he forced the top of her body over the edge. He could have done it quickly, but Clarke was the type of guy that liked to see people suffer. He wanted to watch her squirm, watch her cry and beg for mercy. But she didn't. She did nothing except fix a smile on her face. If it was her time to go, then go she would, but not without style.

Clarke was barely gripping her coat; he was quite careless in wanting to keep hold of her. She watched as his grasp loosened, felt it become less and less...

"Stop it, Clarke," Damien's voice called from the distance. Clarke turned to face the vampire as he ran from the double doors. He lowered his hood, his face was stained black. "We can end this. You don't have to listen to the angel any longer."

"Take one step more and she falls." Clarke was also a huge fan of mind games.

"Doctor, please, return Margot." Damien said, maintaining the sternness in his voice.

Clarke ignored his plea, turning back to the victim in his clutches.

"Did you really think you would win this war, Miss Grant?"

"No," Margot strained to speak. "But as long as people keep fighting, someday, someone like me will."

She paused: "Oh yeah, and by the way, fuck you."

"Spoken like a true rebel." Clarke said sarcastically, before launching her over the edge.

"Margot!" Damien yelled as he ran to the edge of Silvia's domain and watched as Margot's body disappeared amongst the thick red mist that was the sky of hell.

Chapter 21

In-between Lines

Anyone who saw Damien dive through the red sky would probably think he was falling. At least, he was travelling fast enough to be. At the speed he was going, he *should* have been out of control. But he wasn't. He was determined. Damien's eyes flitted from right to left as he bombed through the sky. He refused to believe she would die, not there. He hit thick fog, it was hard to make out what was in front, what lay ahead, where she was...

His eyes scanned the air; his lungs inhaled the thick atmosphere. He didn't know how close to the ground he was, never mind how far he had dived already. And then, as the clouds started to clear, he saw her. Like a shooting star before him, she hurtled to the ground. He was almost directly above her. If he could travel faster, push himself further, he could catch her in time. Damien could then see the dark red sand of the ground. It could be risky, instant death for them both. He braced himself; it was a chance he was willing to take.

Damien, shot like a bullet from a twisted gun, and made a perpendicular turn. If he timed it correctly, Margot would be saved; incorrectly, and she'd fall to her death. He opened out his arms as he tried to generate the friction to slow himself down. He was hoping the hovering shoes he'd taken would be enough to hold the both of them. She was nearing the ground. He almost had her...

The vampire lurched forward as Margot fell into his arms, in too much of a state of shock to find words. The scene would almost be perfect, heroic even, except Margot's velocity made it near impossible to support her. After straining for a few seconds, they were back where they started, falling the last few metres of the decent before hitting the ground hard. "I really don't know how I'm not dead yet." Margot groaned, staring up at the sky. She looked at Damien; she was half lying on top of him. Needless to say, he didn't look too impressed.

"Would you mind removing yourself from me?" he said and she rolled over onto the sand.

"Where the hell are we?" She asked as she turned on her side. The atmosphere was arid. The red sand stretched for miles in the barren, desolate landscape. In the distance, the sky darkened and she could make out silhouettes of strange shapes and dark buildings.

"Welcome to the desert plains of the Underworld." Damien said, as he struggled to get to his feet.

Margot groaned.

"Here," he said, passing her a box of cigarettes as she got to her feet. "You'll most probably need these."

"So," Margot took a deep breath. "What's the plan?"

Damien pointed to a shadowed area where she'd been staring. "Now that we're here, we head that way."

"I had a horrible feeling you were going to say that. So, who lives there?"

"Beelzebub." The vampire replied. "And of course, his city of followers; we just have to find his home."

"Somehow, I don't think my SatNav will help pick up that location." Margot's voice was filled with sarcasm.

"No," Damien said. "But Jade's compass can."

Margot returned his grin; she reached into her leather jacket and pulled out the globe-like object.

"Let's go," he said, turning to face the direction the arrow pointed.

It was clear he was in pain by the way he moved, even though Margot knew he would never admit it. She smiled at him while his back was turned. He had braved the fall for *her*. Something, until recently, she never would have expected from the once awful, unkind vampire. "Hey, Damien," Margot said. "Finally meeting the father making you nervous?"

The vampire rolled his eyes. "Really, Margot, the end of your world could be just around the corner and you're still able to make jokes?"

*

Every door of the hotel was wide open, every room filled with the sounds of battle. Although the creatures of the darkness had fought hard, they were losing. Their base had been invaded and Hurst knew if they weren't careful, their home would soon be destroyed.

Don't let them breach the top floor. He thought hard, hoping his message would get to Frank in time. The demon was worried; he hadn't seen him for a while. Frank was vulnerable enough as it was and with the fight becoming more bloodthirsty by the second, he knew that in terms of being captured he didn't stand a chance. It was scary how things had turned so violent so fast. Even Hurst, the biggest pacifistic of all, had found himself murdering on instinct. He cringed, thinking back to those he had killed. His beliefs had been completely destroyed.

The demon ran down the long corridors, trying to give aid to those who needed it. Hurst looked through a bedroom door to see a man struggling, caught beneath a couple of U.A.S. members.

"Here!" He shouted; he threw a knife, which thudded into the first member's back. Hurst watched as the man ripped his hood off in agony as he dropped to the floor. The other member took a step back, in shock at the sudden turn of events. Hurst watched as the man he was helping reached out, preparing to strike. The demon could bear it no longer and retreated, running out into the battle field once more.

He was met by another U.A.S. Hurst sighed, the Rider hadn't seen him. It was almost too easy as he ran up to the scientist; biting him hard on the leg, pulling back his hood and slitting his throat as he fell to the ground.

"Oh, I am *so* going to hell," he mumbled to himself as he took his few final breaths before losing consciousness. Hurst stared at his face. He looked so young, barely older than Margot and his life had gone. He watched in silence as blood flowed from his mouth and ran down his pale cheek.

It was sad, looking into those blank green eyes, knowing that he would never laugh or cry; never experience life again. He wondered if he had children, a lover, plans made after he left the war. He lay there motionless, never to have the lines of time trace across his unblemished skin. Hurst had come to the conclusion that humans were like paper; pure white but easily marked and crushed.

They were much more than just figures once the hoods were pulled back. It was sickening.

"That's him!" A thundering voice from the other end of the corridor yelled. "One of the leaders, quickly, down there!"

The demon looked up to see a large group of U.A.S. figures gliding from the lift. There must have been twenty of them and they had all been searching for him. He gulped. The closer they came, the more they grew in number. He watched in horror as more members abandoned their victims in their rooms and joined the small army heading for him. For the first time in the battle, he was glued to the spot. He was helpless.

Hurst knew what he should do, what any respectable man would do; face them head on, go down in a blaze of glory, demonstrate his bravery. If it was the end, it should be glorious. However, Hurst wasn't a man, Hurst was a demon and to him, there was nothing glorious about murder. So instead, he did what he thought any honourable creature would have done in his situation. He turned tail and ran.

"After him!" Their leader yelled as the group picked up pace.

With only his adrenalin to guide him, the demon dived into the lift, shutting the doors with seconds to spare. He stared at the excessive quantity of buttons.

"Which one, which one?" Hurst panicked, pressing buttons at random. There was an abrupt bang as a U.A.S. threw himself at the door to try and get inside. Hurst screamed at the large dint in the metal door. The small lift began to shake. He wasn't moving.

"Come on, come on!" Hurst squeaked, but it was no use. There was another loud bang and the lift shook again. Hurst looked up through the vent. Two White Riders were on top, trying to cut the cable. The safety net of a lift had become his cage, his death trap. Hurst listened.

He prepared for a rapid descent and closed his eyes.

There was a bang and the demon was prised from the death trap and into someone's arms. He didn't look. He didn't want to anymore.

He heard the lift crash below him and cringed. Whoever had saved him placed him down somewhere hard and cold. Hurst finally opened his eyes to find himself in one of the hotel vents. He looked up to see the twisted face of Frank, his blank eyes, staring at him.

"Frank!" Hurst said.

"Shhh!" Frank whispered angrily, pointing above them. They were still in the elevator shaft, in a vent just off the main corridor.

"Is he dead?" Hurst heard a deep voice call from above.

"He must be; no one could survive that fall."

"Frank, you're alive!" The demon said once the coast was clear.

"It's funny that you're the only one who seems pleased about that," Frank said, gasping for breath. "Most of me enemies are getting pretty annoyed that I won't die."

They crawled through the ventilation shaft to the nearest light source; an office, guarded by a White Rider.

"Yeh ready?" Frank whispered.

The demon nodded and they leapt into the room.

"God forgive me," Hurst mumbled, he took off his cross and hit him over the head. The White rider collapsed to the floor.

"I wish yer'd stop doin' tha'" Frank complained, feeling around for the door.

"Oh, shut up," Hurst squeaked, bracing himself for the fights that hadn't even begun.

"Hey, I saved yer life; I'm sure that means I have rights or summit now?" Frank protested.

Hurst sighed, "Come on, let's go."

*

"Well," Barbie sighed. "This is definitely inconvenient."

Inconvenient wasn't quite the word he was looking for. He was standing on a small wooden square, floating over the top of the city of angels. There were no chains to bind him, there was no need. He couldn't move; he couldn't even sit. Stepping a few inches forward meant sudden death. He would shudder to think about it if his body would only allow. Wolf was in the opposite situation. He was chained to a large pole suspended next to the transvestite's small platform. He could feel his wings being sliced every time he attempted to move. When he didn't reply Barbie spoke again.

"I'm sure it's going to be okay." His words were of little comfort.

"Barbie, please, just be quiet." Wolf strained to speak.

"Well," Barbie thought for a moment. "It can't really get any worse, can it?"

"That's extremely comforting," Wolf said. "No, it can't really get any worse lad. In fact, the only way it could probably get better would be for me to turn into a human and for you to jump off that bloody ledge you're standin' on."

Barbie gave a heavy sigh and looked down at the angel city.

"Barbie," Wolf said. "You know I didn't mean that, so don't ya dare think about it. This isn't over."

"A few words of encouragement?" A voice from behind them said. Barbie turned to see Anthony gently beating his wings as he turned around to face them. His white cloak was longer than any Barbie had ever seen as it fluttered in the air. Then again, the transvestite forgot that those people didn't wear clothes fashioned for those that were earth bound. As he lowered his hood, Barbie was reminded of the U.A.S. His dark eyes cast down upon them as though waiting for some sort of answer.

"Do you not think we have questioned her methods before?" He looked down on them. "Of course we have, however, unlike you; we will know how to act when the time is right."

"The time to act is now!" Wolf shouted, clenching his hands hard to stop himself from crying out in pain.

The judge laughed. "You are criminals, you are not rational people. You do not abide by the good in this world."

"If she keeps preaching, there won't be any left." Wolf's breathing had become heavy.

"Save your strength for the Under World." The angel's eyes darkened. He gave one final look towards them before beginning to drift away.

"Just tell me one thing," Wolf called after him. "Tell me how you'll know when she's gone too far."

The angel paused in mid-flight; he turned his head back towards them.

"I thought you'd know the answer to that," he said with a sly and malicious grin.

Wolf didn't reply; he didn't want to give him the satisfaction of teasing him any longer. He was tired, he was worn out. He was done.

"The shaman of the city, the oldest of our kind, the one who saw this world rise, had a vision."

Barbie sighed, surely it would have been quicker just to say the shaman, but he didn't want to ruin the dramatic effect so he let him go on.

"We asked him about what he had seen and he drew us a picture of a girl. When the dark angel comes, he said, then that is when we have to strike."

"And this girl, what does she look like?"

The angel raised his hands to his temples and closed his eyes. At first, Wolf thought he was being sarcastic, and then he saw light puffs of white smoke drifting in front of him. It was coming from his nose, his ears, his mouth. It all came together in the sky; it began to form a picture. Wolf stared as the image of a girl wearing black clothes, with hair and skin as white as an angel's hung in the air. He stared closer, to see the way her hair flew in front of her face, the way she grasped her leather jacket as she struggled across the plain, the fear and determination in her red eyes. She wasn't an angel; she wasn't even from that world.

"You've made a mistake." Wolf said. The angel broke from his trance and the small figure of Margot Grant disappeared in the air.

"I make no mistakes," the judge said fiercely before turning away and leaving the two of them as immobile as they were before.

For a while, no one spoke. There was nothing to say. There was no point in conveying their frustration to one another. They already knew how the other felt. There was nothing worse than knowing your home, your friends and your life were being destroyed below your very feet, while you had to sit and await your fate for a crime you didn't commit. Wolf thought of using Face to communicate; then he questioned its point. There was nothing they could do for them up here. It was all a waiting game. Pointless.

"This isn't right," Barbie said, watching the angel fly away. "It seems like everything good in the world has just disappeared."

*

The sky began to darken around them the closer they got to the Devil's home. In a mile it had grown so dark that it was hard to see where they were walking. Margot watched her long shadow slowly disappear into the blackness every time she took another step.

"Okay," Damien whispered. "We're about to enter the city's outer circle. This will be a lot different to the desert so please don't be alarmed."

"What is it with cities? Why does he have to live in a bloody city?"Margot replied angrily.

"Did you really expect the devil to live in some quaint shack in the middle of nowhere? Of course he lives in a city and a heavily guarded one."

"What can we expect?" she questioned, reaching for her gun. Damien put his hand on hers.

"Leave that," he warned. "These creatures can see better than you. Just stay close."Margot sighed; anyone would think he was trying to act 'macho' or something. She looked down for her shadow. It had gone.

The atmosphere changed. Everything was colder. Margot felt exposed as she walked. She didn't need to ask Damien, she knew they were there.

"Our destination is right over there."

Margot followed his pale finger to see a high stone wall lit by wooden torches. She tried to keep her eyes focused on it, to ignore whatever surrounded her. It was harder said than done. Margot felt like she was being watched. Tall strange shapes were coming into focus. Margot could feel energy all around her; she could sense the presence of those hidden in the darkness. It was the side effects of 'Face'. She knew it; without the drug, she wouldn't be aware. It was a gift in a way; Margot's senses had been heightened, like she'd been given a special power.

"Damien," she whispered. "We're surrounded by things, I can feel them."

Damien slowed down; he had moved so close to her that they were practically embracing.

"Just stick to this path," he said quietly. "All we have to do is get past the wall."

Margot tried to stay calm, she didn't want to admit she was frightened, but the truth was she was petrified. She wasn't used to those sorts of senses; they were making her more paranoid the further they walked. She reached for her glasses and Damien stopped her again.

"Your sunglasses won't work down here. This is no ordinary darkness. Like the light, it is powerful. It cannot be stopped by spells or human gadgets."

Margot shrugged, "Alright," she said putting them back in her leather coat, "I hate it when you talk like this."

Something had just caught the corner of her eye, something that wasn't human.

"What was that?" She whispered to Damien.

"Probably just the defence system working against magical creatures; he doesn't want the whole world entering his city. It's probably in your head."

In the distance a figure sprang into the air, latching onto one of the many tall figures that lingered in the darkness.

"That wasn't in my head." She reached for her gun once again. "Something moved."

"Margot!" The vampire shouted louder than intended. Suddenly a low hissing noise began to rise from all around them. It grew louder as more creatures joined in. What they were, Margot didn't know, what she did know, was that she was running low on her mental powers and couldn't afford to miss whatever she was shooting at. She could feel the hairs on the back of her neck stand up as it grew louder and closer. She could see Damien looking around them. She envied him, with his eyesight he could see what was going on. He just wouldn't tell her.

"Stay calm and keep walking slowly." He said in a lower voice, pushing her to walk in front of him.

"What's behind us?" She asked, still gripping her gun tightly.

"Just keep walking." He continued to push her forward, constantly turning to look behind him. They picked up the pace, despite Damien warning her to maintain an element of calm.

"Don't run," he kept repeating in her ear. "Just walk quickly, stay on the path."

"Okay," Margot nodded, turning round to face him. She gasped in horror. He was gone.

Margot tried hard not to panic as she turned her head in every direction, hoping to see the vampire somewhere across the landscape. *Where the hell would he have gone?*

She breathed deeply trying to come to terms with the situation. The hissing became louder; she could hear scuttling. Something was following her and whatever it was, it had taken Damien. Margot could not remain calm for much longer. She could sense a presence; angry and tortured souls, black-hearted criminals and deathly creatures surrounded her. Even though she couldn't see them, she knew they were there. There was no escape.

Something latched itself onto her back. She could feel its claws digging into her skin, even beneath her leather jacket. Margot shook her body hard and fell to the ground as she tried to shake the creature off.

"Get off of me!" she screamed, loosening its grip, before firing her gun behind her. There was an ear piercing scream as the creature darted away.

She could feel life squirming around her. She thought her action had woken up every creature in the strange land. She heard whispers emanating from the darkness; growls and screams filled the night. Margot heard Damien's voice in the back of her head so clearly, it was almost as if he was saying it to her right there and then.

'Stay calm, don't run. Stay calm, don't run.'

But Margot was in no state of mind to stay calm, nor to stay still. After hearing another scream in the distance, she gripped her gun and ran.

It was chasing her, they were chasing her. The faster she picked up the pace; the closer she could feel them moving in, gaining on her. Margot looked towards her target in the distance; to the wall and its gothic torches. She then realised that it had also disappeared. Margot took a deep breath. She had strayed off the path. She was no longer running in the right direction. But she couldn't stop, couldn't change course. Whatever was following her would continue to chase until it had hunted down its prey. *There has to be some way out.* There must be some way she could trick them; throw whatever it was off her trail. She turned behind her, hoping to see something shift in the darkness, hoping to see some reason to keep on running. She slammed into something hard and collapsed.

She lay there for a few moments, grasping her face, waiting for her vision to come back into focus. She knew they would be here soon, she had to get up, to keep running, but she didn't have the strength. Margot glared up at the large object as it came into focus. It looked like a tall building, but she knew that couldn't be right. There was no need for it, no reason to be there. Margot could feel the hairs on the back of her neck begin to stand up again when a large pair of stone wings hovered above her.

"Over there!" A sinister voice yelled. Margot listened as the stampede of whispers gained on her. She was surrounded. With great effort, she edged her body backwards, trying to move as fast as she could away from the beast in front. Something grabbed her from behind and hoisted her onto her feet.

"Get off!" Margot screamed, trying to escape. She tried to hold in her scream as she ran past the stone creature, right into another one. They were everywhere.

Everywhere Margot looked, everywhere Margot turned; she was surrounded by the grotesque stone figures of the Brontangus.

"Stop running!" The voice called again.

"Leave me alone!" Margot screamed. She would not go down without a fight.

"Margot," the creature called again. "It's me Damien."

Margot froze as an arm reached out and patted her on the shoulder.

"Damien!" She said, flustered. "We need to leave!" She didn't even question where he'd been, she didn't care.

"Margot, calm down." Damien sounded annoyed.

"But we're being followed, by an army or something. I can hear them!" Margot yelled. *Why wouldn't he listen to her?*

"No, we're not." He replied, frustrating her more.

"Damien," Margot panted. "You don't understand, I can hear them, I can hear them. They're coming after us. Something's chasing us."

"It's 'Face'," Damien said. "We're picking up on the thoughts of souls trapped inside the Brontangus. Hurst said it was dangerous."

"But something grabbed me!"

"That would be the demon I found. He's waiting for us. Morn has agreed to take us to the city; for a price, of course."

Margot nodded. She felt her cheeks turning red, as embarrassment swamped her. She had been made a fool of by her own invention. She had displayed her fear to the world, or at least the Under World. It was definitely a first.

"Where are we anyway?" She said, desperately trying to regain her cool.

"A Brontangus graveyard."

Margot ran her fingers through her hair as she looked around at their surroundings. She could see the creature's silhouettes in the distant blood red sky of the desert. There must have been hundreds of them, filling the second circle of the Under World. She could feel her pulse racing.

"Are they safe?" She asked, lowering her voice.

"No safer than the ones that have been recruited for Silvia. However, these are watched over by the Devil."

"Oh, great." Margot said with an air of sarcasm.

"Damien!" They heard a voice shriek in the background: "Are you coming or not?"

"Guess it's show time." Margot said. She frowned and kept a firm hold on her gun as they went towards the city walls.

Morn was a demon, but he was nothing like Hurst. Yes he was small and red, yes he spoke in a high and twisted voice, but unlike Hurst, there was something about him that was darker. Margot watched as his yellow eyes gazed upon them in the darkness, listening as he cursed to himself again and again. It made her feel uneasy.

"Human in the Under World," he muttered. "Whatever next?"

Margot pretended she didn't hear the remarks and stayed close to Damien as she stared at the compass in her hand. It was beginning to glow. They had almost reached their destination.

"Put this on." Damien said, taking off his cloak and handing it to her.

"Damien, I'm okay. Why do men always think they have to take their coat off as a manly gesture?"

"There was no 'gesture' intended," Damien's voice was firm. "These creatures, aren't like those on the island, they won't take too kindly to seeing a human in here."

"Right," Margot sighed, throwing the cloak around her shoulders and lifting the hood.

"We're here." The demon said. He turned his ugly head to face them. Margot watched as the dim light coming from the doorway cast over his wood-textured face. She continued to stare as he twisted his face into a grotesque smile, glaring with his yellow, pointed teeth which were bared in his wide grin. They had reached the wall.

There were no guards by the doors. Nobody wanted to break in, no-one sane at least.

"Try not to arouse suspicion." Morn hissed as they stepped through the gates. Margot held her breath; they were surrounded by creatures moving through the streets of the Circular City. The creatures were very similar to the ones on the island and surprisingly didn't scare Margot as much as she thought they would. But she could tell the difference between them. They were harder, unfriendly, more pointed at the edges. Everywhere she looked, she could see eyes glaring at them as they entered the city centre.

The streets were more old-fashioned than Margot had expected. As soon as she walked through the gates she saw a market stretched out on the dusty ground before her. The demon directed them down one of the middle passages, towards the centre of the city. The area and the people were ragged. She looked at the crumbling stalls as she passed them, keeping her hood firmly over her face. The tables were dirty and lit by mouldy candles. The sheeted roofs were covered in layers of grime and were torn and falling down in places. It was ironic that they thought they needed them at all, there was no sun light; what did they need shading from; the darkness? Damien pinched her arm as she lingered. She had been staring at a stall that traded gruesome things in jars.

"Roll up, roll up! I have just acquired some humans from the prison of Izsafar." The shout came from a slimy man from down the street.

Margot's heart skipped a beat as she stared at the small cage he was pulling behind him. Sure enough there were crippled, skinny figures huddle together. Margot could see their white hands clinging to the dirty bars. They didn't seem like humans, not any more. Without thinking, she wandered towards them, moving in front of the crowd to where the creature and his assistant stood. Margot watched as he stepped forward, turning to the small gathering. If she moved quickly, opened the cage when he wasn't looking... Margot's feet left the ground as two large hands grabbed her from behind.

A man with a large pig-like head was staring her in the face. Blood dripped from his snout and beady eyes as he breathed down her neck.

"Just what do you think you're doing?"

Margot gasped at the stench of his breath.

"Nothing's free here." He said, catching a glimpse at her ghostly white skin beneath the hood. "What are you?" He asked and pulled her closer to him.

"Nothing for you to be concerned with," a cold voice from behind said. Damien grabbed the back of her cloak with such force it knocked her to the floor.

"You have no right-" The pig man began but on seeing Damien's bared teeth, he backed away to his slimy master. Damien lifted her off the ground and whisked her round a back alley so quickly she didn't have time to take a breath.

"Why didn't you do that before?" She said.

"Because the devil would sense my presence, and now he'll expect our arrival," Damien snapped. "And after all, do you know how long it takes before I can do things like that? Especially, after our little journey has weakened me."

"Little journey?" Margot said, pulling her hood off.

"You ought to be more careful," Damien glared at her. "You'll get yourself killed. Those people were human traders; they'll catch you and sell you quicker than you can blink. Then who knows what will happen."

"He was going to sell them? How can you be okay with that?"

"I thought you would have learned by now, you cannot save everyone."

Margot turned away from him as she thought back to Jade. The image of him lying there would never truly leave her thoughts, no matter how much 'Face' she took.

There was the sound of footsteps as Morn appeared round the corner. "What are you doing?" he hissed.

"Good question." Damien folded his arms.

"You're liabilities, the both of you. I shall go no further with you by my side."

"That is fine with me," Margot said, dusting herself down. She wanted nothing to do with him.

Morn turned away to the corner then paused.

"Damien, one more thing," The demon held out his wretched hand.

"Of course," Damien said, slipping something gold and shiny into his rough palm. "Now leave us, and remember your promise, not a word."

After one last glare, the demon scuttled off into the dimly lit streets.

"So, now we're in, all we have to do is find *him*." Margot said, looking around.

"Somehow I can't see that being too challenging." Damien smiled, pointing a pale finger into the distance. She followed its direction. In the centre of the city was a large gothic castle, reaching high into the black sky.

"That," Damien said. "Is the home of the Devil."

*

Arabina stirred under the sheets. She didn't know how long she'd been asleep; she didn't know where she was. She wondered where the others were, wondered if they were still alive. Arabina didn't know how she felt towards them anymore. She turned over to see Lucy fast asleep on the bed next to her. Arabina ran her fingers through her thick black hair, smiling. There was something special about that girl.

Arabina didn't stay with women any longer than one night. She had never had someone go out of their way to care for her, to look after her. Or at least, no one she'd noticed...

She sat up, thinking on that thought. Had people cared for her? She thought of Barbie, who had warned them when her chapel was about to fall. Of Hurst, who had followed her loyally through thick and thin, defending her, staying close by her side. And last she thought of Damien. Damien was the most loyal of all. He was the one who took her into hiding, who warned her, who tried to stop her going to Izsafar and taking them all with her. It was her fault. It was all her fault. If she hadn't gone, or made the decision because of something as stupid as pride then none of it would have happened. They *had* cared, they had all cared. She'd just been too blind to notice.

Arabina felt a pang of guilt hit her in the chest. She looked down at Lucy, knowing she'd have to leave her. It was not in her nature to be selfless but it was time to change. Arabina slipped out of the silky white sheets and got to her feet. She could feel her energy returning. She might just have enough magical charge to fly out of where ever she was and find the others. After all, who knew what horrific danger they were in?

*

"So, any ideas as to how we're going to get inside?" Margot whispered.

"Not a clue," Damien answered. "I was hoping you'd be able to give me some input."

"Well I don't know, Damien, why don't we have a look in my travel brochure to check the correct procedure… oh wait…"

"Margot," the vampire snapped. "Now is really not the time for sarcasm."

"Well, look at it!" Margot exclaimed, gesturing to the building before them. "How the hell are we gonna get in there?"

Damien gave a deep sigh, she had a point. Everything about the building seemed impregnable. It was patrolled by guards in red hooded cloaks. The castle reached high into the sky and was made of a dark grey stone with gloopy-looking black slime. It was jagged and one half looked as if it was going to fall down. Around the castle there was a bottomless moat. Margot looked at it from a safe distance. Why a moat? She wondered for a while. Surely you could get no closer to hell than the Under World? Where else was there left to fall? She gazed again at the building, it was impossible.

"Okay," she whispered. "We need to acquire those red cloaks the guards are wearing."

"And how do you propose we do that? These people are the Devil's watch. They're just as powerful as the angels, we have no chance."

"I agree," said a deep voice from behind. They turned to see a tall hooded figure looming over them. Margot gulped, scared of what sort of a creature would be under its uniform. It was half the size of a Brontangus and twice as scary. They were much more menacing at such close proximity.

"What business do you have here?" He asked, grabbing the back of their coats.

"We're here to see the Devil." Damien replied.

"Well then," the watch member said, lifting them off their feet. "I'd better take you inside then."

"We can walk," Margot said, as the he carried them over the drawbridge.

"Very well," the creature said, dropping them on the floor.

"Jesus," Margot muttered, getting to her feet. "This place is like being in an old school horror film."

Damien shot her a 'do not open your mouth' glare as they walked through the entrance.

Everything was cold and very medieval. The creature led them to a small room, gesturing them to sit on a stone bench in the corner.

"Wait here," he said. "Mary over there can check your appointment time."

He wandered back towards the doors to resume his post.

Margot raised her eyebrows. "Did he just say 'appointment time'?"

Suddenly her ears were drawn to the sound of clicking coming from the far end of the room. They turned to see a woman sitting behind a desk. On sensing their glares, she raised her head, she was annoyed.

"Yes," said the receptionist, in an irritated tone. "Do you have one?"

As Margot and Damien approached the desk, Margot realised that the women was out of place. She was caked in make-up and her white hair was scraped back in a severe style. Margot could hear gold jewellery catching her computer keyboard as she typed; it matched the two gold rings hanging from her pointy ears. That was the only evidence that helped Margot come to the conclusion that she must be some sort of elf.

"Yes?" She repeated, looking away from the computer screen.

"We need to see the Devil," Damien said.

"Appointment time?" she asked sharply.

"I wasn't aware the Devil had a receptionist"

"Well, what a shame, looks like you don't have one, let me check when he's next available." She turned back to her screen, tapping vigorously at the keys. "Okay… he's free the morning after the Angel's Court, in fifteen human years."

Margot wanted to scream. They'd travelled all that way to be told they could see the Devil in fifteen years? She knew opening her mouth would only make things worse and therefore thought it best to stay silent and behind Damien.

"Unfortunately, it's rather urgent." He said, leaning over the desk. "We cannot wait fifteen human years."

There was a loud bang as the doors at the far end of the room flew open and a man covered in snakes ran past them towards the entrance of the castle. Mary sighed with boredom as his screams echoed throughout the building.

"Well, it looks like your lucky day, it appears one of his meetings has been cut short." She opened a drawer under the desk. "You'll need name and race badges, so we know what you are. Please state your information."

"Of course," Damien smiled. "Damien. Vampire."

"Oh," Mary giggled, as she wrote out a name badge. "And what about her?" Mary shifted her eyes to Margot. "Lower your hood madam; the devil must know who he's meeting."

Margot gulped and removed her hood. She watched the elf's eyes light up.

"Well, say your name," Damien said. "We haven't got all day."

"Margot," she said but was interrupted by Mary. She bit her lip as the elf sat up in her chair.

"You're very pure looking to say you live in the Under World. What is your race?"

"She's a harpy." Damien replied.

"Hey!"

"Is there a problem?"

"No," Damien said through gritted teeth, as he glared at Margot. "Everything is fine."

"If you're a harpy," Mary said. "Where are your wings?"

"They were taken from her," Damien replied. "Taken after she stole from the angels and that's how she came to be here. However she's extremely embarrassed about the whole situation."

"Fine," Mary said, writing out her name badge. "Take these, go up to the top floor, straight down the hallway towards the golden doors. You can't miss them. I'll let him know you're coming."

Damien nodded and she giggled one last time, before resuming her typing as they left.

"Thanks for that," Margot glared at him, once the elf was out of ear shot. Damien grinned in response. His face resumed his normal expression when they looked at the twenty seven flights of stairs they would have to climb.

"This...this...is stupid," Margot panted as they finally made it to the top floor. The castle maintained its medieval look, although it grew more grandiose the higher they climbed. They paused at a red marble floor leading towards two golden doors at the end of the hall.

"This must be it," Damien said, looking around. The stair rails had turned golden. There were stone guards positioned every two metres down the corridor. It had to be it.

Margot took a deep breath. "Well, what are we waiting for, then? Might as well get this over with."

They walked towards the double doors, not bothering to stare at the paintings of torture on the walls. Margot's heart raced; the whole point of being there lurked behind the doors in front of them. All she had to do was open them.

"Now keep calm," Damien spoke softly, preparing to turn the handle. "I doubt he'll fall for the harpy excuse and I don't think he'll take too kindly to having a human in his midst."

"Damien," Margot rolled her eyes, "I know, I'm not Arabina-"

She stopped in mid-sentence, because Damien turned away. It was still a raw subject. Just before he opened the door, she watched him hesitate.

"What's that noise," the vampire wondered. Margot screwed up her eyes, she could hear it too. It sounded like a soft drum beat. She shrugged and put her ear to the golden door.

"Beats me." She said, resting her hand next to her gun. "Let's just be careful, I didn't come here to wait around and elf-face can go screw if she thinks we're sitting here for fifteen years."

Damien nodded. She was right; they had no choice; it was now or never. He turned the handle and they stepped cautiously inside.

As the door opened, they were blown away by the loud dance music that hit their ears and the vast amount of smoke that filled their lungs.

"What the hell?" Margot choked, as the door closed. The room was so smoky, it was impossible to see anything. They battled their way through the mess on the floor, holding their arms out so as not to bump into anything. The floor was covered with multi coloured beanbags, throws, empty bottles and pieces of rubbish. They had no idea where they were going. The plan was simple; follow the music. Margot slipped on something wet, she looked down to see a half-eaten carcass. She directed the vampire's eyes to it. But they continued.

Damien tripped over something in their path. It was a large black box- a speaker she told him; they were close.

"Where the hell is he?" Margot yelled over the noise.

Damien didn't reply; his eyes were fixed on something else. Margot frowned, turning to see what he was staring at. It was the most bizarre sight of her life.

Before them the smoke had parted to reveal the most bizarre scene. She may have experienced being chained up by a necrophiliac, fed on by a vampire, chased by a Brontangus; but nothing that she had seen or experienced in the strange realm compared to what was in front of her. A grotesque yellow creature was dancing vigorously; it was smoking and eating something that resembled an arm. Margot gulped, that couldn't be *him* could it? They watched in silence as the demon danced around in the smoke. He switched from seventies to fifties swing, then to something Margot thought shouldn't be legal. As he twirled round, doing a half pirouette, he noticed them standing there, gobsmacked.

"One moment!" The devil yelled. "I'll just turn it down!"

Margot watched him go to the speakers him and press the off button. The room fell silent. The devil wafted his hand about trying to clear the smoke.

"Please," he smiled, revealing his pointed teeth. "Take a seat." He clicked his fingers and two beanbags appeared behind them. Margot didn't move her eyes from the creature as she sat down.

His yellow eyes were watery; his hands were worn. His dank, yellowy skin was the colour of filth; it looked like some sort of rotting vegetable the way its bumps and bulges turned darker in places. Margot stared at the small horns on his ugly bald skull.

"I'm terribly sorry, I thought I had the afternoon off," he said, taking another puff of whatever he was smoking. "Now," the creature said. "What can I do for a vampire and harpy such as yourselves?"

Margot and Damien stared at each other before speaking.

"Sir," she said. "You're never going to believe this but…"

As Margot spoke, Damien thought of those on Manhaden's surface. Those who were fighting, those who were dying… Every word that came from Margot made the situation more real, more intense. Yet the longer they spent in that room, the more distant he felt from it. It seemed like a long forgotten nightmare, stretched across the minds of millions.

"…so you see," Margot concluded, taking a large intake of breath. "We need your help."

"To stop Silvia," Damien added. "And send the humans back to their world." Margot felt her stomach lurch. She hadn't told the vampire what she had seen in the castle. After his words, they both waited in silence for the creature's verdict. The Devil turned from them, stroking the bottom of his chin as he pondered. Finally he looked back in their direction.

"I'm going to be honest," he smiled at them. "I don't really care."

The Devil shrugged, making his way over to a dressing table hidden amongst the smoke behind them. Margot's mouth dropped open.

"No? Just like that?" She whispered angrily to Damien. "We came all this way for him to turn around and say *no?*"

"Margot," Damien said. "Will you please sit down?"

"No," she turned back towards the Devil. The vampire's ears picked up people climbing the main stairs, it wouldn't be long before they were intercepted, taken away for their efforts.

"Excuse me!" Margot yelled, moving through all the smoke to where the creature sat. "Dude!" She called.

"Yes," he said. Margot stopped; he was wearing a long brunette wig on top of his head. "I do love human wigs," he said before turning back around. Margot gave an exasperated sigh. The creature was either completely crazy or just near damn impossible to reason with.

"It's really important you help us," she insisted.

"And why would that be?" the Devil asked, rolling another cigarette.

Margot gulped before she replied. She hated grovelling and asking for favours, but they were desperate.

"We need you," she struggled to say through gritted teeth.

"Child," the Devil turned to her, he had changed the style of wig to a pink bob. "I have lived for many years, seen many a problem and tried to avoid nearly all of them. I wish for no war on the angels, believe it or not, I'm actually quite peaceful. You are young, things like this drive you to do something, I've seen far too many situations like this, it will pass. I plan to stay away."

"What about your daughter?" Margot asked sternly.

Before the creature had chance to answer, the doors burst open and in flew three of the devil's red hooded guards. She sighed as they glided towards her and Damien. The game was up. They had lost. She lowered her head; she would not lose any more dignity through grovelling. It wouldn't be long before they discovered her true identity and then she was as good as dead anyway. Margot felt a cold hand touch her shoulder-

"Wait!" The Devil yelled. "Leave them, leave them!"

Margot raised her eyebrows as the creatures around her backed away towards the doors. She couldn't see the vampire, but was sure he was as confused as she was. She looked at the yellow creature; the Devil's glare had changed. He no longer had the same carefree look as minutes before. The look in his watery eyes was that of concern, agitation.

"Where is she?" He asked as the large doors slammed. "Where's my Gloria?"

"Gloria?" Margot said. "I'm talking about Arabina. You know, Queen of Manhaden?"

"Of course!" The Devil said. "Sorry, my Gloria's an angel; I assumed it was her who was in danger when you mentioned the issue. Now, what has happened to my daughter?"

"Well," Damien said, stepping out from the smoke. "We are unsure of her whereabouts and current state."

The Devil looked as though he was about to collapse.

"My guess," Damien continued. "Is that she is either in hiding or has been captured. Silvia would let us know if she had killed her."

"Very true," the Devil nodded, sounding a little more relieved. Margot could see his hands shaking as he held them close to hide half of his face. "And what of the people on Izsafar? And the others in the castle, what was it like there?"

Margot turned away before replying, "They're all dead." She spoke calmly. "I've seen it for myself; I've seen them all lying dead."

"Surely not." The Devil shook his head.

"I *know* what I saw." Margot yelled.

"No Margot," Damien interrupted. "You do not understand, the Devil has a point. She would never do something like that. Although corrupt, it was never her intention. Torture yes, but not kill."

"But Jade watched people die!" Margot exclaimed.

"Yes," Damien sighed, sounding impatient. "But it was never the angel that killed them."

"Be quiet, both of you," The Devil said. He sat down on a nearby beanbag. He needed to think fast. "Silvia wouldn't be so obvious to walk around mindlessly killing, and that's if she killed anyone at all."

He scratched his wig. "We need to get an army of creatures and bring the fight her way, I just don't know where she's gonna be."

He passed back and forth, deep within his own thoughts. "I can imagine her hiding on Izsafar, staying in that castle is too obvious. She would need to blend in, look human, something to -" He paused, looking at Margot and Damien who were swapping concerned looks with each other.

"What?" The Devil exclaimed. "Did I say something wrong?"

*

Arabina's hand was on the door handle, she was ready to leave. Sighing, she turned back one last time to glance at Lucy, still asleep in the bed. No, she had to do it. She had to leave her, or she feared she'd stay there forever. She turned the handle as quietly as possible.

"Evie?" A voice whispered from behind her. Arabina turned to see the dark haired woman stirring in the bed.

"Where are you going?" She asked, stretching as she rose.

"I'm sorry, darling," Arabina said softly, turning her back on her. Suddenly, there was a warm hand running down her back and another making its way around her shoulder.

"Don't go," Lucy whispered in her ear. "Don't go, you'll die. Stay, stay with me."

Arabina inhaled deeply. She closed her eyes as she turned around, finding Lucy's mouth. Her lips were like nothing she'd ever felt before; they hit her like morphine, filling her with ecstasy as she led her back towards the bed. Arabina threw her on the bed, tearing off her tight fitting black top and undoing the lacy bra underneath. She watched as the pale chest moved up and down as Lucy tried to catch her breath. Arabina leaned to her neck, kissing down her body until she reached her nipple. She sucked hard. Lucy moaned as Arabina moved her hand between her legs. Lucy would let her go no further and instead, she flipped her over, sitting astride her and stripping Arabina in the same fashion. The Devil's daughter grinned; she had been waiting for that moment for a long time.

Suddenly, Lucy moved her mouth from her neck to Arabina's ear.

"Let's play rough." She whispered, and dragged her nails down both sides of her back. Shivers cascaded down Arabina's spine.

"Sure." She smiled as she slapped Lucy across the face. Lucy gasped, taken aback by the response. After a moment, she thrust Arabina back onto the bed, stripping her fully naked.

"Yeah well, how would you like me to do this?" She yelled inserting her fingers fully inside. The Devil's daughter screamed with pleasure.

"Well," she moaned in return. "How would you like me to strangle you?" Arabina reached up, putting her hands around Lucy's throat.

They rolled about the bed; sweat slicked their skin as the foreplay continued. Arabina groaned as she hit Lucy across the face again. The dark haired girl hit her back and pinned her to the bed so that she could suck and bite her neck. Arabina thrust her head back and moaned. It wouldn't be long until they were having full blown sex. Every muscle in her human form was tingling, she was elated. It was as if Arabina was transforming. She wondered if Lucy felt the same. She lifted her head forward again, preparing to let her eyes travel down Lucy's perfect body but as she pulled the woman's hair, she found that the strands she held were pure white. The colour of her hair was changing, along with her form...

Arabina grabbed Silvia's hair and threw her to the floor.

"Don't think I don't know who you are!" Silvia yelled, scrambling to her feet. Arabina stared at her hands; they'd changed back to their original dark colour. The angel shot up from the floor, grabbed her and threw her against the headboard.

"Oh sweetheart," Arabina replied through gritted as the angel leapt on her. "I knew who you were all along."

Silvia laughed at her words; she had the upper hand as her glow became brighter. Arabina was being crushed under the angel's weight. It was a trap; that's what it had been the whole time. Arabina felt the anger building up inside of her. The angel would not win, she told herself.

Without warning, Arabina spat in her face, blinding Silvia for a few seconds. A few seconds was all she needed, she rose from the bed, and ran for the door.

"Not so fast," the Angel's voice screeched. Arabina was flung through the air towards the window at the edge of the room.

There was a thud as her naked body hit the glass and she slid to the floor. Arabina was dazed, she needed to stand up. She grabbed for the curtain, hoping to gain some sort of support. It ripped; she fell back to the floor and took the material with her.

Arabina groaned as she tried to struggle to her feet. The atmosphere in the room had changed and Silvia was no longer interested in her. Arabina stared out of the window to see what had captured the angel's gaze. She didn't know what was more alarming; the blood red sky, the stormy castle grounds or the hordes of creatures in the air. Before them, millions of Brontangus had taken flight and were headed towards Izsafar. Silvia's army had turned on her.

*

"Fall back! Fall back!" Hurst screamed from the hotel window. He stood for a moment, glaring at the uncountable white figures that poured through the hotel's open doors. It was no good; it would be the end of them. Hurst knew they had to defend the portal to save the others.

"Hurst!" He heard Frank call from the stairs. "Hurst quickly! We're blockin' off every route te the top of te stairs!"

The demon ran to the door, climbing the final flight, only to hear the creatures blocking up the doorway behind them. They could run no further. They had reached the top, the last floor of the building. Hurst ran to Frank's side, he was facing the window at the top of the staircase. Many others stood next to him, wounded creatures from the darkness, all there to defend the room.

"I'm here, Frank, I'm here." Hurst put his claws on the blind man's shoulder to let him know of his presence.

"I think," said Frank slowly. "We don't have much of a chance."

There was the sound of banging below. The U.A.S. had almost breached their defences.

"I know," the demon sighed, staring out at the fight. He could see Frank's demon dog attacking at least ten at a time. "At least we found a use for your pet." He smiled.

"Stupid bastard," laughed Frank. "I should 'ave been nicer to 'im really."

Outside the screams were growing louder.

"You were fine," Hurst smiled. "I can imagine it's annoying when your pet's always trying to kill you. You were as nice as you could be."

"Gonna be lonely without you an' Damien an' tha'," Frank voice was strained over the increasing noise.

"Yeah," Hurst said. "Well I wasn't much help, a bit of a coward if you ask me."

"You di' a pretty good job from where I was standin'" Frank rested his hand on the demon's shoulder. "When the time was right, you showed 'em all."

Someone screamed down below. Things were about to get nasty.

"Would you have done anything different given the chance?" The demon turned to him.

The banging grew louder.

"I'd quit drinkin'"

"Really?"

"Hurst!" A creature called from the bottom of the stairs. "We can't hold them for much longer!"

"No!" Frank laughed. "No I don't suppose I would."

The banging was unbearably loud. Hurst heard the breaking of wood and the smashing of windows. They were coming for them.

"Everyone!" Hurst yelled over the noise. "Stand your ground; do not let them past. They have got this far but they will not get any farther. I'm so proud of you all, you who have made it to the end."

There was the sound of U.A.S. shouting as they ran up the stairs.

"Wait," Hurst screamed. "Wait... hold your ground-"

Suddenly it fell silent. The fighting stopped. There was no more running up the stairs, no explosions or spells. All that could be heard was the lonely scream of a dark creature, falling from the building and crashing onto the hard ground below.

"Wha's goin' on?" Frank whispered. "Why 'ave they stopped?"

"The Brontangus," Hurst stammered. "We're surrounded."

*

High above the seas of battle, two hopeless figures remained chained to the angel's sky.

"There's nothing good left in this world Barbie because there was never any to start with. Humans talk of angels and demons like they mean something deep and spiritual. Well, I tell you, I've come across many and they don't. They're just creatures, exactly the same as you and I, just trying to make their way in these confusing worlds. Right and wrong are the real concept of myths and legends. They don't exist, they have never existed and, if people stopped following the conventions of what they were raised to think was 'right,' then people like you and me would have a much easier time. Let's hope they don't find Margot, let's hope and pray."

"Why?" Barbie asked. "We need her; it's the only way they'll believe us. If humans knew we were here-"

"We do," the angel agreed. "But if they find out she's not one of them. They'll kill her."

Chapter 22

The Devil in Action

The ground beneath Margot's feet began to shake.

"What in the Devil's- in my name is going on?" the Devil clicked his fingers, clearing the smoke from the room to reveal his fascinating décor. Margot wasn't interested in the bodies, array of speakers or the mountain of rubbish. What did focus her attention was coming from the window. Outside, hundreds of Brontangus were taking to the sky and soaring high above the Under World.

"This cannot be!" the Devil yelled; his chilled persona evaporated. He turned away from the window and sat on a multi-coloured throw. Margot looked to Damien unsure whether to go over to the creature's side or not.

"I think," the creature sighed, returning to his original calm attitude after the initial shock. "We seem to have a bit of a situation on our hands."

Damien looked at the ceiling, exasperated. If it wasn't for the fact that he was the Devil, he'd make a sarcastic comment. The Devil closed his eyes, muttering something under his breath.

"Don't panic," he said. "I've called up my lead guards; we'll try and straighten this out."

"I thought your guards were meant to be watching these creatures." Damien said.

"They were," the Devil whispered. After a moment, he spoke again. "There could be only two reasons for this, each as unlikely as the other."

"And they are?" Damien said.

"Well either the guards let them loose or-"

The Devil never finished his explanation, as three guards burst into the room.

"Sir, what do we do?" One asked as they glided towards him.

For a while, the creature did not answer. Margot had a scary suspicion it was because he didn't know the answer; none of them had a clue. She groaned, the longer they stood there, the more time they were wasting.

"I am guessing," the Devil said. "They'll be looking for revenge on those that imprisoned them."

"Meaning?" Margot asked.

"They'll be heading for the Over World and most probably be looking for Silvia on the way."

"So they'll leave Izsafar alone then?"

"HA!" He laughed. "Far from it my dear; they'll tear the whole place down, whether she's there or not." He looked Margot in the eye: "Do not forget harpy, a lot of them were bound to a lifetime of servitude there. It made the hell they were already living in just that little bit worse."

He turned away from her and approached his guards.

"Gather an army!" the Devil yelled. "We must take the fight to them. This is bigger than Silvia now; these things are out of control. They'll tear the whole world apart."

"But the angel," Damien said.

"…will still be there once this has been dealt with, if you find her on the way then so be it."

"With all due respect sir, I do not think you-"

"No, vampire," the Devil interrupted, his watery eyes fixed on Damien's icy blue ones. "It is you who does not understand. There will be no world to search if they have their way."

He turned away and yelled his commands.

"Assemble an army! Quickly, go! And gather me ten creatures to assist me, the vampire and harpy will be making a short detour to the castle."

"I wish you hadn't called me a harpy," Margot muttered as she moved to the vampire's side.

But Damien wasn't listening, instead he was crossing to the other side of the room; with his eyes closed, he concentrated.

"What are you doing?" Margot said. "We have to help fight!"

"One moment," Damien said sharply. "I am just trying to contact the others through 'Face'. We need to make sure they know-"

The window smashed and a large stone hand reached inside. Margot collapsed to the floor, putting her hands over her ears. The room was filled with the screeching of two Brontangus. They cried out so loud, Margot thought she'd never be able to hear again. Then, out of nowhere, something hit her hard on the head then threw her up in the air. In the background she could hear the Devil shouting out his orders. They seemed like a million miles away.

"Go quickly! Run now, gather them quickly! We shall deal with this!"

Everything went cold around her and Margot dropped to the floor.

She passed out, as a large claw moved closer. Everything was fading, turning black.

"Margot!"

Margot heard a cry in the distance. She was being pulled across the floor; she felt two cold arms reaching around her.

"You're okay, they've gone now," Damien's cold voice whispered in her ear. Margot looked up to see the vampire staring down at her. He looked away as soon as their eyes met.

"Thanks," she muttered quietly. She rolled from his lap as she began to regain consciousness. Margot turned to look at the room, it was ablaze.

"Is everyone alright?" the Devil yelled. Margot saw his figure standing amongst the flames. He was calming the fire with water from his long fingers. Once it was finally out, an awkward silence filled the room.

"Sorry about your room," Margot said, rubbing her head.

"They did me a favour, it was a mess," the creature replied.

Outside they could hear the distant cry of Brontangus flying into the red sky. The attack had come as a shock. They had fallen dumb when hit with the cold reality of what awaited them.

"Well," Margot said. "Time to leave boys."

"Are you sure you still want to do this?" the Devil was shocked.

"Of course I do!" Margot said, offended.

"Margot Grant is it?" He asked, as he pulled her to her feet.

She nodded, regaining her balance. After all she'd been through; one knock to the head wasn't going to stop her.

"Well Margot Grant, I've heard a lot about you. I was wondering when we'd meet." Margot's pulse quickened as he continued: "They say you're reckless and they were right. Have you seen what you've done? You broke into Izsafar, broke into Silvia's castle and the Circular City, you slipped past all my guards and-"

Margot bowed her head, waiting for her punishment.

"You're the toughest human I've ever met." He smiled. And for the first time in a long time, Margot was taken aback.

"Oh please," he rolled his eyes. "I am the Devil, you know. A little anarchy never hurt anyone. Now quickly, run through to the next room and take your pick of weapons, you'll find they don't need mind power to work. Quickly!"

Margot nodded, sprinting off without question.

"Wow," Damien muttered. "That bump on the head actually made her follow orders."

The Devil turned to him. He faced the vampire with a serious expression.

"That was no coincidence, they wanted her for something." He stared at Damien. "There's a lot more to Margot Grant than meets the eye. I don't think I need to explain that to you."

"I don't know what you mean," Damien replied.

"If I was you I'd make a move quickly, you may live forever but she certainly won't."

The doors burst open and Margot returned. Her arms were full of a variety of guns.

"Right then," she grinned, throwing one to Damien. "What are we waiting for?"

"We need to move quickly," the Devil said. "I can deal with one or two, but once we get to the hundreds we may have a problem." He turned to them. "Grab an arm."

"What about the guards?" Margot exclaimed.

"No time."

Damien and Margot stared at each other as he held out his yellow scaly arms. Awkwardly, they gripped one each.

"We're heading to the castle."

*

"What te hell do we do Hurst?" Frank exclaimed. "They're gonna kill everyone!"

"I'm well aware of that, Frank," Hurst said. He frowned and looked at the clouds. The creatures had stopped fighting. They were gliding through the bright sky. The crowd on the ground watched in silence as they came closer. No one moved. No one spoke. They stared in awe, waiting, just waiting for something to happen. And then, out of nowhere someone sprang from the crowd; some stupid U.A.S. member who thought himself invincible.

"Get back in line!" he yelled. One of the Brontangus let out a low rumbling sound. Without warning, the stone creature reached out its arm and batted him away like a fly. It had begun.

A catastrophe had hit Izsafar. All had gone wild. No one knew who to fight; no one knew what to do. The U.A.S. had turned and fled. On the battle grounds it was a free for all. Hurst watched as creatures panicked and turned to attack their own kind. It sickened him.

Hurst paced, trying to think of some sort of strategy. It was bad, very bad. As the demon watched the chaos from the window, he was powerless. They were no longer fighting for freedom of choice; they were fighting for their lives. It was not how it was supposed to be. If only there was some way they could beat those things, if only there was some way the mindless violence could be stopped!

An idea hit Hurst. It was radical, it was stupid, it was crazy, but it just might work.

"Stay here." Hurst said. He screwed his hand into a fist and smashed the window.

"Hurst?" Frank yelled, "What are yeh doin'?"

"Something I should have done a long time ago," Hurst said, climbing through. "I'm calling a treaty; the only fighting we're doing with these humans is alongside them."

"Oh fuck, the pressure of leadership has sent 'im crazy. Hurst!" Frank yelled after him, "I told you couldn't handle the stress of a high positioned job! Hurst!"

*

"They're on Izasfar!" Wolf said; "The Brontangus, they're free. They've been freed."

"How do you know?" Barbie asked.

"Damien's just communicated with me via 'Face'. This is bad. This is very, very bad. They're angry; they're going to destroy everything."

"They might be nice?" Barbie said, trying to give the angel some sort of comfort.

"Barbie," Wolf glared at him. "These things are evil souls that have been tortured and sentenced to be trapped in a stone prison for eternity. I highly doubt they're going to want to spend their new freedom gardening and having dinner parties with old friends."

He stared out into the distance. "Oh no, my lad, they're gonna be angry. They're gonna work their way up until they get to the Over World. Then we'll be doomed."

"Oh dear," was the only reaction Barbie could give.

"Stars and skies!" A cold voice exclaimed behind him. "What is he complaining about now?" Anthony had returned and was more smug than before.

"You must listen to me!" Wolf said. "The Brontangus-"

"Yawn, yawn, yawn, I'm bored of your stories Wolf, the whole court is." The angel flew higher than necessary so he could look down on them. "That's why we came to the decision, we're imprisoning you. You will be one of these creatures soon enough, then you can talk to your heart's content."

"Look," Wolf said. "Do what you want, but they're free, they're coming to get you. You need to do something."

The angel threw his head back and cackled.

"I'm being serious! They'll make you wish you weren't immortal!" Wolf yelled.

"You see, Wolf, this is what I'm talking about. Hanging around with these humans has made you 'lose it', so to speak." The angel paused. "You know perfectly well there is only one way the Brontangus can be free, and that could never happen."

He flew off, leaving Wolf to deal with his own fate.

"You need to listen to me!" Wolf screamed after him. He turned to Barbie: "Oh it's hopeless, completely hopeless!"

"Calm down, I have a feeling hope is nearer than you think." Barbie said, gazing out into the distance.

"Barbie," Wolf sighed. "I hate to tell yer this lad, but no one is coming to save us."

"I wouldn't be so sure of that."

The angel turned to him, a confused look on his face. "What are yer talking about?"

He turned his head.

In the distance, sailing across the peaceful skyline of the city was a ship; a ship without a Capitan. There was only one destination it could possibly be heading.

*

"Well, here we are," the Devil said as his feet touched down on the marble courtyard. There was an eerie atmosphere surrounding the castle; a quiet that contrasted with the stormy skies above. The doors were open; someone had left in a hurry. The harsh wind blew Margot's hair about her face. It was time.

"Let's go inside," she said, making her way towards the entrance.

"Margot wait," Damien said. "We can't just go charging in there. We don't know who we'll meet." He turned to the Devil for support.

"Damien's right." The Devil turned to the doors. "We don't even know our way around."

"One step ahead of you," Margot smiled, pulling the Jonovicator from her pocket. "So Damien, you should go back to the prison cells, see who's left there and free any living human, while me and-" She paused, trying to find a suitable name for the Devil.

"Please, call me Bub," he said.

"While I take Bub to the laboratories, Jade's marked a main control room here. I think it's important."

The Devil shrugged: "Sounds good to me."

They ran towards Silvia's throne.

"Meet at the top of the passage way," Damien yelled as he ran towards the dungeons.

*

Alone, Arabina sat on the edge of the King-size bed. There was a devilish smile on her lips. Black coils extended from the palms of her hands and wrapped around the body on the floor; the body of a broken dictator. Silvia didn't speak; she was wrapped in the silk bed sheets, rolled up like a cream cocoon. Only her white hands were visible and their glow was fading, much like her rule over Izsafar. Arabina entwined her one last time, making sure she was unable to move, before levitating her to the bed and sliding her under the covers. There she lay and would do so for a while, until her judgement came.

Once again, Arabina moved towards the door. There was no one to stop her, no beautiful female to change her mind. She sighed and looked at the cream cocoon that lay motionless in front of her. Maybe it could have become a butterfly if given a chance. The Devil's daughter could feel the tears welling in her eyes as she took one final look at the woman that had entranced her since they had met. A loud bang broke her train of thought. Someone was in the building. She had to leave and find the others.

*

"I can't destroy this, Margot," the Devil said.

They sat on the floor of the waiting room. The artificial sunlight shone through the stained glass roof, beaming down on them. It sickened Margot, it was the first time they had seen Silvia's work. The Devil wouldn't let her step inside 'The Room,' he wouldn't let her go near it. In his opinion, Margot has seen enough horror to last her a life time.

"So what do we do?" Margot said.

"We wait for Damien to return. Then I shall destroy this and the human

371

power source."

"Why not now?" Margot was becoming frustrated.

"Because," the Devil said. "If I do this, it will probably kill us. We need the best chance of survival."

"Oh."

She wasn't quite sure how she felt about that. It was the ultimate sacrifice. She wasn't sure she loved the human race that much. Margot shook her head, she had come so far - it was the right thing to do. A dark figure caught her eye and Margot looked up to see the vampire strolling across the hall alone. They got to their feet.

"Damien, I hope you're ready to run, because-"

She looked at the stern expression on his face. He continued past them, and leaned on the banqueting table.

"You are right." He sounded exasperated. "They're all dead."

He leaned over the table. Margot and Bub looked at each other. Margot's stomach turned as the image of the little girl rocking back and forth in the cell came back to her mind. It hadn't been a hallucination, it was real.

"I'm sure-" the Devil began.

"No," Damien turned to him, his eyes hard as flint. "Margot was right, I have seen it. She's destroyed them all; the whole castle is full of bodies."

The situation was looked increasingly dire as the seconds ticked by. Damien didn't turn away from Bub. He wanted him to know how serious the situation was; he wanted him to feel the pain, the loss. And as the silence continued, the Devil finally understood.

"We're running out of time," Margot spoke out, she looked at their surroundings: "Destroy it, destroy it all."

"We will make sure generations to come have no memory of this horrible place." Damien said, staring out into space.

"Right, glad we're all in agreement then," the Devil said.

He turned back to the vampire explaining what he had to do. Damien said nothing, but nodded his head. Margot could feel her knuckles whiten with every word uttered. But she wouldn't leave him there; she wouldn't let the Devil be crushed alone, not the same way they had left Frank. Bub beckoned them back down the corridor, as close to the exit as they could go. They refused to go any further. Their pride would not let them.

"Can't you do this from outside?" Margot asked.

The Devil shook his head. "Sadly it wouldn't work, she made it so it has to be destroyed from the inside, it's suicidal."

"Well guys," she said. "It's been sweet."

Damien still refused to look at her. He put his arm around her waist, getting ready to run when the time came. She sighed, there was a high chance they weren't going to survive the blast and he still wanted to be ignorant? Margot thought they were long past that stage.

"Okay!" the Devil yelled, raising his arms. "Prepare yourselves, kids!" He began muttering complicated incantations at the red door. At first, Margot thought nothing had been accomplished; she was embarrassed at the tightened grip she had around Damien. But, just as she relaxed her body, it happened.

The floor began to shake, the pictures fell from the walls, glass smashed as it hit the floor; the lights flickered and went out. In the background, Margot heard an explosion. Before she had chance to turn around, Damien had fled with her in his arms.

The castle was moving like it was alive; every passage had been changed, every brick collapsed. Damien had to turn back because of the destruction. Although Margot was blind to the damage around her; she could hear the smashing of chandeliers, the splitting of wood and crumbling of stone. It was shocking how quickly the beautiful structure was falling around them. There were like five year olds, lost in a hall of mirrors. A flash of light caught Margot's eye. She turned to see a fireball closing behind them.

"We have to find the Devil!" She yelled over the noise.

"No," Damien replied. "We reach ground; we are still in the laboratory."

"But he could be back there!"

They were in one of the main rooms. Margot was sure of it. She could hear hospital beds clattering as they were thrown about and the sound of guns exploding as they were hit by the flames. Damien was beginning to slow down, the quick turns had taken their toll, he wasn't sure how much longer he'd be able to carry her.

The fire had caught up with them and it acted as a light in the chase. It was shining on a large broken pot. In its shadow Margot could see a yellow figure tampering with the structure.

"Keep moving!" It yelled as they sped past. "I've just got to release this."

"That's Bub," Margot said. Suddenly, she leapt out of Damien's arms, dropping to the floor. Margot got to her feet and headed back to help the Devil.

"Margot Grant," Damien hissed, going after her.

The task of dodging the debris was made more challenging because the floor was uneven and kept throwing her into the air as she moved. It was difficult to steady herself.

"Bub!" She called out to the figure.

"Margot, get back!" the Devil yelled. He was climbing the sides of the structure. "You'll be destroyed by the fire."

She looked back at the blaze, it was mere metres away. "What are you trying to do?"

"Smash this to release the mind power!" the Devil yelled back. "Try and find a weapon from the side!"

Margot rushed around in the darkness, trying to find something, anything to free the human thoughts. Something caught her foot and she stumbled to the ground. She heard a crash next to her; rubble had fallen nearby. Margot tried to scramble to her feet, but she was unable to move. In the background the Devil was still desperately trying to break the pot. It all seemed hopeless. The only thing Margot could see at that point was the fire burning towards her. Suddenly, a beam of blue light pierced the container. The pot crumbled. Damien pulled her to her feet as a bright white light erupted.

"What's happening?" She whispered in the vampire's ear.

"I'm not sure," he said. The light became more prominent and circled around them.

"It's okay, we've done it," they heard the Devil call. "These people will guide us to freedom. Go towards them!"

Confused as to what he was talking about, they stepped into the light and their feet lifted from the fire around them.

Away from the horrors of the underground, the well in Silvia's garden began to quiver and shake. Had they got close enough to it, they'd have been able to hear the chattering of the bricks, the liquid rising, and the sound of the Devil screaming with joy. The well collapsed and sprayed out a bright white substance that took hold of them.

"Well," Margot said, as she fell to the ground. "I didn't think we were gonna make it."

The Devil collapsed next to her: "Me neither," he grunted. "I'm getting way too old for this."

"What have you just released?" Damien asked. Already on his feet, he reached his hand out to the white substance, which floated out of the castle grounds and trickled towards the stormy skies.

"That, my friend," said Bub, jumping to his feet. "Is all the human thoughts that the angel has taken. I've transformed them into gas; it's much easier to transfer them back to their owners that way."

Margot stared at the sky. "That stuff has been in my gun." She felt guilty, as ghost-like faces rose above them, returning to their bodies. A thought occurred to her. "But Izsafar is powered on that stuff... that means."

"It won't be long before Izsafar is destroyed." Damien finished her sentence.

The Devil said: "We need to move, my guards should meet us at the entrance and then we'll head to Izsafar." He looked about the beautiful garden and muttered: "Disgusting."

The grounds of the castle were empty. Margot wasn't sure if she was grateful for that or worried about the horrors which waited above. Once again, the ground beneath them rumbled.

"To the castle doors!" Bub said and ran across the grass.

"Bub!" Margot yelled: "It's the other way!"

"Of course!" the Devil replied.

Margot could hear the castle walls cracking. The devastation was rising; it wouldn't be long until the whole building collapsed.

"We should follow," Damien said.

Margot didn't move. "Thanks for saving me back there."

Damien paused; he didn't look at her. He ignored her. Margot refused to move. She was sick and tired of his behaviour towards her. End of the world or not, he needed to acquire some manners.

"Just what is your problem, Damien?" Margot yelled. "Why won't you look at me? What is it with you? You've never liked me! Anyone would think I'm pure evil!"

Damien did not reply.

"I'm talking to you!" Margot yelled, refusing to move out of the garden.

"Margot, Damien!" the Devil called to them: "We need to leave! What the hell are you doing?"

"Damien!" Margot screamed amid the commotion. "Look at me!"

Without warning, the vampire turned on his heels and marched towards her. His icy eyes looked her up and down; his glare was as serious as always. He grabbed her shoulders and yanked her towards him and kissed her hard on the mouth.

For a moment they stared at each other. The red eyes had warmed the ice and the blue had tamed the wild.

"Damien I-" Margot began, but her words faltered. She thought he'd hated her, always thought he'd wanted her dead. But-

Once again, the Devil called out. "If you stay here, you are going to die!"

Without another word, they ran towards the castle.

The floors shook, the tiles rose as the floor split and cracked, Margot could see bits of brick chipping from the detailed ceiling. They didn't have much time.

"Quickly!" the Devil yelled. "Quickly! We'll never make it to the entrance!"

They followed, finally catching up with him. He stopped and Margot and Damien almost ran into the back of him.

"Why have you stopped?" The vampire asked. He didn't realise the reason was standing directly before them. Standing in the doorway, dressed as her old self - Arabina.

Margot could feel her pale cheeks turning even whiter. She glanced in Damien's direction. He was as calm as always. At the opposite end of the corridor, the Devil's daughter was silent and still. It was a bizarre moment for them all.

After a few seconds, the Devil walked towards her, his arms open wide, a smile on his face.

"Father!" She yelled, preparing to embrace him.

"Arabina!" Instead of accepting her embrace, he grabbed her wrist and dragged her along behind him. "No time to talk! Catch up later!"

They ran back through the throne room, towards the last corridor. Soon they would be free. Soon they would be able to help the others.

"We're almost there!" Margot said as they turned the final corner. "The doors are just round here!"

"Did you really think you'd get away that easily?" A cold voice echoed in the doorway. Before them was Doctor Clarke with a Brontangus on either side of him.

"Move out of the way, Clarke," Margot ordered. "Who is that dumpy human?" the Devil whispered to his daughter.

Arabina cracked her knuckles: "An old friend."

The floor shook again. If they didn't get out soon they'd be buried under the rubble. Clarke didn't move a muscle, something told Margot he had no idea of the danger they were in. It was also clear he had no idea he was standing before the Devil.

"If you would please, step aside," Damien said and walked towards the door.

"Ahh, well if it isn't the traitor," Clarke said. "I knew you'd return."

"Don't be a dick, Clarke," Margot yelled, following the vampire. "The building is collapsing."

Both men ignored her comment. They kept their eyes fixed on each other; if looks could kill, Margot could imagine both of them dropping to the floor.

"The building is going to collapse?" Arabina said in the background. "She'll be crushed."

"I don't care who you are or the powers you possess, Rider, you're not going anywhere." Clarke laughed, looking at the Brontangus on either side of him.

"Doctor, I give you one last chance, let us pass or we all die." Damien's voice was slow and firm. It was getting harder to hear him over the rumbling noise of the castle.

"The U.A.S. was fine, everything was fine until that stupid bitch and Jade Wilde interfered!" Clarke screamed.

"Don't you dare talk about Jade like that!" Margot screamed, pulling a gun from her pocket and firing at the professor. The impact sent him out of the door to slide across the marble outside.

"Quickly!" Damien beckoned. "Outside."

The Brontangus charged at the group. Margot watched as the Devil and his daughter nodded at each other and lifted their arms, casting charms on the creatures. Their stone became stiff and their movement stopped.

"Go!" the Devil yelled. "We can deal with this!" He took them further into the building, towards the unsteady ground.

Margot and Damien ran to the exit. Clarke sprang to his feet outside and threw a bomb at them. The arch caved in and Margot took a few steps back in order to avoid the debris. Suddenly, Damien grabbed her waist and carried her out using what energy he had left.

Margot collapsed face down on the marble. Damien loosened his grip and continued towards the professor. The vampire flew at him so hard the two collapsed on the floor. She ran towards them, her gun in her hand. For the first time, her hand shook; the two of them were so close to the edge, one shot could easily knock them both down to the Under World.

"Margot, stay back!" Damien cried.

Clarke grabbed him by the throat and lifted him off the ground. The vampire was struggling; there was a high risk that they would never leave that awful place.

"Finally," Clarke gloated: "The Dark Rider shall be no more." Margot watched as he pulled a wooden stake from his pocket. He must have been waiting for that moment for a long time.

As Clarke, pulled his hand back to prepare to stab Damien, he faltered and shook. His power was diminishing. Izsafar was finally dying. The professor's shoes stopped working and he fell to the ground. Damien gasped for breath as Clarke's grip loosened. The roles reversed. The vampire pounced on the professor, holding him down by the throat. They were inches away from the edge; one false move and either party could fall. Margot ran towards them.

"She would have- she would have-" Clarke stuttered as he gasped for air.

"She would have what?" Margot shouted as she crouched down to face him.

"Turned me... into a Brontangus," Clarke continued: "I didn't want to do it... I had no choice."

Margot could hear the words gargling at the back of his throat.

"Please... don't do this." He pleaded with them. Damien pulled the man

377

up, lifting his feet off the ground.

"Humans like you are the reason there are angels like her." Damien spoke through gritted teeth. Margot saw his canines grow.

"Margot, help me!" Clarke screamed. "I was your boss, your friend!"

"You are no friend of mine, Dr Clarke."

Damien tore his throat apart.

*

In the middle of the chaos, the tiny demon stood on the roof of the hotel. His legs shook as he scanned the area. Where was Wolf? Where were the angels when they were needed most? Everything he believed in had been taken away. There was no point hoping for help from higher beings. It was every man for himself. The Brontangus were in full force. Hurst watched them tear apart every creature they could find. Blood filled the land, blood that should never have been shed in the first place. He was perplexed, angry at the destructive nature of those around him. If they continued like that, they'd destroy themselves. There'd be nothing left. They had to join forces with the U.A.S. It was the only way. Together, they could beat the Brontangus, and help each other.

"Everyone!" Hurst screamed at the top of his lungs, "We need to work together!"

No one listened.

"Guys!" Hurst tried again: "If we all just work together! Hello? Attention!"

It was no use, they wouldn't pay attention. They were too busy fighting for their lives. Hurst looked to the sky.

"Where are you?" He yelled. "Where are you when we need you?"

Suddenly, in the distance he heard the crash of thunder. Hurst looked towards the mountains. Black clouds were making their way over the mountain range. Margot and Damien had done it! Izsafar was falling.

Hope was here.

The demon looked around and a smile formed on his face. It was getting darker, it was dying. He watched as the trees wilted and the grass turned a filthy shade of brown. A white mist rose from the ground. If the demon had been there, he would have known it was the humans' thoughts returning to them at last. Someone grabbed Hurst's shoulder. The demon turned to find Frank wobbling by his side.

"Frank? Wha-"

"Thought yeh might need this." He said, handing Hurst a small device. "Megaphone - I took it off one of the U.A.S."

"Thanks, Frank," Hurst smiled and turned to the crowd. "Let's try this again."

*

"Quickly lad, untie us!" Wolf said as the boy flew from the ship. He, like Wolf had returned to his original angel form and looked so much more majestic for it. His long hair was white and flowed behind him, his pale blue eyes concentrated as they tried to break the chains that held his tutor.

"These are angel bound chains, only another angel can break them," he said as he snapped Wolf's in half. They turned to the transvestite and lifted him off his ledge and onto the ship.

"Full speed ahead!" Wolf yelled, as the ship plummeted down to Izsafar. It whirled through the pure clouds and down below the angel city. It wasn't long before Barbie could see small dots zooming towards them from the city. *What was that strange formation in the sky?* He ran to the back of the ship, to examine it closer. Then he realised. If Barbie's eyes could widen with shock, they would have done.

"Wolf, they're following us." He said, running down the ship towards the two angels.

"Perfect," Wolf smiled.

*

"We need to get to Izasafar, now!" the Devil shouted as he ran from the building.

"Where's Arabina?" Margot asked, looking around for his daughter.

"There is no time for questions!" Bub answered, glancing at the stormy sky. "My army is ascending and so should we."

Margot nodded, he was right. As she looked towards the clouds, she saw the red hooded creatures, flying up towards the storm. Damien wiped the blood from his mouth as he approached them.

"Are you alright?" Margot asked, trying not to sound concerned.

He nodded as he took the Devil's side. "Never better."

*

"They're gaining, Wolf, they're gaining." Barbie said, looking from the back of the ship. Sure enough, the army of angels was coming into focus.

"Good!" Wolf yelled. "Let them see what they have done. The ship continued to descend until the island was finally in sight. It looked nothing like it once did. He could see the land of Izasafar, writhing within the darkness of Arabina's kingdom. The mountains trembled as they tried to sustain the might of the human prison. There wasn't long left. Wolf could feel the ship shaking as it picked up speed in the descent. It was good; if they travelled any slower they'd be caught.

*

Margot held her breath as the Devil thrust her and Damien into the water. There was more swell than normal. The sea swayed back and forth, creating a whirlpool-like current. Around them, the world shook. They were amongst many red figures, swimming to the surface, preparing to fight.

*

As Wolf and Barbie flew closer to Izsafar they could hear Hurst's voice echo through the sky.

"We need to work together!" He squeaked. "It is the only way we can survive. Forget about your quarrels, forget about what separates you; your past. I see you all as equal individuals. Everyone has the right to live. Do not give up your right now, just because you carry false hate. We have been turned against each other by those beyond our power, but now we have the chance to fight together, now we have the choice to live."

Slowly but surely, the crowd stopped and turned to one another. The demon had spoken the truth and they had listened. The creatures of darkness took the hands of the humans; the U.A.S. drew back their weapons and turned to the Brontangus. There had to be a way to defeat the creatures.

The demon turned to Frank, "It's working Frank; it's actually working!"

There was a sudden shout from the distance as many humans, freed of the constraints that once bound them, ran towards him. Hurst was so overwhelmed, he could feel tears forming in his beady eyes and had to hold back his whimper.

"You're crying ain't ya?" Frank sounded disappointed.

"No!" Hurst squeaked, a little too high.

"Oh Hurst," Frank sighed. "It ain't even over yet!"

*

Margot and Damien burst to the surface of Izsafar; their only greeting was the burning buildings and the sound of screaming.

"Well," the Devil was confused. "Apart from the light, everything seems to be in order."

"As much as I hate to intervene, your observational skills do not seem to be up to scratch. Just when was the last time you saw humans fighting and Brontangus ripping the place to shreds?"

"Good point," Bub agreed, turning to his army. "Right, get out there and-"

He paused as one of them raised a finger to the sky behind him. The Devil's face fell.

In the sky above him soared an army of angels who had just noticed his presence.

After centuries, the Over and Under Worlds had finally come together.

Chapter 23

The lonely girl in the human prison

"Are you happy now?" Wolf screamed at the angel army. "In the search for perfection, you have created a monster!"

The ship crashed into the rocky sea, almost tipping over as it swayed and lurched, trying to keep afloat.

"This is madness!" Gabriel exclaimed, dumbfounded. They had flown into what could only be described as a catastrophe. It's not often that armies get to the battlefield and don't have a strategy, but the angels didn't have a clue what they were doing. Everyone was at war, the earth around them was collapsing in on itself and its leader was nowhere in sight.

"Where is Silvia?" the angel yelled. His army was silent. No response was appropriate; no one knew the answer.

"For once," the Devil shouted. "I can take no part of the blame. I am completely innocent."

The angel glared at him. Something caught his eye; a pale female, with white hair and black clothes. It was her, the angel from the prophecy, the one who has caused all the destruction. She was the only one who held the key to stopping the creatures.

"Get the girl!" He screeched, pointing at her.

A large group of Brontangus caught sight of the army and charged towards them. The angels screamed with rage as they tried to fight the stone creatures off.

"Time to move!" Margot said and ran in the opposite direction.

Damien followed, leaving the Devil to command his army.

"I'm taking Margot into hiding," he yelled as they ran past.

The Devil nodded at them, and then turned to the figures behind him: "Right then, you know why you're here! Protect these people from those beasts. Guard the sky!"

Damien and Margot ran across the battlefield; dodging Brontangus as they raced to find a safe place. What she had witnessed threw her completely out of sorts. She had gone there with a clear idea of what had to be done, but after witnessing the chaos, she had no clue on where the hell to start. There was no sign of Silvia, a group of angels were chasing her and to make matters worse, Brontangus were swarming over the already wild landscape.

The ground beneath her cracked; Damien pulled her back as the land lifted into a mound and the ground before them split to create a fissure. Some were not so lucky; they watched as three U.A.S. members were caught off guard and fell down to the skies of hell.

"The hotel!" She yelled. She ran back up the mound and prepared to jump over the other side.

Meanwhile, on the roof, the small demon was still giving pep talks.

"That's right! Fight, fight like you've never – ARGH-" He screamed as a Brontangus dived at him and Frank, missing them by a hair's breadth.

"Maybe it's time ter get off the roof now?" Frank asked.

"Never!" Hurst squeaked, raising his hands to the sky. His eyes turned back to the landscape below. "Hey, look! Look over there!"

"Well, Hurst thars tis thing called bein' blind."

"Oh, sorry Frank," The demon apologised. "But it's Margot and Damien, they're coming towards us. They look strange… oh my goodness!" Hurst reached for his megaphone, at last understanding what was going on. "Damien, Margot look out!"

They turned to see a host of angels heading straight for them.

Across the other side of the field, Wolf and Barbie had also spotted it and were in the ship, charging full steam ahead towards the chase.

"Dive straight through the middle! We'll cut them up!" Wolf yelled, urging the ship to increase its speed.

"Wolf," Barbie said. "This guy asked if he could join us."

Wolf jumped back when he saw who was standing in front of him.

"Hi," Bub said. "Nice to meet you, I'm the Devil."

"Everyone, hold on!" Wolf yelled. "Lad, you know what to do."

Barbie gripped hold of the rigging around the ship's mast. What was Wolf planning? He didn't have much time to think before he became light headed and the heels that he wore began to slip down the deck. The vessel was turning on its side; making it look like some sort of horizontal sky scraper. Wolf punched the air; the little beauty could take on anything.

The angels screamed as they were hit by the ship and thrown off course. Some turned back to tear the ship apart, smashing the thick windows and ripping out the insides of rooms. Wolf cringed as he watched cutlery, paperwork and other household objects fall to the ground. Barbie was holding on to the rope for dear life.

The distraction was just what Margot and Damien needed; they dived through the revolving doors of the hotel and fell into the reception. The building was empty. Like the day of the massacre, only the dead remained. Margot ignored their vacant faces as she dived into the nearest room.

"Get in here!" She shouted. "Bolt the door."

"They'll be here soon," Damien said, trying to make a barricade with the wardrobe, while she drew the curtains. "Someone must have seen us enter the building."

He paced the room, trying to think of a plan. She ignored his words; Margot could feel herself slipping into yet another 'Face' vision.

"There must be something we can do," Damien said, not noticing. "Some plan we can come up with…"

The walls began to tremble.

"We have to get out…now!" Margot shouted, running to door.

"Why?" Damien asked.

"I had a vision," she said, dragging things away from the door. "The hotel is gonna come crashing down, we'll be crushed."

"We know you're in there!" A voice called from outside. The angels had left the ship and were circling the building.

The structure trembled for the second time. Without questioning, Damien helped remove objects from the door until they could finally open it. They ran down the corridor. A white light flashed across the exit to the reception. They stopped in their tracks.

"What was that?" Margot whispered.

"Keep running," the vampire hissed. But it was too late, they'd been spotted.

Before Margot knew what was happening, an angel shot down the corridor towards them. She pointed her gun at the ceiling and fired continually until all her ammunition had been used. It caved in, creating a barrier of debris between them and the creatures.

"Stairs, Margot, let's get to the stairs." Damien said, pushing her forward.

The skies of Izsafar were growing darker and after the third tremble, the lights of the hotel went out. Margot and Damien were running through darkness again. As Margot threw the door open towards the stairs, the floor tipped.

"It's happening!" She yelled, as she and Damien attempted the stairs. She thought of Frank and Hurst on the roof and her heart sank. The further they ran the more the hotel moved, until it was swaying.

"Why are they so determined to chase us when there's a herd of Brontangus wrecking the place outside?" Margot hissed. Bricks were falling from the ceiling, down between the flights of stairs.

"Just keep moving," Damien said, turning to see she had stopped. He rushed back down the stairs to find her rifling through her leather jacket.

"Margot!" Damien said. "Is this really the time, to look through that, that toy?"

"I'm looking for something important!" She snapped, taking the Jonovicator from her pocket and opening it out. "I've just realised something. It could help us"

"Can it not wait?" Damien replied, exasperated. "The building is swarming with angels!"

"Just one moment!" Her eyes were fixed on Jade's journals, she was reading voraciously…

Then, many things happened at once. A lot can happen in a moment, and in that particular moment, three different, salient events took place:

The first thing that happened was Margot Grant had a complete brainstorm and thought of an idea how to stop the destruction.

The second and third things to take place weren't as grand; a group of angels grabbed hold of them and the hotel collapsed.

Everything happened in slow motion for Margot Grant, as she was dragged across the dirty ground. She turned her head to the right. War surrounded them. Explosions and fighting continued across the uneven and darkening land. Judging by the sight, the Brontangus were winning. She turned to her left, only to see Damien's cold eyes staring back at her. Margot could feel something warm trickling down her face; she was bleeding. How much, she did not know, nor did she care at that point. Every sense she had had become redundant, every brain cell. Her whole body ached.

"We've got them, sir," a voice from above said. Margot was thrown before their leader. He stared down at her, he was angry and unimpressed.

"All this trouble," Gabriel said, lifting her head to face him. "For one God forsaken human?"

Without thinking, she spat blood in his face. He jumped back in disgust.

"Where is Silvia?" He demanded. "I want somebody to explain to me what the hell is going on here!"

"It's that group!" Margot heard another angel exclaim. "That bunch of criminals from the West."

Margot could feel many eyes suddenly fall upon her. With great effort she turned her head to try to see what was going on.

Next to her, her friends were also captive. Margot looked in horror at the blood dripping off Barbie's swollen face. They had all been beaten, they lay bleeding on the floor. And that was supposed to be the work of angels?

"Now," the lead angel continued. "What are we supposed to do about these winged beasts? If we're not careful they'll take their destruction to the Over World!"

Despite her pain, despite her agony and hurt, Margot Grant would not give in.

"Set them free," she muttered.

"What?" The lead angel asked; sarcasm clear in his tone. "I think the human is trying to say something."

"SET- THEM- FREE!" Margot screamed. The group around her fell silent. Gabriel let out a dark and evil laugh.

"Set them *free?*" He cried. "You are as bad as they say. They have been trapped for a reason."

"I didn't understand before," Margot struggled to speak. "But I do now. It all made sense in Jade's journal, in what I've learnt in Haszear. They aren't evil, they're just tortured souls. You know, I realised how the first one must have escaped. They can only be released by a normal creature if the creature that touches them doesn't judge them. Jade never judged or hated anyone, no matter how annoyed he got, therefore upon touching one of those creatures, he set their soul free." She paused. "Set them free, they just want to be released. Stop their suffering."

Many of the angels turned to one another. The girl spoke sense.

"You are the most twisted person I have ever met." The leader laughed. "What on earth makes you think I would release those wretched creatures?"

"You may not, but I sure as hell will." Bub said, stepping forward. Many of the angels drew back in horror. None of them wanted to be anywhere near the Devil.

"You wouldn't dare!" The angel hissed at him.

"Hells yeah he would!" A familiar Spanish voice boomed in the distance. "And so would I!" They turned to where the hotel had been to see a beautiful woman standing in the ashes, holding a familiar figure in her hands.

"The Devil's daughter has captured Silvia!" One of the angels said.

"Silvia has caused more trouble on my island than I dare to say. Not only has she stolen my land, she's built killing machines, turned mankind against itself and murdered thousands! Without those so called 'traitors' you'd probably have no land at all. If you ask me, they're heroes." Arabina walked towards them as she spoke.

"Also," she said, just as Gabriel was about to talk. "Before you go jumping down my throat, bitches, you may say I've captured her, I'd prefer to use the phrase 'saved her life' after her castle was about to collapse on her."

"Arabina," the Devil whispered to his daughter. "You do know she is immortal, right?"

She nudged him. "Don't ruin my moment."

"Preposterous!" the angel leader exclaimed. "It's your friends' fault this has happened! Look at you all! How you managed to mess up this system, I'll never know! You're cowards, outcasts; the lot of you!"

"And what, if you wouldn't mind me asking," Damien said in his cold tone as he was released from the grip of the angels. "Have you done for the Over World apart from bringing the wrath of the Brontangus upon it?"

Margot tried to hide her smugness. Yet again, Damien's cheek had prevailed. There was a large amount of mumbling going on between the angels. It wasn't long before Margot also felt the grip around her loosen and before she knew it, she was being placed gently back on the ground. Barbie lifted her to her feet and put her at his side. Many of the angels were leaving their posts to stand behind them. Margot looked about their group and smiled. They had done it. They had won the angels over and there was only one last thing left to do before Izsafar fell into the darkness.

"Okay," the Devil turned to the crowd behind him. "You know what to do-"

"You can't do this!" The lead angel hissed, interrupting Bub's instructions.

"Oh God," the Devil placed his head in his gnarled hand. "Are you still here? Right before I forget, someone seize this annoying person and Silvia, while we're at it."

Arabina jumped backwards as two angels yanked the still unconscious Silvia from her arms.

"What will happen to her?" she asked, running over to her father.

The Devil stared at his daughter. The worry and desperation on her face frightened him.

"Well," he began. "As angels don't die, the only thing I can think of is to have her turned to stone; there's no way she'll be allowed back to the Over World."

"Please, father," Arabina said, clutching the Devil's hand. "Please don't do this."

"Arabina?" Hurst asked, approaching his mistress. Barbie turned to Margot, although his face was blank, she knew what he was thinking. They were all as confused as each other.

Arabina ran to her side.

"I don't understand it," the Devil said. "She killed all those humans, took your land. She practically imprisoned you and your people and you want me to spare this angel?"

"But… you hate Silvia," Margot said. "You said it yourself?"

In the arms of the angels, Silvia began to stir.

"I didn't mean to kill those humans," Silvia finally spoke. "They wouldn't stop screaming. Then they began attacking each other. Such destructive creatures…"

The Devil chose to ignore the comment. Instead, he turned back to his daughter, who was kneeling by the angel's side.

"What is the meaning of this?" He asked quietly. "This 'thing' has caused more damage than the entire Under World."

"I love her." Arabina replied.

If it were not for the constant explosions filling the sky, the whole of Izsafar would have fallen silent. Margot turned to see Damien's reaction. As always, his face was stern, he gave nothing away.

"This is ridiculous," Margot stepped forward. "There are a million people here waiting to tear her limb from limb. She should go down with Izsafar."

"I agree!" Hurst yelled.

"No!" Arabina shouted. Behind her, the crowd grew restless. "If she can't go home," she continued. "She can live in Manhaden with me."

The Devil turned away in shock.

"Arabina," Hurst said nervously. "She tried to kill you."

Wolf stepped forward. "No Hurst; that is not our way."

"But-"

"Too much has been lost on this land. We cannot teach those that are dead." Wolf said.

The Devil clasped his hands together and paced. Finally he stopped and spoke very quietly: "Very well then, she is yours to take."

"Strip her of her wings, permanently!" Gabrielle yelled to his guards.

There was the horrible sound of ripping and an ear piercing scream filled the air.

Many angels cheered.

Silvia was dropped to the floor and ran straight to Arabina's arms.

"She's your prisoner now," the angel glared at them. "She's free to tread where she wants here, providing your people don't destroy her."

"I'll remember that," Arabina looked at the stony faces around her. They knew she would not change her.

The sky was growing darker. The mountains were shaking as stones fell from their rocky sides. The sea was a storm as it crashed against the torn land. The Brontangus danced around the destruction, the humans screamed and the U.A.S. and people of Arabina's land ran for cover best they could. The paradise was to be no longer.

"So, Bub, what do we do now?" Margot asked, stepping forward to stand beside the Devil. He smiled back at her as gently as his face would allow.

"You?" He laughed quietly. "You six have done enough work for a lifetime of servitude to this realm."

He raised his arms to the sky and a white light shot from each hand towards the stone creatures. Margot looked around her to see the angels copying. One by one, the Brontangus froze in mid-air. They dissolved and disappeared. Margot could see small white dots in the distance, floating high above the land before disappearing. Where they were going to next, no one knew. She sighed as more tiny lights appeared. It made her think of Jade Wilde and where he had gone. The pain and realisation hit her that she would never see him again. The lights over Izsafar faded and all became calm as the land continued to darken.

"Well, we did it guys." Margot said. Barbie walked over to her, taking her hand and squeezing it tight to his. He was joined by Hurst, Frank, Wolf and Arabina. Together they stood close, waiting for the mountains to fall. Finally, the vampire made his way over. Margot caught his presence and once again their eyes met. They continued to stare at each other until everything fell into complete darkness.

It was finally over. There was nothing left.

Epilogue

The other end

In the darkness of Haszear, amongst the noise and chaos of the night, a small group of people stood on a high ring of hills. Candles had been carefully placed to circle the gathering. Another circle of candles had been lit in the centre to surround something much different. In the centre of that circle lay Jade Wilde, hidden under the lid of a black coffin.

Anyone who had travelled with the group would know that was where it had all begun. It was where the chapel had collapsed, where the real fight had started. Yet, there they all stood, as silent as the body that lay before them. Margot looked from face to face. They were all there; they had all come to join her in the event. She smiled. Even Wolf and the Devil himself had decided to join her in the time of mourning.

"Well," Margot said and stepped forward. "Jade Wilde."

She sighed. "I don't really know where to begin. Jade was more than a work colleague to me, so much more. He was my inspiration, my brother, my friend." They remained silent around her as she paused. The only thing she could hear was rustling coming from nearby bushes. Margot ignored it and continued. "Jade was the only person who supported me with my science and the only one who believed in my ideas. He was kind, un-judgmental and always willing to help; even when forced into doing things like taking untested drugs."

Damien and a few others shot her questioning looks.

"Jade Wilde was a very special man, but I never told him any of these things." Margot tried to hide the trembling in her voice. "In fact, I don't think anyone did and it's a shame that he'll never know this. However, Jade wasn't just a man, he was a symbol of hope and will be remembered by many as the force that drove this rebellion and the courage that kept us afloat when everything seemed to fall into the ruins."

Margot paused again and looked over her shoulder. The rustling was getting louder; she was sure she could hear many things moving about in the undergrowth. "And like many a hero, he didn't live to see his cause prevail. His mark will not be forgotten. Now I know he's not the first and won't be the last to die, but to me, Jade will always be the most important person that has ever set foot in my life and I don't think things will ever be quite the same now he has gone."

Margot took a few steps backwards. Barbie, Wolf and the others began to break into a slow clap. Then, half way down the hill, someone else joined in and then someone else until the clapping became so loud Margot could barely think. Her jaw dropped as she heard the roar of a crowd and the cheering of what sounded like the whole island. Margot turned to see thousands of creatures on the hills, all around. They were led, by no other than the angel Silvia, herself and were all carrying something that projected light; whether it be candles, torches or burning branches. She turned back to the group, completely bewildered.Margot looked back at Barbie in pure horror. *Had all these people just witnessed her speech?*

"Ahhh, my subjects!" Arabina exclaimed, walking forward. Damien rolled his eyes, Arabina may be a changed demon, but it'd be a lie to say that she didn't like the lime light.

"Finally, muchachos! We are free!" The crowd filling the hills screeched in celebration. Once they were silent, she continued. "My actions as a leader have been wrong; I have not cared for you as I should have, I have not watched over you. Instead I fled into hiding. I abandoned you, but I promise I will never let that happen again. As long as I am your leader, I will watch over you."

She turned to her father and smiled as he nodded in approval. "Now, a lot of creatures who I never thought in a million moons would surprise me, have done. One of them is the amazing Hurst, who led me and my army into battle. That is why I have decided to make him my second in command to ensure that I don't mess up again. Hurst, step forward please."

Everyone turned to the demon as he stepped forward. No one laughed at him; no one taunted or yelled names. Instead, they stared with admiration for the small creature. As he stepped next to his leader, he bowed before her and burst into tears. "Oh Hurst," Arabina rolled her eyes lovingly. "Come on, get it together."

He sniffed and wiped his eyes with one of his long sleeves. "In these hard times, even our supposed enemies, the angels," Arabina gestured to Wolf. "Have stepped forward and helped us. From this moment on, Wolf will always be welcome in these parts. Whereas Gabriel can go fuck himself."

The crowd all sniggered at that comment. So, maybe she'd not completely changed, Margot thought, amused.

"From this day forward," Arabina silenced the crowd. "I release Barbie from his curse and thank both him and Damien for their servitude. May no one here ever cause them harm. However, the most important person here is our human friend, Margot Grant. Without this woman, we would still be in captivity, without this woman, I'd most probably be dead. This is the one woman that changed everything. Let her name never be forgotten. Let it be shouted to the skies."

With that final word, the crowd got down on hands and knees to bow to Margot Grant. Margot turned back to look at the others and to her shock, they were also on the ground. Even Damien.

"I erm- ermm, well thanks, but erm," she cringed, playing with her hair. Arabina went to her side, taking her hand.

"To Margot!" she yelled and the crowd imitated her cry.

Although lots of things were uncertain about her future, Margot knew there was one thing that would remain the same. Unsure if it was 'Face', the journey or the loss of her best friend; she had been changed forever. Whatever she did from that point, there was no going back. Margot watched the people of Manhaden leaving the hillside. In a way, she envied the simplicity of their lives. Easy living would be something that she'd never experience. The funeral was over, Margot had done what she'd set out to do - and more. It was time to move on, she was done. She looked up as Barbie approached. Margot could feel a lump in her throat as the transvestite broke out into a sad smile.

"So you're definitely leaving?" He looked down at her.

"Yeah," she replied. It was almost a whisper. "Yeah, I am."

"You'll always be my friend, Margot," he said. "I'll miss you."

"Barbie I-"

"Don't," he said, hugging her tight. "I understand." Margot looked up to see silent tears running down the transvestite's face. She noticed he was no longer wearing his gothic attire. Instead, he wore a bright green flowery dress with a large straw hat to match.

"Barbie," Margot laughed, breaking the tension. "What's with the outfit? I thought the curse was broken."

The transvestite shrugged. "I guess I just like dressing this way." He lifted up one of his big black boots and tried to pop his foot. Margot laughed.

"So, what's next?" He asked.

"No idea." She sighed. "You?"

"I'm going to the Earth with Wolf. Now that Faith has been laid to rest, there's nothing left here for me anymore. I'm going to try and leave this darkness behind me."

"Yeah, but isn't the Earth-"

"Under construction," Wolf said, strolling towards them. "You're looking at the new deputy head of the Over World. It took us a while to decide what to do with the Universe."

Margot raised her eyebrows. "And what was the outcome?"

"Well there was only one thing to do. We've had to erase the memories of those living there, take away their technology, and start the whole process over again."

"Wolf, I thought they offered you the position as Lead Angel of the Over World, why are you spending your time with us humans?" Margot said.

"Pftt," the angel shook his head. "Gabriel can keep his job; I've never fancied myself as top angel. Besides, I like working with you humans, you keep me and Barbie on our toes.

Margot heard Frank and his demonic dog making noise in the background.

"Don't yeh even think 'bout it!" She heard Frank's voice. "After all I've bin through and you wanna drag me off again ARGH! DAMN DOG!"

They burst into laughter as he was dragged into the darkness.

Margot turned to Wolf. "This all seems like a great idea and all, but, what happens if it starts all over again? You know; the wars…"

"We shall just have to wait and see, let's hope, for their sake, they do it correctly this time." He smiled one of his all-knowing smiles and embraced her. As Margot pulled away, his gentle eyes met hers. She knew it would be the last time she'd ever gaze upon them.

"You are welcome here anytime. Although humans will not know of your good deeds, you and Jade Wilde will be known amongst the creatures of Haszear as the two who saved us all."

Margot smiled sadly as theywalked into the distance. She was alone. Not just on Earth, but in the whole of the eighty one worlds. Everything had just become ten times bigger; she didn't know if she could keep up.

"Good always powers over evil, hey?" she muttered to herself. "Guess they're not as evil as they thought."

"Touching, very touching, at one point I half expected you to cry." A cold voice came from behind her.

"Come to say goodbye?" she asked in a sharp tone as the vampire came round to face her.

He smiled, extending his hand. "Cigarette?"

"I quit," she replied, pushing the box back at him. "Life's too short."

He looked shocked.

"Shame you lost out to angel-pants over there," she nodded towards Silvia and Arabina. "It's funny how things work out."

"Isn't it just," he agreed.

"Well," Margot sighed, "I know we didn't always get on, but it was nice meeting you. I'd best be getting on." She turned and headed towards the town.

"And where will you go?" The vampire called after her.

"Away from all this," she called back. "Maybe I'll go back to Earth, start a band or something, settle down in New York and help Barbie, or finish Jade's work, haven't quite worked it out yet."

"A quiet life for Margot Grant?" The vampire laughed. "How can you go back? I know you Margot, you'll get bored. There'll be no action, no adventure on the Earth anymore."

She saluted sarcastically, still not turning around. Without warning, the vampire sped after her to lean on a dead tree that blocked her path.

"Damien," she tried to hide her smile. "What do you want?"

"I just thought you'd be bored." He shrugged, looking away from her.

"You're really bad at this," Margot folded her arms.

"I don't know what you're implying," his gaze became cold. "If you think for one second that I have feelings for you-"

Margot went over to him, moving her face close to his. He didn't pull away; instead he leaned in and kissed her.

"Shame about that," Margot raised her eyebrows. "Because I was actually starting to like you."

"How do you feel about travelling the worlds? There are a million things out there that I'm sure you'd love to see. We could take a ship." He called after her.

Margot's face lit up. "Okay, I've got nothing on."

She turned to the land for one last look before following the vampire into the darkness.

The tired hands on an ancient clock face may stop turning, but time stops for no man. It's eternal. The rivers would never stop flowing, or the trees flourishing. Life would carry on around her.

Margot knew that deep down in her heart, it was time to move on. And that was exactly what she did.

Earth year- 3159 – Two years after our story has ended

"Mum! Mum!" Byron yelled, running along the beach. It was a pleasant summer's day and he and his mother had been walking along the quiet shore line for quite some time. She sighed, looking over at the sunset. It couldn't get much better.

"What is it?" she called after her son.

He was running towards a small lemonade stand that stood at the shore. "Excuse me," he said, jumping on the seat and leaning over the counter. "Can I get a drink please?"

"You certainly can," a croaky voice behind the counter said. The boy looked up to see Barbie smiling down at him. His flowery dress blew in the wind as he moved to the dispenser.

"You're that author, Barbie," the mother leaned over the table, putting the money in his hand. "You wrote that book, the one about the legend of Margot and Jade?"

"Sure did," Barbie smiled, taking off his straw hat.

"Can you tell it me, please, please, please?" the boy said.

"Byron!" his mother exclaimed.

"No it's okay." Barbie smiled. "Are you sitting comfortably?" he asked the boy.

Byron nodded, sipping his lemonade. Next to him, his mother took a seat.

"Well then," said Barbie reaching behind the counter to find a copy of the book. He sighed, turning to the first page. "It was a quiet day, a really quiet day, too quiet: in fact, it had been too quiet for a very long time…"

Lightning Source UK Ltd.
Milton Keynes UK
UKOW04f0944151213

223026UK00002B/71/P